Praise for *Wife Goes On*

"A celebration of s   umorous, heart-
felt homage to the   ."—Arianna Huffington,
bestselling author of *On Becoming Fearless*

"*Wife Goes On* is a hopeful romp of sex, humor, and friendship."—Bruce Bauman, author of *And the Word Was*

"Like Olivia Goldsmith before her, Leslie Lehr has done the
impossible: She's made divorce into a winning, funny, and in-
spiring activity, if one fraught with the sadness of mistakes made
and lives changed. *Wife Goes On* isn't fictionalized self-help or
mundane chick-lit; it's about loving, escaping, and living again,
the hard road to finding relevance . . . and the joy found in oc-
casionally running over every rut and divot in that very same
road. Just like real life."—Tod Goldberg, author of *Simplify*,
Living Dead Girl, and *Fake Liar Cheat*

"Sexy and fabulous!"—Jerrilyn Farmer, author of the bestselling Madeline Bean mysteries

"*Wife Goes On* is a tantalizing romp through the world of the
newly divorced featuring a group of women who are vulnerable,
smart, resourceful, wonderfully resilient, and wickedly funny.
Anyone who's been through a bad breakup will recognize the
heartaches and triumphs that rise from these pages."—Hope
Edelman, bestselling author of *Motherless Mothers*

"Underlying the sass and verve of Lehr's prose are trenchant
insights on relationships, friendships, and motherhood—not
to mention the kind of wisdom that comes from hard knocks
plus a few good laughs!"—Samantha Dunn, author of *Failing
Paris*, *Not By Accident*, and *Faith in Carlos Gomez*

"Leslie Lehr is a truth teller—a rare writer who untangles the
realities of women's lives without flinching while making you
laugh, cry, and nod in understanding with every word."—Leslie
Morgan Steiner, editor, *Mommy Wars*, and daily online work/
family columnist for washingtonpost.com

WIFE GOES ON

LESLIE LEHR

KENSINGTON BOOKS
http://www.kensingtonbooks.com

KENSINGTON BOOKS are published by

Kensington Publishing Corp.
850 Third Avenue
New York, NY 10022

All Kensington titles, imprints and distributed lines are available at special quantity discounts for bulk purchases for sales promotion, premiums, fund-raising, educational or institutional use.

Special book excerpts or customized printings can also be created to fit specific needs. For details, write or phone the office of the Kensington Special Sales Manager: Kensington Publishing Corp., 850 Third Avenue, New York, NY 10022. Attn. Special Sales Department. Phone: 1-800-221-2647.

Kensington and the K logo Reg. U.S. Pat. & TM Off.

ISBN-13: 978-0-7582-2241-1
ISBN-10: 0-7582-2241-6

First Kensington Trade Paperback Printing: March 2008
10 9 8 7 6 5 4 3 2 1

Printed in the United States of America

For my girls

ACKNOWLEDGMENTS

Many thanks to Mollie Glick and her talented associates at the Jean V. Naggar Literary Agency, and to my editor extraordinaire, Danielle Chiotti, at Kensington Press.

Unspeakable gratitude goes to those who encouraged this former wife to get a life, including Louise Fischer-Kohan, Janet Robertson, Winston Perez, Cathy Kazan, and Lisa Vaughan. Members of the "club" whose friendship inspired this story include Janet Orloff, Sheryl Braunstein, Jeri Harman, Dawn Snyder, and Dy Bessee.

Others who lit the path to living happier ever after include Hope Edelman, Leslie Morgan-Steiner, Sally Wofford-Girand, Andrea Chapin, Karen Waldron, Craig Anderson, my friends at the Writers Program at UCLA Extension, my fellow Amethysts at Antioch University, and the amazing members of the Women's Leadership Council of Los Angeles.

Valuable research came from many sources, from the formal issues addressed by attorneys Wendy Forrestor, Linda Gross, Peter Nichols, and Leslie Hirschbaum, to the fun parts from Kim Sheridan of Pure Romance, Inc., Nancy Kiley from the Nordstrom Lingerie Department, Evans Louis at Mi Piace, and John Logan at SafeGuard Guaranty Corporation.

Most of all, thanks to my beloved daughters, Juliette and Catherine, for enduring so many dinners of Tahitian Tuna Toss—here's to making your own dreams come true; to my mother, Dr. Claire Lehr, and my sister, Tracy Lehr, for providing a safe haven in their hearts; Dr. Jay and Janet Lehr for helping me see; and for John Truby, who taught me that there's more to every story, even mine.

Did it ever occur to you that "wife" is a four-letter word? The first time I cringed at the sound of it, I knew my marriage was over. But I refused to get a divorce. Maybe it was partly my fault for devoting so much to my kids and to the asshole snoring next to me that there was nothing left. But this was no starter marriage. Sure I was miserable, but I made a commitment, damnit.

The truth is, I was afraid to be alone. Then I heard my daughter swear she'd never get married and I realized sticking it out wouldn't win me Mother of the Year. If I wanted my kids to be happy, I would have to show them how. So I tore off those golden shackles—and found out I wasn't alone. I had joined a club that I didn't know existed. I never wanted to join this club, but now I'm glad I did. Everywhere, there are members who have paid their dues, know the secret handshake, and are reaping the benefits of real friendship . . .

Welcome to Club Divorce,

Diane Taylor

Part One

INITIATION

You know you're in the club when . . .

Chapter 1

DIANE

. . . you wish you had married for money.

"I hate you," Diane said. She sat down on the velvet settee her husband had proposed to her on eighteen years earlier. She would miss her grandma's antique furniture even more than this beautiful Brentwood estate, sold on the verge of foreclosure.

Steve yanked her white cotton briefs down her unshaven legs and over her feet, then tossed them over his shoulder. The flat circle of a poker chip pressed against the straining denim of his pants pocket. "A deal's a deal."

"You would know," she said. He was an asshole, but it was nice to see him on his knees. Plus, she hadn't had sex in two years. She dropped the legal documents and leaned back until all she could see was the chandelier. At least she wouldn't have to clean those crystals again, she thought, as his gray head lowered out of sight between her legs. She flinched. A jolt of electricity surged down her naked thigh and burned the sole of her left foot, making her toes cramp.

Her Volvo horn honked from the driveway. She opened her eyes and struggled up to peek out the living room window. The sky above the palm trees was nearly dark.

"The kids are fine," Steve said.

Diane hesitated, then reached for the collar of his Hawaiian shirt and pulled him up on top of her. He was a little heavier than she remembered, but he still had all the right parts. She yanked down his zipper. What harm was there in a quickie? Then his mouth was on hers and he was inside her and it felt so damn good. They had made love 1,999 times in this house. Might as well go for a record before she reset the counter to zero. According to those books at Barnes & Noble, she could be there for a very long time. Right now she had an itch the size of Disneyland, and who could resist the Happiest Place on Earth? A sheen of sweat broke out beneath her T-shirt. She felt the warm flush of blood inside her chest.

The car horn faded behind the sound of her panting. This was the true meaning of wedded bliss. Steve knew exactly how she liked it: how hard, how fast, even how to make her ears ring.

No, that was her cell phone. Her hand automatically groped for it on the floor.

"Mother," fifteen-year-old Quinn whined from the car. "What's taking so long?"

"I'm . . . coming," Diane said.

What a woman will do to get her divorce papers signed.

Two minutes and a gulp of water from the kitchen faucet later, Diane dragged a potted palm out the front door of the house. She felt dizzy, but not from the sex. She couldn't believe this was really happening. That could not possibly be her shaky hand locking the double door for the last time. That was, however, her key chain with the kids' pictures and the Ralph's club card attached. Diane wiped her fingers on her sweatpants and pried the house key off. Perfect. Now she had a complete set of broken nails to go with her broken family.

She kissed the happy face house key good-bye and put it under the welcome mat for the new owner. Then she looked across the overgrown yard to make sure the kids were okay.

They were still waiting in the filthy Volvo station wagon parked in the driveway next to the Brentwood Realty sign. The sign was already surrounded by weeds. Diane had felt awful when she let the gardener go last month, but to hell with the Homeowners' Association. Diane was no longer a homeowner.

In the car, Quinn and her nine-year-old brother, Cody, were pinned between moving boxes. Cody was engrossed in his Wii, thank God. Quinn was painting on lip gloss as if she had a date, which she sort of did, with a whole new life in a tiny rent-controlled apartment a few blocks away in Santa Monica.

The wrought-iron gate next door clanged open. Diane jumped behind a square porch column as headlights swept past. The last thing she wanted was for her neighbor, Olivia, to come home from the neighborhood picnic—if you could call a catered barbecue a picnic—and spot Diane fleeing in the dark of night like a criminal. The T-shirt sticking to her back might as well be an orange jumpsuit stenciled with the number 16,000,001. Diane might be a statistic now, but she was not one of them . . . those walking clichés, those bitter divorcées. Diane was not a quitter. She was a starter, that's all. Starting over. With a mountain of debt, two kids, and a deadbeat ex who had fucked her in more ways than one.

Diane pushed a lock of faded bottle-brown hair behind her ear and prayed for Olivia's gate to close. The kids were restless and they were already late "vacating the premises," but if Olivia saw Diane, she'd run out to say good-bye. And if that woman brought over another plate of those god-awful crème de menthe brownies, Diane might have to run her over. She was tired of hearing how a reliable maid could save a marriage. A reliable husband would be a better bet. Not that she was the betting kind; she left that to Asshole.

Diane knew what people like Olivia thought: that Diane was one of those brides who got married with their fingers crossed behind her back. But that wasn't true. Diane had not eloped, planned a prenup, or shouted her vows while jumping out of an airplane. She had a proper church wedding—except for the usual obscenities exchanged between her mother and step-mother whenever they were on the same side of the Rockies. Which was why Diane truly meant it when she swore "till death us do part." Unfortunately, her husband refused to keel over on his own accord.

Ex-husband, she reminded herself, now that the papers were signed and sealed in the envelope in her hand. Or did she have to suffer the name Kowalski until the L.A. County Court recorded her failure for posterity? She used to think divorce was the easy way out—that people got lazy and didn't try hard enough. When other couples bit the dust, she and Steve used to feel superior, as if sticking it out were the key to happiness. But now, after eighteen months of torture from fancy lawyers and forensic accountants, she knew differently. Happiness was the key to sticking it out.

The blare of the Volvo's horn shook Diane from her reverie. She saw an upstairs light flash on at the colonial across the street. Faces peeked between the curtains above a jumbo American flag. She knew what they were thinking: *the Kowalskis are at it again.* At least the screaming was over. Diane waved to the kids to lay off the horn, but who was she to demand loyalty? If there were only her life to consider, she would have split a long time ago. And her stomach wouldn't be cramping like a permanent state of PMS.

Diane glanced at the plastic Cinderella watch she had borrowed from her daughter. Time to move. She hurried to the custom-made oversized mailbox and pulled out her last pile of mail at this address. Aside from the bills she couldn't pay and the catalogs she could no longer order from, there was a padded envelope from London, the home of her old business school roommate. A belated forty-second birthday present? Or had her friend read between the cheerful lines of Diane's e-mails? She pinched the bulge. Didn't feel like a self-help book, thank goodness; Diane had read them all.

Diane pinned the mail under her arm, picked up the potted palm, and hurried across the front yard toward the car—just as the sprinklers went on. Oh hell, she knew she had forgotten something. Besides her panties.

Diane shoved Scout, the black Lab, to the backseat and wedged the plant into the front next to the pet crate. Inside, their black cat, Boo, was hissing at a bottle of red wine that Diane had swiped from the otherwise fully stocked, climate-controlled wine cellar. It would be Two-Buck Chuck from here on out, so what the hell. Let the new owner sue her over a missing bottle of Montrachet. The bright side of bankruptcy is that no one can touch you. Still, she didn't want to set a bad example for the kids. One criminal in the family was enough. Scout barked again and nearly trampled Cody to get to the window. Diane couldn't pull the dog back from smothering her son. She tapped her daughter's sunburned shoulder. "I need your help, Quinn."

"Ouch. Okay, but don't get me wet." Quinn dropped her copy of Hawthorne's *The Scarlet Letter* and opened the back door. A sleeping bag rolled out onto the driveway.

"I meant help with the dog."

"Can't Daddy take Scout?" Quinn asked. She retrieved the sleeping bag and climbed back in, tugging Scout's tail until the beast sat. "I want a purse poodle."

"You know Daddy's apartment doesn't take pets." Theirs didn't either, until she pawned her Cartier watch for the extra cleaning deposit.

"Isn't Daddy coming with us?" Cody asked.

Quinn sniggered.

Diane shook her head and toyed with her wedding rings. Asshole offered to have them cleaned just before the end, but she had wised up by then. He would have pawned them and claimed they were stolen to get the insurance money. Still, she couldn't take them off; her finger felt naked without them. "He said he'll pick you up for a barbecue tomorrow." Diane wrung the excess water from the hem of her sweatpants and climbed into the driver's seat. "Seat belts."

"Can you turn on KROQ?"

"I'm hungry," Cody wheezed.

Diane dug his inhaler out of her purse and tossed it back. "Give me a minute, you guys. It's been a long day."

"I am so sick of this whole divorce," Quinn said.

Diane met her daughter's eyes in the rearview mirror. She looked just like her father back when he had long hair and played the drums. Diane smiled at her, but Quinn was back to bickering with her brother as they pushed the dog back and forth between them. The cat hissed in her crate. Diane sighed. She was sick of the divorce, too, and it was only the beginning.

Diane tilted the mirror back from where the palm frond had tweaked it. Who was that scrawny woman in the mirror? Diane's hair was a frizzy cloud and her eyes were ringed with circles as dark as Quinn's mascara. And how long had she had that smudge of dirt on her forehead? It looked like a "D"—like the scarlet letter, announcing her failure to the world. Diane was marked for life. A long, lonely life.

Diane caught a glimpse of Olivia coming out of the gate next door. She jammed her key in the ignition. Diane was in no mood to make nice with a woman who had no idea what she was going through. The truth was, Diane had been lonely for a very long time.

A moving truck lumbered up to the curb. The night air seemed to thicken and settle over the car like a blanket. Everyone quieted down, even the animals. Diane took one last look at the only home the kids had ever known, and blinked back her tears. She had to set a good example. Act like this was an adventure. She lifted the collar of her T-shirt and rubbed the smudge off her forehead. Then she revved the engine. "Say: good-bye, house."

"Good-bye, house!" The three of them waved.

There was no turning back now; she had to make the best of it. In L.A., that only meant one thing.

"Who wants IN-N-OUT burgers?"

The kids shouted, "I do! I do!"

Diane laughed at those two little words. She hadn't had an appetite in months, but now her stomach was growling. She cranked the radio to the classic rock station. Then she hit the gas and sped off into . . . she had no idea what.

Chapter 2

LANA

. . . you avoid men who are too good-looking.

Lana loved salsa dancing. She loved how the red lights made her skin glow, how the clavé beat showed off her years of ballet, and how the short flippy skirts flashed her long legs. La Bamba was the best salsa club in L.A., more than worth the trek downtown through the Fourth of July traffic. Here, you were twenty-nine forever and all you had to do was dance. Most of all, Lana loved the touch of a stranger's hand on her hip, the intimacy without the emotion, 1-2-3, 5-6-7. It was like disco without the drugs, like sex with your clothes on. A total rush.

Friday was Ladies' Night, so the room was full of muscular men in tight black pants and shiny shirts. Lana towered over the shorter ones, so she was visible from every angle. Her glossy hair—dyed black this month—brushed her bare shoulders. She held it up to cool her long neck as she chose her next partner. Lana had danced with five different men tonight, but young Raul had the strongest hands and the smoothest moves. He also had the smoothest head. Lana's ex-husband had spent so much time fussing over his long locks in the mirror that she was now only hot for the hirsute. Plus, she had just read a study proving that the testosterone missing from a man's hairline tended to collect below the belt. Lana suspected there was even more to their machismo: bald men tried harder.

Raul spun her left and right, forward and back, but as he steered her by the hips, it stung. During her Hollywood days, Lana had endured chemical peels and fat injections, high heels and hair removal, but nothing compared to this lingering burn from getting her tattoo removed.

She blew Raul a kiss—he admitted his real name was Richard—and headed to the bar, squeezing past heavily perfumed tables filled with women of all shapes and colors, a democracy of dancers. A meritocracy, rather; you couldn't fake the footwork. Lana waved the hem of her spangled black skirt to get some air. The bartender poured her a martini with five olives before re-filling a wineglass for the divorcée next to her.

At this point, Lana could spot them without checking for rings. They were the ones trying too hard. This one was cos-tumed in head-to-toe black with the requisite funky earrings and eyeglasses of an Intellectual. Lana tugged at her red bra strap and toyed with the idea of referring her to Dr. Levine, her cosmetic surgeon. There was practically a law about looking forty in L.A., and this babe was breaking it. Lana was already twenty-nine—and she planned to stay that way forever.

A harried waitress squeezed by with a plate of beef taquitos. She scanned the noisy crowd and raised her eyebrows at Lana, who cringed and shook her head. Lana's body was her temple, and she would never defile it with fried food.

Another divorcée—a new one, by the looks of her turquoise sequined skirt and perfectly matching shoes—fumed as she joined her friend. "He called me a tease. Said I shouldn't wear a dance skirt until I learn how to dance."

Lana laughed and nearly choked on an olive. Widows got it together right away, maybe since they were single by accident, but divorcées, handicapped by guilt, were slow learners. And these women were everywhere, wearing designer duds to yoga class, then struggling to do a down dog; spending hours study-ing upholstery fabric, then settling for beige canvas. When Skirtwoman glared at her, Lana apologized and mentioned the free salsa classes the club offered on Sunday nights. What this woman really needed was a class on How to Have a Life. She turned away, but both women glanced back at her. Lana knew what was coming.

Intellectual passed her friend the wine, then signaled the bartender for another. Skirtwoman turned to Lana. "You look familiar. Any relation to that actress who—"

"No," Lana interrupted. "But I get that a lot." Fortunately, the half-life of actors was shorter than that of shooting stars. You could flame and burn out and no one would remember that you even existed. Unless you were married to another star, that is. Then it was like planets colliding, the debris drifted for eternity. She smiled and glanced in the mirror over the bar to tame her $300 bob. It was expensive to hide in plain sight, but it was easier than going home to Boston a complete failure. Besides, Lana loved L.A. "I work at a furniture store. Ever been to Mecca?"

"Sure," Skirtwoman said. "That must be it."

"Wonder what happened to that actress," Intellectual mused. "It's like she dropped off the face of the earth. Not that you can blame her."

Lana tried to maintain the friendly smile, one of dozens in her repertoire, but she was tired, and her hip hurt. She needed something to dull the pain, or better yet, something even more painful. Lana knocked back the rest of her martini, waved at the bartender, and ordered a shot of ouzo. Two years and eighty-one days since she fired her film agent. There should be a twelve-step program for recovering actresses.

The band slowed to a mambo, and Raul tapped her hip. Lana yelped, but no one could hear her over the conga drum. Maybe the wound was infected. She suggested that Raul ask Skirtwoman for a dance. When he whirled the woman away into the crowd, Lana gulped down the shot. Then she reached up beneath her skirt to smooth the bandage on her hip.

She should never have gotten the damn tattoo in the first place, but she'd wanted to surprise Lucas on their first anniversary. That Dickens quote came to mind: "It was the best of times, it was the worst of times . . ." Blah, blah, blah.

Lana had fallen hard for Lucas on the set of that Haggis movie. The two of them were inseparable, living the good life in Malibu Colony. Lana's mother, a professor of English literature in Boston, was not impressed by the swans at the Bel Air Hotel, where they got married. She warned Lana that only swans mated for life; it was a bad idea to marry an actor.

Lana just laughed, bought her mother a subscription to *Us Weekly*, and flew her home first class. Everything was perfect until she got pregnant and Lucas took a job playing Caesar on a film shooting in Italy. Lana lost the baby before the press got wind of her pregnancy, but Lucas sent her a beautiful pair of emerald earrings that matched her eyes to cheer her up. He even e-mailed her the first set of dailies so she could see what she was missing. She was so touched, she branded her hip with their wedding date in Roman numerals, then got on a plane to visit him on the set.

When Lana boarded the plane and saw that her Haggis movie was screening in first class, she took it as a sign. Granted, most people recognized her from that movie where she played a supermodel puking her guts out, or from *People* magazine as the "wife of," but Lana had studied at the Royal Academy, where she played more Shakespeare than her pretty husband could pronounce.

Just before the plane touched down in Rome, Lana ducked into the cramped bathroom and changed into a slave toga and sandals identical to those rented for the film from Western Costume, then donned a dark wig. When the jet landed, she stuck out one of her long legs, all laced up in leather, and hopped in the first taxi that stopped. Decked out as an extra, Lana sashayed right past the location manager outside the Coliseum. She had no problems slipping through the flaps of the tent blocking the set from the tourist area; the problems started after that. If only she'd called ahead and had the studio limo pick her up. If only she'd dressed as Caesar's wife. If only she'd stayed home. But no.

Lana—known as Lacy back then—sauntered right past the lunch caterer, who was grilling a whole disgusting lamb over an authentic-looking spit. She looked at the Pretty People over in hair and makeup, held a finger to her lips to keep them quiet, and strolled right past the studio executives—the Suits, they were called, since they were dressed too well to do anything more than get in the way—staring at the bank of video monitors mounted behind the camera. The klieg lights burned hotter than the Suits' tempers when the production went a minute over the schedule. For a cast and crew living in hotels on location, with equipment shipped from New York and London, time was truly money. Lana arrived just as the portrait photographer from *Vanity Fair* stepped onto the white sand and held his light meter over the taped X for a quick exposure reading.

The camera hovered overhead, filming a wide-angle shot of slaves carrying a plinth on which Caesar kissed a nubile slave girl. Lucas looked amazing; his bare chest gleamed with baby oil, his pectoral muscles were highlighted by an airbrush artist, and his bleached hair was brushed down over his massive shoulders.

"Cut!" the director called from the crane.

Several of the crew members had noticed Lana by now, and she could hear the Pretties whispering. Cherry Baby, with her pink pageboy, waved. Then she whispered in the ear of Marlene, wardrobe stylist extraordinaire, whose hair was held up by a wooden clothespin. Lana stopped just long enough to hug them hello and have Cherry deepen the black kohl rimming her eyes. When she stepped away from them, Lana stood up with her perfect dance posture. Sure enough, cameras started flashing. Lana dropped her chin to her bare shoulder and posed. Let the poor things make a few extra bucks selling photos of her romantic reunion with Lucas.

As the motion picture cameras were shut down, the costumed extras set down the plinth. A prop assistant collected wooden spears and plastic knives. Grips started winding the black electric cables. The shoot was a wrap—except that Lucas was still kissing the slave girl. Talk about Method acting. A few crew members whispered behind Lana as she straightened her skirt, and she wondered why they were being so quiet when the cameras weren't rolling. Usually when a shoot ended, all hell broke loose and you had to shout to find your ride back to the hotel. Then Lana turned back toward Lucas and it all became clear, as his Scientologist friends would say. The nubile slave girl wrapped a spiderlike leg around Lucas's six-pack waist, clearly familiar with the territory. Lucas threw off his helmet. He stuck his tongue in her mouth and slipped his hand down her toga, then leaned in closer to ravage her in front of the entire crew.

He always did like an audience.

Lana screamed and grabbed a spear from the prop assistant. Flashbulbs popped. The prop guy tried to pry it from her hands, but it was too late. Lana broke free and threw the spear as hard as she could. Someone yelled for Lucas, and he pulled away from the bimbo. The tip of the spear missed him as he turned, but the tail feather sliced his cheek, and Lucas lost his balance. Blood dripped down his face. The bimbo screamed and jumped back. The Suits started swearing and talking about insurance. Lucas sat up, dazed, then spotted Lana in the crowd.

Lana was starring in her own movie now: *Revenge of the Jilted Wife*. She gave Lucas the finger, drew up to her full six feet and marched out, pausing only to grab a bottle of ouzo from the craft service table. The crew parted like the Red Sea around her. The women applauded as she passed.

The scene was on the Internet within minutes. *Entertainment Tonight* replayed it for weeks. In retrospect, it was not Lana's finest moment. If only her reaction had been a bit more original. Something classy. Something that made her famous for something other than Divorce.

Lana had once read an article that claimed that 72 percent of men cheated on their wives. She was simply the first to have her breakup instant-replayed on *Entertainment Tonight*. As soon as she saw the clip, she hacked off her signature hair and fled to London, where nobody cared. Lucas never saw the tattoo. Lana now thought of it as her sell-by date.

It took Lana's entire savings to keep the tattoo artist quiet.

She paid no attention to the Web site that sprang up to praise her, nor to the debates on Charlie Rose. The studio should have paid her for the extra publicity, but she was young and stupid and humiliated, whereas Lucas's pockets were so deep his lawyers could have strung her along for years. Lana didn't have years, she had a lawsuit from the bonding company that covered the expense of keeping the crew in Italy while Lucas's stitches healed. So after a year in London, she took the settlement, paid them off, and came back to L.A.

When she realized she was broke, she thought of burning his house down. Actually, she almost did burn his house down one drunken night, but he never proved it. So she hid. She had no interest in coming clean to become another "Born Again" bad girl. That type of career move took a high-priced publicist to pull off—and rehab was so cliché. Finally, another year had passed, and she blended into the scenery enough to brave a tattoo parlor and have the damn date removed.

Lana winced and tugged her spangled skirt back into place. The worst of it was, the fan magazines agreed that the scar on Lucas's cheek made him even more manly. Lana's scar ensured that she'd never do another nude scene. Maybe that was a good thing.

"You okay?" the bartender shouted over the salsa beat.

Lana nodded and plucked another olive from her empty martini glass. She should have listened to her mother. Four years later, she still got a big kick out of saying "I told you so." She didn't actually say it out loud, she just smiled that snarky, knowing, Miss Haversham of *Great Expectations* kind of smile. But she was pleased when Lana traded her emerald earrings for her loft in the artist district downtown. That turned out to be an excellent investment, both financially and personally. Not one of her black beret–flinging, red lipstick–wearing, graffiti-praising neighbors on the paint and poetry circuit watched *Entertainment Tonight*.

Lana scanned the dance floor. Raul's chest looked hard and inviting. He saw her and headed over, passing the divorcée in the sequined skirt, who was now twirling with a new partner.

Lana turned to her friend and raised a perfectly plucked eyebrow.

Intellectual nodded. "This is so good for her. First holiday without the kids."

Lana smiled and gestured to the bartender, who handed over her motorcycle helmet. She took Raul's hand and led him through the crowded dance floor toward the exit. Halfway there, she tapped the shoulder of Skirtwoman. She was dancing flirtatiously with her partner, a light sheen of sweat across her forehead. She smiled up at Lana. "Happy Independence Day!" Lana shouted over the music. "See you Sunday."

Chapter 3

BONNIE

. . . you hate your white picket fence.

The phone was ringing. Bonnie couldn't spot it in the trail of toys Hayley left beside her brother's crib, so she stayed put in the rocking chair while the baby sucked the life out of her. Her breasts hadn't been this sore since spring break at Ohio State, after she fell asleep on the roof of the Delta Gamma house while sunbathing topless.

Bonnie needed to get baby Lucas down for a nap so she could get dinner ready. He looked so cute grasping a strand of her dirty-blonde hair that she prayed it wasn't her husband calling on the way home from the airport, and rocked harder. She knew she should be grateful that their nine-month-old had such a healthy appetite; he took after his daddy that way. Unfortunately, Buck was more enamored of her baby-making belly than the rest of her. He said it was like sleeping with a pony keg. Even if that was a compliment, it sure wasn't romantic.

The oven timer went off. Hayley, her three-year-old, screeched from the kitchen. "Mommy! The noise is hurting!"

The scent of burnt chocolate wafted into the nursery. Bonnie yanked her son off her nipple, snapped shut her nursing bra, and buckled her overalls before standing up. Whoa, too fast. Her head was spinning.

"Be right there, Princess!" she called. When the stars cleared from her vision, she thumped the baby's back and stumbled over a plastic Cinderella carriage trying to get to the crib. There was no time to wait for a burp, so she set him on his tummy, pulled the crib side up until the lock clicked, straightened the zoo-patterned bumper, and ran out. The baby's squalls made her heart hurt, but they were soon drowned out by the buzz of the oven timer.

When Bonnie got to the kitchen, Hayley was nowhere to be seen. One tray of peanut butter buckeyes for the neighbor's barbecue was on the table, but the bowl of melted chocolate was missing. A brown puddle was hardening on the counter. Bonnie turned off the oven timer and pulled down the metal door. Smoke rushed into her eyes, then the alarm blared.

"Shoot!" cried Bonnie. After a three-diaper shopping trip for Buck's homecoming, the fridge was so stuffed with his favorite foods that she'd stored the candy in the stove and completely forgotten about it when she preheated the oven for the meat-loaf. At least she remembered to use his mother's recipe with Lipton's onion soup this time. Bonnie opened the window, climbed a chair to unplug the smoke detector, and then dumped the charcoal mess in the trash. She looked around. "Hayley, where are you? Want to lick the spoon?"

Bonnie's old Homecoming Queen crown—with only a few seed pearls missing—rose up slowly from behind the chipped tile counter. Hayley's blonde bangs appeared next, then her three-year-old face, streaked with chocolate. "I did already."

Bonnie opened her mouth to scold her daughter, but Hayley was already crying. Bonnie squatted down and hugged her. "Oh, Princess, we have tons more chocolate chips. That's why Mommy shops at Costco."

A truck horn honked outside. Bonnie released her daughter and looked out the window past the overgrown lawn at the Fourth of July decorations she had strung along the white picket fence. She made Buck buy this house because it reminded her of Ohio, but it wasn't the same without her old friends and the family next door. When Buck's red truck pulled up the driveway, Bonnie snapped the shutters closed. Shoot. He was early.

Bonnie reached out to wipe her daughter's face and the red-and-blue T-shirt dress they'd tie-dyed his morning before grocery shopping. There was no time to change; she'd do that before they went to the neighborhood block party. She fluffed her hair and pinched her cheeks and tried to look like something more than a baby maker. Then she wiped the counter with a damp sponge and sprinted to the living room.

She hid her stack of movie star magazines and opened the scrapbook to her birthday page. She wanted to show him how she put in his photo so he wouldn't feel bad about missing her twenty-fourth. Then she ran to the front hall and straightened the new photo of Hayley hugging her baby brother. She dusted the one of Buck in his scarlet-and-gray Ohio State football uniform, which hung next to her Homecoming Queen photo. She hoped he wouldn't mind that she had moved them to the hall. The other photos of his football glory days were back in her hope chest, where they belonged. That was then, this is now. Why rub it in?

Buck was still unloading his suitcase and a cardboard carton when she peeked out the window, so she kicked a sneaker into the closet and ran back to the kitchen. She shoved the meatloaf in the oven, stuck the tray of buckeyes in the fridge, popped open a Budweiser, dashed into the front hall, and opened the door just in time. "Welcome home, honey!" She got on tiptoe and leaned up against his beer gut to give him a kiss. She still carried a bit of baby weight, but he looked like he was stuck in his second trimester. He still had that big-man-on-campus confidence, though. Hayley hugged his knees.

"Howdy, girls!" He gave her a squeeze and traded the cardboard carton of Charles Chips for the beer. "You're looking at the new West Coast Quality Control Manager."

"Congratulations! Did you get a raise, too?"

"All in good time," he said. "When's dinner?"

"Soon," she lied. "Want to see the baby?" She led him down the hall to the nursery.

Buck ducked under the doorway, then tripped over the Cinderella carriage. He frowned and gave her a look. Bonnie kicked the carriage out of the way, picked up a stuffed giraffe, and turned toward the crib. The baby was covered with spit-up. "Jesus Christ, what's going on here?"

"He's been a bit colicky today," she explained. She scooped up the baby. A spurting noise came from his diaper, then that unmistakable odor hit the air. Buck winced and backed out of the room. Bonnie cleaned up the baby, trying to stay positive. Then she heard the squeak of the oven door and Buck swearing so loudly she could hear him all the way from the kitchen. Bonnie should never have promised to make meat loaf today. There just wasn't enough time. Besides, there would be perfectly good food at Cathy's barbecue down the street. Not to mention those delicious chocolate éclairs from the Gourmet Grocery.

The truth was, Bonnie hated to cook. She enjoyed baking sweets, but after making dinner for her father all through high school and college, she thought she was done with meat and potatoes. Every New Year's Day, she cooked chili for the Rose Bowl party, where she and her friends cuddled up under wool blankets and watch the football game play out under the palm trees in Pasadena. During those long gray Ohio winters, she dreamed of moving out to sunny California. Bonnie had girlfriends who moved across the country on their own, but she didn't need to be that brave. Buck promised to make it happen.

The year he played in the Rose Bowl, she had never felt so proud. So she planned the wedding, and Buck was true to his word. Unfortunately, Bonnie had forgotten to plan anything *beyond* the wedding. And being a bride turned out to be a lot like being a beauty queen. It all sounded so romantic until your life was no longer your own.

Bonnie pulled an OSU onesie over the squirming baby and hurried to the kitchen. Out the window she could see neighborhood families strolling down the sidewalk carrying foil-wrapped bowls. She hoped Buck still wanted to go to the block party. Cathy's parties were always fun—and Bonnie was dying to get out and talk to some grown-ups. Or even some teenagers. Anyone who knew the entire alphabet without singing it. If only that included her husband.

"All I want is a hot meal on the table when I come home from work. Is that asking too much?" He opened his prescription bottle and took another Vicodin. Poor guy's neck would never be the same. Bonnie cradled Lucas's soft neck; she'd never let him play football.

"I'd like that, too, honey. The only hot meal I've eaten lately is . . ." Bonnie shrugged, she couldn't remember the last time she'd had a hot meal. "Hold the baby and I'll make the salad. There'll be burgers at Cathy's, you know."

Buck aimed and tossed the can in a high arc to the trash bin. He flashed a peace sign, but he meant: two points. "I turned down a room key from a smokin'-hot bartender last night."

"You're still a hottie, I know. Now, wash your hands so you can take the baby." Bonnie said. She got the cutting board from beneath the stovetop.

"A little appreciation would be nice, is all," Buck said, from the sink. "This promotion is a lot of pressure. If the product is too salty or not crunchy enough, we lose business."

Bonnie laughed. "What do you do, taste potato chips all day?"

Buck gave her a chilly look.

"I'm sorry," she said. "I was kidding." She took a deep breath and peeked in the oven. Yup, the meat loaf was still raw. She heard a beer tab pop behind her. If she weren't nursing, she'd be tempted, too. She hoisted the baby on her hip and stared at the cracked stars-and-stripes salad bowl she'd found at the 99-cent store. "Can't we eat at the party and save the meatloaf for tomorrow?"

Buck was leafing through the mail on the counter. "Nah, I just want to stay home and relax. Maybe have a little fun." He dropped the mail, gave her a hug, and ran his hand down her back beneath the straps of her overalls.

Bonnie had spent five lonely nights under the Amish quilt on their king-size bed, pining for the warmth of her husband's embrace. But now she just wanted five minutes to herself. "Oh, honey, I'm too tired to be any fun." She pulled away and with a sigh took the salad fixings out of the fridge with her free hand. "Take him, will you?"

"You're always fun," Buck said. Instead of reaching for the baby, he took another sip of beer. "Remember how we used to sneak into the stadium and do it in the VIP section after practice? That was fun." He plucked a cherry tomato from the basket and popped it in his mouth.

Bonnie shrugged, kicked the fridge shut, and banged the faucet on with her wrist so she could rinse the tomatoes. "I wish it was more fun now."

"We're just getting started, honey. The more the merrier, Mom says. Maybe we'll make another baby tonight." He kissed her cheek and went to get his suitcase from the hall. He put it by the laundry room for her. Then he sat in the overstuffed recliner just beyond the kitchen and clicked on the TV as if he were Master of the Universe.

Bonnie felt like molten lava was running through her veins as she dumped the tomatoes into the salad. One fell to the floor, and Bonnie stepped on it on her way into the living room. She switched off the blaring box, then put the baby in his arms.

"Hey, I want to watch the news!"

"Here's a news flash: no more babies. You don't even help with this one." She wiped the squished tomato off her flip-flop.

"What are you, a feminist now?"

"Don't give me that."

"Good, 'cuz that really worked for your mom, didn't it?"

"Leave her out of it." Bonnie put her hands on her hips. "I remember a time when you didn't want babies at all."

Buck cradled the baby, silent a moment. "Don't talk about that."

"Why not? It didn't happen to you."

He gave her a dark look and put the baby on the floor to

crawl. Big whoop. If she'd wanted the baby underfoot, she'd have put him on the floor herself. Buck went into the kitchen for another beer. Bonnie followed him, and started chopping celery. She chopped faster and faster as she got more agitated. She knew she was treading on dangerous territory, but she couldn't stop herself from asking, "Don't you ever think about it?"

"What are you going to do, blame me forever?"

"I don't blame you at all, Buck. We were too young. But you can't pretend it didn't happen."

"Why not?"

"Because—it's July." She tossed the knife in the sink.

"So?"

"So. That baby would be six years old this week—and all the babies in the world won't change that!" She felt tears breaking loose. She wanted him to wipe them from her cheeks and then take her in his arms and make it all better.

But he didn't. Instead, he said, "Maybe you're right. We shouldn't have any more children." He lowered his voice, as if Hayley wouldn't be able to hear him. "Truth is, you're not doing so well with these two." He grabbed his keys and went to the front door.

Hayley passed him as she skipped in. "Look, Daddy!" she said, holding up a picture.

Buck patted her on the head and kept going.

Bonnie picked Hayley up, holding her like human body armor. She straightened the crooked crown on her daughter's head, then followed Buck to the door.

She might be disorganized these days, maybe even a bad wife, but she tried really hard to be a good mother. And where she came from, good mothers provided fathers for their children. "Don't leave!"

The baby started crying. Bonnie set Hayley down and pointed for her to find her brother. "C'mon, Buck, I'm just tired. Did you notice the new portrait? At least check out the scrapbook." Bonnie grabbed his arm. "I love you."

He pulled away. "You love my paycheck."

Bonnie tried not to laugh. "Right, because we're living in Malibu eating lobster every night."

Buck opened the door.

She blocked it. "I'm sorry! Maybe we just need a time out."

"What am I, three? I'm another kid for you to clean up after?" He shoved her out of the way and opened the door. "To hell with it. I work hard for you and the kids and—I'm done. Find another sucker. I quit." He grabbed the suitcase in the hall and left, slamming the door behind him.

"Wait!"

The baby was wailing now. Bonnie looked from the door back to the kitchen, torn. She ran to the kitchen, scooped the baby up from the floor, and looked out the window over the sink. The truck was already squealing out of the driveway. Buck had stormed out before, but not like this. Not with a suitcase. And not without dinner.

She felt frozen. Helpless. But there was no time for that. The baby was starting to squirm and Hayley was back, tugging on her. Bonnie splashed water on her face and pasted on a smile.

"Mommy, look." Hayley held up a drawing of their house with the white picket fence.

To Bonnie, it looked like a cage with white picket bars. "Very nice, honey." She gave her a kiss and stood up. "How about a walk?"

Outside, neighbors were enjoying the beginning of the Fourth of July weekend. Bonnie pushed the stroller down the sidewalk, and though she nodded at the older couple walking an enormous poodle in the other direction, her hands were shaking. Bonnie had tied her hair back with Hayley's Hello Kitty ribbon and put on her matching tie-dyed T-shirt dress, but she didn't feel any better. She felt like she was watching herself walk down the sidewalk; an out-of-body experience.

Bonnie had known better than to bring up the abortion. Buck couldn't even say the word—had made her promise to keep it a secret. But every once in a while, the memory of that day came creeping back . . . telling the nurse that she was really a good girl, she did love the father . . . hearing that enormous black woman next to her in the recovery room shrieking, "Mama!" Bonnie didn't dare tell her own mother. She was the only one in central Ohio who didn't adore Buck, but all of Bonnie's friends swooned at the mention of his name—and Bonnie was the one who got to marry him. At the time, she felt like she'd won. Right now, she couldn't remember why she'd entered the contest in the first place.

Bonnie strolled along, forcing herself to smile at folks as if her husband hadn't just left her. She and the kids always took a walk this time of day, when the light was soft and the air was cool. The magic hour, the movie magazines called it. There was nothing magical about it tonight.

Hayley pedaled her tricycle past a yard full of kids twirling illegal sparklers, while Bonnie trailed behind. The golden streams of light were like arrows, all pointing to her. She was a headline in *People* magazine: "Beauty Queen Abandoned by Ex-Football Star." This was *so* not happening to her.

The aroma of USDA Prime beef rose from her neighbor's yard. If she closed her eyes and imagined more space between the houses, she could pretend she was in Ohio. Buck was gone so much, she might as well live back there anyway. If she and the kids caught the red-eye flight tonight, tomorrow she could show Hayley how to stuff crêpe paper in chicken wire for the neighborhood float, then show off the baby while drinking Yoo-Hoo at the ice cream social, and take them both to hear her old high school choir perform before the fireworks.

A basketball rolled into the street. Sweaty teenagers raced down the driveway in front of Hayley's pink tricycle to fetch it. Bonnie hurried to catch up. "Hayley!" she cried. Hayley stopped pedaling and rang her My Little Pony bell. Brring brrring! She held her tiara on while she leaned over and plucked a small American flag from the row bordering the grass. "Put that back, Princess, that's not ours."

Kyle, the teenager whose noisy graduation party got shut down by cops last week, ran over, pushing the blue bandanna up his sweaty forehead. His buddy followed, his bare chest glistening above UCLA basketball shorts. Buck hated the Bruins. Kyle stuck a flag in each handlebar of Hayley's trike, turning it into a parade float. "It's okay, Bonnie, she can have it."

"That's so sweet." She'd never get used to being called by her first name. California was so progressive. Once upon a time, she couldn't wait to be called Mrs. Fornari. Now she felt like she'd earned it. She sniffed and looked up. Kyle's friend was smiling at her. Maybe she should have said: Thanks, Dude—or was it Dog now? She was only a few years older, but she felt ancient. "Say 'thank-you,' Hayley."

"I have a turtle," Hayley said.

"Turtles are cool." Kyle smiled. "There's a surf contest at Zuma tomorrow," Kyle said, looking at Bonnie. His friend shoved him. He turned back to Hayley. "I mean, if your mom and dad are taking you to the beach. Turtles live there."

His friend scoffed. "It ain't Hawaii, dude."

Kyle threw the ball hard at his friend. "I meant the tide pools at Leo Carillo, jerk-off."

"Daddy went bye-bye," Hayley announced.

Bonnie forced a chuckle and yanked Hayley's trike forward. "We haven't made plans yet. Thanks again!" When she glanced back, Kyle was still watching. He waved. His friend yanked him back toward the hoop. Bonnie couldn't help relaxing just a little. She must not look quite as hideous as she felt.

Red and blue balloons were tied to Cathy's mailbox next door. Bonnie put her arm out for Hayley to wait as an SUV pulled up in the driveway. She could make out the laughter and Bruce singing "Born in the U.S.A" from the backyard. A familiar-looking couple got out of the SUV and carried a sheet cake up the driveway. Bonnie was halfway up the driveway when she lost her nerve. She yanked Hayley to a stop. No way was she going to any party now. Last thing she wanted was questions about where Buck was tonight. Or tomorrow night. Or ever. Blinking back the tears once again, she turned the stroller toward home.

The house was empty. She threw out the meatloaf, gave the children baths, and put them to bed. She wondered where

Buck would eat dinner. And where he would sleep. She wondered if another "smokin'-hot" bartender would offer him her room key. She almost hoped that he'd take it.

She found the phone in the nursery and dialed her father's number. She was dying to talk to somebody, but she was too ashamed to call her sorority sisters or the women she'd met at Mommy 'N Me. She heard her father's voice, gruff with sleep, and hung up. He wouldn't understand.

She wandered aimlessly, then flipped through some magazines. She skimmed *Parents* until she saw an article about single parenting. She polished off a dozen peanut butter buckeyes, then she picked up *People* for news about Lucas Hatteras. Buck thought it was a sissy name, but what did he know? He wanted to name the baby Buck Junior, like his dick.

Bonnie went into her room and opened her hope chest. Her great-grandfather had carved it for her mother, who passed it down when Bonnie got engaged. She dug between the books and letters to her white lace wedding album. She flipped through the pages, stopped at one of her in her wedding gown, and stared at it for a long time. When she finally looked up, it was late, and she saw a starving coyote run down the street. It was a sign that meant more than just hot weather in the hills. Tomorrow there would be posters describing missing cats nailed to telephone poles around the block. Buck called them coyote menus.

He wasn't coming back. This was real.

The baby let out a squall, and she went into the nursery to feed him. Afterward, she let him sleep in her arms while she rocked and rocked. She heard a wailing sound. As it grew louder, she realized it was coming from her.

Her husband had left her.

Bonnie was a reject, like a potato chip that was too salty, or not crunchy enough. She put her son back in the crib, hugged the stuffed giraffe to her chest, and sat back down. She listened to her babies breathe. She rocked until she had bitten all her fingernails down to the flesh; until the morning paper hit the driveway; until the curtains glowed at dawn.

Then she heard Buck's truck roar into the driveway. Hayley

stirred, but didn't awaken. Bonnie peeked out the windows. He was back.

She tossed the giraffe in the open toy box, ran toward the door, then stopped. She looked at the pictures hanging in the hallway and heard his key scrape in the doorjamb. She tiptoed back into their bedroom. Then she slipped under the quilt and pretended to sleep.

Chapter 4

ANNETTE

. . . you buy your own damn flowers.

The windows in the Century City tower across from Annette's thirty-second-floor office glowed in a red, white,
and blue flag pattern for the Fourth of July weekend. She loved
holidays—but not for the lights. She loved being in the office
when the phones weren't ringing, buying property before it
went on the market, and hiring movers to unpack in the dead
of night. Annette was a counterprogrammer.

She popped a chocolate Kiss in her mouth as the last bank of
lights over her glass desk clicked off. The super had turned the
power off again. She hit Save on her computer as the screen fiz-
zled to black and she held her breath until it sprang back to life
on auxiliary power. The Chambers file had fast-saved, thank
God. She clicked the file closed, then fastened the pearl buttons of her St. John knit jacket before rising to a stand. "Hel-
looo?"

The door opened, and a wiry Mexican man leaned in. His
eyes opened wide at the sight of her. After nine years of legal
practice, she was used to this reaction from men. She used to
think it was because she was black, but she had come to understand that sex trumped color every day of the week. Men were

distracted by the sight of her shapely legs under the glass conference table. She never wore pants; they were uncomfortable
on her curves. Plus, she wasn't opposed to using everything in
her arsenal: God gave her legs at the same time as brains, after
all. At the moment, however, they were draped in darkness.

"*Pardon, Señora,* I thought this floor was empty."

Annette sniffed in the glow of the computer screen. This was
a new janitor. The regulars knew to check with her before making any attempts to save electricity after hours. Annette didn't
offer up any pleasantries. She was well aware of the benefits of
keeping one's mouth shut until the time was right. Just today,
she had received a private investigator's report that proved the
tennis-pro husband of one of her clients had four kids from
three other wives. Naturally, her client was furious, but Annette
explained the financial benefit of hiding one's feelings and
using the information in court after the plaintiff had asked for
a generous settlement. It was never safe to show emotion.

If only Annette had applied that wisdom to her own life.

Annette sat back down as the man yanked a bandanna from
the pocket of his white coveralls and mopped his forehead. She
reached for the photograph of her daughter, illuminated by
the ring of light from her monitor, then piled it, along with var-
ious folders, into her Prada briefcase. The janitor stammered
about orders to limit utility bills during the holiday. She sniffed
again but said nothing. Far more money would be saved turning down the frigid air-conditioning every day, but her male
partners set the thermostat for the comfort of three-piece Italian suits, so Annette was used to summer colds. During ten
years of practice, Annette had learned to pick her battles. This
one was not worth fighting.

Annette waved the janitor out and took one last look at the
Dissomaster on the computer screen. The formula was used by
the courts to calculate a fair balance of support from one
spouse to another. In reality, it was bullshit. Annette's law professor at Stanford was right: the fair came once a year and only
to the highest bidder. That described her typical client, but this
particular client was the head partner's niece, a stay-at-home

mom. Annette didn't know how anyone in Los Angeles could live on the amount displayed on the screen. Legally, after nine years, the woman was due support for the rest of her life. Unfortunately, the calculation was based on her projected earnings for a college degree she never used while raising five children. According to the Los Angeles County guidelines, the support this woman could depend on amounted to less than what Annette paid to feed her ex-husband's cat.

Annette worked hard to support her ex-husband's cat; she had no choice. She had won some big cases over the past few years while Jackson painted and partied and took care of Morgan—with the help of Carmen, her housekeeper, of course. But since Jackson didn't sell enough paintings to qualify as actual income, Annette was legally bound to maintain the lifestyle she had given him. The irony was, she had to work so hard to keep up that the family court ruled that she was not available often enough to share custody beyond every other weekend and Wednesday nights. And since Jackson lived in the house, she had no proper place to care for their daughter anyway.

Now, however, Annette had taken the first step toward demonstrating that she could provide a home for her daughter. She closed the Dissomaster, printed the Chambers file—a nice, neat case with a clearcut prenup—and slipped both in her briefcase to study at home.

"Home," she said aloud. She liked the sound of that.

After six months of camping out in the Century City condo normally reserved for partners visiting from the East Coast, Annette was finally moving into a real house with a real yard. She took her Mercedes key ring out of her purse and admired the happy face house key. She had bought the home and everything in it from a client desperate to sell. He was a gambler whose wife had wasted their savings trying to prove he had simply hidden the money, not lost it. It was ironic that she tried so hard to prove her husband was evil rather than stupid. Ultimately, they were forced to sell the house to pay her firm's bill. A win-win for Annette.

Annette glanced at her Movado watch. Carmen should be

finished unpacking the boxes from storage by now. Annette wanted everything perfect for Morgan's arrival in the morning. She might be an expert at delegating at work, but she would not delegate motherhood. Especially not to her ex-husband. Call her sexist, just don't call her late for her weekend with Morgan.

Annette turned off her computer, grabbed her briefcase, and hurried down the dim hallway, trying in vain to get a clear signal on her PDA so she could call Morgan to say good night. In the office lobby, one of his oil paintings hung askew. Annette pushed the enormous canvas horizontal to the ground, just as Jackson had done the day they met at his gallery show. She'd been so delighted to date an artist back then. He was so sensitive, so romantic, so different from the black executives she usually dated. She should have known better. She should have gotten premarital counseling, asked for a prenuptial agreement—or listened to her mother and not married a white man. But no, Miss Smarty-Pants thought she knew it all. Worse, she thought she could do it all.

Now she had to.

Ten miles and thirty minutes later, she was at her new home. The empty moving truck pulled away from the curb as Annette pulled into the circular driveway, and stepped gracefully out of the car. Away from the city, the stars blinked like strobe lights. Annette knew they might be nothing more than movie premiere spotlights over in Hollywood, but she made a wish anyway. She admired the clean lines of the California Craftsman and nodded at the man hoisting a large American flag on her veranda-style porch. It was a perfect match to the one on the flagpole fronting the colonial across the street.

Annette exchanged a wave with the family relaxing on the rooftop deck. Perhaps they could see some early fireworks from there. If all went well, next year she and Morgan could join them.

Carmen met her at the door, wiping her hands on her apron. "Good evening, Ms. Gold."

"It is indeed," Annette said. "Nice to have you back." She smiled at the small Salvadoran woman whom she relied on as much as her law partners relied on their wives. In a perfect world, everyone would have a wife; if only it weren't so hard to be one. "Could you please have a gardener mow this overgrown lawn first thing tomorrow?" Annette knew it would cost twice as much as waiting for a weekday, but she wanted to fit into the neighborhood like a proper family, not some pathetic single mother who couldn't keep a husband happy. Despite the legal dissolution of millions of marriages, there was still a stigma for divorced women.

Annette would be a perfectly respectable neighbor. She and Morgan would stroll along the sidewalk with her bunny carriage. They would wrap twinkle lights around the square pillars for Christmas. They would dress up and trick-or-treat. Maybe they would even get a dog. Carmen opened the door for Annette and she went inside. In the foyer, movers were hanging another Jackson original above the mahogany entrance table, but they had it upside down. She pointed until they corrected it, then listened to them complain in Spanish. She didn't care. All men cared about was money, and she was paying these two quite generously for their muscle, not their opinions. She nudged the frame up another half inch. As much as she resented her ex, the few things she got attached to meant a lot to her, and this five-foot-square burst of indigo was one of them.

She picked up a green apple from the enormous Harry & David gift basket sent by her law firm. Annette was generally tight-lipped at the office, but it was no secret that she was excited about her new home. She took a bite, then turned and faced the living room.

Carmen frowned, expectantly. "You like?" she asked in a dubious tone.

Annette surveyed the shabby velvet furniture and shook her head. "You can give it to your cousins, if they'll take it."

Carmen shook her head. "Maybe you sell it on eBay."

Annette nodded. It was antique, after all. But she needed to move it quickly, so she could buy sleek modern replacements.

Carmen pointed at the apple.

"Enchiladas in the icebox. I go now."

"Thank you, Carmen."

Carmen got her enormous purse and ushered the movers out. Annette shut the door and punched Jackson's number into the PDA once again, but there was no answer. Annette unlocked her briefcase and put a photo of Morgan down beside the fruit basket. She touched the glass over the dark curls springing from her daughter's head. She would never straighten them like her own mother had, to help her fit in. She wanted Morgan to be an original. She'd fought hard for the pregnancy, after all; a hundred grand worth of failed fertility treatments, finally resulting in a surrogate. But Annette loved Morgan as though she had given birth to her; Morgan was like a piece of Annette's heart outside her body.

She took another bite of the green apple and headed upstairs. Due to an old knee injury from playing basketball at UCLA, Annette wasn't a huge fan of stairs. She leaned on the hand-carved banister and took her time to admire the tongue-and-groove landing.

Upstairs, logs were arranged in the fireplace of the master bedroom—a real fireplace, not the fake gas kind at the company condo. Her four-poster bed fit perfectly. Carmen had placed a Chanel lipstick by a tall white orchid on her vanity table. She checked the label to be sure it was "Fire," a duplicate of the shade she kept in her purse. Then she tossed the apple in the trash and made a mental note to give Carmen a raise.

Annette walked in the cedar-lined closet and ran her hands along the smooth shoulders of her suits. They were lined up by color, the black ones fading to pinstripes, then charcoal. The slate skirt was out of place, so she pulled the hanger out and slipped it back in by the lighter fabrics two suits down. Shoeboxes with coordinating high heels lined the shelf above, but one of the lids was askew.

Annette pressed the lid down, but it wouldn't budge. She took down the box and looked inside. A dark fabric was stuffed around a stiletto heel. Since Annette hadn't done the packing, she assumed Carmen had simply put it there by mistake. Annette pulled the filmy fabric out, and the memories rushed back. She sat down quickly, before she fell. It was the peignoir she'd thrown away over a year ago. That was no mistake.

Annette rubbed the fine black fabric between her fingers. It was as if she was back at the beach house, with the Siamese purring on the bed. She could practically smell the salt air and hear the hypnotic rhythm of crashing waves. Normally she prided herself on total recall, but this was a memory she'd rather forget.

She'd been working so much that she and Jackson had become little more than roommates. She'd wanted to do something special to make it up to him. She took an allergy pill and opened a good bottle of Vouvray. She poured them each a glass and looked out the picture window at the last traces of twilight. The waves rose and fell in frothy white rows beyond the deck. A dolphin cast a long shadow as it leaped across the surf. Annette put on some mellow jazz, but not so loud as to wake Morgan, who was asleep in the back bedroom.

Annette tapped her nails on the rim of Jackson's wineglass as she set it on the bedside table by his reading light. He checked the time on the Rolex Submariner watch she'd bought for his birthday, put his book down, and took a sip. She felt his gaze as she walked away and knew he was watching her through the glass bricks as she lowered her naked body into the bath. She rubbed baby oil into her skin, from her breasts to her curved hips, then down her toned legs. She dried off quickly, shook her dark hair out of the shower cap, and clipped it up in a bun to give him access to her long neck. He used to make her come just by kissing it.

She couldn't wait to taste his tongue in her mouth tonight, feel him press against her breasts and slide between her legs. She snipped the price tag off the sheer peignoir with a cuticle scissor, slipped it over her head, and strutted like a model toward the bed.

Now was Annette's chance to make him forget those lonely nights when he called and interrupted her meetings with long descriptions about the sunset and the rainbow of pigment he

would blend to portray it. Now was her chance to make him forget those who kept him company when she didn't take his calls.
Oh yes, Annette knew there had been other lovers, but she was
willing to forgive him this indiscretion. As a divorce lawyer, she
knew that adultery was merely a symptom of neglect. It was not
the worst thing that could happen.

Annette climbed under the linen duvet. She lifted the cat off
the covers and put her arm around her husband's suntanned
chest. He was a good father and a very sexy man. She would do
her best to please him. Jackson stroked her hair for a moment,
then closed his eyes. Annette caught her fingers in the curly
hair on his chest. She snuggled up and brushed her soft lips
against his neck. She moved her leg over his and reached below
the covers. She stroked him for a moment, then cupped his
balls. He didn't respond. She put her hands on his shoulders
and kissed him full on the mouth. He pushed her away, picked
the cat up and set her between them.

Annette sneezed and sat up. "What is it, Jackson? Are you
punishing me?"

"No."

"No, what?"

"No, thank you."

"Excuse me?"

"It's not you."

She looked down at her voluptuous figure. Damn straight it
wasn't her. She could give up law and have a career modeling
lingerie, for Christ's sake. But the line he used was so old, so
cliché—and so wrong—that none of her clients dared to use it
anymore. She was pissed. She could ask if he was taking antidepressants or if he needed Viagra or had male menopause or
wanted couples counseling, but it would make no difference at
the moment. Right now she just wanted to have sex and it was
obvious that it wasn't on his agenda.

She grabbed the covers, rolled over, and tried to sleep, but of
course that didn't happen. She went out on the deck and looked
at the waves. For the first time, Annette felt helpless.

The next morning, while Jackson was in the shower, she found a watch under their bed. It was a rubber sports watch with the Ironman logo. A man's watch.

Annette had no problem with homosexuality—this was Los Angeles, after all and Jackson was an artist from West Hollywood. In her head, she knew that a person mattered more than their sex. But in her heart, she wondered what had she done wrong as a woman to lose her husband to a man. Jackson said the change in his feelings wasn't personal, but of course it was. She heard the shower stop and waited for him to appear from behind the glass bricks. Now was the time to confront him. But why bother? It didn't matter who he loved if it wasn't her. And all evidence pointed to that same conclusion: Jackson no longer loved her. *That* was the worst thing that could happen.

Annette sneezed, shaking herself out of the memory. The Kowalskis' cat must have slept in every corner of this walk-in closet. She plucked a folded Kleenex from one of her suit jackets and blew her nose. Why couldn't Jackson have been like every other husband in town and fucked the nanny? She could understand the attraction of nubile youth and a nurturing instinct. She could have competed with that. She could have interrupted her meetings to take his calls about the sunset; she could have swept him away on romantic vacations to art galleries in Europe.

Annette jabbed a hole in the peignoir with her nail and ripped it in half. What kind of divorce attorney was she to ignore such horrible odds? It was one thing to believe in love, quite another to count on it. *Naïve* was just another word for *stupid.*

She peeled herself off the closet floor and dropped the negligée in the trashcan. There would be no more mistakes. Annette had no need for a sexy nightgown. She could pay for her own dinner, thank you very much, and sex was overrated. When she wanted to be touched, she booked a massage.

Annette sighed and found the hanger with her silk pajama pants and blouse. She changed and went downstairs. In the kitchen, gleaming copper pots hung above the granite island. Computerized invoices lay in a pile by the sink. Thanks to Carmen, the Sub-Zero refrigerator was packed as well. Tomorrow, she and Morgan would celebrate with hot dogs and lemonade and all the Popsicles a little girl could eat. She remembered a wine cabinet from her tour and found it off the pantry. High time to celebrate her housewarming.

Annette dialed the beach house once again then opened the door to the wine closet. Ahh. Row upon row of bottles were turned label up, in order of vintage. Except . . . there was a bottle of Montrachet missing from the second row. The stainless-steel racks had been full last month, Annette was sure of it. She made a note to ask Carmen about it and picked out a spicy Shiraz instead. Annette gave up on the beach house phone and tried Jackson's cell.

He answered immediately. "Howdy."

"Jackson, you can't just not answer the phone. I have every right to say good night to my daughter."

"Your daughter?" Jackson replied. "Don't you mean our daughter?" He went on about how he took such good care of Morgan and all Annette did was pay the bills. Annette toyed with the light switches on the wall and yawned. She could hear his damn cat yowl in the background.

"Fine, *our* daughter," she said into the PDA. "Please put her on."

"It's bedtime," he said. "You have three minutes."

"Don't tell me what I . . ." Annette heard him put down the phone. She looked through the window by the back door. The backyard was lit up with twinkle lights now, like fairyland. The rose garden led to a playground complete with a regulation basketball hoop. A vine-covered fence surrounded the Jacuzzi and the pool and what had to be a faux waterfall. There was even a guesthouse off to the side. The place was deceivingly small from the street; back here it was a frigging hotel. An understated one, expanded slowly and carefully and with excellent taste—except for the furniture. Go figure.

Annette chuckled at her good fortune as she walked down the steps outside and strolled between rose bushes, searching for a basketball. The crickets sang in unison.

Jackson came back on the line. "She's asleep. She wasn't feeling good after the chili dog, so Leo let her lie down on the hammock. I didn't want her to have the chili dog in the first place, but you know how persuasive she can be. She got that from you."

Annette nodded until she realized what he said. "Did you say Leo's hammock? Isn't that in Big Bear?"

"Well, yes, but—"

"Yoo-hoo!" a friendly voice called out through the night.

Annette looked around but didn't see anyone. She shook it off and returned her attention to the argument at hand. "Jackson, this is my holiday. Unless you want to be arrested for kidnapping, you'd better bundle her up, get in the car, and have her back in L.A. tomorrow."

Annette held the Treo at arm's length to avoid the squawk of Jackson's voice. The down side of being a partner in a law firm was that your ex got half the business. The up side was you could file a motion during a holiday weekend. Annette found the basketball. It was wet, but it had some bounce left. She threw it, and missed a shot she could have done blindfolded ten years ago.

There was a shuffling noise, or maybe a hitch in the hum of the pool motor, but Annette ignored it. She'd get used to the new sounds soon enough. She clicked up the volume on her Treo and headed for the plastic castle nestled under the oak tree. The pink shutters reminded Annette of the one she'd circled in the Sears wish book when she was a child. Now her daughter would have it all. If only Jackson would let her. "Jackson? Did you hear me?"

"Yoo-hoo!" There it was again.

"I heard you," Jackson said. "I'll send you a picture if that'll shut you up."

"It will until morning, thanks," Annette said. She sat down on a swing and clicked to download the image. Sure enough,

Morgan was asleep with her stuffed bunny. Such a sweetie. Annette clicked back to the audio channel. "Eight A.M. And she'd better be wearing sunblock."

Jackson hung up so fast, she wasn't sure if he'd heard the last part. Ingrate. When she stood up, the rubber seat swayed. Annoyed, Annette grabbed it. She pitched it into the air as hard as she could. The chain jangled as the seat flew around and around the stained-wood frame, clanging until it stopped short. Then it dangled above reach.

There was another scuffling noise, this time beyond the wooden gate. Annette snapped her PDA shut and tiptoed over the wood chips, to the cement path.

She peered over the gate. A shiny red bow lay crushed on the walk. A foot away was a clear Tupperware container of—were those brownies? Annette listened to the crickets for a moment, then opened the gate. She loved brownies. And they went so well with red wine. Now she had all the fixings for a celebration.

If only she felt like celebrating.

Chapter 5

DIANE

. . . the man in your bed is nine years old.

Diane locked the car in the smelly garage of the Pacific Palms apartment building. She shifted her backpack and Scout's leash and picked up the potted plant while the kids played a weary game of hide and seek between a dented Dodge convertible and a shiny Kia. They'd come back for the boxes later. "Grab your stuff and let's go, you guys." She pulled Cody out from behind the faux Spanish arch.

"Ouch." He lifted his arm to show off his latest injury, a long red scratch.

Diane looked around the corner and spotted the enormous bougainvillea plant. It grew like ivy on the other side of the arch, coloring the stucco wall with clusters of fuchsia blossoms. Dark spikes were hidden among the verdant leaves. "Beauty comes at a price."

Quinn lugged the cat crate through the arch into the court-yard. She pointed to the planter by the tiled fountain. "I like the orange flowers on those stalks. They look like roosters."

"Birds of Paradise," Diane said. She admired the Spanish bungalow–ambiance of the exterior; it reminded her of Spain and Greece and all those places she hadn't seen since backpacking through Europe after college. But the interior of the apartment building was horribly generic—just like Diane was now. Through the single-paned windows of the building, she could see the other apartment dwellers drowning in the glow of their televisions. She pressed the elevator button, but it didn't light up. "We'll have to take the stairs."

The wrought-iron stairway was bathed in the moonlight, but the kids didn't find it the least bit romantic. They complained with every step until Diane heaved open the fourth-floor security door. Cody dropped his duffel bag and peered down the stark white hallway. "Where's the Coke machine?"

"It's not a hotel, honey. We can have our very own refrigerator with our very own Coke."

"You never buy Coke," Quinn said.

"That's because it's bad for your teeth." Diane said. "I'll make an exception tomorrow and we'll have a picnic on the beach."

"It will be crowded."

"It will be fun."

"But Mother, I hate the sand."

Diane studied her daughter. When did she become "Mother"? And how could she have birthed such a mall rat? "I'll teach you to surf."

The kids both stared at her. "You can surf?"

"*Mother* has many hidden talents."

"I hope one of them is getting our house back."

Diane didn't answer. She hadn't told them about their father's gambling addiction. It was bad enough telling them about the divorce and that they had ten days to pack up their old life. When they were eighteen, she would explain that their father was a criminal. Or maybe she would say he was a victim, which was the gospel according to the Gamamon groupies. Or, she would call it an illness, or whatever official term the mental health industry was using then to maintain pharmaceutical treatment for a simple lack of discipline.

"Mommy, what's this?" Cody started reading: "E-V-I-C-T-I—"

Diane smiled, the universal disguise for panic. Then she

dropped the plant and ripped the document off the door. How could they be evicted before moving in? Stupid question. She should have paid the damn deposit in cash. She clutched the paper to her chest, hoping Quinn hadn't read it yet. She stepped back over the fallen clots of potting soil.

"It's a mistake, honey." She tried her key, but it no longer worked. She pulled the iPod ear bud out of Quinn's ear. "Watch your brother while I find the landlord, alright?"

Quinn slumped to a seat against the thin wall. Scout whimpered and put her nose in Quinn's lap. The cat hissed through the cage. "Hurry," she said.

Diane turned and ran down the hall. She tripped down the stairs, praying that Mr. Orloff, the Russian landlord, was home. When she reached the door by the pool marked MANAGER, she heard men's laughter. She took a deep breath and knocked.

A series of chains rattled from inside, then a swarthy man with safety-pinned spectacles opened up. Behind him, three other men sat around a poker table piled with cufflinks, plastic Jesus figurines, and a six-pack of generic cola. An exotic brunette nearly burst from her polyester blouse as she set a tray of sandwiches on the card table beside a sweating bottle of vodka. One of the men lifted a slice of bread and mumbled. A baby squalled from the back room.

"Nyet, Natalia!" the landlord scolded.

The woman's eyes flashed at Diane, then she withdrew.

Diane wanted to smile, but the landlord was already checking her out. She couldn't very well unbutton her T-shirt to win him over. Not that it would. She smoothed her hair back, but she knew she looked like shit. Maybe he smelled Steve on her. This was a good reason to wear her wedding rings—it kept creepy men from bothering her. It was like those invisible electric fences and the collars for zapping dogs.

Diane held up the eviction notice.

"Check bounce," Mr. Orloff said. "Boing-boing."

Diane smiled sweetly and tried not to inhale Mr. Orloff's cigar breath. Fucking Steve. She should have closed that account long ago. "I'll take care of it in the morning, I promise."

"Is holiday."

"Please, sir," Diane said. "I've got two exhausted children who just had the rug pulled out from under them."

"Vat rug?"

"It's an expression—never mind. Please don't make us sleep in the car. Your garage smells like urine."

"Fine, what you haf deposit?" He raised his unibrow and leered at her diamond engagement ring. Diane covered it. She was saving it for Quinn. Or food money, if she didn't get a job soon. But without a major credit card, a hotel was not an option, and Diane had already called in all her markers—to use Steve's poker lingo—from her married friends. They even avoided her at the last PTA fundraiser, despite her record-breaking haul for the school. It was worse than when the three of them had chicken pox: the kids could play with the other infected kids, but the delivery boy left the grocery bags on the porch and ran. Apparently, divorce was contagious.

Diane pulled her engagement ring off. "This is worth a year's rent."

Mr. Orloff snorted and started to close the door.

Diane jammed her sandal in the opening. "Six months?"

He opened the door. "Three months," he said. "Is used. Cursed. Plus, it make trouble with wife." He tilted his head toward Natalia, who was back with the mustard.

"Fine. Three months—and that six-pack of soda."

"Is deal," Mr. Orloff said. He traded her useless apartment key for a shiny brass one.

Back upstairs, wrinkled clothes from Cody's duffel bag were strewn next to him in the hall. He held up his new camp T-shirt. "I hate volleyball camp. I don't have any friends there."

"You will, Cody. Give them a chance." She held up the soda. The kids jumped up and reached for a can.

"For tomorrow." Diane lifted it out of their reach. Then she unlocked the apartment door and peeked inside the empty space. It looked even smaller than she remembered, and there was no sign of the kids' beds. There were, however, boxes full of old files she should have thrown out. Diane led them inside and shut the door. "Okay, today."

She handed out the sodas, not as a bribe so much as a distraction. Anything to avoid hearing Quinn say the place "sucked." Diane would be hard-pressed not to agree. Thank goodness she'd trusted her mother's intuition and kept their sleeping bags handy. Or had she merely learned to expect the worst?

Quinn opened the pet cage. The cat drew back. "See? Even Boo hates it here."

"Just shush and drink your Coke," Diane said.

"It's not Coke. Besides, I prefer Pepsi."

Diane longed for the contraband bottle of wine, but she needed to stay alert long enough to unpack a bit. She found a saucepan and set it on the stove to boil water for tea. She had a flash of the Eleanor Roosevelt saying on one of those schmaltzy plaques her mother had sent. Something about not knowing how strong a woman is "until she gets in hot water." One of the pleasures of moving was having to throw that crap out. Especially the ones that rang true. She reached for Quinn's can of soda and took a long swig. "Okay," she said to the kids, "let's get moving." She hustled the kids back to the car for more boxes.

An hour of complaints later, Quinn and Cody retreated to their empty room. For the first time, the kids had to share; for the first time, Diane didn't. She shook flowered sheets out of the plastic packaging. Then she tore the tags off her air mattress. Diane never did remove the tags off the California King-size pillowtop she shared with Steve. She was afraid of the mattress police. She was afraid of everything then.

She flung the crisp sheets out, causing the mattress to bump into the wall and bounce off. Why not be honest and call it a pool float? She tried to press the polyester creases down, then stepped over the packing boxes to tuck the edges under. Hip-hop music erupted from the hallway. "Go to bed, Quinn!"

"It's a holiday!"

Diane sank down to the makeshift bed and flipped through her pile of mail. "It's almost midnight. You'll wake your brother."

"I'm awake!" Cody called.

"Don't be!" Diane called. She sure didn't want to be, but after staring at the stained cottage cheese ceiling for a half hour, her mind was still too flooded with to-do lists to sleep.

She sat up, switched on the light, and looked through the mail. A catalog from a valley furniture store was inside. There was a Web site, but Diane wasn't about to order furniture on-line. Who in their right mind bought furniture without seeing it? She put the catalog aside—and felt something rectangular. A credit card. Diane squealed.

"You okay, Mom?"

"Yes, Cody, go to sleep!" Diane thought the bankruptcy had hit every credit reporting service, but evidently this store slipped through the cracks. Diane could cancel her order for that generic rental furniture. No more compromising. She could be practical and still have pretty things, right? All it would take was a quick trip to the valley, either by congested freeway or winding canyon roads. In any case, tomorrow they would shop.

Next, she picked up the padded package from her friend. Diane had forgotten about it. She ripped the package open and pulled out a bubble-wrapped cylinder.

"I can't sleep," Cody called.

She yelled back. "Try harder. Good night!" She tried not to pop any noisy bubbles, and unwrapped a black silk pouch. After untying the drawstring, she pulled out a small purple cylinder. Bizarre. Diane twisted the top. It buzzed.

Startled, she tossed it in the air. It fell on the floor and buzzed in a circle. If she didn't know any better . . . well, she didn't know any better. But there was only one thing it could be: a vibrator.

Hip-hop music erupted again from the hallway. Diane scooped up the vibrator and slipped it under the sheets just as Quinn appeared at the doorway. She kicked a cardboard box of clothing over the threshold, then cocked her head. "What's that noise?"

"Ceiling fan," Diane said. Quinn looked up at the motionless blades. Diane snatched the catalog and shoved it toward Quinn. "What do you think of this furniture?" Diane sat down to block Quinn's view of the vibrator and twisted the darn thing off.

"Ugly," Quinn said. She dropped the catalog on the bed and kicked the box closer. "This is yours."

"How do you know?"

Quinn opened the box and pointed at the clothes. "Ugly."

"Is that ugly, too?" Diane pointed at her phone in Quinn's hand.

"Oh, sorry." Quinn handed Diane the phone. "Daddy said to call."

Diane put the phone down and rooted through the box of khaki shorts, skirts, and pants. They were hers all right. Camouflage. Underneath them was a large, dusty box. "Quinn, wait!" She dusted it off and opened the cover.

When Quinn reappeared in the doorway, Diane showed her the vacuum-packed bridal gown. It was still white. "You still want this? I meant to ask you before packing up the car, but it's just taking up space unless you want it for your hope chest."

"Hope what?"

"It's an old-fashioned thing. Furniture handed down for generations. Used to be, every girl had a trunk to collect things for her trousseau."

"Her what?"

"Her special wardrobe for when she got married."

Quinn burst out laughing.

Diane couldn't blame her. "Not very empowering, is it?"

"Oh, don't give me that feminist stuff. I told you, I'm never getting married."

Diane felt the urge to strangle her daughter. "Feminism is why you have that choice! Anyway, what if you change your mind?" The desire for grandchildren struck Diane for the first time. Then again, Quinn wouldn't have to be married for that, either. Oh, hell. What was left to count on, besides wrinkles? She tapped the white bridal box. "Should I save this? Or do you think it's bad luck?"

Quinn looked again at the gown's stiff bodice and lace trim.

"Considering the fact that it's truly hideous? Yeah, I think it's bad luck."

"It's nineties style—I thought you loved the nineties."

"Just because it's old doesn't mean it's classic."

"Now you know how I feel about disco." Diane closed the box. "Promise me you'll get premarital counseling. I'll pay."

"You mean Daddy will. Doesn't he pay for everything?"

"No, he does not." Diane tried to control herself. Steve's idea of child support was like when the school cafeteria called ketchup a vegetable. But she didn't want to burden Quinn with what a loser her father was. She could barely admit it to herself. The only thing Diane had salvaged was his life insurance. Now he was worth more dead than alive.

If only she were a widow.

Quinn was waiting for an explanation, but Diane was going to be quiet if it killed her. Being a mother sucked. Quinn was right; "suck" was a good word.

"Whatever."

"Quinn." Diane reached out to touch her daughter, but Quinn pulled away to study her nails. Diane took a deep breath. "I'm really, truly sorry about all this."

"All what? This dump?"

"Yes, but more than that. We'll get out of here, I promise. But . . . I feel like part of my job as a mother is to provide a good home—and that includes a father living there."

Quinn looked up. "Oh, Mom, you're so twentieth century." She flounced out.

Diane wasn't sure if that was a bad thing in this case. But, like Quinn said: whatever. Not much she could do about it now.

" 'Night, Mother," Quinn's voice trailed from the hall.

"What, no kiss?" Diane chuckled.

Quinn's door slammed.

Diane's cell phone rang. She looked at the caller ID and groaned. Steve always knew just when to ruin her mood—which was pretty much every time he called. If she didn't answer, it would bug her just as much. She would wonder what he wanted and get ready for a fight. "What?"

"I just . . ." Steve sighed. "I just want to know, do you miss me?"

Diane was tempted to say yes; she didn't want to hurt his feelings. Some habits were hard to break. Like managing his home, running his business, and having her checks bounce. When Diane grounded her children, she was always careful to remind them that their behavior was bad, not them personally. They could choose to behave better. But that easy out didn't extend to adults, not when they made bad choices repeatedly. A pattern was a sign of character—or lack thereof. She looked through the glass door at the first stars in the sky. She wished for what could have been.

She could hear Steve's breath on the phone as she lowered her gaze to the apartments across the alley. Most windows were dark; people were out having fun. It was her turn now. She needed to be honest and cut the cord. Did she miss him? "No," she answered. There were many things she missed, but not him, not anymore.

There was silence on the line. "I'll pick up the kids at ten."

"No, Steve, I told you: I made plans for tomorrow. You can have them for the fireworks."

"I hate fireworks."

"Just show up this time, okay?" Diane snapped the phone shut. If it weren't for the kids, she'd get an unlisted number. If it weren't for the kids, she'd have a real ocean view by now. If it weren't for the kids, she'd be lost. She'd stayed for them, but ultimately, she left for them.

She went out to the five-foot-long balcony. Telephone cables were strung like trapeze wires between the three-story buildings. She could see people moving around in the newly renovated condo across the way. Still, there was the unmistakable scent of salt in the air, and above the building, stars sparkled across the night sky. Diane climbed over the rickety chaise abandoned by the last resident and pressed her back against the porch railing. Now she could see around the corner of the building across the alley. She grabbed the railing and leaned her head out. Eureka!

A perfect slice of ocean was visible just over the fringe of palm trees. The moonlight shimmered on the water. She stepped up to sit on the railing, hooking her knees between the bars and pressing her back against the wall. If she tilted her head, she could sit and enjoy the view. Her neck cramped a bit, but this was doable. Yes! She had an ocean view. Proof there was a God.

Someone giggled. Diane looked down to the alley below. A young couple was leaning against the building, kissing. Diane watched, remembering those giddy first flickers of love. That's what she missed. What if no one ever kissed her like that again?

She caught herself rubbing her wedding ring. When she looked back, the guy's hands were down the girl's pants. Next the girl would be pregnant, the kids would be screaming, and he'd be asking: what's for dinner? Diane went inside and slammed the sliding door shut. She didn't want to be such a pessimist. But happy? Could she really be happy all by herself?

Well, there was one way to try. She dug under the sheets and found the vibrator. Then she ran to the bedroom door and listened for Quinn's music. Nothing: they really were asleep.

She should spend her time unpacking, but that could wait until morning. Tonight was all hers. She had a giddy feeling, like she'd eaten all her vegetables and it was time for dessert. Diane tried to remember where she packed the candles. She rooted through some boxes and found one mixed in with her clothes, but she had no matches. She plugged in the bedside lamp. Nothing. She lifted the shade—no light bulb. So much for ambiance; she didn't even have a radio. The reggae music wafting from a nearby apartment would have to do. She found her emergency flashlight, turned off the fan, and climbed under the scratchy sheets.

Diane had never tried a vibrator, but how hard could it be? She did try to masturbate once in the bathtub after watching *The Vagina Monologues*, but it was like being hypnotized—it felt too obvious. Diane opened up the folded instructions, but the print was too tiny to read, so she dug her glasses out of her purse, held the flashlight above the instructions, and studied the diagram. Hmm, didn't look anything like a Georgia O'Keeffe painting. She flipped to the written instructions. *This clitoral stimulator is designed for* . . . yikes! Enough directions. She slipped the vibrator beneath the covers, keeping her eyes focused on a crack in the ceiling.

The door squeaked open and Diane jumped, then relaxed. It was only Scout, who settled herself on the carpet with a sigh. "Good girl," Diane muttered.

Concentrate, Diane said to herself. Maybe she needed to be drunk. She focused on the soft beam of moonlight falling across the bed from the sliding glass door, and she could hear the ocean in the distance. She turned on the vibrator and imagined the water. Of course, the water was cold now. Okay, think Hawaii: a powdery beach with warm waves lapping gently over her tanned and polished toes. Diane was in a bikini, overflowing the top, with a gold chain around her hard tummy. Hey, it was her fantasy. She tried to come up with a face. Not Steve's. She imagined herself in a spangled gown at some Hollywood party with gold dust on her cheek and George Clooney on her arm. Without the beard. Ah, that was better.

She turned the vibrator on high and pressed it gently against herself. She dipped her wrist so that the head circled just the right spot. Okay . . . that was good. That felt nice. Mmmm. She groaned.

Scout growled.

Diane lost it. Damn dog. She took a deep breath and tried again. Okay, there it was again. Sort of warm. Really warm. Okay, that was really the right spot. She moved her hips, then wondered if her hand should move while her hips were still, or vice versa. Then her hips were moving and her hand was moving and she stopped wondering because she had to breathe so she opened her mouth wide and pressed her head back into the pillow and pressed the—

"Mommy?" Cody's voice snapped her back to reality.

Diane's hand froze. She turned off the vibrator and sat up. Cody stood at the end of her air mattress. Scout stepped up on it. She snapped her fingers and pointed. Scout stepped back down and left the room with her tail wagging. If only the kids were trained so well. She caught her breath enough to speak. "What's wrong, honey?"

"The cars are crashing."

Diane reached down underneath the polyester sheet, trying to locate her panties. "That's the ocean, honey."

"Where are the sharks?"

"In the water, far away."

Cody just stood there.

Panties up, Diane patted the empty space beside her. Cody launched himself over to her. The air mattress lurched. Her head bumped against the wall. Diane pulled the sheet up over her son and stroked his head. It was after midnight, so it wasn't long before she heard his steady breathing. Living closer to the beach might be better for his asthma. See? She was a good mom.

She grabbed the vibrator, slipped it in the pouch, and ran to the bathroom.

The bright light woke her up. Diane kneeled down and opened the cabinet beneath the sink. Since they were sharing, this was the one room she had completely unpacked. She reached way in the back beneath the leaky drainpipe and pulled out a box of jumbo tampons, the kind her daughter would never use. She jammed the vibrator pouch inside and hid it back behind the pipe.

When she stood back up and washed her hands, her wedding band twirled around her finger. It looked odd alone, without the diamond engagement ring. Heavier, somehow. Diane wondered how much it was worth. Funny, how quickly some things lost their value. Her marriage hadn't been all bad; it just wasn't good enough to continue. This was her life, her one chance beneath that moon out there to be happy, damnit. What if she had forty years left? What if she only had one? The ring pinched like a miniature handcuff.

She pulled off the gold band and tossed it in the toilet bowl. It plunked into the clean water and sunk quickly. She flushed the handle before she could change her mind. She watched the water circle and go down the rusty bowl. The tan line on her finger practically glowed in the dark.

Diane leaned close to the mirror. When had she gotten that wrinkle on her forehead? If only she hadn't fought the divorce for so long. The expression, "I gave him the best years of my life," didn't sound so stupid anymore. Diane looked old, tired, and pale. A day at the beach couldn't hurt. It would be fun. And fun was exactly what she wanted—with or without batteries. She couldn't help but laugh.

Ah, that felt better. Beyond the broken blood vessels in her eyes, Diane saw an old, unmistakable gleam. That was the person she missed. There was no "D" on her forehead now, just a woman with her whole life ahead of her. Her second act, anyway.

Cody was snoring. Diane yawned, climbed in bed, and put her arm around him. A burst of noise rattled the sliding glass door of the porch. Earthquake? A flash of light caught her eye between the curtains. Above the building across the alley, a burst of silver hung in the sky like tinsel. It was midnight, the start of Independence Day.

Here, in this cramped apartment, the world was wide open with possibilities. Diane listened to the waves crash a few blocks away beyond the Pacific Coast Highway. She imagined the empty parking lots and the gritty sand. She closed her eyes and heard mermaids singing underwater.

Part Two

CLUB MEMBERSHIP

You know you're in the club when . . .

Chapter 6

LANA

. . . you can spot another member with 90 percent accuracy.

Once the fireworks were over, the furniture industry was as bored of summer as Lana was with her lover du jour. Clearance prices on white canvas couches were signs of lost profit in that who-the-fuck-turned-the-lights-on sort of way. They wasted space on the showroom floor until the fall chenilles arrived, just as the same hard-bodied surfer boys wasted Lana's precious time before she could find someone new.

By July, the day shift at Mecca seemed to drag on forever, and today Lana's patience was wearing thin. When a bargain-hunting housewife set her mismatched stars-and-stripes napkins on her counter, Lana locked her cash drawer and pointed her to Eli, at the next register. He was young and patient and full of plans for the future. Lana refused to think ahead to Friday, let alone the next Fourth of July; each hour that passed only made her frown lines grow deeper.

When the tall, dark hottie cruised in from the mall entrance and rolled his Sea Island cotton cuffs up over his hamhock forearms, Lana felt oh-so-much better. She fluffed her short black hair in the reflection of a gilded display mirror, slipped her lavender bra strap back under her sleeveless black turtle-neck, straightened an amethyst earring, and gave him a sexy smile. Straight men didn't shop alone unless they really wanted something. Lana's job was to make sure they got it. She cranked the Mecca Mix CD on the stereo hidden beneath the maple counter, eager to earn her commission. After all, what was the fun of being the store manager if she couldn't get what she wanted, too?

Provided she sold furniture, of course. Which meant she should get rid of the Kowalski family, who was camped out on the display couches at the mall entrance, before they scared away other customers. She caught the hottie's eye and lifted her perfectly arched eyebrows before mouthing "Be right with you." Then she winked.

He nodded back.

Lana swept the ring of fabric samples from the counter, straightened the shelf of silver picture frames, and salsa-danced past the leather club chairs toward the entrance. Her stilettos clicked across the marble tile.

Mrs. Kowalski glanced over, set her pocket calculator on her scribbled catalog and lunged to clear the half-eaten food court hamburgers and empty Slurpee cups from the coffee table. Lana shouldn't have let the kids eat in the store, but she felt sorry for women who wore baggy sweatpants outside the gym— or in the gym, for that matter. Lana learned the benefits of a good wardrobe with her very first acting role. Once in costume, it was so easy to play the part. It worked that way in real life, too. Lana straightened the name tag pinned to the top of her store apron and smiled patiently as she looked across the mess to Mrs. Kowalski's teenage daughter.

The spoiled brat was sprawled across the Rossmore armchair taking pictures of herself on a sparkly cell phone. She had spent the last hour clipping photos from her pile of celebrity magazines without bothering to pick up the pieces on the display rug. Prior to that, she had obviously hit the M.A.C counter at Nordstrom. That peacock eyeshadow job was the signature style of the transvestite who saved Lana the last tube of Viva Glam lipstick during the half-yearly sale.

Lana rested her perfect ass on the smoked-glass coffee table. Patience was the most difficult virtue to fake. "Any more questions? We close in a half hour."

When Lana spoke, Mrs. Kowalski bumped the brat's ankle. Startled, he looked up from some electronic game and knocked over his nearly empty Slurpee cup. Red liquid sprayed across the white canvas cushion. "Shit," Mrs. Kowalski blurted.

Her daughter giggled, the little bitch.

Mrs. Kowalski reached toward her daughter's movie magazines, then hesitated, unsure of how best to distract Lana from the stain. Since they had arrived two hours ago, the woman had already charged and returned an entire living room set; she couldn't make a decision to save her life.

As the woman finally reached down and swept aside some magazine scraps, Lana noticed the fluorescent tan line on her wedding ring finger. Ah, yes, it was just as Lana suspected—the woman had already made the decision to save her life. "Can I give you a hand, Mrs. Kowalski?"

"Please, call me Diane. If I wanted to be called Mrs. Kowalski I wouldn't be shopping for furniture at all. Diane took a deep breath and started rubbing the red spot with one of those paper squares that the food court passed off as napkins. The spot smeared into a stripe. "I'm so sorry about this—I thought canvas was stain resistant."

Lana pressed her French-tipped acrylic nails on the customer's shoulder to stop her. "Not too many fabrics can resist Red Dye Number Five."

"How much is it?"

"Forget it. But may I suggest you consider slipcovers? Dark ones? They last longer than most marriages." She paused as a woman studying a wedding registry walked past, then she offered the ring of fabric samples. "I don't usually do this, but why don't you take this home and think about it?"

"I don't have time to think about it."

Her daughter snapped her phone shut. "Does that mean we can go home now?"

"Home?" Diane Kowalski's eyes widened at her daughter's slutty makeup. "Five minutes. Clean up your trash."

"It's not trash. I want my new room just like my old one, with a wall collage of movie star pictures."

Lana peered past her. The hottie was back in the dining table section now. She stood up to go. "Any more questions?"

Diane reached for the magazine held hostage in Lana's hand and peered closer at her unlined face. "Did anyone ever tell you—"

Lana smoothed her skirt and rose to her full six feet. "I meant about the furniture."

"Oh. Sorry. I'm a little out of it lately. I'm getting a"—she shielded her mouth with her hand and whispered—"divorce." Her eyes veered to the egg-sized amethyst on Lana's left thumb. "Are you divorced? Not to pry, but . . ."

Lana sighed. Poor woman didn't have a clue. "You're new. Soon you'll be able to tell with one glance." She waved around the large store. A perky couple in striped polo shirts were stuck trying to get out of a doublewide recliner—definitely married. A chubby woman with two inches of gray roots and a flag-embellished sweatshirt studied the area rugs—definitely married. As if she needed confirmation, Lana spotted the flash of a diamond eternity band as the woman swung each hanging rack to one side.

Lana had a ring bigger than that once. Much bigger. It would have paid for a condo near the sailboat jetty in Marina del Rey. Or a house in Manhattan Beach, south of the airport, where the flame from the offshore oil derrick lit the sky at night. She was a fool to throw it away. Even in L.A., good looks didn't guarantee a cushy lifestyle. Then again, money didn't guarantee happiness either.

The pretty gal sniffing candles at the Helston table was definitely divorced. She was confident and put together in a floppy hat with a matching flowered skirt—an honest-to-God *outfit*.

She didn't look sexy in the way that attracted men, but she did look pleased with herself. It was true that women had more time to dress when they didn't have to take care of a man, but it wasn't to attract men. Lana knew well that it felt good to look good. And then the irony of ironies: confidence attracted men.

Diane stood, frowning as she tried to smooth the creases from her khaki pants. Lana had seen a hundred women in that mom uniform, as if it were a sign of superiority that they were too busy to care. But obviously, this Diane person did care. She looked up at Lana. "How long did yours last?"

"Six months," Lana said. "We met at work, but then . . . he met someone else at work."

Diane shook her head. "I meant the furniture."

"Oh." Lana had lied about owning the furniture. Why buy furniture if you rarely sleep at home? Lana was just acting, to make the sale. "I couldn't bear to keep it. Besides, styles change. I like to mix things up."

"Not me," Diane said, rubbing a chenille square against her cheek. "I want something that will last."

"No, you don't," her daughter said. "You got rid of Daddy."

Lana froze.

Diane put down the fabric sample ring and took off her glasses. She folded them and shoved them in her backpack. "Go wash your face. And take your brother." She pointed to the washrooms in the back of the store.

Lana quickly flipped to another page in the catalog. "Great Traditions is classic," she told Diane. "And with the store charge, it's ten percent off." The hottie waved to her from across the room. Lana didn't have to imagine what it was like to be alone. Thank God she was over it. The ex. Lana flipped to a flowered print on the sample ring. "The chintz is cheap—it's discontinued."

Diane wrinkled her nose at the hideous print. "I can see why."

Lana leaned over and lowered her voice. "I can do thirty percent. Call it a Divorce Discount."

"Deal," Diane shrugged. "We have to sit somewhere." She

gathered her things, including her daughter's cut-up movie magazines, and followed Lana to the register. "Sorry about the mess. My ex was supposed to pick the kids up for lunch, but he . . . had a meeting."

Lana nodded and copied the fabric code off the chintz square. "Twelve-step?"

"Yup," Diane smiled. "Assholes Anonymous."

Lana laughed.

The hottie approached the register and reached past Diane for a catalog. He nodded at Lana and left. Both women watched the ripple of his shoulders as he turned, his shirt swinging loose over his designer jeans, the peek of bare ankle above his Italian loafers. *Oh, well,* thought Lana as he disappeared from sight. Diane whispered as she handed her credit application to Lana. "So, what do you do about sex?"

The man decked out in Dodgers gear at the next register looked up. Lana caught his eye and winked before lowering her voice to answer. "Are you kidding? Men love divorcées. We're so *grateful.* Plus, we're hot."

She smiled at Diane, but the truth was as plain as her white T-shirt: Diane was not remotely hot. She had good bones, though; with a little help from Lana, she might be lukewarm.

Clocks chimed from different places in the store. The Dodger fan put his hand on his wife's elbow. "Game's on, Brigette. Time to go."

His wife shifted the cobalt vase in her arms. "But, Frank, it's the last one."

He took the vase from her and set it on the edge of the display table. "Dodgers win, I'll raise your allowance. You can buy two." He hustled her out of the store.

"That's one advantage of being divorced." Diane smiled at Lana. "No one telling you what to do."

Lana nodded and called the store credit office. She tried to make nice with them about Diane's mysterious lack of major credit cards, but none of the ID cards Diane gave her listing her roles as PTA president, Walk for Life chairman, Girl Scouts of America trustee, and Little League Moms of L.A. helped raise her credit limit. When Lana saw the Wharton business school MBA alumni card, she demanded to speak to the supervisor. Then she covered the phone and handed the cards back to Diane. "Quite the go-getter, eh?"

Diane shrugged as she filled out yet more forms promising her firstborn in exchange for a few hundred dollars' worth of store merchandise. "Sometimes, when you're good at something, you end up doing it even if you don't like it. Then you like being good at it—so you do it even more." She slapped the fabric samples around the wheel. "Then you forget what you liked doing in the first place."

Lana nodded and waited for the supervisor to get on the line. She understood. When she started this job, she only did it for the commission. Then she found it was fun to match furniture up with people, to help them define their identities, or create entirely new ones. She could help Diane figure out who she was after being a wife for so long. And yes, for a former actor, there was comfort in taking control. Call it manipulation, but Lana was well aware of the power in her smile.

The credit office supervisor finally got on the line with Lana, but he was no help at all. "Look, we sent her the card. If we don't honor it, she'll have every PTA member in Los Angeles boycotting the store. Yes, I'll hold." She looked up to see Diane's reaction, but Diane was staring at the mall entrance, swearing under her breath.

"Problem?" Lana said.

Diane tucked her T-shirt in and frantically smoothed her hair. "I'll say. If it weren't for that woman, I wouldn't need your ugly couch."

Lana looked over Diane's shoulder at the Chanel-clad customer gliding toward them. She had better posture than Lana, who had studied ballet for ten years and yoga for six. And while Lana was no stranger to cosmetic surgery—tofu could only go so far—this woman's skin was as smooth as milk chocolate. Her curves were so seamless, it seemed her entire being was Botoxed.

Men stepped back in her wake as she cleared a path through the store. Not a soul would approach her; they wouldn't dare. "Don't tell me: the ex's mistress?"

"Worse: lawyer." Diane looked positively green.

The woman clicked her way to the counter in her Jimmy Choos. "May I help you, ma'am?" asked Lana. The slight frown told Lana she should have said "miss."

The woman set her briefcase down and picked up a catalog. She flipped through it once, then turned back to page two. "Yes, thank you. I'd like the Contempo group in—Arctic Linen."

"Which pieces?"

The woman set down a Platinum American Express card printed with her name: Annette Gold. "All of them."

Lana and Diane both looked at her. "Must be fun to spend other people's money," Diane murmured.

"Good afternoon, Mrs. Kowalski." Annette pushed a tortoise-shell bobby pin deeper in her tight bun. "How nice to see you again."

Diane ignored her and turned to Lana. "I never used to say what I was thinking."

"That's because you were married," Lana said. She put the hold Muzak for the credit office on speakerphone and rang up Annette's order.

Diane nodded. "That's how I stayed married."

Annette retrieved her credit card from Lana and spoke to Diane. "It's not always in your best interest."

Lana watched Diane's reaction. She seemed desperate to ignore Annette, but curiosity finally won. "What's not in my best interest: saying what I think, or staying married?" Diane asked.

Lana wanted to know, too, but a voice squawked from the speakerphone before Annette could answer. Lana kept her professional mask on and thanked the credit manager before hanging up. "You're approved, Diane. Two weeks for delivery."

"Thanks, but I can't wait two weeks. My kids are camping in an empty apartment." Diane glared at her ex-husband's lawyer.

Annette set an envelope of cash on the counter. "How much for delivery tonight?"

"I hate you," Diane said. "Even if it's not in my best interest."

Annette sighed, picked up a Mecca pen, and dashed off her address on the delivery list.

Lana read the address aloud. "Five-seventeen Malibu Cove?" She looked up, surprised. "I went to a party there once. White with a blue tile roof right on the beach. Fabulous party! But I thought it was some artist's place, Jackson something."

"Jackson Knight. My former husband. May I?" Annette reached for the delivery list to make a correction.

Lana vaguely remembered the painting Lucas brought home to their house in Malibu Cove that night: streaks of purple. No doubt Lucas collected a fortune for that piece of crap. At the party, she'd thought for sure Jackson was gay. Now, after meeting his tight-ass ex, she was sure of it.

Annette read Lana's name tag and uncapped her fountain pen again. "Not to worry, Lana, I'm sure there will be many more fabulous parties at the Cove."

Lana thought of the beach house she had shared with Lucas. It was in the actual Colony, home to moguls and mansions, and there was always a party nearby. Oh, what she would do to live on the beach again. When Annette finished writing her new address, Lana pushed the clipboard holding the list toward Diane. "You forgot the apartment number."

Diane nodded. She took the list and glanced at the new address Annette had filled in. "Twenty-seven seventy Larkspur? That's *my* address! At least, it was until last week."

Annette buckled her briefcase shut. "I beg your pardon. Didn't Mr. Kowalski tell you I bought the property?"

"If Mr. Kowalski was in the habit of telling me anything, that house would still be mine!" Diane slammed the clipboard on the counter.

Lana tried her most comforting smile—#46—at the customers looking their way. It wasn't enough. Half a dozen potential sales slipped past her and out of the store. Great. At this rate, she'd never make her quota. To make things worse, Diane's brats galloped back in. Lana knew one thing: she had to get this family out of her store.

The two surrounded their mom, but it was the boy who reached for her. Wide-eyed at how her hand was shaking he asked, "Mommy, are you okay? Daddy says you have mental-pause."

Diane turned on her son, eyes narrowing into slits. He backed up and scurried behind the cobalt vase on the table.

Quinn clapped her hands to her freshly scrubbed cheeks. "Oh, my God, is this going to happen to me someday? Being a woman sucks!"

"Stop using that word!" Diane said, then turned back to her son. "Cody, come back here!"

Cody ducked to avoid his mother's reaching hand. His elbow swung wide and hit the vase. It crashed to the floor. It only took a moment, but it seemed like slow motion as shards of cobalt glass rained down around him. He looked around, his face white with panic. "I didn't do it!"

Quinn giggled.

Diane pulled Cody away from the mess and checked the small cut on his wrist. She gave him a hug, then dug out her sanitizer. She sighed. "I'm sorry, honey. I haven't slept in months." She smiled strangely as she cleaned up his wound. "Actually, last night was the first time I did get any sleep."

Lana braced herself for a meltdown—Diane screaming at her kids, begging for sympathy—but it didn't come. Instead, Diane pulled herself together like one of those zombies in Lana's first film. She had an eery, unearthly calm. She put her arm around her son, then reached into her backpack for her wallet as if nothing could surprise her. She was war-weary, ready to put this behind her and move on. Diane stood up and looked at Lana. "How much do I owe you?" she asked.

Even Annette was impressed. She met Lana's eye for a brief moment before resuming her ice queen act.

Lana quickly looked away. That moment of humanity made

it all the more apparent that each of them was putting on a show. Protecting themselves. It was a sign of survival, Lana knew, but not necessarily a good one. Eli approached with the push broom and Lana shook her head at Diane. "You don't owe anything. Just promise you won't sue us."

They both looked at Annette.

Annette's PDA rang. She answered, and checked her watch. She nodded to the person on the other end, as if they could hear her, then whispered to Lana. "Call me about the delivery," she said. "Thank you for your time." She left her business card and cleared a path as she glided back out of the store.

"I guess she's not keeping my grandma's antique furniture. Probably already sold it for a fortune," Diane said.

Quinn whined to Diane. "Can we go home now?"

"There's that word again. Just a minute, honey. I need my receipt."

When Lana looked up, a petite young mother with a child in a soft carrier was doing the baby rock in front of the counter. The woman probably had no idea she was doing it, just as she seemed oblivious that her ponytail was caught under the shoulder strap of her stained Winnie the Pooh diaper bag. She detangled a tiny finger from a lock of her strawberry blonde hair, smoothed the waistband of her baby-blue velour warm-up suit, then smiled. Lana saw past the baby weight and caught her breath. Some women worked at it, some women bought it, and some women were born with it. Lucky bitch. And Lana meant that in the nicest way. "How can I help you, miss?"

"Mrs. Fornari. Howdy. I don't want to bother you. But could you tell me the price of the coffee table in the window?"

"Five hundred ninety-nine. You have a wonderful eye, Mrs. Fornari; that whole line is exquisite." Lana heard a hiccup and leaned over the counter to find the source. A miniature blonde clone in a tiara and matching warm-up suit clung to her mom's knee. Mrs. Fornari patted her daughter's back and fretted, glancing back at the window display.

"Sorry, but I need something a little less, you know . . . a little less."

"The Aspen, over there by the couches, is nice at three-fifty."

"The corners are too sharp. I really like that one in the window." She stopped rocking, took a deep breath, and pulled a credit card out of her diaper bag.

Lana swiped the card and frowned. "This card has been denied, Mrs. Fornari."

"Call me Bonnie," she said, and burst into tears. So did the little princess. And the baby. Lana rushed around the counter with a box of Kleenex. Bonnie took one.

Lana tried to ignore the baby, who was staring up at her with his freaky big eyes. "I have a floor model in back." She looked up and prayed Diane would still be standing there. Help! she called silently.

Diane smiled at the hysterical woman. Maybe all that PTA experience was valuable after all. "Excuse me, does your little girl like to color?" She dug a broken crayon and an eyebrow pencil from her backpack, and grabbed a catalog from the counter display.

Bonnie hesitated and gave Diane the once-over.

Lana got her act together to smooth things over. "Don't worry," she said. "Diane is an upstanding member of the community."

"Used to be," Diane said with a smile. She kneeled to the girl's level and put her hand out.

The girl hopped over. "I'm a princess."

Diane nodded. "Quinn's a teenager. It's the same thing." She led her over to the sheepskin rug.

Quinn smirked and put her arms out. The princess plopped right down on Quinn's lap and they started coloring together. Took one to know one, Lana guessed.

Being worshipped was always nice. Lana vaguely remembered that feeling. She also remembered the joy of making a sale, so she turned back to Bonnie. The pathetic creature had relaxed at the sound of her daughter's giggles, thank God, and was dabbing her eyes with the tissue with her free hand. Lana pulled the baby gently from Bonnie's arms and handed him over to Diane as well. She was an old pro at the baby rock, so the baby stayed blessedly calm.

Lana heaved a sigh of relief and led Bonnie to a stack of furniture in the storage area near the bathrooms. She pointed out a brown coffee table with a scratch on the side. "It's clearance-priced at three hundred dollars, but I can do another ten percent if you open a store charge."

"I don't know—I'm separated. If things work out, I'll wish I splurged on the nice one. Isn't the scratch bad luck?"

"No, it's good luck, Mrs. Fornari, because that makes it cost less. And you need something to put your baby pictures on, right?" At this point in the day, Lana needed another sale, any sale. She already had the Slurpee stain to deal with. If she could break twenty-five grand, Winston, the owner, would be thrilled. Plus, she couldn't let this sweet young thing stay married for a freaking coffee table. The girl was probably five years younger than Lana even lied about, and clearly not from L.A. And with two kids already! Lana had read about the red states, but she had no idea people still bred so young there. Talk about retro. Had she ever been to a Hollywood premiere, or to La Bamba, or even to the Beverly Hills Saks? Why breathe?

Bonnie zipped her hoodie up and down, unsure of what to do.

Lana kicked the large wooden knob. It cracked. "Oh look—the drawer knob is broken, too. I can do forty percent. Deal?"

Bonnie left her zipper up and gave Lana a grateful smile. "Deal."

Lana removed the knob along with the sales tag. "Don't tell my boss, but you can pick up some pretty glass knobs at Target." She led Bonnie back to the counter where Diane was checking the figures on her receipt. She shouted to Eli. "Carry-out!"

Bonnie got out her checkbook and looked up. "Oh, no,

thank you. It will never fit in my Jetta." She reached to take the baby back from Diane. "Will it, Lucas, honey, noooo."

Lana flinched and dropped the knob. Now it really was broken—in two pieces.

Bonnie looked closer at Lana. "You know, you look like Lacy what'sername—that actress who burned Lucas Hatteras's mansion down." She rocked baby Lucas and laughed at herself. "Not that a movie star would be working in a furniture store, but there is a resemblance."

Lana smiled, this was her best smile, #5—benign. It involved an innocent widening of the eyes, one of the few in her repertoire that required her entire face to pull off. Possibly because she only used it when she was screaming inside. Lana set down the bill, but Bonnie wouldn't shut up. She just put baby Lucas on one hip and wrote a check with her free hand.

"My sorority sister, who runs Lucas's fan site, made us boycott that toga movie."

"Is that so?" Lana plucked the check off the counter. It had one of those insipid cartoons on it: *Love is . . . holding hands.* Ick. When Lana looked up, Diane was staring at her. A small smile danced around her lips. Lana ignored her.

Bonnie slipped the checkbook back in her baby bag, still chattering. "Yup. I bought the DVD, though. I mean, hello, togas? Lucas Hatteras didn't wear a shirt once during the whole movie! My husband's chest used to be . . ."

Lana waited to hear the comparison between this woman's husband and her ex, but the poor pathetic thing got quiet, then burst into tears . . . again. Lana pushed the Kleenex box closer to Bonnie and pleaded with Diane, "Do you mind hanging out for a minute while I process her order?"

Diane looked back to see that her kids were occupied, then shrugged and set down her purse. She guided Bonnie to the club chair nearby. Lana would have offered a Zoloft, if she still took them. Tempting thought.

Bonnie sat down and unzipped her hoodie. She slipped the baby under her T-shirt, and closed her eyes in what looked like a rush of nirvana. Diane slipped a toss pillow under Bonnie's elbow.

Lana didn't want to stare, but she couldn't help watching. It must feel different from having grown men suck on you. She hoped to find out someday.

The metal security gate squeaked. Lana winced at the noise and looked over to see Eli pulling it down to close the mall entrance. Lana checked her watch. When she looked up, Diane stood there.

"You are going to deliver her coffee table, right?"

"Impossible." Lana pulled her black motorcycle helmet out from beneath the counter to prove it. "What's it to you, anyway?"

Diane packed up her receipts. "Been there, that's all. Am there."

"Me, too. So what?"

"So, it shouldn't be so damn hard, should it?" Diane asked. She snatched the last two *Star* magazines from the sheepskin rung where Quinn was still coloring with Hayley. Diane shuffled to put the right magazine on top, then slapped them both on the counter. "Maybe this will cheer her up. Perfect for that table, don't you think, Lana? It is Lana, isn't it?" She turned the photo around so that Lana could see the raven-haired actress who stole her husband and tapped the cover. "Friend of yours?" Diane asked.

It was clear from the smile on Diane's face that she knew exactly who Lana was—or who she used to be, anyway. Lana sighed and put her helmet away. She was all out of smiles now, customer or not. "I'll see what I can do, *Mrs. Kowalski.*"

Diane hesitated, then cracked up.

Bonnie zipped up and came to the counter. "Thanks for your help." She lowered her voice. "I might be, you know, getting a . . . the D word."

"Divorce?" Diane asked. "Welcome to the club."

Bonnie pulled away. "I don't want a divorce."

"Who does?" Lana wrapped up Bonnie's order. On an impulse, she handed her Annette's card with the paperwork. "Just in case. I wish I'd used her."

"Tell me about it," Diane said. She picked up her purse and called to her kids. Bonnie put the baby back in the carrier and went to get Hayley. Diane turned back to Lana. "Tell you what," she said. "I'll drop off her coffee table if you move up my delivery date."

"I have a feeling you'd do that anyway." Lana said. "Besides, I could lose my commision."

Diane picked up the magazines. "You could lose more than that," she said, lowering her voice. "Sixteen years of marriage to a compulsive liar taught me how to spot an imposter. I know who you are. Besides, I've been staring at your wedding picture— the one with all the swans—on my daughter's wall for the past two years. If you help me out, I won't tell Bonnie she named her baby after your ex-husband."

Lana had no choice but to agree. For some reason, she trusted this woman. She bumped her up on the delivery list, then sent Eli to move the coffee table out to Diane's car. Still, it was a relief to finally say good-bye and pull down the steel gate.

Back inside the empty store, Lana found the stain remover and tried to scrub the pink spots off the couch. She gave up, flipped the pillow over, and picked up the last magazine scraps littering the floor where Quinn had been sitting. When she stood up, she saw the hottie peering through the window.

She smiled, letting her gaze sweep over his hand. No ring, but that didn't mean anything; only women had to publicly declare their bondage. Her stomach was growling for a nice plate of farm-raised salmon, maybe some organic greens sautéed in garlic. She had a hunch this guy wouldn't mind the garlic. When he pointed at the black dining table, she beckoned him back inside the metal pull-down gate.

He ducked under. "Thanks. Hate to leave empty-handed when I've been thinking about this all afternoon."

"That would be a tragedy," Lana smiled. "But what's to think about? The design is classic." She put her finger on her collarbone then traced it down to her hip with practiced nonchalance. He watched it graze her curves. Then he flicked his hair back; an easy mark. Lana read that women needed twenty-four hours of foreplay to disconnect their brain and redirect the nerves from their head to their hot button. Men only needed three minutes. In her experience, it was more like three seconds.

Lana led him back to the display and leaned between him and the table. "Dress it up with a pretty tablecloth—or with nothing at all." She sat on the edge of the table and crossed her legs. She smiled, the ever-popular #7 for sincerity. "I have this table."

"You do? Is it big enough for company?"

"Depends on the company." Lana put her hand on his arm, a casual touch, but enough to get him thinking about the two of them on that table, naked. Lana tilted her head and toyed with her earring so he could admire her neck. How can a man hit the bull's-eye if he can't see the target? "You might need the extra leaf."

"Let's find out," he said. He leaned in for a kiss.

Lana let him kiss her, then slowly pulled him back against the table. This was how she liked it, sandwiched so that there was nowhere else to go. She slipped her long skirt up slowly, revealing her legs inch by inch, then waited for him to press her knees apart. She slid back a bit, congratulated herself on the choice of table. It was the perfect height for the horizontal mambo. She closed her eyes and let him kiss her neck. She felt the band of her panties pull tight before he ripped them off. Then she heard the telltale zip of his trousers. That unmistakable sound of blatant desire always made her wet.

He eased into her, gently at first, then with a violence that made Lana gasp. She clung to him and felt her body slam against the table. She closed her eyes against the fluorescent light on the ceiling. This was what she wanted, full penetration. She wanted to feel the pounding deeper, harder, all the way to her heart. This man was perfect for her, an expert at obliteration.

He groaned.

She smiled.

The back door squeaked opened and a familiar voice called, "Hello?"

Lana froze. So did her hips.

Hottie started to protest. She put her hand over his mouth and pushed him down, down, down, out of sight.

Winston, her boss, waved over the high counter. "Hi, there. How'd we do today?"

She saw his blue eyes and the shine of fluorescent light where his halo of hair stopped. Good thing he was short. She waved back. "Great," she squeaked. Hottie was under her skirt now. She wanted him to stop, but he clearly had other ideas. Tempting ones.

"You okay?"

"Mmmhhh," she answered. She did not feel okay; she felt awful. It wasn't just because he was her boss—she could work anywhere. Who cared, it wasn't as if she had kids to feed. Winston did, though, and she didn't want him to think the worst of her. "Be right there! Love the new mix CD!" She squeezed her legs together.

Swear words emanated from below. Hottie appeared, rubbing his neck. "Sorry," Lana whispered, and she truly was. The man had talent. She straightened her skirt and reached in Hottie's pocket for his wallet. "Credit card," she whispered.

Winston called to her. "Lana? Did you close out?"

She hopped off the table, hurried over to the register and ran the credit card through the charge slot. The hair on the back of her neck stood up in the cool of the air conditioner. Or maybe it was him. No, that couldn't be. Winston was nice, but to Lana, "nice" was shorthand for "boring."

"Last sale," she said. "That's twenty-six thousand this afternoon." She smiled innocently. She should have won the fuck-

ing Oscar. Or maybe she just did. She broke into a sheen of perspiration—flattering on her, thank God.

Winston nodded, meeting her eyes for a moment. Hottie
strolled up to the counter, and Winston stood up a little taller,
much as that was possible. "Only serious shoppers come out on
a beautiful day like today."

"Oh, give her more credit. Brilliant saleswoman."

Lana smiled. She had smiled so much today, her cheeks were
sore. All of them. "That's the table, the leaf, and six chairs,
right . . ." she glanced quickly at the name on the credit card,
"Mr. Lawrence?"

Hottie grinned. He was smooth, but up close, not as good-
looking as Lana had originally thought. She noticed a few
flakes of dandruff on his collar.

Winston nodded in approval while Lana handed the credit
card back along with the delivery list. "We're looking at about
two and a half weeks for delivery."

"Will you be delivering it personally?"

She felt Winston's gaze on her and chuckled for his benefit.
Hottie scrawled his address on the delivery list, then pulled a
business card from his leather wallet. When he held it out to
her, she recognized the round imprint of another condom.
"Enjoy your table."

"I already did," he said.

Winston didn't even look at her. Instead, he smiled amiably
at the customer and walked him to the front. Then he locked
the gate down. He stooped to pick something up as he passed
the dining room table. *Shit*, Lana thought. If he knew, he would
fire her for sure.

Winston brought her amethyst earring back and placed it on
the counter. His eyes were calm, but she could tell there was
more lurking beneath the surface. She wished she knew what it
was. Winston hid his solid chest under cotton button-downs, his
hard thighs beneath baggy pants, but he was actually an impos-
ing force. He was like a mild-mannered Clark Kent hiding his
superpowers. Lana felt like Kryptonite.

She put her earring back into her ear as if puncturing a new hole. That would be less painful than this situation. "Sorry about the couch."

Winston emptied the register and zipped the receipts into a bank pouch. "Happens."

Lana tried to smile, but her lips refused to cooperate. She quickly sorted the stack of papers to the proper drawers. She picked up a Bic lighter a customer had left behind and flicked it on. It flared like a torch. She adjusted it down, but still, there was something alluring about a hot, flickering flame.

"Good work moving the coffee table." Winston looked up at her. Lana put down the lighter. For one glorious moment, she imagined he would kiss her. The thought came out of the blue, he was so not her type, and yet . . . he took her hand in his. She closed her eyes and leaned down toward him. Something was pressed into her hand. She opened her eyes. It was half of the broken drawer knob.

"The buyer might want this. There's Crazy Glue in the drawer. Walk you out?"

Lana couldn't help but chuckle. She had five inches on him, even without her heels. "I'll be fine."

He nodded and rolled his shirtsleeves back down, and with that simple gesture, he became just the boss again. "I'm taking the twins to the beach tomorrow, so I won't be in." He walked out, turning to wave. "Take home a CD if you want."

Lana leaned against the counter, but she didn't wave back. Why bother? When the clock struck the hour, she grabbed her helmet from the shelf below. Then she laughed at herself—what was the hurry?

While Lana fixed the knob and waited for the Crazy Glue to set, she flipped through the ring of fabric samples and found the navy chenille. She brushed it against her cheek. Lana had told Diane that she liked to mix things up, but maybe that was just a habit. She had gotten used to rented furniture and temporary hair colors and spontaneous sex. She turned to the mirror behind the counter and smoothed her flawless skin. No matter how rested Dr. Levine kept her looking, Lana was tired.

She'd had enough of dining tables and restaurant closets and airplane lavatories. She wanted someone to love. Someone who would take her home and hold her until morning.

Lana picked up the knob and admired her handiwork. It would hold together better than the rest of the table. Lana put it in her bag and cleared the counter. She knew better than to dream. If she wanted someone to count on, it would have to be her.

Chapter 7

BONNIE

*. . . you talk about personal things to strangers—
and they are no longer strangers.*

Bonnie lifted the stroller over the crack in the sidewalk past Cathy's tidy ranch house, and headed toward home. She had hurried to leave the mall before it got too dark for their evening walk, but now she wished she hadn't. From the familiar line of cars parked at the curb, it was clear that Cathy was having another party. This time, Bonnie had no choice about going; she wasn't invited.

At the sight of Buck's truck, Bonnie nearly ran the stroller into their freshly cut lawn. Buck was probably talking trash about her with Cathy's husband, Tom, right now. Cathy did everything but wipe his big fat Bruin butt, so of course he would hate any wife who got away with less. Plus, jocks had that team loyalty—how else could they run head first into a pile of human bricks?

Bonnie had never admitted how ridiculous she thought football was: a bunch of grown men chasing a stupid ball. She had the same opinion of baseball, basketball, and soccer, all those multimillion-dollar games that glorified men playing with their balls in public. Bonnie just liked the cheerleading outfits.

Buck thrived on the glory, even after he retired his jersey.

Bonnie should have had a clue on their honeymoon when her brand-new husband invited half the hotel over for beer and onion rings every night. He would never let go of his football memories, and she would never be more than his head cheerleader. That used to be enough. Bonnie marched onward, barely hesitating when her own lawn came into view. It needed mowing. She was only separated. It had only been a month. Yet, she might as well put a yellow quarantine tape around the place.

"Mommy!" Hayley waited for her at the corner of their peeling white picket fence. American flags still stuck out of her handlebars. Bonnie caught up and wiped some of the paint chips off the warped wood. She had begged Buck to repaint it after the rainy season, but then it was basketball season and then baseball season, and Bonnie was too busy with the new baby to do it herself. It was a disgrace to the neighborhood—just like Bonnie. They should have gotten the plastic kind. If only she could be the plastic kind, too, like Barbie. Buck would love that.

Bonnie set the brake on the stroller and marched to the fence. She kicked it.

"Hey!" A woman's voice cut through the air. "What did that fence ever do to you?" Bonnie whirled around to see a filthy Volvo wagon backing up in front of her house. The words "Wash Me" were smeared on the back window. Bonnie pulled Hayley out of the way as the Volvo pulled into her driveway. When the door opened, Diane, Quinn, and Cody climbed out. Bonnie's scratched coffee table was wedged in the back.

"Howdy." Bonnie held the front door open as Diane and Quinn brought the coffee table through. "This is so nice of you," she said, wincing when they banged into the portrait of her daughter that hung in the foyer. The phone rang. She let the machine pick up.

Diane stared at the gorgeous black-and-white photograph of Hayley. "Can I get the name of your portrait guy?"

"That would be me."

"How did you get her eyes so big?"

"I turned the lights down, is all." She led them into the great room, which was never that great, just a living room/dining room with nothing in between. Beyond the baby blanket spread out on the floor and the pile of family scrapbooks beside it, the room was completely empty; Buck had taken it all. She encouraged him, really, to ease her guilt at not letting him come back until they had sorted things out. She hated all that brown stuff, anyway.

"Where do you want the table?" Diane's voice echoed.

"Anywhere is good." Bonnie's voice echoed back.

Cody carried a cardboard box inside, then looked around slowly. "Did you get robbed?"

"Oh, no, honey. I'm . . . um . . . redecorating, that's all."

"Me, too," Diane said. "Shabby without the chic." She flipped open an album. "You should do my albums. I'm one of those bad moms—I haven't printed one picture since I got a digital camera." She opened the box Cody carried in.

Quinn opened the box Cody carried in and took a videotape from a neat stack. "This is for you, Princess," she said to Hayley.

Cody snatched the tape—a pirate movie—out of her hand. "That's mine!"

Quinn turned on him. "You little turd, we don't even have a VCR anymore."

"Hayley does. You guys want to watch that?" Bonnie turned to Diane. "Buck took the DVD player. He's staying with a buddy. You have no idea how hard it is to find a furnished apartment in L.A."

"Oh, yes, I do," Diane said. "But we should go."

"Come watch it in my room!" Hayley led them down the hall to her pink paradise. Poodles covered the bedspread and a pink plastic multimedia unit rested on a toddler-sized table. A turtle in a tray with a plastic palm tree craned his skinny neck and blinked at them.

"What's his name?" Cody asked, picking it up.

"Mr. Turtle," Hayley replied, taking the turtle from him. She saw Quinn check out the feather boas hanging in the open closet and dashed over to shut the door. "Those are mine!" she cried.

Bonnie crossed her arms. "Share, honey."

Pouting, Hayley handed the turtle back to Cody, then selected a pink boa for herself and a white one for Quinn. Then she ran to her VCR and blocked it so that only she could hit Play.

Bonnie smiled and exchanged a knowing look with Diane.

"We have to watch the Mommy video!" Hayley said, then hit Play.

The screen glowed with a harbor full of white sails at sunset. A fresh-faced Bonnie, crowned by a halo of daisies, exchanged wedding vows with a handsome young Buck in a gazebo covered with twinkle lights.

"Sorry," Bonnie said. "Hayley found that tape yesterday." She pointed Hayley toward the pirate tape.

"That's okay. So romantic. Is that Marina del Rey?"

Bonnie nodded. On the tiny screen, a large fishing boat motored past in the background. A man's voice called out, "Don't do it!"

Bonnie blinked and hit Stop. She cleared her throat. "Why don't you watch your pirate movie instead, Princess?" She brightened and turned to Diane. "Can I offer you a Diet Pepsi?"

"Can I have some?" Cody asked, scratching his neck like crazy.

Diane lifted his collar. A rash bloomed across his chest. "Oh, honey, why didn't you say something? Generic detergent—sometimes you get what you pay for."

"I have some Benadryl," Bonnie said. She helped Cody change into an OSU jersey that hung to his knees, then left him to the pirate movie and led Diane down the hall to the bathroom.

Diane stopped to look at a picture of Bonnie's Delta Gamma pledge class. "I was in a sorority for a little while."

"Which house?" Bonnie asked.

"I don't remember. They wanted me to wear pantyhose, so I quit. I don't really like clubs, unless I'm in charge."

Bonnie laughed and led her the rest of the way down the hall, past photographs of Buck in all his Big Ten glory.

"You know, if you ever want to talk . . ." Diane's voice trailed off.

"Thanks, but we're just taking a break." Bonnie was polite, but firm. "The three of us are a lot to be saddled with, you know?" She opened the bathroom door. "Besides, marriage is supposed to be hard."

"Sure, but how hard?"

Bonnie handed Diane the medicine bottle with a tiny plastic cup. "We'll work it out. I don't want to be alone at forty." Bonnie saw Diane's hurt look—was she forty? How weird to be friends with someone who could be her mother. Diane probably had a whole life before having kids. Free love and cool concerts and a real job where assistants brought her coffee on demand. Bonnie was jealous. Still, she felt bad for the "old" comment. "I just don't want to be one of those, bitter, hot-to-trot divorcées."

Diane dropped the cup. Pink liquid splashed on the tile floor.

Oops, Diane must be one of those, too. "I'm so sorry! I didn't mean . . ." Bonnie hid her burning cheeks by leaning down to wipe up the mess on the floor.

"It's okay," Diane said. "But we should go."

Bonnie stood up, wringing the towel in her hands. "I'm sorry. You just don't seem like one of them."

"I'm not sure there is a *them*," Diane said. "There's only *us.*"

"No," Bonnie said. "Not me."

The phone rang, but Bonnie didn't budge beyond pouring a new cup of medicine.

"Want me to get that?" Diane offered.

Bonnie shook her head, then ran for the kitchen. When she got there, she reached to turn the volume down on the machine, but it was too late.

Buck's voice sighed heavily over the speaker. "C'mon, baby, pick up. I know you're there. Call me." Buck paused, as if about to leave an endearment, but instead his voice grew cold. "Cunt," he said. The machine clicked off.

Diane moved into the kitchen doorway, car keys still in her hand.

Bonnie could see the pity on her face. But she didn't want to hear about it. Then Hayley squeezed through and attached herself to Bonnie's leg. She put a hand on her daughter's head, hoping she hadn't heard that word. "What is it, honey?" she asked, keeping her voice upbeat.

"I'm hungry."

Bonnie avoided Diane's eyes and opened the fridge. On the top shelf sat a pack of hot dogs, two juice boxes, and a gallon of milk. On the bottom, there was a max-pack of pork chops and a six-pack of Budweiser. That was it. Diane looked over her shoulder and she could tell what she was thinking: the fridge was as empty as the great room. Bonnie opened the freezer and felt Diane's hand on her shoulder.

"Want some help? I could broil the pork chops."

Bonnie shook her head. "I hate pork chops," she said, a little too loudly.

Diane pointed at the tray of buckeyes resting on a frozen pizza box. "What are those?"

"Buckeyes. They're candies, you know, peanut butter dipped in chocolate?" Bonnie relaxed, back in her comfort zone now. "They're supposed to look like the eyes of a male deer, you know, the eyes of a buck. That's what the state tree was named after. Buck eyes. Not that there are many left. The pioneers used most of the wood to build their cabins, but that's just as well, since the leaves look like marijuana, so I'm told. Anyway, they're a tradition back home." She stopped babbling and turned to Diane. "Want some?"

"Sure, thanks."

Bonnie took out the candies with her free hand and kicked the door shut. When she opened the lid of the Tupperware container, her eyes filled with tears. "I just never thought it would happen to me."

Diane nodded and got out the milk.

"He's not a bad person. He just isn't sure if he wants to be married, you know. He's only twenty-four."

"How old are you?"

Bonnie blushed and patted the baby's back. "He thinks I'm punishing him, but that's not it."

"I waited, too." Diane set drinking glasses down on the

counter. "It's hard to give up a sure thing. Even if the thing isn't what you really want."

Bonnie leaned against the counter while Diane poured the milk. "I don't know what I want. I did a pro and con list like in *Marie Claire*, but they didn't add up."

"Exactly. How do you compare finding the toilet seat up in the middle of the night against going to bed alone for the rest of your life?" Diane carried the glasses to the kitchen table. "I even tried a deal breaker. I told Steve—that's my ex—he had to quit gambling for thirty days. But it was football season, so he didn't think that counted. He was so proud of telling the truth that I felt bossy for telling him what to do. I still couldn't bring myself to say the D-word. He lied so much, I thought I was the crazy one. When we fought, I'd hear Quinn's door lock and not think anything of it."

Diane looked at the colorful picture frames on the windowsill over the sink. She picked up the frame that held the old newspaper clipping of Bonnie wearing a tiara on a parade float, the same one Hayley was wearing. "Then Quinn went to her first dance, in real high heels with gold ankle straps. She spent a month of babysitting money getting fake nails—I thought it was ridiculous—and a ceramic hair straightener. She spent all day getting ready for this boy, Danny. She looked so grown-up in her long rose-colored dress. She hadn't worn pink—let alone a dress—since she was Hayley's age. And Danny was sweet, gave her a wrist corsage of tea roses, not just carnations. But all night long I worried. Not about drugs or sex . . . she knew better than that."

Bonnie watched Diane put the picture back down. "But if that boy ever lied to her with a straight face . . ." Diane turned and looked at Bonnie. "She didn't know better than that."

A car horn sounded next door, bringing both women back to the present. They may not have been the same age, Bonnie realized, but they were more alike than she'd ever imagined. She smiled at Diane and grabbed a pizza box from the freezer. "Pizza?"

"Perfect," Diane said, waving Bonnie away and putting the

pizza in the oven. "Do you drink wine? I have a bottle in the car that would go great with the pizza. Actually, it would go great with anything. You can have one glass, right?"

There was a knock on the front door. Bonnie froze, terrified it was Buck. She watched Hayley run past, holding on to her tiara, squealing with glee. Feathers from her pink boa wafted to the floor. Bonnie picked one up.

The doorbell rang again.

Bonnie just looked at the feather.

"Want me to get that?" Diane asked. "I'm going to my car to get the wine, anyway."

Bonnie shook her head. She walked slowly into the front hall and over to the door. She stood on tiptoe to see through the peephole.

Outside, the pink sky glowed behind a dark figure dressed in a black jumpsuit. It looked like Cat Woman. Or a psycho killer. Bonnie checked the deadbolt, then flipped on the porch light. It was the saleswoman from Mecca, holding up the drawer knob, all in one piece. Who knew they had such good customer service? Bonnie opened the door.

Lana put the knob in Bonnie's hand. "If only Crazy Glue fixed everything."

Bonnie nodded. They both stood there until Bonnie remembered her manners and invited her in. "Lana, right?"

Lana looked from the hallway into the great room. The empty space looked even larger now that Quinn was sitting cross-legged next to the coffee table. She barely looked up from painting her nails. "Can I interest you in a stained canvas couch?"

Diane walked into the great room, chuckling. "Not yet—I was going to ask if I could have my divorce party here. I want to celebrate getting my name back."

Quinn looked up sharply but didn't say anything. She finished polishing her nails in short, angry strokes.

"You mean your father's name?" Lana asked. "Just do what I did—make it up."

Diane feigned surprise. "You mean Lana's not your real name? What is?"

Lana unzipped her aero suit and stepped out, unbunching her skirt from one leg. "I forget."

"Well, my real name is Taylor," Diane said, "and I happen to like it."

Bonnie sat down next to Quinn on the blanket and fiddled with the baby monitor on the table.

Quinn closed the nail polish bottle. "What's wrong with my name?"

Diane winced and put her arm around Quinn. "Nothing, honey. You have that great alliteration going for you. But I only took the name for you—and you're big, now, right?"

Quinn flounced down the hall toward the bathroom.

Diane watched her daughter disappear down the hall and sighed. "She knows it has nothing to do with her, right? I just want a whole new . . . everything. Starting with a decent job."

"Tell me about it," Bonnie said. "What am I supposed to do with two babies?"

Lana plopped down to sit on the floor and crossed her legs. "You guys ever hear of housekeepers?"

Bonnie looked at Diane, who could afford one until recently. They both turned on Lana, but she held her hand up before they could utter a sound.

"Stop! I don't want to hear any of that mommy wars crap. It's so passé."

"Wait till you have children, Lana. Won't be passé then."

Lana started to say something, then shut up. She snatched the knob from the top of the coffee table where Bonnie had put it and screwed it back into the side drawer. Bonnie raised her eyebrows at Diane, who shrugged and picked up where she left off. "Yesterday I got laughed out of an interview for an entry-level management job—in what used to be my lucky suit."

Bonnie thought of her favorite *I Love the Nineties* episode. "Omigod—shoulder pads?"

"No! It was a skort." Diane grabbed her car keys. "That's it. I'm getting the wine." She marched outside.

Bonnie looked at Lana. "What's a skort?"

Lana shook her head. "You don't want to know." She sniffed the air. "Do I smell pizza?"

Diane was back before Bonnie finished checking on dinner. And she was still on a tirade. "When I got my MBA, employers said I was overqualified for entry-level work. Now that I've raised hundreds of thousands of dollars without a paycheck, I'm too inexperienced for anything but." She set the wine bottle on Bonnie's coffee table.

Lana picked up the wine and read the label. "Look who's crying poor, drinking Montrachet?"

"It's not mine. I mean, it used to be mine, but . . . the rest of it now belongs to my ex's lawyer."

"Annette Gold, from the store?"

Diane nodded and peeled the corner of the label down. Bonnie recognized the nervous habit. She did the same thing with beer bottles. "Bonnie, do you have a corkscrew?"

"One corkscrew, coming up," Bonnie said. She headed for the kitchen.

"Let me help," Diane said. They gathered picnic supplies from the kitchen and spread another blanket on the floor of the great room. Bonnie always liked this room, with the high beam ceilings and the French doors to the backyard. She was getting used to the echo of voices.

Once they were settled, she handed the corkscrew to Diane. "I don't know why folks make such a fuss over wine." Then she threw a suspicious look at Lana. "Or are you one of those connoisseurs, too?"

"Nope," Lana said, cutting the pizza. "But I know a thing or two about tequila."

Bonnie laughed. "So, why did you get divorced?" She passed out napkins and winced. "I'm sorry. I don't have any friends who are divorced."

"Really?" Lana asked. "I don't have any friends who are married. And contrary to what my dear mother thinks about airing dirty laundry, we should compare notes. Secrets don't protect anyone but cheaters."

"I wish my husband cheated," Bonnie said. "It would make everything so much easier."

"If only that were true," Lana mused.

Diane glanced up at her, then poured the wine into jelly jars.

"You really loved your ex, huh?" Bonnie asked.

"Never again." Lana passed out slices.

"You don't believe in love?"

"Oh, I believe in love, but marriage was invented when people died at thirty."

Diane nodded. "They die at seventy-seven point three now. I ran Asshole's insurance company. Actually, I *was* Asshole's insurance company. My soon to be ex-asshole."

"No one needs two," Lana said.

They all laughed. Bonnie was relieved that the mood had lightened. She gave a napkin to Lana, who pressed it against the grease before taking a bite of pizza.

Quinn returned while Diane was pouring everyone wine. Diane smiled at her, but Quinn pretended not to notice. Bonnie gave her a slice of pizza and watched her tear the layer of cheese off and hang it over her mouth. She reminded Bonnie of a baby bird. She understood what Quinn was going through, and it wasn't easy, ever. She wondered how Hayley would react if things didn't work out. But she understood Diane's side, too. Bonnie tried a sip of wine from Diane's cup: blech. "Buck doesn't like insurance. He says it's like betting against your own team."

"I heard about this company, Safeguard Guaranty? They sell marriage insurance. Brilliant, huh? If it catches on, no one would stay married just for money," Diane said. She looked at Bonnie.

"That's not true," Lana said. "The longer you stay married, the more it's worth, right?" She took a CD out of her satchel.

Bonnie intercepted Hayley on her next dash around the room. "Go get your boom box and come back for pizza, okay, honey?" Hayley nodded and ran off to get it.

Diane smiled. "Your daughter has such adorable outfits."

Bonnie nodded. "Hayley has better clothes than I do. They're cheaper."

Diane sipped her wine. "I had to throw out most of Quinn's baby clothes when we moved, but I kept this one pink romper with an elephant on it."

Quinn's eyes widened. "The trunk lifted up."

Diane nodded and put her hand out in front of her nose. She raised it up and imitated the elephant. Quinn joined her, then the two of them cracked up.

Bonnie smiled at the sentimental moment. "You guys should let me take a picture of you together. Cody, too, of course. Tell you what, I'll trade you photos for an hour of babysitting."

"How much do you pay after the first hour?" Quinn asked.

"Who has the business degree, you or your mom?" Lana teased. They laughed.

Hayley came back with the boom box and they played Lana's CD. Lana got up and started wiggling her hips better than a belly dancer. Bonnie would like to be that uninhibited, but she hoped it wasn't some stripper dance. There were children present, after all. "What is that?"

"Salsa. It's perfect for Diane's divorce party. Here, I'll teach you."

Bonnie threw a wary glance toward Hayley and let herself be pulled up. She tried to relax as Lana pushed her hips back and forth to the salsa beat, 1-2-3, 5-6-7 . . . It was way harder than cheerleading, all loosey-goosey, then skipping a beat. Diane checked Cody's rash, then danced with him. She caught Bonnie's glance and smiled.

Bonnie had always been sociable, but she would never, in a long Indian summer, have picked these gals as friends. Diane was old. And Lana was too glamorous to be real. They had absolutely nothing in common. And yet . . . they seemed to have everything in common.

It was a relief to know she wasn't the only one who had spent weeks crying into her pillow, aching so deep inside you were sure it would never end. This wasn't like losing a boyfriend. It was losing your life. But how could you tell if it was worth the agony of ending it? Bonnie was not going to cry now. She refused. She listened harder to the music and counted, 1-2-3, 5-6-7. She focused on Lana's hand guiding her hip. Then she stopped counting and let the music take her. It was so good to have music and laughter in her house again.

A few twirls later, the front door swung open, and a hot draft of night air swept into the room. Lana stared over Bonnie's shoulder and missed a step. Bonnie pulled away and turned around. Lana turned down the music.

Buck was standing in the foyer. He crossed his arms over his chest. "So, you're a lesbian now?"

Bonnie was tempted to laugh, but he was serious. If only. Buck didn't look quite as scary with her new friends there. They glanced furtively at her, watching to know what to do. They didn't see a Big Ten football hero, the Prince Charming of a million midwestern girls' dreams. They saw an unshaven, beer-bellied jerk a few years past his peak. And for the very first time, so did Bonnie.

Diane stood up. "I believe you're trespassing."

"No, he has a key," Bonnie said, wilting. "It's his house, too."

"Damn straight." Buck's eyes flickered over Cody in his huge OSU jersey.

Quinn reached to cover Hayley's ears, but Hayley pulled away—too fast. Her tiara fell to the floor and broke in half. She started sniffling.

Quinn knelt to retrieve the pieces. "Oh, Hayley, my bad," she said. "Mama will buy you a new one."

"But it *is* Mama's!" Hayley cried. Sensing the fight in the air, Lana helped Quinn hustle the kids out of the room.

"What the fuck is going on here, Bonnie?" Buck yelled.

Bonnie just stood there, trying not to cry. She had no idea what to do. Usually Buck told her.

Diane looked at her. "Bonnie, you don't have to—"

"Who the fuck are you?" Buck glared at Diane.

Bonnie blushed at his language. Diane crossed her arms and

raised an eyebrow at Bonnie. Thank God she hadn't seen her fat lip last week. He hadn't hit her on purpose, she was sure of it. He'd turned too quickly and she'd been standing too close, that's all. Buck was still waiting for an answer. Her heart was practically in her throat, but she willed herself to speak. "She's my friend."

Buck frowned.

It would be so easy just to let him come home. Bonnie shoved her hand in her pocket and felt something small and flat. She took a deep breath and smiled. Bonnie believed in luck and fate and all the things that became destiny. This was a perfect example. She pulled Annette's business card out of her pocket and stepped closer to show him. "And that's my attorney."

Buck blanched and lowered his voice. "It was an accident, baby, you know that."

Bonnie heard Diane and Lana gasp behind her.

She stood her ground. It may have been an accident, but that didn't mean she would ever let it happen again. "What do you want, Buck?"

"Dinner's all. C'mon, baby, don't do this to me."

She met his eye. "You're late."

Hayley burst in with the mended tiara. "Look, Mama! All better." She dug the tiara into her mother's scalp.

Bonnie winced and gave her daughter's tear-stained cheek a kiss. Then she straightened the tiara on her head, went to the freezer, pulled out the max-pack of pork chops, and brought it to Buck.

"Here's your dinner," she said. "Hayley? Give Daddy a kiss good night, honey."

Hayley skipped over and scrunched her lips up for a kiss.

Buck gave Bonnie a dirty look as he kissed their daughter, but he said nothing more, just took his pork chops and left. Bonnie locked the door behind him.

When she returned to the kitchen, everyone followed, quiet

for a moment. Then Lana applauded. Diane gave her a hug. Bonnie grabbed a jelly jar of wine off the kitchen table. She drank it all in one gulp.

"Careful," Diane said. "That's like fifty bucks' worth."

Bonnie wiped her mouth with her hand. "Worth every penny."

Chapter 8

ANNETTE

. . . you start a savings fund for your children's premarital counseling.

Annette pulled the silk coverlet on her four-poster bed up over her daughter's small shoulders. Nine more hours until Mrs. Braunstein took the second-grade roll call; Annette planned to enjoy every minute of it with Morgan, even if she was asleep. Annette would miss her next weekend of custody due to a conference in D.C. She was giving a talk billed as: The Ice Queen Cometh. It had been scheduled a year ago; she couldn't back out now. She never backed out of commitments.

Unfortunately, neither did Jackson. Morgan's dad was so rigid about their custody agreement, Annette would have to wait two weeks to have her overnight again. Who knew such a creative guy could be so anal? Annette laughed at the gay pun, then scolded herself for being politically incorrect. If she weren't so full of rage, she might be more understanding.

She decided not to take her sleeping pills, since she had poured a generous glass of wine. She needed to relax. She didn't want to be one of those bitter women who kept coming back to sue their ex-husbands over the time-share or the golf clubs or the fucking cat. Annette didn't want to be bitter; she wanted to be oblivious. If it weren't for Morgan, she could.

Annette sat at the vanity and creamed her makeup off carefully. She glanced at her daughter in the mirror as if the child would disappear if she didn't keep a close watch. After all those hormone shots and that snotty surrogate, she hated to spend even a moment apart. Annette smoothed moisturizer into her skin and scolded herself for taking the wrong tactic during the divorce process. She tried to reduce her support obligation by making Jackson take vocational tests to determine what work he was qualified for. He was qualified to be an artist. A paint-by-numbers artist, if the moving men's opinion mattered, but the furthest thing from a businessman. Annette could probably sell his paintings to her clients if she tried. Hell, she could sell Morgan's crayon drawings just as easily. But the concept of helping the man who rejected her gave Annette a migraine. And she had too many of those already.

Annette buttoned her silk pajamas and climbed into bed with her laptop, settling in next to Morgan. She had turned off her PDA to enjoy her daughter's company, but now that Morgan was asleep, it seemed silly to move her back to her room just to take care of a little business. She was surprised to see an e-mail from that hysterical young mother who was referred by the gal at Mecca. Bonnie Fornari was in a similar position to Annette's partner's niece, but that was a political favor. Annette couldn't afford to take cases from single parents with no assets; she would refer Ms. Fornari to less expensive counsel.

She would have done the same with Diane Kowalski, had she been her client. She still might have lost the retirement fund and the college tuition savings, but surely not the house. Unfortunately, Mrs. Kowalski was a determined opponent. Forensic accountants were expensive. So were tax specialists, real estate agents, therapists, actuaries, appraisers, and everyone else eventually involved in a complicated divorce. Annette could have told Mrs. Kowalski that her husband was telling the truth—at least about losing it all. But Annette worked on a need-to-know basis: what her client needed to know. What happened between him and the plaintiff was not Annette's business. Literally.

Annette sneezed as she e-mailed Mrs. Fornari the link to a

database of local family law practioners. Few of them listed rates or availability or updated their information, but what more could she do? Her gratitude to the gal at Mecca was the only reason she didn't pass the chore on to her assistant in the first place. The whole grouping of sleek furniture was delivered so quickly that Carmen had to scramble to put the ugly antiques in storage.

She sneezed again, then grabbed a Kleenex and blew her nose. She admired the stone fireplace, and thought of how lovely it would be in the winter. Why not now? So what if it was summer, the air-conditioning was on and she hadn't figured out how to shut it off yet. It was her house, what the hell? Annette got out and rummaged through the drawers for some matches. No luck. She finally found the electric lighter and the key to the gas line in the china bowl on the fireplace mantel. Then, trying to recall what Carmen had written in her long list of household hints, Annette slipped the key in and turned it, starting the flow of gas. She lit the kindling. The fire flared out and caught immediately—it was gorgeous. From the bed, her computer dinged, signaling a new message. Annette tossed her crumpled Kleenex in the fire and sat on the bed to see who was e-mailing after hours.

It was a thank-you note from her client, Paul Chambers. The court had expedited his dissolution papers, so she had messengered them to him earlier in the day.

You're welcome, she typed. *I wish all my cases ended so well.*

The computer dinged. Paul was online right now. *You are being modest*, he typed. *BTW, how is the new home?*

Annette looked around. The fire crackled, but was it smoky in the room? Annette shook her head. If the overgrown lawn was any indication, the Kowalskis probably hadn't had the chimney cleaned, either. *Lovely*, she typed. *I'm in bed admiring the fire right now.* She smiled and hit Send.

Sure enough, he responded immediately. *What are you wearing?*

Annette laughed and looked around, as if to share the ridiculousness of the question. But there was no one to share it with. So she typed back, what the hell? *You can't ask me that. I'm your lawyer.*

Not anymore. Talk to me. I'm lonely.

Try a porno site. Isn't that where you met Wife #2?

Ouch, he typed.

Try online dating.

Gold diggers, he typed. *You?*

Female lawyers don't get hits. Men think we're argumentative.

No, they don't.

Yes, they do.

I see your point.

LOL.

So lie.

I don't lie.

Ever?

No.

Then what are you wearing?

Annette laughed, then went downstairs for another glass of wine. They had only spoken business before, so she was flattered by the flirting. The paralegals swooned when he came into the office. His investment firm was on the cover of *Business Week* twice last year, so he had a rock star rep.

Annette thought she heard Morgan coughing upstairs, so she poured a glass of water. As she was walking back through the foyer, the shriek of the smoke detector pierced the air. Smoke billowed down the stairs.

Annette dropped the water glass and the wine bottle and sprinted up the staircase. Her eyes teared up. Annette didn't see any fire as she ran into the room, but she couldn't see anything—including her daughter. She squinted, to no avail.

"Mommy?" Morgan's voice was high and frightened. She coughed.

Annette crouched down and moved farther into the bedroom, arms outstretched, reaching for her child. "Right here, honey. Get on the floor and crawl to Mommy."

After several frantic moments, her hands brushed something soft—Morgan's pajamas. Annette scooped her up and

rushed out. She stumbled in the darkness and fell on the landing. Pain shot through her ankle as she pulled on the railing to
stand up. Her bad knee buckled. She shifted Morgan's weight
and rushed the rest of the way down the stairs and out the door.

Sirens screamed in the distance, gaining volume as they approached. Annette stumbled off the porch in a daze and crossed
the lawn to the driveway, looking back only to see smoke pouring out of the windows. Olivia, the neighbor, was already on the
sidewalk across the street offering brownies to the gathering
crowd. Within minutes, the sidewalk was full. Annette accepted
a blanket from someone who disappeared back into the crowd,
but she kept her distance, more from shock than embarrass-
ment. She sat with Morgan in her lap and stroked her hair until
the fire truck pulled up. She struggled to a stand to greet the
ambulance behind them. A paramedic leaped over the thick
white hoses and put an oxygen mask over Morgan's mouth and
nose.

"Is she okay?" Annette asked.

"She'll be fine, ma'am. Give us some room." He strong-armed
her out of the way and buckled Morgan into the stretcher.
Other firemen ran hoses into the house in front of them. Annette limped behind him.

A Volvo wagon sped up to the curb and parked by the ambulance. The dirty window rolled down, revealing the Kowalski
woman. Morgan was grinning from behind her mask as the
paramedic tickled her. Thank God. Now that Morgan was out
of danger, Annette stepped away to give Diane hell. "You've got
a lot of nerve showing up here."

"What did *I* do? Tell one of your minions to update your
emergency list, will you? The alarm company woke me up." Annette followed her gaze to the house. "I didn't think you were
home."

"I was home alright, with my daughter—who is strapped
onto a stretcher right now, thank you very much. Can't wait to
sue your bony white ass." Annette limped back toward the ambulance.

"Your daughter?" Diane's voice broke through the cacophony of concerned neighbors and busy firefighters. When Annette looked back, the woman was climbing out of the car in a flannel bathrobe and fuzzy slippers. "Will you stop being a complete bitch for a minute? You can't blame me for this. You signed off on the inspection."

They looked back at the house. Upstairs windows were being broken. Glass rained on the porch roof. Yellow helmets and silver-seamed jackets flashed through the smoke. Annette hurried back toward her daughter.

Diane called after her. "How did it start?"

"You tell me. All I did was turn on the gas."

Diane turned to Annette. "Can I ask you a stupid question? Before you lit the fire, you did remember to open the flue, right?"

Annette stopped short.

"Okay, not such a stupid question."

Only a stupid answer, Annette thought. But she said nothing. Not because she was in the habit of being quiet, but on the grounds that she could be incriminated. Jackson was right: she was a horrible mother.

"Mommy!" Morgan was sitting up on the stretcher.

Diane looked beyond Annette to the stretcher. "She's adorable. Hard to believe you bore that child."

"I didn't," Annette said. "But she's mine. At least until her father hears what happened tonight." She took a step and winced.

Diane reached out to help her.

"Who's going to tell him?"

Annette glanced back, but it was too dark to see the expression on Diane's face.

A paramedic approached her. "Can I take a look at that, ma'am?"

Blood had dried in streaks on Annette's foot, her ankle was swollen like a balloon. All sensation had returned. Annette was relieved to feel the pain, to take the hit her daughter avoided. She felt the familiar ache in her knee, too, as the paramedic helped her hop up onto Morgan's stretcher. Annette pulled Morgan over onto her lap and extended her leg gingerly for the paramedic. But this pain was nothing compared to the fear of losing Morgan, especially now, when she was so close to getting her back. Annette hugged her daughter close until she squirmed. When she looked up again, all she could see was the taillights of Diane's Volvo.

Who would tell Jackson? That was the best question of all.

Chapter 9

DIANE

. . . you realize that the man who said "There are no second acts" died young.

Diane yawned and dropped her purse on the floor where the couch would go, if and when the damn thing arrived from Mecca. She couldn't even remember what the chintz fabric looked like, but she had the feeling that was a blessing. Between attempts to update her résumé, Diane had seen so many reruns of *Martha* that she could make a slipcover from a bed sheet blindfolded. And she had the number of the delivery service memorized, but she could never get a live person on the line. It was time to call Lana at the store and complain. No doubt Asshole's lawyer, Ms. Gold, already had her new furniture, although after tonight it would probably smell like smoke. Diane chuckled. Who didn't know to open the flue before lighting a fire? And it was odd to see Miss Pencil Skirt in pajamas; odder still to see her as a mom.

"Mom?" Cody ran to her.

"What is it, honey?"

He whispered in her ear.

"I can't hear you, say again?"

His eyes darted back to the room he shared with Quinn.

Then he pointed to his crotch. "Quinn is missing a part. Won't her legs fall off?"

Diane bit her lip to keep a straight face. "I think her legs will be fine, Cody. Don't you worry, okay? Go to sleep now."

"I can't. She won't turn the music down."

Diane sighed, and followed the hip-hop beat toward the kids' bedroom. Maybe being forced to hear this awful music would cause Cody to rebel and be a rocker. Diane could only hope. She braced herself and opened the door.

A poster of an Indy 500 racecar was taped to Cody's wall, and Quinn's side of the room was already covered with magazine clippings. Dozens of airbrushed women with perfect skin stared out at her with bored expressions. The one by the door hinge was definitely Lana. Diane tucked Cody in and turned off the light.

"Mother! It's too early to go to sleep," Quinn protested.

"Good night."

"Can I get my belly button pierced?"

"No! It's a scar from your umbilical cord. It's sacred."

"It's mine now."

"Not until you're twenty-one, it isn't. Besides, you screamed when you had your ears pierced. Stop stalling and go to sleep."

"Okay, but can we please just get cable like normal people? The TV reception here sucks."

"It sucks, Mom," Cody chimed in.

Diane winced at that word. "Oh, for heaven's sake. I'm working on it. Do you have any idea how much cable costs these days?"

"Mom, do I have to go to summer school?"

Diane turned the light back on and sat down on the bed. "You do have to take chemistry over, honey, might as well get it out of the way."

"It wasn't my fault the beaker blew up. My stupid partner put the wrong element in."

"Doesn't always matter whose fault it is," Diane said, looking around the tiny bedroom they shared. You still ended up in a shitty apartment. "We just can't do the softball travel team again this summer." It was hard enough to drag Cody all over the state every weekend, but the cost of hotels and fast food added up quickly. Ever since Title X passed, the dads had gotten involved in girls' athletics and made things even more competitive. Not Steve, though. His absence made it hard to compete at all. Which was ironic, since now her daughter would need the scholarship that the softball players traveled to qualify for. Yet Diane suspected that if you added up the expense, it would more than cover the cost of tuition at a state school. "You can still play high school this fall."

"I'm sick of softball. I just want to do something fun. Why can't I just go to the beach every day?"

"I'm sorry, honey." Quinn was too old for camp and too young for a job, but she still needed supervision. Diane had to keep her busy somehow. "Chemistry will be a good opportunity to get used to your new school and meet other kids."

"Stupid kids who flunked out."

"No, honey. Some kids take extra classes to make room for an elective. Strange but true." Quinn rolled her eyes, but she let Diane kiss her goodnight on the cheek. Diane kissed Cody again, then pulled their door closed and headed to her bedroom. She was a whole three steps down the hall when Quinn yelled, "Nana called twice!"

"Thank you! Goodnight!" Great. Just what she needed, another pep talk from her mother, who spoiled her grandkids with fancy electronic gifts instead of helping to pay the rent. Diane went to the bathroom and brushed her teeth. Last thing she needed now was a dental bill. Why was it so hard to get dental coverage? She had paid a fortune to fix Asshole's teeth way back when. By the time her mother met him, he looked so good she was only interested in learning if he had a single older brother. Diane's dad wasn't much better, curious only about Steve's handicap on the golf course. It's not that they didn't care who she married; they trusted her judgment. But she had fallen for good looks and free weekends in Vegas. Diane no longer trusted her judgment about anything.

Diane flossed. She hoped the kids had flossed. She used to remind them every day, but after a while the words are meaningless, so she could only hope that despite any genetic propensity for soft teeth, her good hygiene would serve as an example. Diane suspected the same theory held true for marriage. Quinn and Cody weren't more prone to divorce; on the contrary, they would likely stick it out in a bad relationship longer, or marry later, or not at all. How would she ever have her own grandchildren to spoil? The real difference was that Diane was a lousy role model. She had shown them how to floss their teeth but not how to choose an appropriate mate.

Back in the bedroom, Diane dropped her sweatpants on the floor and flopped onto her air mattress. Her coffee-stained T-shirt doubled as a nightgown. The toilet was running again. A plumber was number five on her list. A decent mattress was number nine. She was still at number one: get a job.

She pushed aside the newspaper classifieds and the coffee cups and the numbers on human resources specialists who hung up on her all day. She had even stood up as she spoke with them—she'd read a magazine at the grocery store checkout that said standing up made you sound more confident. But it didn't make her feel more confident, especially when the only answer she ever got was "no." She had e-mailed her résumé to three employment agencies and no one called back. She even perused opportunities on her alumni Web site, but she was hopelessly unqualified. Her old B-school classmates, the ones who didn't have kids, were running Fortune 500 companies now. Even Lisa, her rowdy roommate, was vice president of a bank. She had three kids and proper help. Diane needed proper help, too. And not just with her kids or her résumé.

Diane slipped under her bedcovers. As optimistic as she was when the blue sky was full of possibilities, the nights were scary. There was only one thing guaranteed to make her feel better. She had become so dependent on her battery-operated prescription for a good night's sleep that she kept it by her bed. One orgasm and she could sleep despite the noise, the floor, and the threat of food stamps. She had to send Lisa a thank-you note.

Diane pushed the vibrator under the covers and turned it on. Ah, the hum of happiness. She was a pro now, knew the exact spot where her nerve endings were closest to the surface of her skin. She glanced at the clock to see if she would beat her new record of an orgasm in two minutes and twenty-two seconds. Ready, set . . .

Nothing. She clicked the on-off button. Still nothing. She snuck in Cody's room and pilfered an AA battery from his game drawer, then snuck back to her bed and tried it again. No go. Diane shook it, twisted it, and pounded it, but it was broken. In less than three weeks! Cheap piece of crap. She threw it across the room. It banged into the wall and landed with a thud.

"Mom? Are you okay?"

"Yes, honey, go to sleep!" Diane called. She went in the bathroom and searched her medicine cabinet for melatonin, but she was all out. Just as well, that made her as groggy as actual sleeping pills. What if Cody had an asthma attack and she couldn't drive to the emergency room? Diane pressed a warm washcloth to her face, then looked at her blotchy skin. She was not only a middle-aged divorcée but the kind of pervert who used sex toys.

This was *so* not her life.

Diane patted her face dry and reminded herself how many times she had caught Steve masturbating. She felt better. It was only fair, right? It was healthy, right? Soon Cody would be doing it, too. Oh, joy. Diane looked at the clock. Only two minutes had passed, but it wasn't a record. She slathered her skin with moisturizer, wishing she could call Lisa, but it was only mid-morning in London, and Lisa was at work. She couldn't chat about vibrators until lunch. Or tea, or whatever it was they did there, besides know a thing or two about how to get a good night's sleep.

She tiptoed to the kitchenette, where her computer was set

up. She tried to log on, but Quinn was online. Diane IM'ed her daughter: *Go to sleep, Quinn!*

Immediately, the Dollface icon disappeared. Diane typed her screen name—Moms"R"Us—and Googled the brand name of the vibrator. She found the Web site easily and tried to order a replacement as fast as possible while keeping an eye on the door in fear that one of the kids would come in for a glass of water. So what if her toy had lasted only three weeks? That was twenty-one nights of uninterrupted REM cycles. When she tried to type in her shipping address, there was a snag. Evidently there were stores all over Europe, but they didn't ship to the U.S.

Diane boiled water to make Sleepytime tea. She Googled "Sex Toys AND United States" while she waited. Immediately, a popup of a threesome appeared on her screen. She hit Close as fast as possible and prayed her kids wouldn't accidentally click on this link tomorrow. She tried again and found a former radio deejay with an intriguing array of products, but the disclaimer said something about a mailing list. How would Diane explain to Quinn what a cock ring was for? Something to help keep her legs from falling off? Decoration, like a belly button ring? Sounded painful. What if she already knew what it was? Diane shuddered at the thought. She clicked on the next computer link.

The next listing was a Midwest-based company called Pure Romance™. They offered an amazing array of products, from postchildbirth Kegel exercise aids to lingerie that rivaled Victoria's Secret. Best of all, the founder looked nice, like a regular housewife. If this conservative-looking, middle-aged mom thought sex toys were okay, and found enough like-minded women for the company to become a Fortune 500 legend, then Diane felt much better about the whole thing. Unfortunately, Diane couldn't order anything online without a credit card.

Diane went back to bed, but she couldn't sleep. It wasn't just the lack of an orgasm, or postmarital stress, or even the frustration of bankruptcy. It was this whole new world of possibility.

After tossing and turning for an hour, she started jotting down ideas. When the sheets were so twisted she had to get up to fix them, she pulled on her ratty bathrobe and returned to the kitchen.

Diane was out of coffee filters, but that didn't stop her. She spread a paper towel in the coffeemaker, brewed the entire ten-cup pot, and scoured the Internet again. She found lots of cute novelty items, but she kept coming back to Pure Romance™. They had bachelorette kits, couples toys, lotions for low libidos—even a book about how to give blowjobs. What a good idea . . . Diane heard Quinn cough and covered the screen in case she came in for water. That was not a book Diane wanted her daughter to know about. Divorced women didn't need to know that, either. Or did they? No. Right now, Diane was more interested in her own pleasure. It was her turn.

Diane found contact information for a West Coast rep and e-mailed her. She got a message back so quickly—the woman had a new baby and was working as she nursed—that she picked up the phone and called her. She begged the woman to ship a vibrator overnight for payment C.O.D. It was an emergency—in so many ways.

The woman understood and invited her to be a local sales rep and earn products for free. Diane considered the offer for a moment as she scrolled through the sales information. But she didn't want handcuffs or lingerie and she didn't want to sell them, either. She was interested in a few items from several different sources, products that would be especially helpful for women who were suddenly single. Maybe it was the badly filtered coffee, but inspiration hit Diane with the same jolt as the moment she realized she had to get a divorce. This was a long time coming, and a shocking idea, but a logical solution to her problems: Diane would start her own business. She needed to take charge of her life, to be the boss in more ways than one.

After dropping the kids off at camp and school, Diane went to the library and checked out as many business books as she could carry. Then she raced back to the apartment and dug into the last moving boxes. She found her old business files and skimmed her notes about developing marketing strategies and business plans. Business had changed in the last decade, though, so she went back online and researched everything she could think of, from advertising to inventory. Her most entertaining challenge was a company name: Sweet Dreams was taken, and Toys"R"Us would sue. She liked Party in My Pants, but what if Cody heard it? Boyfriend in a Box was cute, but the whole point was that you didn't need one.

The kids didn't mind having pizza delivered for dinner and putting themselves to bed, so Diane just kept working. The last time she had stayed up two nights in a row was for a Burning Man concert in the desert out past Palm Springs. She had felt fine after that wild weekend in her twenties, but now she felt like that forty-foot man burned in effigy. Then she read that some toys were illegal in Mississippi, but you could buy a gun there without a background check. Anger fueled her for a few more hours.

Diane surveyed the scraps of paper covering the counters and wished she had an assistant to organize her notes and a wife to clean up and go grocery shopping, but the only way she'd ever be able to afford that kind of help was to let a few things slide now. Asshole used to brag that he'd saved her from the workforce, that businesswomen were like crabs in a barrel, pulling each other down to get ahead. They *were* crabs, Diane agreed, but the only reason they couldn't get ahead was that they were too busy skittering sideways to take care of everything else. Not Diane, not anymore. Time to look further than the next home-cooked meal.

By the time the kids came into the tiny kitchen looking for breakfast, the printer was spewing out copies of a business plan. Diane had eaten all the Pop-Tarts, so she passed out multivitamins and grabbed her purse. "Who wants McDonald's?"

After breakfast, Diane went back to await the C.O.D. shipment of sex toys. Intimacy enhancers, she reminded herself. Relaxation aids. Despite her lack of sleep, she felt awake, alive, and incredibly confident. It wasn't the two pots of coffee that fueled her but the adrenaline rush of confidence. How she had let Steve convince her that she couldn't survive without him, she would never know. It was as if he had kicked the legs out from under her when she had her arms full of babies, and all she could do was sit on the floor and wait for his help. Which, it was apparent to her now, she didn't need. She felt the way she did back in B-school, ready to take on the world.

Ninety minutes later, Diane pulled into the parking lot of her bank. She brushed the dog hair off her old khaki skirt and painted her lips in the reflection of the rearview mirror. Then, she grabbed her proposal folder, took a deep breath, and climbed out. She forbade her armpits to sweat in the blazing heat as she tried to remember how to walk in high heels across the blazing pavement. She smiled confidently at the bank guard who opened the heavy door.

Once inside, she drank two more cups of bitter coffee while waiting for her turn with a small-business loan officer. To the right, a distraught woman with a run in her pantyhose was trying to close a joint account and open a personal one. Diane recognized the legal documents in the woman's hand, as well as the terrified look in her eyes. She had struggled through all that same paperwork and was still struggling to get her ex's name off the telephone bill without paying a new deposit. She smiled sympathetically at the woman. She was tempted to give out her phone number, but the woman hurried out before Diane decided. Now she felt bad. If all went well with this meeting, she would have her number printed on a business card. Then she could offer emotional support—as well as relaxation aids, and maybe even a part-time job.

Diane approached the area where the loan officers worked. There were two at their desks this morning. The Persian woman looked stern as she shook her head at the applicant sitting at her desk, so Diane chose the other officer, an older man with a bushy mustache and a rainbow-printed tie. His nameplate said Mr. Santos, and a picture of a pretty young woman rested on his desk by a coffee mug that read: Mr. Excitement.

Mr. Santos smiled as Diane sat down. She laid out her spreadsheets and pie chart, hoping he didn't notice her sweaty fingerprints. She wanted to blame her nerves on all that caffeine, but truth was, she was scared to death. The last time she sat down in a bank, she'd learned her husband had looted their savings account. The last time she had asked for a business loan was, well . . . never.

Mr. Santos picked up her business plan. "We get dozens of requests each day for global marketing capital, but this looks more like door-to-door sales. A little behind the times, aren't you?"

"No, sir, it's a party-based business where the part-time salespeople work on commission."

"Where would you find people to do that? Even students like guaranteed pay."

"Some people need flexible hours more than a minimum wage."

"Who?"

Diane tried not to vent her frustration. Fucking idiot. "You don't have kids, do you?"

"Sure I do, and two grandchildren." He pointed proudly to a baby picture of twins on his desk. A pretty blonde who could have been their mother beamed from a frame next to it.

"Then you remember how kids get sick at school, or need a ride to gymnastics, or to the store to get posterboard . . ." The man shrugged, clueless, so Diane skipped ahead. "In any case, I'm familiar with this workforce. I simply need seed money to invest in a core line of products that will serve as samples."

"You expect customers to pay in advance for candles and bath oils they could buy at Target?"

Diane squirmed. "Well, sir, these are special candles and relaxation aids that Target doesn't carry."

"How will you market a niche product for such a select customer base?"

"There are millions of divorced women, sir, right here in Los Angeles. The biggest advantage of my brand is in focusing on this specialized and highly motivated demographic. As a member of this group, I can confirm that we are rarely singled out in a positive way. We respond strongly to the marketing strategy

I've outlined, which includes both word of mouth and Internet social networks." First the neighborhood, then the world, Diane thought, as she felt her underarm deodorant fail. "Sir, if you approve my loan, I guarantee I could make a return on your investment just from the women here at the bank this morning."

Mr. Santos perked up and looked around the bank at the dozen women armored up in their business suits. Then he read the name on the folder in front of him. "Instant Pleasure? What is the product, exactly?" Diane opened the proposal for him. She hoped she wouldn't have to demonstrate for him, too.

He flipped through her spread sheets. "I have to say, your credit rating is less than stellar, and I don't see how these products differ in any way from items on the market. Do you have pictures?"

Diane reluctantly pulled another folder out of her old briefcase. She showed him a few printouts she had downloaded from the Internet. She started with the least harmless-looking device, a silver ball connected to a remote control switch. "This is a massager."

"A bit small, isn't it? What's it for? The back of your neck?"

Diane brightened. "That's one area, yes."

He flipped to a picture of plastic lipstick. "What's relaxing about lipstick?"

"It's not really a lipstick. It . . . um, vibrates. It just happens to fit nicely in a woman's purse.

"And divorced women need these massagers why?"

Diane wanted to say it helped them recover from dealing with condescending jerks like him, but she just smiled and handed him a copy of an e-mail her doctor had sent attesting to the negative physical effects of marital stress.

He dismissed the e-mail and looked at her directly. "You seem intelligent and well prepared, Mrs. Kowalski. Do you have a sample product, by any chance?"

Diane winced, and not just at her name. But thanks to overnight shipping and the emergency cash she kept in the cookie jar, she was ready. She pulled her chair closer, opened her briefcase, and set the black velvet pouch on Mr. Santos's desk. She recited the spiel she had practiced. "This product is a circulation stimulator designed to promote good health. It can also be used to enhance intimacy between partners in order to maintain the relationships that are the very basis of our society." She chewed the lipstick off her lip and untied the drawstring. She pushed it toward him.

Mr. Santos nodded and reached inside. He pulled out the plastic cylinder, then jumped to his feet. "In my day," he roared, "that was called a dildo."

The people nearby all looked toward them, whispering. Diane reached over and slipped it back in the pouch. She felt calm now. Her confidence grew. It may have been difficult to trust her old business acumen to ask for money, but she was used to unreasonable men. She smoothed her skirt over her knees. "Fortunately, that day is past, Mr. Santos." She took her glasses off and looked at him. "As you know, men have an advantage in being self-sufficient with their, um, circulation, so these products strengthen the vast numbers of female workers also responsible for providing our country's tax base."

He finally looked up from the pouch on his desk. "You're saying dildos are good for the country?"

Diane bit her lip until a woman took her children by the hand to the safe deposit box. Then she corrected him. "Vibrators. Yes."

"Let me get this straight," Mr. Santos said. "You want me to invest ten thousand dollars in this? Why not call it what it is: porno for the Tupperware set?"

The caffeine was wearing off and Diane's head began to pound. She should have chosen the woman loan officer. What was she thinking? Diane stood up—maybe it gave you confidence in person, like it did on the phone. She pointed to the photo of a young woman on Mr. Santos's desk. "I'm sure your daughter is aware of the benefits."

He stroked his mustache. "That's my girlfriend."

Diane looked closer and scoffed. "You want me to believe that your sagging sixty-year-old penis can satisfy a twenty-five-year-old girl? You Viagra-swilling hypocrite!"

She saw his hand reach for the button under the desk, but by then it was too late. She was on an all-night, greasy-food, bad-coffee roll. And there was no way she would shut up now. "How dare you patronize me with your male supremacy, while you stick it to a woman who could be your granddaughter. I bet she'd buy my products. And what about your ex-wife?"

A strong hand gripped Diane's arm. "Ouch!" The guard who had nodded so pleasantly as she entered the bank was now just as pleasantly escorting her out. "Hey! I have an account here!" Diane had never been kicked out of a bank before. She had never done a lot of things before. She struggled to free herself enough to put her things back in her briefcase, then heard a strange sound.

Behind her, the Persian woman was clapping. One by one, all the female tellers joined her. Diane glared at the guard and he let her go. She straightened her blouse, held her head high, and marched out.

She felt tall and powerful until the bank door closed behind her and the guard escorted her to her crappy old car. Then she shrank back to size. Still, she had her pride. She thanked him politely, tossed her briefcase on the passenger seat, then made him wait as she lowered herself—all ladylike with her knees to-gether—before swiveling to her seat behind the wheel.

After the guard shut her car door, Diane put her key in the ignition to turn on the air-conditioning and made a show of taking her time to sort through her Wayne Dyer CDs. When she looked up, he was still standing there, sweating in the hot sun, waiting for her to exit the lot. He was just doing his job. She opened the console between the seats and picked up her Tic-Tacs. She rolled down the window. "Breath mint?"

He blinked and shook his head. She rolled the window up, chuckling. She picked out a CD that was overdue at the library. His soothing affirmations were the perfect accompaniment to the squeal of her tires as she sped out of the parking lot. She saw the bruise on the jiggly part of her underarm. She needed to find a new gym. And a new bank.

Diane had an hour to kill before picking up Cody from

camp. It was enough time to go grocery shopping, but she didn't bring her coupons. And she couldn't bear to go back to their stuffy little apartment to get them. The place itself was bad enough, but now, covered with piles of business plans, it would feel too much like failure. Diane pulled up to the light but wasn't sure which way to turn. She was tempted to stop by Mecca and commiserate on a soft couch in the air-conditioned store, but Lana was so poised and pretty. Diane looked like shit.

Instead, she splurged on a blended coffee and parked at the beach to watch Cody finish his last game of volleyball. Beyond the courts, a fully dressed man was scouring the sand with a metal detector. She wondered how many coins he would collect. Not enough to loan her money for her business; she would have to think of another way. She moved the driver's seat back and opened the window.

A soft breeze flowed through the car. Sailboats threaded the horizon in the distance. Diane closed her eyes and despite all the caffeine, she fell asleep. Cody woke her up when he climbed in the car with his sandy towel and his lunch bag full of wheat-bread crusts. She looked at him, bleary and a little out of it.

"What's for dinner?" he asked. He sounded so much like his dad, she wanted to slap him. "I'm sick of spaghetti."

She chuckled, regaining both her wits and her memory of what happened at the bank. "That's why we call it pasta, sweetie." She ruffled his hair until he pulled away.

"Can we visit our old house?"

"Let's go see how Quinn's first day of summer school went, instead. We can pick up some Popsicles on the way." He nodded, so she pulled up at the next 7-Eleven. The truth was, Diane didn't want to see the old house. It was too painful. And she didn't want to tell him about Annette's fire last night. She just wanted to go home. Home, another four-letter word.

As soon as Cody had a Popsicle in his sandy fist, he started back in. "Please, Mom? Can we just drive by?"

Fortunately, they were already pulling into the parking garage. "I appreciate your good manners, honey, but Mommy is tired."

"Please?"

Diane picked up her briefcase and the box of Popsicles and got out of the car, wondering how to explain. She decided to take the easy way out. "I love you, but the answer is no."

"Okay, but just tell me why?"

Diane snapped. She was finished with the politically correct parenting. "Cody, I really don't want to see that woman who lives there now."

Cody dragged his beach bag down the hall. "But why?"

"She's just not a nice person."

Quinn heard their footsteps in the hallway and opened the door. Her eyes were all sparkly and happy. *Oh God, please don't let her be on drugs*, Diane thought. "Hi, honey."

Quinn smiled mysteriously and opened the door wide.

Cody walked behind her, still chattering. "Remember what you said, Mom? You gotta give people a chance. Maybe she's not so bad."

Diane looked past Quinn inside the apartment. Her grandma's antiques—all the furniture she had lost with the house—was piled inside.

Diane walked in slowly, rubbing the scarred velvet of her favorite settee. "You're right," Diane said. "Maybe she's not so bad after all."

Chapter 10

LANA

. . . talking about money isn't taboo, it's research.

Lana shook her hair out from her helmet and hurried past the loading dock behind Mecca. She was usually the first one in during the morning shift. Something was wrong. Delivery men she didn't recognize were unloading furniture from a cube van. They were using furniture pads instead of bubble wrap. And when she walked into the store, the air conditioner was already blasting.

Winston was all dressed up, waving his clipboard at her from across the store. Lana liked how he dressed with such care. He only had half a dozen nice shirts that she had seen, so Lana predicted the day by it, like a horoscope. Today, Winston was wearing his charcoal dress pants, the ones that hugged his tush just right. He also had a baby blue dress shirt rolled up to his elbows, with a blue-and-white striped tie. The pants were excellent, the shirt was right up there, but the tie she wasn't so sure of. Yup, the tie was a bad sign; there was no doubt about it now. That was Guy Franklin trailing Winston.

Guy was the prop assistant who had tried to pry the spear from Lana's grip back in Greece. If he hadn't been in such a hurry, she might not have thrown it at all. Okay, that was a lie, but still. He had probably used that infamous job to rise through the ranks. If he was dealing directly with Winston, he must be the art director, designing his own sets now. Or the furniture, in this case. Lana stepped back from the counter and pressed closer to the wall, out of sight. She prayed he wouldn't spot her. She should have left Los Angeles and moved back home like her mom said, but Boston? The weather made her hair go flat.

"Morning, Lana," Winston said. As he approached her, she could hear him humming, some nursery rhyme the twins learned in preschool, no doubt. He came around behind the counter and slipped in front of her to put a wad of cash in the bank pouch.

"What's up, boss?" Lana asked.

"Big studio rental."

"Big mistake, Winston. You'll never get your stuff back in one piece. That's what I've heard, anyway."

"At fifty percent of retail, plus insurance for loss and damage, I'll take the risk."

A screech filled the air and Lana winced. Eli had opened the mall gate for the first customers of the day. Lana recognized Diane Kowalski among them. *Soon to be Taylor*, Lana corrected herself.

Winston put his hand on Lana's bare shoulder. It wasn't a hairy paw or a manicured pretty-boy hand. Aside from a few rough cuticles, it was the kind of hand she was glad to have on her shoulder: warm.

"Don't worry, Lana. I can handle the studio rental. You take care of retail."

Lana nodded. He took his hand away and walked off to meet Guy at the nursery display. Lana turned away quickly and put on her apron. She glanced in the mirror wondering if it would be enough of a disguise. Her hair was a good ten inches shorter now. She mussed it for effect.

"Lana? You alright?"

She turned to see Diane. "Of course, how are you?"

"I'll be good if it's not too late to get a full refund." Diane put her receipts on the counter.

"Don't tell me you changed your mind again."

"No. My old living room furniture mysteriously showed up yesterday."

"You mean the antiques? Wow. I didn't realize that woman had a soft spot."

Diane shrugged. "She has a daughter she's crazy for. Custody issues, though."

"Bummer," Lana said.

"You're lucky you didn't have kids."

Lana didn't respond. Diane knew a lot, but not everything. She checked the delivery schedule. "Your furniture's already on the truck, Diane. Which means you'll be charged a restocking fee."

Diane frowned. "How much?"

"Twenty percent," Lana said.

"I still need the bed, but I'd rather wait and get a really nice one when—" she caught Lana ducking her head as Winston and Guy passed again. "Someone you know?" Diane asked.

"Used to." Lana replied. She caught Diane's raised eyebrow. "You know what? Forget it." She swiped the receipt from Diane's hand. "How's the job search going?"

"Fine. Well, not so fine. I was going to start my own business, but I had a little problem at the bank."

Lana looked at Diane. She still looked like a PTA president in her khaki pants and white T-shirt. At least it wasn't the suit with a skort. She laughed out loud at the thought of it. "Guess they figured the Girl Scout cookie market is already covered, huh?"

Diane frowned. "Actually, I was thinking of a product line for bigger girls," she said, leaning over the counter and lowering her voice. "Know anything about sex toys?"

Lana's finger paused over the credit button on the register. "I know a thing or two about that one on *Sex and the City*, and the one with the rotating heads and the little . . ." She looked up. "Oh my fucking God, are you going to sell sex toys?"

Eli, who was helping two older women at the silverware cart, coughed and shot her a look. He had no idea how interested they might be. Older women were far more liberal than the young ones. They no longer cared what people thought.

"I'd like to, but I couldn't get a loan."

"So?" Lana asked.

"So. End of story."

"One rejection and you're ready to quit? Talk about thin skin. Do you have any idea how many rejections it takes to get a gig in this town? And it has nothing to do with anything. Maybe the guy had a fight with his wife, maybe they want someone younger, maybe . . ." Lana caught herself again and shut up.

"What are you talking about?"

"The loan officer. Go to more banks. Or find a private investor. No offense, but maybe you just aren't wearing the right clothes, Diane. You have to look the part to get it."

"Fine, I'll hit Goodwill on the way home. Quinn finds some great stuff there."

Lana shook her head. She tapped her finger on the computer key, then pulled it off. She squinted at the receipt. "You know, this is not a rotating charge account."

"Meaning?"

"Meaning it's not your usual payoff term with interest accruing every month. Not for two months anyway."

"Meaning?"

"Meaning, this is essentially a free sixty-day loan."

"I know, Lana, I went to business school. I ran a company for fifteen years. But this is a credit. And it's not enough to start a business."

"That's where you're wrong, my friend." Lana glanced over at Winston, then lowered her voice. "If I give you the refund in cash, it's enough for a new wardrobe. If you're going into business, you need it."

"I don't get it."

"You still have to pay the credit card bill when it comes. But meanwhile . . ." Lana tapped the computer in all the right boxes. So what if the deposit would be different? The books would add up the same. She took a stack of hundreds from the bank pouch and put the credit slip inside. She saw Annette's name on a receipt. "As for real money, I'll bet Annette knows some investors."

"She's a divorce lawyer."

"Rich people get divorced all the time."

"So I've heard. If only I could meet one. A tall, dark, hand-some one."

"Those are overrated," Lana said. "But you should call An-nette. She did give that furniture back to you, right?"

"Doesn't mean we're friends. It was a gesture, that's all."

"Fine," Lana said. "I'll call her. You know what? I bet those studio guys would rent some paintings from her husband. That's a good excuse to call her, right? Might put her in a good mood."

"My own grandma's furniture is one thing, but I don't want to owe that woman. I can handle things myself." Diane said. She eyed the cash envelope. "Most things."

Lana chuckled. "Fine, do it your way. But here in Hollywood, who you know beats what you know every time." Lana held out the cash envelope.

Diane held up her hand to block it. "Maybe this isn't such a good idea."

Lana sighed. "Sorry, I'm in a bad mood today. Let's get out of here and do some retail therapy. There's someone I want you to meet." She set the money down and handed Diane a pen.

Diane signed for the money. "Okay. But remind me again why you care?"

Lana took her name tag off. "For one thing, I appreciate your silence about my, um, former life. For another thing, after

giving you that cash, I might be needing a new job." She struck
a sexy pose.

Diane laughed. "I'm not talking about a porno Web site,
Lana; it's more like Avon ladies."

"Cool, I can do Vanna White." She smiled sweetly and rolled
her wrist to point at the counter. "Or the briefcase babes on
Deal or No Deal." Now, she stuck her chest out, pursed her lips,
and pointed to her crotch. Diane laughed.

Lana waved to Eli. He looked around. There were only a few
walk-ins on weekday mornings, and from the looks of the furniture leaving the store, there wouldn't be much inventory left to
sell. He nodded.

Lana steered Diane out of the store and into Kitty's Closet,
the boutique a few doors down. She introduced her to Kitty, an
older woman with eyeliner a half inch too high. Lana used to
think the old lady was tacky, until a few months ago when her
eyesight started to go. What a nightmare! If there was ever an
action that gave away a woman's age, putting on glasses to read
a menu was it. Now Lana simply ignored menus and ordered
whatever she wanted. Chefs in L.A. were used to making special
meals. So Lana understood that Kitty wasn't tacky at all, she just
couldn't see to put her makeup on or to read radio scripts.
Which was why she had set up shop here in the mall, using her
smoky voice on sexy soccer moms. It was endearing.

And, just as Lana suspected, when they told her about Diane's
business plan, she wasn't the least bit shocked. "Why should
men have all the fun?" Kitty purred. "Tell you what: if you have
something small that comes in a pretty box, I'll give you some
shelf space."

"Can you do that in a mall?"

"They do it in London. Isn't that so m'love?" she said in a
perfect British accent.

Lana replied in kind. "Quite so."

They laughed, and Kitty continued. "Once Victoria's Secret
sees there's money to be made, they'll be next."

"See?" Lana said. "Now we have to make you look the part."

Lana channeled Marlene, the gal who used to dress her. That woman could make a paper bag look sexy. Lana sat on the love seat she'd sold to Kitty at a discount, and piled up the clothes Diane would purchase at an equally favorable discount.

Half an hour later, a petite seamstress with a tomato pincushion on her wrist kneeled on the carpet, pinning Diane's hem. Lana circled her, studying every inch. "Just one more thing, Diane."

"What? I love the leopard print and the cinched-waist jackets. It's so different."

"No, it's still your colors, tan and black. But the fabric is important. And the tailoring. And remember—only one accent piece. You want the *sophistication* of a big cat, you don't want to look like one."

Diane looked at the price tag and winced.

Lana turned it so she couldn't see. "Better to have three great outfits than ten crappy ones. Especially jackets. Every time you wear a jacket it raises you a notch above the crowd."

Kitty draped a few long necklaces around Diane's neck. "But don't forget to have fun with it, doll."

Diane nodded, then twisted her head around to see Lana. "So what was the one more thing?"

Lana shook her head at the panty line creasing the linen trousers Diane was wearing. "The panties have got to go."

"But I love my briefs," Diane said. "They're comfy and classic."

"Classic for a five-year-old."

Kitty rearranged the jewelry counter. "Don't insult my granddaughter. She prefers Little Mermaid."

Diane laughed. "Would it be better if I got them in a print?"

"No, it would be better if you burned them," Lana said. She looked at Kitty for reinforcement.

Kitty winked at Lana. "Panties are a statement, doll. They say who you are. Don't you read *Vogue*?" She pulled an assortment of lace panties out of a drawer and laid them across the counter.

"But nobody sees them." Diane stepped off the pedestal and picked up a hot-pink thong. "And they're expensive."

"Damn right. They're for you. Panties are power." Lana turned to Kitty. "What are you wearing, Kitty?"

Kitty smiled. "Leopard print. Sheer." She batted her fake eyelashes. "I'm feeling flirty today. How about you, doll?"

"Basic black thong. Simple, strong, and sexy."

Diane held up a boy-cut style embroidered with a Superman logo. "Panties are like mood rings?"

"Bingo."

Lana held up a pair of red silk panties. "Power panties."

Diane held up a black string bikini that tied on the side. "Panties with intent?"

"She'll take one of each." Lana supervised the transaction while Diane changed back to her street clothes. She dug Diane's phone out of her purse before handing it back. "Time to call Annette."

Diane nodded in a what-the-hell way. She took the phone outside the store where she could get a clear signal.

Kitty gave Lana a small bottle of Perrier from her fridge under the counter. "Any progress with the boss?"

Lana spun the rack of earrings and shook her head.

"Why don't you just fuck him, doll?"

Lana put her hand on her notorious hip. "Oh, Kitty, you know better than that. You can only fuck the ones you don't care about."

"So *that* was my mistake." Kitty laughed and made out the bill by hand.

Lana waited for Diane to hang up. She had lied about the black thong. Beneath her swishy white skirt, she was wearing white lace bikinis with rosebuds on the front. She was feeling delicate. Too delicate to face her past or a future she'd never have.

Diane came back in. "She wants to see the proposal, but it sounded like she has an investor in mind."

Lana handed Diane the fur-trimmed shopping bag and gave her a smile—a small smile, #16, for sincerity. "Come on, I have a buddy at the spa downstairs who wants a deal on a new desk."

Diane swung the bag over her shoulder. "So?"

"So, let's go get our hair done."

Diane smiled.

Lana smiled back, but there was no number for it. The smile of friendship was real.

Chapter 11

BONNIE

. . . your stupid old hobbies don't seem so stupid anymore.

The policeman rapped on the driver's side window of Bonnie's Jetta. She rolled it down. "Howdy, officer, can I help you?" There had been a dead deer in the canyon pass, a young buck with a small rack of antlers. Maybe the police were looking for clues about which car had hit it in the morning fog. She peered over her hood at her front bumper. It was clean, thank goodness.

Several cars slowed to rubberneck as they drove past toward the Malibu courthouse. "You made an illegal turn at the light, ma'am."

Bonnie turned around and watched three more cars make that same left and drive past. She whispered. "Looks legal to me."

The officer frowned. "Not between seven and nine A.M."

Bonnie glanced at the dashboard—8:50, and it was already 83 degrees, ten degrees cooler here on the coast than in the valley, except for under her arms. She handed him her license. She didn't usually go to Malibu this early in the morning, so she didn't know. She only came this way once in a while to stop at the Country Mart, where the kids could enjoy the playground while she splurged on a smoothie. She looked in the mirror to check on Lucas, asleep in his car seat. Thank goodness Quinn was able to babysit Hayley this morning.

She looked up at the officer. Three more cars made an illegal left turn and passed them. This must be her lucky day.

Bonnie could have gone to the Chatsworth courthouse, but she thought the lines might be shorter at Malibu. What did rich people have to fight over? Bonnie wiped her clammy hands on her overalls and picked up the pile of legal papers she had printed from the Web last night. "I'm sorry, officer. I'm on my way to file a restraining order and I didn't see it." She made a show of checking on the baby sleeping in the back seat and putting her finger to her lips so he would speak quietly.

He didn't. "Registration?"

The baby woke up and began fussing. The officer didn't give a darn. She used to get out of tickets with a smile. Maybe if she had visible bruises. But all she had was a list of threatening phone calls. She had worked really hard to look normal—only her nails, bitten to the quick, were proof of anything amiss. The officer wrote out a ticket and directed her to the correct parking lot at the courthouse. So polite.

Once inside the courthouse, Bonnie found the anteroom with windows like a post office. After twenty minutes of reading arrest warrants on the wall, it was her turn at the Information window. The enormous woman on the other side took one glance at Bonnie's cracked cuticles and patted the back of Lucas's Snugli. She acted like getting a restraining order was no big deal. Maybe it wasn't, to her. She probably saw it every day. What a scary thought. Scary world, rather.

The clerk tapped her impossibly long, blue rhinestone–studded nails on the form. "Anger management should be a requirement of marriage," she said. "Mm-mm. Think of the taxpayers' money it would save. 'Course, I might be out of a job." She laughed and printed out a map to an entirely different courthouse, ten miles down the coast in Santa Monica. When Bonnie's cell phone rang, the clerk pointed her index finger at the sign prohibiting cell phones.

Bonnie thanked her and put her phone back in the diaper bag with a sigh of relief. She had never had such a good excuse not to answer Buck's phone calls. Bonnie was so pleased for the few moments of peace, that she didn't mind the drive to Santa Monica nor the nonrefundable parking fee in the lot that the courthouse shared with the Civic Auditorium.

After an hour of waiting around there, she learned that she was still in the wrong place and had to drive another twenty miles up the 405 through the jammed Sepulveda pass and over the hill to Van Nuys. The third time would be the charm, she hoped. There was absolutely nothing easy about any of this— except for spending her morning free of phone harassment. Talk about a silver lining. Bonnie chuckled as she drove.

Once there, Bonnie bounced the baby as she stood in line to answer questions. The clerk said she really should be downtown at the main L.A. County Courthouse, but he took pity on her. He read the same questions off the list that she had already filled in online on the Do It Yourself Restraining Order form: "Was she afraid of Buck?" and "Would he ever hurt the children?" Bonnie just wasn't sure.

No matter what, she couldn't bear to hear the phone ring one more time. She didn't dare answer, not knowing what he would say, nasty or nice. She didn't want his accusations on the home machine either—he was toxic. Every time he left a message, she erased it. Bonnie pulled the fabric of her shirt away from her armpits and blew air between Lucas's Snugli and her chest. Didn't whoever made up those stupid rules understand how humiliating this whole process was? Bonnie hadn't done anything wrong. Then she remembered that Dr. Phil show about codependency and wondered if she had. But how could being nice be wrong?

Three hours, a diaper change across a dirty sink, and a lecture from an antipacifier mom later, Bonnie clutched five more forms. One was stamped TRO. Temporary Restraining Order. The clerk handed her the last form, stamped with a date.

"What's this one for?"

"That's your court date. The judge will decide if the restraining order will remain in effect."

"How?" Bonnie asked.

"Doctor reports, witnesses, any physical evidence you have."

Bonnie wilted. She had no evidence of anything, no proof at all. She had erased all of his crazy phone messages. Shit. Now she had to hope he did it again and keep the recording. Bonnie felt sick as she watched a fly buzz around the head of the clerk. The smell of his kiwi-scented shampoo mixed with the sweaty crowd made her nauseous. She loosened her belt beneath the Snugli and wiped her forehead with a baby wipe. If the police were collecting so much in traffic fines, why didn't the air-conditioning work?

She turned her cell phone back on for the drive home. The beep tone indicated she had two messages. And now she had to listen, in case they were evidence. Just as she decided to put the phone on vibrate and deal with it later, the phone rang again, startling the baby awake. She didn't recognize the number, but she picked up anyway.

It was the attorney whose number she had gotten from Annette Gold's assistant. She couldn't see Bonnie until next week. That felt like forever to Bonnie, who so desperately wanted advice. She'd even surfed the Web for information but only got depressed by the chat rooms full of people complaining.

On the way home, Bonnie stopped at Target for milk and more baby wipes. When she pushed her cart past the hardware aisle, she remembered what Lana had told her, and looked at pretty glass knobs for her coffee table. Target was always a bargain, but she could never leave without spending a lot more than she intended. What she really needed was a few rows over. She headed to the electronics department and bought a tiny tape recorder.

An hour later, Bonnie pulled past her peeling picket fence and into the driveway. Kyle, the adorable high school graduate from down the street, was mowing her front lawn, bare-chested. He smiled and waved at her. She waved back.

Finally, her overgrown eyesore of a yard would look semirespectable again. She wondered if Buck would try to beat up Kyle if he saw him on the property. She hoped Buck was more rational than that. She would be ashamed for a nice kid like Kyle to get mixed up in this mess.

She put the baby down for a nap, then greeted Quinn and Hayley, who were playing Princess in Hayley's bedroom. She had been dubious of Quinn at first, but she was proving to be a first-rate babysitter, and Bonnie was grateful. She was in the kitchen unpacking her plastic bags when she heard pounding on the front door.

For a moment, she was giddy with fear. If it was Buck, he would know from her face that something was up. But when she peeked out the window, she saw that it was Diane, looking fabulous. Her hair was cut to her shoulders, styled and streaked, and she was actually wearing lipstick. She looked like Diane's younger, prettier sister.

Bonnie opened the front door with a smile. "Sorry, lady, I think you have the wrong house," she said, pretending to shut the front door.

"Hey!" Diane poked the toe of her pump in the opening.

Bonnie laughed and shouted over the drone of the lawn-mower, "Just kidding. But you do look different. I mean, you know, pretty."

"Thanks. How'd it go?"

Bonnie's smile faded. She tried to keep her hands from shaking as she shut the door behind Diane. "It was pretty brutal. But I know what I need to do, so that's a relief."

"I'm proud of you, Bon. That was a big step."

"How can I feel proud about getting a restraining order against my very own husband?"

Diane put her arm around her. "That title doesn't give him the right to behave however he wants. I just saw him at the grocery store. Don't worry, he didn't recognize me." She handed Bonnie a sloshing can of lemonade concentrate. "He was having a fit because the buyer wouldn't stock some Midwest brand of potato chips."

"He does have a temper," Bonnie said. "Thanks for the lemonade. Once he gets the restraining order, we'll be on bread and water." She walked back to the kitchen. "Plus, I want to give Kyle something cold to drink before I get arrested for child endangerment."

As if on cue, the lawn mower noise stopped. Bonnie looked out the window at Kyle. He adjusted his headphones, then wiped his sweaty forehead with his red bandanna. He was adorable, no doubt about it. The lawn mower started again.

Diane followed Bonnie's gaze and whistled. "He's no child. But I can't believe he's working in that hundred-degree heat. What are you paying him?"

"Nothing. He volunteered." Bonnie found a plastic Kool-Aid pitcher and mixed up the lemonade.

"Oh, really?" Diane said.

Bonnie blushed as she stirred. "He's eighteen, way too young for me."

"That's only six years, Bon. Guys do it. In fact, I have my eye on a young trainer at the gym." Diane laughed at Bonnie's shocked expression. "I'm kidding. By the way, if you still want to join a gym, let me know. The gal who works there gave me a discount."

Bonnie got out the jelly jars. "She's in the club, too?"

Diane nodded and poured herself a glass. "Some very happy divorcées out there, Bon."

"Probably just adrenaline from all that jumping around."

"Whatever it takes," Diane kidded.

The lawn mower started up again and they both looked out the window. "Think I should make him wear a shirt?"

"Please don't." Diane answered. "Just get him to paint your fence before you break his heart, okay?"

Quinn and Hayley bounded in for a drink. "Quinn, honey, would you mind taking this glass out to the boy mowing the lawn?" Bonnie asked.

Quinn drew back. "He looks sort of busy."

Bonnie looked at Diane, then put the glass in the refrigerator to chill. "He *is* busy, you're right. We'll wait until he's done." Bonnie wanted to be busy, too, to not think about where she was this morning, how she had betrayed the father of her children, and what the consequences would be. She sighed and took another look at her friend. "Diane, you look so pretty. Can I take your picture?"

"Why?"

"Just for fun."

Diane shrugged. "I have a meeting with an investor that Annette knows next week. Guess I could use a picture to put on my business card and brochure and everything. Maybe I won't need it, but . . ."

"Maybe you will. You were a Girl Scout, weren't you?"

"Yup: 'Be Prepared.'"

Bonnie sighed. "Me, too. If only I'd been prepared for this."

"There is no way to prepare for this."

Bonnie nodded and went to the linen closet for a plain bedsheet. She thumbtacked it to the wall at the far end of the great room to make it look like a photographer's backing. Then she draped a matching sheet on a kitchen chair and dragged it over. She sent Hayley for her boom box and jammed in the old Marshal Tucker CD—the one CD she'd hidden from Buck. He took all the others when he left, including her dad's OSU marching band CD. So it was either Marshal Tucker or Quinn's hand-me-down Hakuna Matata. Some day she'd buy some sophisticated music. Not salsa, something with a violin. "Want me to make your eyes big like the one of Hayley in the hall?"

"No, I need something professional for the business."

"What kind of business?"

"I'm still working on that part. But, you know, respectable would be good."

"You look very respectable, Diane. I wish I had your magic wand."

"Talk to Lana."

Bonnie nodded. She might just do that before her court date "Okay, sit down."

The dryer buzzed in the alcove off the kitchen. Bonnie nearly dropped the camera.

Diane saw the slip. "You okay?"

Bonnie nodded. "You mind if I just fold the laundry before it gets all wrinkled?"

"Sure," Diane said. "I'll go check on the kids." She wandered down the hall to Hayley's room.

Bonnie waited until Diane was out of sight, then put the camera down and ran to the laundry room. She pulled Buck's clothes out of the dryer as fast as she could and started folding.

"Bon?" Diane found her. "Want some help?"

"No, I can handle it."

"Okay. But those clothes look sort of big for you."

Bonnie kept folding. She didn't want a lecture, but she was up for a fight. "He can't earn a living in pink shirts, Diane. I get dibs on the house, because we made the down payment with money my mom left me. But I need Buck to pay the mortgage, so this is our deal."

"But you just filed a restraining order. Why are you doing his laundry?"

"I don't want him to know anything's up until next week, when the sheriff's deputy serves him."

"Bonnie, what are you waiting for?" Diane asked.

Bonnie threw a pair of jeans in the basket and looked at Diane. "This is my life, do you not get it? Or maybe you just want everybody to be divorced so you can feel like it's okay!"

Diane was quiet for a minute. "That is not true." She picked up one of Buck's T-shirts, folded it, and set it on the pile.

Bonnie opened her mouth, then closed it. They folded in silence. She looked around the corner at the kitchen phone. She dared it to ring. When she looked back, Diane was tugging at her panty line. She grabbed the next T-shirt and started folding. "Didn't you change detergent after Cody's rash?"

Diane nodded. "Can I ask you a weird question? What kind of panties do you wear?"

Bonnie stepped away from Diane and folded a T-shirt. Maybe Buck was right, and these women were perverts. "I don't know."

"Sure you do."

Bonnie pulled her overalls aside and peeked down. It was

dark, so she unbuttoned the side and pulled the pale blue cotton into the light. Script letters spelled out: *Wednesday.*

Diane nodded. "It's Friday."

"So? It's hard to keep up." At that moment, Quinn trekked through the kitchen with Hayley on her back, giggling all the way. Bonnie liked having a babysitter. Next time, she'd leave Lucas home, too. Except, she didn't want a next time. She wanted Buck to come home and for her to forget any of this ever happened. What was she doing?

Diane reached for another T-shirt and started folding. "I'm taking a poll. A panty poll. I just changed the kind I've been wearing for, like, twenty years. Oh God, now I sound like Quinn: like, like, like. So, anyway, why wear days-of-the-week panties?"

Bonnie handed Diane the other end of one of Buck's sheets. What kind of panties was she supposed to wear? Hers were a bargain at Target, a whole week of panties in one package. And they came in different colors, so every day felt special. Bonnie liked feeling special every day, even if it was only from her panties. But she could do without the psych lecture. She folded her corners up to Diane's corners. "The days make me feel organized."

Diane chuckled as they folded the sheet in quarters. "Even though you don't wear the right pair on the right day?"

"They're clean. And I was born on Wednesday, so these are my lucky panties." Just as Diane brought her sheet corners up to Bonnie's, the phone rang. Bonnie dropped her end of the sheet on the floor. She burst out in sobs; long, racking sobs.

The phone rang again and the machine picked up. They listened to Buck's muffled voice. "I love you, baby, let me come home."

Bonnie felt her hair being stroked. "Is there anything I can do?" Diane asked. "Besides shut the fuck up, I mean?"

Bonnie laughed through her tears, then pulled away. She wiped her nose on Buck's clean sheet. "He says I'm crazy, and it's true. He's making me crazy. 'I love you—I hate you—I love you—I hate you.' I can't stand it!" She picked up Buck's undershirt and wiped her mascara-ringed eyes on it. "Yesterday, Hayley called her preschool teacher the 'C' word."

Diane laughed. "Is she?"

Bonnie laughed, too. "Well, she can be a bitch. But no, not the 'C' word. No one deserves that."

Diane nodded. "Have you talked to anybody, Bon? I know someone who's really smart. She made me feel like I wasn't crazy, like I'd be okay. Do you have insurance?"

Bonnie was right about Diane being old. She rambled on like Bonnie's mother used to, except her mom analyzed everything: a sad person had to be depressed and a moody person had to be chemically imbalanced. Bonnie didn't want to be an insect pinned in anyone's display case. "I talked to the priest. He told me to pray."

Bonnie was suddenly thirsty for lemonade. She picked up the clothes basket and headed toward the kitchen. She wiped perspiration from the creases beneath her milk-laden breasts and poured herself a glass, trying to ignore the flashing red message light. "Let's do your photo." She gulped down some liquid and put the laundry basket by the front door.

Right on cue, the phone rang. She heard his voice again and ran to turn down the volume.

"Bonnie?"

She could hear the growl in his voice; there would be no terms of endearment this time. Shoot, she didn't have the tape recorder set up yet. She poured more lemonade and took it to the kids.

She knew she was acting manic—that's what her mom would say—but she couldn't help it. She went in Hayley's room and admired the picture Quinn and Hayley were coloring, In the nursery, she moved the stuffed giraffe away from Lucas, who was sucking in his sleep. Then she dragged the standing lamp back into the great room.

Diane followed for a moment, then stopped short. Bonnie looked back to see what happened. "Should we go?"

Bonnie looked back at her. "No, please. I want to take your

picture. But not with that worried look. Relax." She led her to the makeshift studio in the great room.

"Okay, I'll try. I'm not good at posing, though." Diane sat on the sheet-draped chair.

"Don't worry, I am. I did all the yearbook pictures in high school and for my sorority."

"I thought you were a prom queen."

"It was a nice change from having my picture taken, believe me. And my kids practically pose on cue now." Diane laughed while Bonnie snapped away. "Tell me about your kids, Diane. What was Quinn's first word?"

Diane laughed again. Bonnie captured the moment and paid close attention, waiting for the next one. She moved around so that Diane would turn without being told chin up or down or whatever. "Oh my God," Diane said. "You won't believe it. It was on the Santa Barbara Pier the summer when she was barely one. I gave her a lick of my ice-cream cone—and when I took it away, she reached out and shouted 'Mine!'" They both cracked up.

Bonnie kept snapping, moving around and making Diane talk. Bonnie was good and she knew it. She asked her as many questions as she could think of until she spied a bit of cleavage and got an idea. "Let's do a sexy one just for fun."

Diane looked doubtful.

Bonnie ran to Hayley's room and snagged her pink boa and a long rope of plastic pearls. When she returned, Diane was standing up, looking around at the empty, not-so-great room. "When my business gets going, I'll pay you back. But please don't fill this room with furniture yet."

Bonnie put the pearls around Diane's neck. "Don't worry, it's bound to be empty long past your divorce party."

"Actually, I was thinking of something sooner. Ever been to a Tupperware party?"

"Are you kidding? I've been to purse parties, fancy chef parties, and jewelry parties—the hostess gets a free gift, right?"

"Definitely. But the kind of party I have in mind is different." Diane hesitated, toying with the strand. "Folks sometimes call it a 'Schtupperware' party."

Bonnie pulled her hand back. "You mean . . . sex toys?"

Diane nodded. "I know you're a nice Catholic girl, so you don't have to even be here, seriously. I'll rent card tables and chairs and I'll give you money to go to the movies or something. I just don't have the space. If I make any money, I'll pay you for these photos."

Bonnie pouted. "You don't want me to come? I could make chocolate buckeyes."

"I just don't want you to be uncomfortable; you've got so much on your plate."

"Buck won't be able to barge in anymore, if that's what you're worried about. And now you really need a sexy picture."

Diane shook her head. "You know, I'm not feeling very sexy. Maybe let's skip this part. I should take Quinn home so she can get started on her chemistry homework."

"No," Bonnie said. "Just relax. Want some wine?"

"You bought wine?"

"No, but I could." Bonnie looked at the clock. "Tell you what. Go under my bathroom sink and get the first aid kit. Inside is a bottle of red nail polish."

"You keep it there for chigger bites? Doesn't matter; red is sexy, but it will take too long to dry." Diane took off the plastic pearls and held them out to Bonnie.

Bonnie blocked them with her hand. "It's not really nail polish, Diane. But it might give you a nice glow."

Diane's eyes widened, then she burst out laughing. The pearls slipped out of her hand and clattered to the hardwood floor.

Bonnie picked them up. "I'm from the Midwest, Diane. Ever heard of Pure Romance?" She glanced towards Hayley's room. The door was closed, but she lowered her voice anyway. "My sorority sister paid her tuition selling that stuff. How do you think we stayed virgins?"

Diane whispered back. "What about your boyfriends? Jocks aren't known for their, um, patience."

Duh! It was Bonnie's turn to chuckle. "Let's just say, we went through a lot of Chapstick in the winter."

Diane shook her head as if it was hard to believe that a nice girl would know how to give the kind of blow job that would satisfy a two hundred and twenty pound quarterback. Bonnie didn't mind. She was used to being underestimated—she was blonde, after all. She stood on tiptoe and slipped the ropey pearls back over her friend's head. Diane regained her senses as she arranged them over her collarbone. "Does Buck know about the first-aid kit?"

"What Buck doesn't know can't hurt him." There was a knock on the door. Bonnie stopped smiling. "Not yet, anyway." She raced to the kitchen and peeked through the window. It wasn't him, thank God. She heard Diane come into the kitchen behind her. "It's just Kyle." Bonnie said. "Go! Get relaxed for your picture."

Bonnie took Kyle's glass of lemonade out of the refrigerator and pointed down the hall with it. Diane blushed, but headed out towards the bathroom. Bonnie followed her as far as Hayley's doorway. Then waited until she saw the bathroom door close and heard the lock click. Bonnie opened Hayley's door and leaned inside the pink room, where the girls were coloring. "Hayley, you want to give this lemonade to Kyle?"

Hayley shook her head.

Bonnie handed the glass to Quinn. "Take this out and I'll get money to pay you, all right?"

Quinn shrugged and took the lemonade to the door.

When Bonnie returned, she looked out the front window. The glass in Kyle's hand was nearly empty, but he and Quinn were still talking. Bonnie watched Hayley bop around them in the freshly cut grass.

Behind the three of them, the fence was nearly gray where the paint had peeled off. Bonnie wondered if she should ask Kyle to fix it, but it wouldn't be as simple as it looked. Nothing ever was. The paint chips needed to be sanded. The holes needed to be filled. Then the wood needed to be primed and painted and sealed against the elements. But Bonnie was feeling better now. Maybe she could fix it herself.

She could at least try.

Chapter 12

ANNETTE

. . . you don't mind being a sex object. At all.

W̲hat are you wearing?
Annette looked from the sentence on her computer
screen down the front of her gray pinstriped suit to the ace
bandage still wrapped around her ankle. She typed her response: *Leather and lace.*

There was a knock on her office door. She glanced up as her
assistant, Nigel, leaned in with a stack of phone messages. Nigel
had packed up his life and moved from London to L.A. for a
woman he fell in love with on the Internet. When they met in
person, however, it was a no-go. No chemistry, he said. Fortunately, Nigel had far more foresight when it came to screening
her calls. He set the execution copies of the Instant Pleasure
loan contract on her desk. It occurred to her that he had said
something, but she was so involved with her e-mail that she
hadn't even heard him.

"Excuse me?"

Clients loved Nigel's English accent, but it did take a bit more
attention. And Annette's attention was on the screen. She
wanted to stay tuned to Paul Chambers. After several weeks and
several hundred e-mails, she felt they could read each other's

minds. His words were like an intercom in her head. Even though, right now, he was in Paris.

Tres bon. Perfect for the Champs Elysees. Paul wrote.

Annette looked up at Nigel. "I said: you're late." Right now, she was supposed to be in Santa Monica at a chi-chi restaurant called The Mermaid Café with Diane. Nigel loosened his tie. "And your mother phoned again. Shall I ring her back?"

"No thanks, Nigel. See you in the morning." For once, Annette wanted to call her mother herself. Her parents had been married forty years—they'd be so happy she had found someone. Didn't all mothers want their daughters to live happily ever after, and all that crap? She unwrapped a Hershey's Kiss.

Her computer chimed with Paul's next e-mail. *Vous aimez un chocolat?*

Annette laughed and popped the chocolate in her mouth. He knew her so well now. She could ask for truffles, but she felt awkward asking for a gift. On the other hand, her birthday was fast approaching. She wrote: *No thank you. I don't need anything.*

Paul's signature blue type appeared immediately. *I think you do . . . "Often and by someone who knows how."*

Annette laughed again. Even Jackson would be slow to get the *Gone with the Wind* reference. She typed back in pink. *Rhett Butler was talking about kissing.*

No, he wasn't.

Annette grinned. She typed: *Must go.* She put the legal envelope in her briefcase and stood up.

Where to?

Change my panties.

She knew he'd be laughing now, thinking she was kidding about being wet. But Paul affected her in the way no man ever had before, even when he was an ocean away. She really did need to change her panties, or she'd be sitting in a puddle all the way to Santa Monica. Annette had known for years how the power of suggestion could sway a jury's response, but it wasn't until Paul began his virtual seduction that she realized how easily she could be swayed as well.

Bon. Time to catch train. PC

Annette studied those initials for a moment. Prince Charming. She laughed at herself. Still, the coincidence was too delicious to disregard.

Half an hour later, heads turned as Annette limped into the bar at the Mermaid Café. Annette hadn't left the office this early in years. She peered out the picture window past the palm trees to the Santa Monica Pier out the window. The rainbow of lights on the Ferris wheel began to glow. The ocean beyond looked thick and dark, like waves of black licorice.

Annette scanned the well-groomed west side crowd for a frizzy brunette in tired khakis. When a sleek, blonde-streaked woman in a camel suit over a leopard-print blouse waved a martini at her, Annette ignored her until the woman's smile dropped into the familiar scowl of Diane Kowalski. Annette joined her. "Good evening."

"Hope so," Diane said, hailing a waiter. "What's your pleasure?"

Annette studied the laminated wine list and ordered a pricey pinot noir. The cute young actor-type nodded and made his way through the sea of little black dresses.

"Your ankle looks better. How is Morgan?"

Annette passed the contract envelope across the table. "Great, thanks. You look sharp."

"Lana is a miracle worker," Diane pulled the papers out. She put her glasses on and skimmed through it.

"These say Kowalski."

"Until your divorce is final, that's your legal name."

"I just don't feel like that person anymore." Diane took a sip of her martini. "Did you lose yourself when you got married?"

Annette shook her head. She had done the opposite, kept so much of herself that there was no room for anyone else. Or maybe not; maybe it was inevitable. She'd prefer to think she simply married the wrong man. "In any case, you have to sign it with your legal name as of the date of signing. If you repay the loan after your divorce is official, I'll get you a new signature page. You can have it notarized as soon as you have your new social security card and driver's license."

"That's still six weeks away, right? I'll pay it back after the Instant Pleasure party at Bonnie's house next weekend."

"My client will be very pleased."

"So will mine," Diane said. She handed Annette a business card. "I invited half the PTA from Quinn's old school. I figure, all I really need is a dozen women to get started. They'll know moms looking for part-time work. I plan to canvas the west side with flyers this week. You wouldn't have a mailing list of women clients, would you?"

Annette coolly appraised the card and Diane's photo. The woman was mistaken to think that Annette would give out confidential information, but she admired her nerve. Annette looked closely at the picture. It wasn't the usual business shot: Diane's head was cocked to the side, her blouse was unbuttoned and she was twirling a long string of pearls around her finger. "You're very photogenic."

Diane pushed her glasses down to smile at Annette. "Bonnie has an amazing way of relaxing her subjects."

The waiter set Annette's wineglass down and waited as the two of them clinked the crystal glasses together. Then he put down a platter of calamari. Obviously, Diane planned to stay for a while. She gestured to the appetizer.

Annettte waved it away. "I haven't forgotten your discretion about the fire."

"What fire?" Diane smiled. A glass of wine was set on the table in front of her. She showed the waiter the martini glass in her hand, but he pointed past a group of nubile young actress-types to the man they were giggling about.

He was adorable, with a stubbly beard and a black jacket over ripped jeans. He waved.

"Do I know him?" Diane asked.

"Apparently he'd like you to," the waiter replied.

Annette sipped her wine and winced at the bitter note. Not what she expected. She caught the waiter before he left. "Excuse me, could you show me the bottle this was poured from?" He nodded and went to get it. Annette saw Diane look back at

the kind of twentysomething known in her office as a "player."
"Forget it," Annette advised. "He just wants sex."

Diane laughed so hard she had to cover her mouth to keep
from spitting out her drink.

Annette pushed her glass away. "Without commitment."

"Me, too." Diane said. "Sign me up." She downed the rest of
her martini and raised her new glass to toast the young man who
sent it. He nodded. Several twentysomething women swiveled
their bronzed shoulders to scope out the object of his affection.
Diane waved back.

Annette thought she heard her PDA buzz, but the Happy
Hour chatter was too noisy for her to tell. She checked her
watch. "Diane, you already read through a draft at the office;
it's the same terms."

"I still wish I could afford an outside lawyer, but that would
cost more than the loan. You have to admit, there's a conflict of
interest, right?"

Annette smiled. Diane didn't know the half of it. Instant
Pleasure, Inc. was a small, yet solid investment for Paul. And for
Annette. But she was being fair to all parties. In fact, the whole
arrangement was quid pro quo.

The waiter returned with the correct wine bottle. He poured
another taste into a fresh glass, but it was still sour, as if the bottle had been opened days ago. There were lots of excellent vin-
tages on their list, but apparently this clientele preferred mixed
cocktails. Annette shook her head.

"Get her a glass of this," Diane gestured to her glass. "It's excellent."

Annette nodded. Diane's wine cellar was top quality, so she
trusted her judgment on this—just as she did with the truth
about the fire. Annette tapped the contract where Nigel had
put a yellow flag on the signature line. Then she checked her
PDA for the kind of flag that interested her even more. Sure
enough, the red flag was up on her mailbox. Annette uncrossed her legs and crossed them the other way. She was out of
fresh panties.

Train delay. Anything new? Piercing? Tattoo?
Only the one on my inner thigh.
What does it say?
PC. Annette hit Send.

Diane moved the contract aside to get a new cocktail napkin. Annette looked at her watch. Lately, she was even more pressed for time. Paul e-mailed so often, she took her computer to bed. Annette didn't mind. Sleep was overrated.

As Annette watched the mailbox on the tiny screen, she vaguely noticed heads turn as two women approached, a petite gal in a sunshine-colored sundress and a very tall woman in cargo pants. She hadn't realized this was such a pickup joint. If it weren't so noisy, she would refer her clients here. They usually wanted to meet where photographers hung out, across the street at Ivy-at-the-Shore or to the low-key Chez Jay, a few blocks south of the pier. Diane was no gourmet, however; she must have chosen this place for the view. Annette turned to see it again. How long had it been since she had watched a sunset? She couldn't wait to see it from Paul's penthouse downtown. Ah, there he was, back online . . .

Free next Friday?
Never free. Always expensive. Annette smiled at her wit, but was interrupted when Diane stood up to greet the sundress-clad woman with a hug.

"Hope you don't mind," Diane said to Annette. "I left a message with your assistant, but . . ."

Annette offered a Mona Lisa smile. She had no doubt Diane's name was among the messages in her briefcase. She pulled her thumbs off the keypad long enough to shake hands with Lana, the chic furniture gal who resembled a tall coatrack with breasts, and the young client Annette had turned away, who looked flushed and voluptuous—a housewife who had broken free for the night. Annette held one finger up. She needed another minute to finish her virtual conversation with Paul.

Dinner Sunday?
What's on the menu?

What are you hungry for?

Annette hesitated. Here was the moment she was waiting for, and yet . . . she was no dummy. *When was your last physical?*

Last month. Corporate insurance policy. Need evidence?

Bien sur. Annette typed. She could *parlez* with the best of them.

I'll e-mail the blood work. 5 pm?

Oops, forgot. My weekend with Morgan.

Ah, enjoy.

Annette clicked the PDA off. "Sorry about that. What a pleasant surprise."

Lana ignored Annette's outstretched hand and leaned down to hug her instead. She had changed her hair color to platinum, but without makeup, the nerdy eyeglasses made her fade into the flashy Friday night crowd. "How do you like your new furniture? Diane said you might want the fabric treated."

Annette rubbed her sore ankle under the table and nodded. She could still smell smoke in her bedroom at night, but she wasn't prepared to admit that. Her PDA buzzed again, and she couldn't help but break into a sly smile. Diane had proved adept at keeping secrets, but Annette wasn't ready to share Paul yet. "It's always a good idea with children, *n'est-ce pas?* I mean, don't you think?"

Lana nodded and pulled up a chair. Diane dug through the calamari for a piece with tentacles. "We didn't mean to bombard you, Annette. Bonnie has a few questions." She popped the piece into her mouth.

Annette nodded. She understood immediately that this was payback time. Diane had kept her secret about the cause of the fire. As annoying as that was, Annette was pleased about Diane's potential. She would handle the politics of running a business very well. A sip of the wine that the waiter set down only reinforced Annette's opinion. She ordered drinks for the others and put on her game face.

While the others chatted and waited for their drinks, Annette looked beyond them out the window. The sky was dark now, and the carnival rides were all lit up. It was a stunning view. She really needed to get out more often. She would have Nigel put it on the calendar. She looked at the bright-eyed blonde woman, so young, so hopeful, that Annette couldn't help but like her. "Your photo of Mrs. Kowalski is remarkable, Mrs. Fornari. What's your secret?"

Bonnie blushed and turned to Diane. "Practice, of course." She ignored the beer glass the waiter set down and drank straight from the bottle. Diane smiled at her and dipped a calamari ring in cocktail sauce. "You can call me Bonnie, everyone else does."

Annette nodded. "Well, Bonnie, you might consider it as a source of revenue. Meanwhile, how did things work out with Linda Forrest?"

"She was nice, but mediators can't take sides. I still need someone to advise me confidentially."

Annette's PDA buzzed again, and Lana raised a sculpted eyebrow in her direction.

"Middle of a big deal?" Bonnie asked.

Annette nodded. "I'm sorry," she said. "Excuse me for just a moment." She picked up the PDA. Diane muttered something about an intervention. Annette ignored her.

Wednesday at 8? Paul asked.

I'll be at the Instant Pleasure party, protecting your investment.

You're the investment, Annette.

Annette loved it when he actually typed her name. It took the fantasy element out, made it real. She was in serious lust.

You could bring samples.

Annette chuckled. The others eyed her warily. She tried not to smile as she typed. *Would you like that?*

Oui.

She looked at Bonnie, who was pulling a sweater over her sundress. "When is your court date?"

"Next month."

"Let's have a look at your TRO." Annette held out her hand.

"I don't have it with me." Bonnie looked stricken.

"Keep it in your wallet. Also, your daughter's school needs a copy. They need to know the distance your estranged husband should stay away. Once off the property, they can't control him, but they can stop him from seeing your daughter."

"But Hayley's dancing the salsa in a camp show next week." She started peeling the label off her beer. "Buck won't want to miss that. I just want to make him stop calling. Now he says I'm stunting Lucas's growth, because he's not walking yet. He's not even a year old. And everybody knows boys are slow."

Annette ignored the others' laughter. "Accusations are irrelevant, but threats are credible. Do you have evidence of harassment? Witnesses?"

Bonnie shook her head.

"Ask your therapist for a signed note on professional letterhead. You need documentation of changes in your emotional well-being: medications, inability to work, and difficulty in caring for dependents."

Bonnie drew back from Annette as if she'd been slapped. "I have no difficulty taking care of my children!" she cried. Diane put her arm around her.

Annette continued. "Ask the children's pediatrician to document signs of depression expressed via bedwetting or insomnia."

The table was a quiet island amid the conversational roar around them. Lana sucked on the lemon that came with the calamari. Bonnie finished her beer and burped.

Annette sighed. "Whether or not you proceed with filing a motion for divorce, Bonnie, you do have to deal with the legal system now. Restraining orders are serious business. Unless you show proof of why the County of Los Angeles should protect you, the temporary order will expire on the day of your hearing. If all you want is a few weeks' reprieve from the emotional abuse until then, so be it. But then, there's no need to waste anyone's time discussing it. We all have better things to do on a beautiful night like this, don't we?" She couldn't help but glance at her PDA.

Bonnie clutched the table. "I am serious, but Buck will stop once he gets the message. Besides, he'd never get a lawyer for this. He's afraid of lawyers. Plus, he'd have to pay them in potato chips." Bonnie laughed as if this were hilarious and waved to the waiter.

"Call me if you change your mind about the hearing." Annette finished her wine.

Lana pulled Bonnie's hand down. "You trying to get your baby drunk?"

Diane dabbed a napkin at her mouth. "Don't worry, she pumped a gallon for Quinn to bottle-feed him."

"He's starting to like the bottle better than me," Bonnie pouted.

"Maybe that's a good thing," Diane chided.

Lana nodded. "Men don't take tits personally. Real or fake, they couldn't care less."

Diane and Bonnie groaned with laughter.

Annette opened her briefcase and put her hand out to take the contract back from Diane. Office hours were officially over.

Diane started to say something, but stopped at the now familiar buzz.

Four blue question marks appeared on Annette's PDA screen. Annette withdrew her hand and typed in a response: *Monday.*

Why Monday?

It's my birthday. You can be my present.

D'accord. xo PC.

Annette smiled, then looked up. "Are we done here?"

Diane rolled her eyes. "You're worse than my daughter on that thing. Can you put it away for a minute, please? We want to show you something . . . in case it can help."

"Help what?" Annette finished her wine.

"You. Since you're helping us."

"That's business."

Diane shook her head at Annette. "I want to hate you—you do make it easy—but it might be better for all of us to be friends."

"I don't need friends." Annette stood up, slipping her suit jacket back on. She was constantly inundated with invitations to parties and gallery openings and film premieres. Sure she turned them down, she had work to do. Still, she played golf with the partners on Sundays, her dry cleaner thought she was hilarious, and Nigel kept her supplied with chocolate Kisses. Her life was full. When you were Morgan's age, friends were at school; when you're grown up, they were at work. Case closed.

"You may not need friends, but I do," Diane said. "I can't relate to my married friends right now. They just don't get it, you know? Not in the club."

Bonnie interrupted, slurring her words slightly. "Just show her already!"

Lana stood and waved her hands like a game-show hostess at the painting on the wall over the bar. Annette hadn't noticed it at first, but now she recognized the slash of colors against purple. To Annette, it looked like the flashing lights of a migraine. Oh, hell, it was one of Jackson's paintings. "What's going on?"

Lana sighed. "Look, my boss is really pissed at me for giving Diane a cash refund—even though she looks awesome, right? Anyway, business is slow in the summer and he's been renting furniture out to film sets. But they also need art. I promised the owner here exclusive rights to display art being used in the movies and sold through Mecca. So he fills his walls with fine art and shares the sales commission with my boss."

Annette looked around at all of them. So that was why Diane had suggested this particular bar. "You have this all figured out, don't you?"

Diane nodded and folded up her glasses. "I know you think I'm stupid because I don't wear pantyhose or work out of an office. But running the PTA and a business and a family, trying to please everyone all the time, takes a lot of work. So, yeah. This one was pretty easy to figure out."

Lana interrupted. "Look, if Mecca sells enough that Jackson starts earning some income, you could pay him less and get more time with your daughter."

Annette pulled Diane's contract from under her plate and put it in her briefcase. "Keep dreaming, ladies. My custody agreement is binding."

"Actually . . ." Bonnie unfolded a small piece of paper and

read from it. "'If both parties agree that conditions have changed, the agreement can change too.'" She looked up. "Linda Forrest said that."

"I know the procedure," Annette snapped at Bonnie. Then, more softly, she said, "Sorry, I'm uncomfortable with favors as a rule."

Diane toyed with the candle on the table until the smoke rose between them. "I know what you mean."

Lana looked between them and blew out the candle. "Look, do it as a favor to me. I need my boss to not arrest me for giving Diane that refund. And I do not want to be known as that slutty divorcée or—"

Bonnie chimed in. "The pathetic little housewife whose husband left her—"

Diane let go of the candle. "Or the woman who lost her house trying to pay legal bills."

"Or the bitch who lost her daughter to her gay ex," Annette said, looking past them out the window. The sky was completely dark now. She could barely see the horizon line of the ocean beyond the Ferris wheel. Morgan would be taking her bubble-bath, then watching a cartoon before bed. Annette's heart ached.

She looked to the faces of each of these women, so different from her, yet so similar. She pushed the candle away. "Deal." She stood to go. They were silent for a moment, as their eyes met. Annette was not the hugging kind, but she felt a certain warmth emanating from the group. And it was, oddly enough, a group. What had Diane called it? A club.

The waiter delivered another round of drinks. Diane frowned at the new wineglass as he set it down in front of her. The others looked up in surprise, "We didn't order these, either."

"Compliments of the gentlemen." He pointed to the table in the corner, where a new group of young businessmen waved. The flirty young beauties at the table turned around and glared at them. They grabbed their sequined bags and teetered off on their strappy heels. One of them knocked a chair over in her haste. Boom.

The waiter excused himself to right it.

Diane laughed and raised her wineglass. "Good to be back in the game." Next time, this will be champagne." Diane's cell phone rang just as they clinked glasses. She took a sip and put the glass down to check the number. She read it and gave a wry chuckle. "I gotta roll. My kids can't find the microwave."

Annette reached over and shook Diane's hand. "I'll messenger you a copy of the fully executed contract tomorrow."

"Just bring it to the party."

Annette shook her head. "Business meeting."

"On your birthday?"

"I'm baking a cake," Bonnie said. "Chocolate."

"Your assistant mentioned it."

Annette smiled. "I'll try." She glanced at her PDA before putting it in her purse.

"You get a lot of pleasure from your business, don't you?" Bonnie asked.

Annette nodded.

"But it doesn't keep you warm at night," Lana said.

Mai oui, Annette said to herself. It would.

Chapter 13

DIANE

. . . the person in the mirror is starting to look familiar.

The sun was finally burning through the mist over the ocean as Diane drove up Pacific Coast Highway toward Malibu. Cody was at camp, Quinn was at school, and after posting fifty party flyers around town, Diane deserved a treat. She treated herself better now than she ever did when she was married. And this morning, she was splurging yet again, on Starbucks. She was such a martyr back then that the only coffee she drank was Folgers. And since the divorce, it had been the cheap instant stuff, or nothing at all.

True, she drank the good stuff on coffee dates, but that wasn't always a treat. It took six months after her official separation to be interested in men and another six for her married friends to come up with referrals. It was fun when she was in the mood, but she was grateful not to have to endure so many dinners, even if there was free food involved. Over coffee, she met a nice banker who lived an hour away in Pasadena with his toddler, a golf-obsessed producer who was older than her father, and a short accountant who spent an hour on the phone every night helping his college-age daughter with her homework. When

Diane asked the one age-appropriate, geographically desirable, independent divorcé she met why his first marriage ended, he got so angry that he knocked his double espresso on his designer warmup pants. Diane was happy to offer him a Shout towelette and a view of her rear end—without panty lines—as she left.

One of these days, Diane would try online dating, but right now it sounded too much like work. She spent enough time online researching products, designing a brochure and working on her business plan for Instant Pleasure. But she always kept her eyes open, and Malibu was a prime location to explore new leads. She stuffed a few flyers in her purse while she waited in the Starbucks parking lot for a shiny Hummer to pull out. It was bad enough people needed gas-guzzling combat weapons on the suburban streets; they should at least learn to drive them.

Diane checked her appointment book. She was still old-fashioned enough to use paper, or maybe she had learned not to rely on batteries. Diane smiled to herself and decided to include batteries with her products as an extra bonus. She saw that it was an early-dismissal day at Quinn's school, but she still had several hours now that Quinn had reluctantly agreed to humiliate herself by riding her bike. Diane used to ride her bike everywhere, but there wasn't so much traffic then. Or so many freeways. With such an erratic school schedule, Quinn's cooperation was a real blessing. How did moms with full-time jobs keep track of their teenagers?

Diane fixed her lipstick in her compact mirror and got in line. She didn't mind lines the way Asshole did. Even back when she went to a violent movie with him just to have a date, he couldn't understand how hanging out together was part of the fun. But Diane always enjoyed the gift of a few minutes when she couldn't possibly do laundry or pay the bills—this was time she had to herself. When she was married, she'd often read a book while waiting her turn. Now she people-watched and called it market research. Diane was always amazed by how

many people didn't work during regular business hours in Los
Angeles. At least the ones in this neighborhood weren't there
due to unemployment. They were more likely to be resting between movie deals and celebrity guest spots.

Diane yawned as the line moved up. Caffeine would be good.
She was still having trouble falling asleep. She had only received her sample products yesterday, so she hadn't had time to
inventory them, or to try one out. The man in the plaid short-
sleeved shirt in front of her gave his order, then turned back
and winked at her. "What would you like?" He had his wallet
out, which was nice, but when he smiled his teeth were crooked
and yellow. Creepy.

"Oh, nothing, thanks." Diane blushed and held up her wallet, proof she could handle this herself. The man behind her
smiled in commiseration. His teeth were blinding. He had a
bronze tan and vivid blue eyes. Too vivid. Who wanted to date a
man prettier than you? She was starting to feel like Goldilocks
desperately looking for "just right," when he pulled a cell phone
out of the pocket of his suede pants. She saw the flash of a wedding ring and relaxed.

She looked past him at a clean-shaven man in jeans, reading
the *Wall Street Journal.* He ran a bare left hand through the gray
hair at his temple—that was more like it. He looked up at her,
then his eyes flicked away quickly, as if she were invisible. She
might as well be. This was very different than the status quo in
Santa Monica. As much as Hollywood was known for false glam-
our, the women in Malibu shared a more natural brand of
beauty that made Diane feel like she was wearing too much
makeup. She pulled a Kleenex pack from her purse and rubbed
her lipstick off. Where did they all come from, these gorgeous
women? Were they the result of the inner breeding of generations of high school prom queens who came to Hollywood to
be movie stars, or evidence of a lifestyle devoid of financial
struggle? No matter. This man could get anyone. Younger, prettier, bigger boobs. Oh, well.

Maybe she should stop in for coffee earlier, say 7:45 or 8 A.M.

when the older studio executives were just heading into town on the Pacific Coast Highway. No matter what time of morning she showed up, she didn't fit in with the skinny mocha half-something-something-ordering, four-hundred-dollar T-shirt crowd that surrounded her. Finally, it was her turn at the counter. There were far too many choices, so she asked for her usual. "Grande drip, please."

The statuesque cashier blinked as if Diane had just ordered in Swahili. Her name tag, which was pinned to the tight tank top framing her perfectly round bosoms, read: Whitney. Whitney's eyelashes were long and lush, but natural looking. They weren't unlike Lana's lashes, except Lana's were glued on one at a time by a professional. It would take far too many of the hand-painted teacups full of tips on the counter to cover that expense. They must be real. Maybe she was an actress. Or a kept woman. No, there was no wedding ring on her hand. And yet, she had to be thirty—how could she not be married? Diane hated her. "Don't you sell regular coffee here?"

"Not often," Whitney said. "Hang on, we'll brew a fresh pot."

Diane gave her name and went over to peruse the bulletin board. It was covered with ads for house-sitting, purebred puppies, vintage Harleys, surfboards, even a yurt. Damn, Diane had forgotten pushpins. She looked around to make sure no one was looking before covering a want ad for private Pilates instruction.

"Diane?" Whitney called a few minutes later.

Diane went back for her coffee and opened her wallet to find it empty. Quinn must have swiped her last few dollars before school. She'd have to use a credit card until she found an ATM. Ah, the joy of teenagers.

"Oh, no, it's on the house. Sorry you had to wait."

"Thanks," Diane said, with a reluctant smile. It was hard to hate someone when they gave you stuff free. Diane poured nonfat milk in her coffee and glanced back at Whitney as she moved gracefully about behind the counter, laughing with the regular customers. How could she not be married? Or not have been married? Diane was dying to know. She marched back to the counter. "Excuse me, I just have to ask: are you divorced?"

Whitney smiled brightly. "Almost!"

"Me, too." Diane said. She didn't hate her anymore. She felt a kinship with her, and it wasn't just the coffee. Whitney probably got lots of alimony. Maybe he'd slept with her sister and felt guilty or maybe she had a trust fund and didn't need it. In any case, more power to her. Divorced women should stick together, no matter what. "Were you always this happy about it?"

Whitney clutched her belly as if she had appendicitis. "Oh, no."

Whew, Diane thought. "But it does get better, doesn't it?"

"Are you kidding? I can do whatever I want, all the time." Whitney said.

"Exactly!" Diane agreed. Except for the part about kids and work. She pulled a flyer out of her purse and handed it to Whitney. "Maybe you'll want to come to my party." The man behind Diane cleared his throat.

Whitney waved at him. "I got you covered, Sven." She marked up a cup and passed it down the assembly line. Then she looked at the flyer. "Sweet."

"It's not just for divorced people. You can bring friends."

She nodded, studied Diane's photo, then looked up. "Great picture. I need a new headshot. Can I have the number of the photographer? Does he have a Web site?"

"Yes," Diane said, knowing perfectly well that Bonnie didn't have a Web site. That was Diane's new motto, *just say yes.* "It's a she, though. Her name is Bonnie, but the Web site is under construction. She'll be exhibiting her work at the party." Diane was thinking of the photo of Hayley that hung in Bonnie's hallway. That counted, right?

"Sweet," Whitney said again, and stuffed the flyer in her apron.

Diane held her cup up. "Sweet, yourself." She went outside and pushed her way past the perimeter of the noisy group of people on the patio who brandished autograph books and cameras. In Los Angeles, locals made it a point to ignore celebrities, partly to give them privacy and partly to prove how superior they were. But some celebrities always drew a crowd. Lucas Hatteras was one of them.

Diane got a glimpse of his chiseled face as he passed by her car with his entourage. He looked so manly with that scar on his cheekbone. Bonnie would be thrilled, but Lana was still hurt—and seeing as she was the one who put it there—Diane felt compelled to hate him. That's what friends were for.

An hour later, Diane had posted every flyer. She stopped at a light behind a minivan bearing a bumper sticker that read: *Happiness Is Being Divorced.* She couldn't help but honk as the driver took a left and headed off. Diane wanted to speed after the van and talk to the woman, but it was too late, she'd missed the light. Still, it was a good omen. It meant she wasn't the only one. There must be others. She knew a lot of people—she used to, anyway. All at once, a curtain lifted and Diane realized she had boxes full of contact lists: not only Asshole's insurance clients, but school rosters, sports team rosters, Girl Scouts, Boy Scouts—half of them divorced. Diane could only imagine the number of women in need of a good night's sleep. She opened her appointment book and scribbled notes to herself about doing an e-mail blast. She could even contact her alumni association Web site.

A handsome face popped into her mind. Ben Hunter was a man in her marketing class in B-school. He asked her out just after she was just engaged. She should have gone; no deal is done until the contract is signed. Diane had been blinded by her new diamond. Worse, she was loyal to a fault. She decided to track Ben down to ask for his advice. What the hell, maybe she'd hire him as a consultant. Maybe he was even single! Okay, now she knew she'd had too much coffee. If he was still in L.A., he probably lived in the Palisades with a lovely wife and three children and preferred Coffee Bean.

A horn honked behind her. She waved an apology to the driver, turned up her worn Wayne Dyer CD, and sped off. Diane used to laugh at the women who bought armloads of self-help books at Barnes & Noble; now she was one of them. She intended to buy a house. She intended to pay for her kids' college education. But right now, she intended to get back to the apartment and go through those storage boxes.

First, she had to pee. Diane stomped up the stairway from the courtyard, hurried down the hall, unlocked the apartment door, and raced into the bathroom. Ahh, sweet relief. Diane's bladder hadn't been the same ever since Quinn tap-danced on it for nine months. That was fifteen years ago; it should have stretched back to its regular size by now. Maybe it would, if she gave up coffee.

When the torrent subsided, Diane recognized that awful beat that passed for music through the thin plaster walls. Diane washed her hands and imagined being back in a big house with walls thick enough to block the hip-hop beat from the next room. Diane turned off the water. The next room?

She opened the kids' bedroom door. Quinn grabbed her T-shirt and jumped up from the bed. Bonnie's lawn-mower guy sat up and turned around. At least he was dressed. It was the first time in two years that Diane wished Asshole was here. "Hello, Kyle. It is Kyle, isn't it?"

He had the decency—or audacity, Diane wasn't sure which—to nod. He stood up, dwarfing her, and held his hand out as if they were meeting properly. She stared at it in shock. "You do realize this is a statutory offense? Don't worry, you'll get lots of sex in jail."

She grabbed his keys off Quinn's desk and threw them at him.

"Mom, nothing happened!" Quinn hooked her bra and pulled her T-shirt back on.

Diane lost it. "Nothing happened *yet*, you mean. Nothing happens at places where people go on actual dates, like the movies or the beach! You do not go to a bedroom when no parents are home for nothing to happen!"

"I'm sorry," Quinn mouthed to Kyle.

"You will be sorry, young lady. And you, too!" Diane pointed at Kyle, then at the door. Action had consequences, that's why they were here in this crummy apartment in the first place.

Kyle looked at Quinn, motioned that he'd call her, and left. At least he wanted to talk to her again, Diane thought. But it wasn't much consolation, especially when she spied a familiar strap of black lace rising over her daughter's hip bone. "Hey, those are mine!"

Quinn started yanking the thong panties off from beneath her skirt.

Diane held her hand up. "I don't want them now. But you're too young for them."

"No, Mom, you're too old. Girls in my PE class have worn these since middle school."

"But you're not that kind of girl, Quinn." *She didn't used to be,* Diane thought. Damnit. Would this be happening if she still had both parents at home? Was this Diane's fault for getting a divorce?

"It's just the style, Mom, it doesn't mean anything."

"Oh yes, it does. And don't change the subject. You are too young to have sex. It's messy in—so many ways. What happened to you?"

"Me?" Quinn shouted. "What happened to *you?* You don't even pack my lunch anymore!"

Diane blinked. "I've been a little busy trying to earn the money to buy food for your lunch, Quinn. You're old enough to slap peanut butter on a slice of bread, for God's sake. Or to pick up the phone and call Pizza Hut. You think my sole purpose in life is preparing your food? Do you think I'm nothing but a servant? Driver? Human ATM?"

"No, but . . ." She pointed at Diane's designer blazer and high heels. "Who do you think you are? Looking all glam, pretending to be a businesswoman . . ."

"I had a life before you, you know; I *was* a businesswoman." Diane stood up straight and glared at her daughter.

"Oh, really? Was it a porno business, Mom?" Quinn opened her drawer and dug one of Diane's flyers out from beneath the mess. "Is this the real you, with your tits hanging out?"

"They are not! There's nothing wrong with that." Diane snatched the flyer.

"Okay, Mom. Explain this." Quinn whipped out of the room so fast that Diane was standing in there by herself.

Oh, God, Diane knew what was coming. She shouldn't have defended herself before, but now she would have to. The boxes of sex toys arrived yesterday, in plain brown wrappers, but . . . there were an awful lot of them. Too many boxes to ignore. Diane had planned to rent storage space as soon as she did inventory.

She followed her daughter into her bedroom. One of the product boxes was open. Apparently, Quinn had taken the liberty of doing inventory for her. And while most of the items were gels and powders and lavender wands, a few were most definitely not. For example, the one that Quinn was holding. It was a life-sized, flesh-colored, rubber penis.

Diane reached for it, but Quinn held it out of reach. She flipped the switch. The whole flesh-colored cylinder gyrated. Not exactly lifelike, but close enough. Better, even.

"Can't wait until Cody has Show and Tell at his new school. Or, I know: Career Day."

Diane grabbed the rotating penis and switched the power button off, but it just vibrated faster. Startled, Diane lost her grip on it.

Quinn's softball reflexes clicked in and she leaned in for a clean catch. It was throbbing now. Quinn squealed and threw it back at Diane.

Diane wasn't ready. "Oh, shit," she said, and raised her arms to deflect the flying penis.

Quinn started laughing. So did Diane.

The penis hit the floor with a dull thud, still moving. Diane ran out of the room to the kitchen for a screwdriver, then ran back with her eyeglass repair kit.

Quinn stood on the air mattress watching the plastic penis writhe against the thin carpet as if it were a wild animal. Diane couldn't help but think of that loan officer with the mustache—Mr. Excitement. He was right: this was definitely a dildo. There was nothing remotely sweet, nor romantic, nor personally empowering about it.

Diane motioned for her daughter to help. Quinn stepped on it with her bare foot to keep it still. "It tickles!" she shouted.

"That is sort of the point," Diane laughed as she unscrewed the battery compartment. Then she shook the damn thing until the batteries fell to the floor. It died immediately, just like the real thing. The two of them laughed hysterically, until they had to wipe tears from their eyes.

Diane sat down—fell down, really—on the edge of the air mattress. She took off her high heels and patted the space beside her. The mattress let out a low hiss, and began to deflate. Just great. She had to move "bed" up on her list of priorities.

Quinn sighed loud enough to let Diane know how reluctant she was to do this, but she plopped down. Diane saw that Quinn had painted her nails black. How had she not noticed the color change? Was black glam or Goth this week? She wished that kind of question still mattered. But there were bigger concerns now.

She put her arm around Quinn, who, of course, pushed it off. "Quinn, I never said sex was a bad thing. It's just not a good thing until you're ready and you have someone you care about. Then it's healthy and—"

"Then you can't live without it?"

"No, you can." *I did,* Diane thought. "A lot of people do."

"So why is it okay for you and not me?"

"Because I said so?"

Quinn scoffed.

Diane felt her rump sinking closer to the floor. "It's hard to explain."

"Obviously." Quinn pushed up off the flattened air mattress and walked out.

Diane's rump bounced, again, then bumped the floor and stayed there. Ouch. The excitement of the morning had faded, leaving her as deflated as her mattress. She wondered if Quinn would delay real sex longer if she had one of the little battery-operated lipsticks. Or would it just increase her natural desire?

Aargh. Diane wondered if she should send all the products back, repay the loan, and return the new wardrobe.

She picked up her pretty high heels. No, not the wardrobe. She liked this new person she was becoming. Quinn's hormones were not related to her parents' divorce. Diane would take her to the doctor and make sure of it.

Diane needed to rethink this whole idea. But it was too late to cancel the party. If only Quinn still wore Little Mermaid panties.

Chapter 14

LANA

. . . you realize how good an actor you are.

Lana took off her helmet and slipped it over the handlebars of her motorcycle. Nobody would steal it in Malibu Cove. She recognized Jackson's modern white beach house right away, even from the garage side. She took off her Cole-Haan sandals and walked the tight space between a gray Cape Cod and a tan Spanish hacienda to the beach.

It was one of those gorgeous California mornings that hardly seemed real. The rising sun shimmered on the ocean like the spangles on an Oscar gown. Seagulls cried louder than in THX surround sound. Lana pushed up her Oliver Peoples sunglasses and peered down the thin strip of sand past the tightly packed row of houses. Even though it was summer, most of the home-owners used these houses as weekend retreats, so it was peaceful and quiet.

She turned to admire Annette's ex-husband's home from the front. She'd always liked the blue tile roof, but the clear balcony railing was new, probably for Morgan. Lucky girl. God just didn't make beach property anymore.

Lana put her hand above her eyes and backed up into the

shallow water. Now, she could see inside the entire place. And the entire place could see her. Through the floor-to-ceiling windows, she saw Jackson get out of his bed. Thank God he was wearing pajamas. His friend got up wearing a lot less, and disappeared into a back room. One Friday night, when Winston left the store smelling of cologne, he mentioned that he would never have a woman sleep over when his twins were at his home. She wondered if there was a rule about sleepovers for men. She waved.

Jackson yawned and came out on the porch. He was so different from Annette, it was tough to imagine them as a couple. Either she had changed, or the contrast was the attraction. Jackson needed a haircut, but he was cute, with just a bit of a pot belly. That's what Lucas would be like—without the benefit of a personal trainer, nutritionist, and chef.

Lana waved again. "Hi, there!"

Jackson came out on the porch, in skull-printed surf shorts. He squinted down at her. "Private property."

Lana looked down at her ringed toes. She was standing on wet sand. Which meant she was below the mean tide line. Which made this property quite public. Despite David Geffen's nineteen-year battle to keep the plebeians who support his multimedia empire out of his Pacific Ocean backyard, public gates were now open from dusk to dark. Lana scratched her ankle and looked back up at Jackson. He was stretching. "I'm from Mecca. About the other paintings? Ms. Gold was going to come, but she was—"

"Busy, right. Do I know you?"

Lana shook her head of short hair. She wasn't lying, exactly. He didn't know her, not this version of her. Besides, her hair was down to her waist last time he saw her. "Came to a party here once." So had everybody else on the L.A. party circuit. Jackson used to have an open house every other weekend. It was a wonder he had time to paint at all.

He waved her up. Lana brushed the sand off her ass and checked her watch. Where the fuck was Eli? She had promised Winston she'd have the paintings at the store before they opened. She waited for a few oh-so-toned joggers to pass by. A scruffy dog paused to sniff a pile of seaweed, then bounded after them. Lana pulled a string of kelp from her toes and spotted an old man tossing a tennis ball into the surf. A large Lab paddled out to retrieve it. It would be great to have a dog, Lana thought; she did not want to end up a cat lady. No offense to the one-eared stray she already fed. But if she lived here, she would have a smart dog to fetch sticks of driftwood she threw in the waves. If she lived here . . .

Lana chuckled. Wouldn't everyone in the country like to live here? The entire world, maybe? She was lucky to live close enough to enjoy a crab cocktail at one of those picnic tables with an ocean view across the street at Malibu Seafood now and then.

She climbed the weathered stairs up the porch and entered through the open sliding-glass door. Inside, plastic toys lined one wall and large canvases lined the other. Most were splashes of color on soft backgrounds of fading light. Lana was drunk the night Lucas bought his, but from where she stood now, they looked like something Annette's little girl could have painted. Especially without frames.

Jackson's wiry boyfriend, shirtless and in Spandex bike shorts, loped in with a blender full of peach-colored liquid. He was cut like a crystal decanter, but clearly he only drank smoothies. He scratched the bulge of his Spandex bike shorts as if she weren't there and started arguing with Jackson about the music.

"I don't want to get in your way here," Lana interrupted. "Why don't you point out the ones you want to display and I'll tag them."

"No worries." Jackson went over to the stereo. "What do you want to hear?"

She glanced back at the ocean. "The waves would be nice."

"The who?" He glanced back at her and put on paint-splattered glasses to read his music files.

Moron, Lana thought. She excused herself and found the mirrored bathroom. She flushed and washed her hands, avoiding her reflection for possibly the first time ever. When she emerged, Jackson's friend was cranking the warm voice of Rufus Wainright.

I don't want someone to love me, just give me sex whenever I want it.
All I want is instant pleasure, . . .

Lana laughed out loud at the coincidence. Jackson and his boy toy had no idea that the title of the song was the name of Diane's company, the one Annette was helping to finance. Her hips picked up the beat automatically.

Jackson crossed his arms and gazed at her. "I remember you now. Dancing on that table."

Lana stopped smiling. Now she remembered the end of the song, something about sex being easy to find, real friends being hard. She looked at the table she had danced on, or was it the bar? Was her hair already short then? She barely recalled any-thing from those days. She was pretty sure it was after—

"Lo, how the mighty have fallen."

"Speak for yourself," she said, looking back at his work. "Which ones did your kid help you with?" She knew it was a stu-pid thing to say, even as the words came out of her mouth. It was hard to think straight.

She had been so smart, until now. Her worlds were beginning to collide. She tried to change the subject and deflect Jackson's attention. "How much do you want for these?"

"How much did Lucas's insurance pay for after the fire?" Jackson's voice was cold.

"I have no idea what you're talking about." She was grateful to hear banging on the back steps and see Eli roll a dolly through the back door.

"Hey. So which ones are we taking?"

"Take your pick," she said. She pointed Eli to the closest stack of paintings leaning against the wall. On top was a blue canvas, with a bit of indigo on one side.

When he tilted it up to see the pictures behind it, the sun-light shone directly on the blue canvas. A dozen different shades must have been layered in different sections of the textured color. The indigo came to life, full of emotion. The more Lana stared at it, the deeper she fell inside herself. She was sinking down as if in the ocean, deeper and deeper, falling without fear.

Jackson's voice intruded. "Be great to buy the bitch out."

"Excuse me?" Lana said.

"My ex," Jackson said.

"Oh," Lana nodded, pretending that she didn't know he was talking about Annette. She pulled her gaze from the painting. Then she realized what Jackson was saying. He wanted to own the place. Which meant . . . *he didn't.*

Lana wrote out a receipt for the paintings and shook Jackson's hand. She looked at the next pile, wondering how many to take. She saw a canvas with a hint of burnt orange, like a sunrise, and took a deep breath. She thought she'd have to do a whole dog and pony show for Winston, but these were actually good. She could sell the hell out of these paintings. She would compare him to Suzan Woodruff, a masculine interpretation of her voluptuous, mystical acrylics. That's what Annette had seen in Jackson: talent.

"Pleasure doing business with you, Jackson." She wasn't ready for him to know she was doing it to help Annette. Lana needed to sell enough to feed Jackson's ego, so that he didn't shut the sales down to spite her and keep his spousal support up. She gave him smile #21, a flash of such vapidness that it could only confirm what Jackson already believed, just like everyone else, that she was an idiot.

After Eli had hauled the paintings out to the truck, Lana went back down the stairs to the beach. She ripped off her shirt and her skirt until she was wearing only her polka-dot panties and bra. They covered more than her string bikini did, so what the hell. Lana ran down to where the water went from light green to brown and stretched out her arms. She dove beneath a wave. She was excited to sell these paintings. She could sell anything—it was easy when you believed in your product.

That was the problem. She had been selling herself short for a long time.

The riptide caught her and tumbled her upside down. She

held on and kicked back up to the surface. She gasped for breath, but she was fine, she was strong. She dove under like a mermaid, undulating from the hips, kicking until she made her way back up to the bright surface. Then she started swimming. She swam as hard and as fast as she could toward the horizon.

Chapter 15

BONNIE

. . . you wish you had the sex life your ex thinks you do.

"Anything you'd like to talk about?" Dr. Fisher asked.

Bonnie shook her head. She'd been sitting quietly for a while now, sipping water from a paper cup. "Like I said, I just need a letter confirming that I have a DSM-IV anxiety disorder due to my husband calling all the time."

"Call me Louanne." Dr. Fisher straightened the dangling earring that matched the silver and turquoise pin on her poncho. "You seem familiar with this diagnosis."

Bonnie looked at Louanne. What an old-fashioned name for such an earthy woman. She'd use her professional name; that was the only reason she was here. "My mom used to leave her textbooks around. She was studying to be a shrink. She thought everyone was crazy, but she was the crazy one. Isn't that why a person becomes a shrink, Dr. Fisher? No offense."

"None taken. It's a logical assumption about why certain individuals might be intrigued by behavioral studies."

Bonnie nodded. "My husband thinks I take after her." She twisted her neck to check the time. The clock was partially hidden by the box of Kleenex on the table next to the burgundy couch she sat on. It was actually a comfy room, with a pitcher of daisies cut from a garden on the coffee table. She could see Dr. Fisher's appointment book lying open on her antique writing desk and her Sierra Club calendar on the wall. But why didn't therapists just hang a clock on the wall like normal people? Bonnie's neck was getting sore from turning around to look. Nine more minutes until noon.

The deputy sheriff could be parking the patrol car right now. In minutes, Buck would be "restrained" and Bonnie could breathe easy. Or be more afraid. Buck would be less than pleased to have a man in uniform show up at his corporate offices, but Bonnie didn't trust those other estranged husbands exiled to Oakwood's studio apartments to let anyone breach their front line. His office was easier. At lunchtime he'd be eating his bologna sandwich alone at his desk while the others went to Wendy's across the street.

Buck wouldn't dare. They worked at the Wendy's booth at the Ohio State Fair every summer. He would do anything to avoid thinking about the scent of baby powder Bonnie dowsed herself in every day of the year the fan broke. No matter how much he reminisced about "doin' it" in the Buckeyes' stadium before they had the skybox, they had sex for the first time in the meat cooler at Wendy's. That's where she got pregnant the first time as well. Now Buck got angry when she used baby powder on Lucas. He bellyached about how dangerous it was and made her use baking soda instead. But she knew it was just an excuse so he wouldn't have to think about it. If only she could stop thinking about it, too.

She felt her eyes water.

"Can you tell me more about that?"

Bonnie blinked it back. "My mother? No thanks. I know your tricks. You just want to make me cry. I don't feel like crying."

"Okay."

Bonnie wished she had worn a watch. She turned to look at the clock again. Four minutes.

"Can you tell me why you keep looking at the clock?"

"I have to pick up my daughter at preschool in an hour."

"We'll be done well before that."

Bonnie nodded. She wished she were back in the waiting room with all those travel magazines picturing white beaches and blue water. The reading material here on the coffee table consisted entirely of pamphlets on grief. She tried to smile, as if she hadn't a care in the world, but the silence unnerved her. Bonnie sighed. "The sheriff's deputy will be done serving my husband with a restraining order in a few minutes. He's going to kill me."

Dr. Fisher sat up.

Bonnie was afraid she was going to reach for the phone. "No, no, I don't mean for real." Bonnie had to remember not to mention her fat lip. It was a lot of work remembering what *not* to say. Therapists never knew the whole picture; they could misinterpret only what you told them. Bonnie didn't want to get Buck in trouble.

"Then why the sheriff?"

Bonnie eyed her other hand, then sat on it. Nail biting was a disgusting habit. "It was free. I didn't want to do it myself, so what the heck? We pay taxes."

"I meant: why the restraining order?"

"Oh, to stop him from calling all the time."

"All the time?"

"We have kids, I can't just cut him off." Dr. Fisher was waiting for a better answer. Of course she was waiting; Bonnie had already paid her. "Can you just write the letter? Please? Or do you charge more for that? You must have a form letter for court. My mom did."

"Can you tell me more about that?"

Bonnie stood up and looked out the window. "Nice try."

"What do you mean?"

"Honestly, you seem like a good person and everything, but—I really don't care about anything but the letter."

Dr. Fisher just sat there.

Bonnie could not believe Diane put up with this. "Look, my mom got sick after she opened her practice. My dad said the cancer was her punishment for leaving him." Bonnie kicked the table. Shit. She should never have said that. "But that's not the point, okay?"

"Okay," said Dr. Fisher. "What is the point?"

Bonnie sat down on the couch and shuffled the pamphlets. Bullet points listed the biggies: denial, anger, bargaining, depression, acceptance . . . "The phone calls. They don't stop."

"Can you unplug the phone?"

"What if my dad calls? Or a friend?"

"Can you change the number?"

"Not without his permission, because his name is on the account. I did change my cell phone number, but when the baby had an ear infection, I needed insurance information and called him from the doctor's office. The number showed up on his phone. So now he calls that one, too. I can't keep changing numbers. I need him to stop."

Dr. Fisher nodded. "It's reasonable for you to be able to enjoy a peaceful home without the phone ringing."

"Yeah, right. I have a baby and a three-year-old."

"So not that peaceful."

"Not really," Bonnie laughed. "But that's okay. You get what you pay for."

"And what are you paying for?"

"I got pregnant, I married him—I mean, I married him, got pregnant, had children. The usual, you know. But I love my children, so it's fine." Bonnie was very firm about this. She wasn't going to talk about the abortion; this had nothing to do with that. "I want what's 'reasonable.' That's a good word."

"Why do you think he calls so much?"

Bonnie heard the familiar screech of wheels. She got up and looked out the window again. Sure enough, Buck's truck pulled into the parking lot of the office cottage. Bonnie waited for him to get out of the car.

He didn't.

"That him?" Dr. Fisher came up next to her. "Big man."

"Football star," Bonnie said. She smiled, automatically, then caught herself. "He can't come in, right?"

"If he does, I'll have him arrested."

"Don't. He just swears too much, that's all."

"Is that what bothers you: the swearing?"

Bonnie sighed. "Is it time yet?"

"No."

"Am I allowed to talk to him?"

"Not if you want the order to stand. What does he say when he calls?"

"That I'm cruel and ungrateful. Or he calls me names." She looked out the window but then pulled back out of sight. "He thinks I'm 'fucking' every guy alive. Poor appliance guy nearly got beat up for fixing my icemaker—after giving me such a break on the price, too." Bonnie giggled. "Buck says when men meet people, they only have two options: Fight it or fuck it." She stopped laughing. "It was funny when he said it."

Dr. Fisher said nothing.

"Why would he want me, if he thinks I'm a slut? Anyway, it's no biggie. I just don't want to talk to him, and I don't want the kids to hear him. Can't tell when he's going to swear or . . . you know."

"What do you think I know?"

"Sometimes he's nice."

"What does he say when he's nice?"

Bonnie looked toward the window and pushed the words out one by one. "He says life isn't worth living without me."

"What's that like?"

"Bad." She sat back down. "He's a good guy. He means well. He has good intentions."

Dr. Fisher nodded. "Good intentions."

Bonnie crossed her arms. "I know 'the path to hell' and all that. Is it time yet?"

Dr. Fisher smiled.

"You don't understand: he was a star ever since junior high. He doesn't know better."

"Would you like him to know better?"

"Sure, but he won't listen to me," Bonnie laughed. "And he doesn't believe in therapy."

"And you do?"

Bonnie looked up. "He just wants to come home. Maybe I should let him. It would be easier than this."

"Would it?"

"I knew what he was like—he's a big baby. He needs me."

"What do you need?" Dr. Fisher asked.

"I need you to write a letter, geez!" Bonnie took a sip of water.

"Okay, let's talk about the letter. What do you want it to say?"

"That he should stop calling, duh."

"Can you tell me more about the calls? What happens when you don't answer?"

"I feel guilty. You know, selfish. Like I'm a bad person."

"You are selfish for not answering the phone? Or for not letting him come home?"

Bonnie stared at the flowered pattern on the paper cup, then put it down. "The second one."

"Not letting him come home makes you a bad person?"

Bonnie nodded. That was all she could do with the lump in her throat.

Dr. Fisher leaned forward. "That's not reasonable, Bonnie. How does protecting yourself from abusive behavior and taking care of your children make you a bad person?"

Bonnie chewed on her thumbnail. She never thought of it that way.

Dr. Fisher sat back. "I will write you a letter. And it won't cost you any more money. But can you do something, too? Just for a minute, can you take yourself out of the picture? Out of your marriage?"

"But my marriage is my life, my kids and everything. That's who I am."

Dr. Fisher nodded. "Marriage is a big part of your life. But not your whole life: that's what happens between the day you're born and the day you die."

"You mean if I get cancer?"

"No. Everyone dies. What do you want to do before it's your turn?"

Bonnie looked across the room over Dr. Fisher's writing desk to her calendar. She thought of the time lines in her history books: the Civil War battles fought before the Gettysburg Address, Martin Luther King Jr.'s speech before his assassination, the Beatles' songs before John Lennon's murder. How much time to the right of today's date did she have?

When Bonnie sat back, she saw Dr. Fisher's eyes dart to the side. She was looking at the clock. "Time's up, right?"

"I'm sorry," Dr. Fisher said. Her eyes got crinkly above her smile, as if she really was sorry. But she was just doing her job. Bonnie didn't care, as long as she got the letter. Didn't even matter what it said.

She heard the squeal of tires in the parking lot and got up. She pulled the curtain aside. Buck's truck was gone.

By the time Bonnie picked up Hayley and got home, the Party Central van was waiting at the curb. She invited them in, offered them ice water, and showed them where to set up the card tables and chairs. Then she let Hayley rest in her bed while she changed back into her overalls.

Lucas was still at Diane's apartment. She said Quinn was busy studying for a test, but after finding Quinn and Kyle together, Diane was wary of leaving Quinn at Bonnie's.

Bonnie would never tell Diane this, but she was sort of relieved to know that even Diane had problems. Aside from this thing with Quinn, Diane's ex kept changing his mind about taking the kids during the Instant Pleasure launch party. Since Bonnie now had her kids 24/7, she didn't have that problem of fighting over schedules. Then again, it might be worth it to get a day off now and then. Bonnie yawned and brushed her hair. When she opened her drawer for a ponytail holder, and saw the stack of legal papers. How long would it take the deputy sheriff to mail the paperwork proving Buck had been "Served?"

Bonnie laughed. Her mother would call this denial. If she was in the denial phase, then Diane was in the bargaining phase, and Annette was in the anger phase, and Lana was . . . well she seemed happy, euphoric almost. Maybe that was depression. Or denial, Bonnie wasn't sure. But they were all in some stage of grief. Bonnie's mom acted all those ways when she got divorced, too; that's why she seemed so crazy. Bonnie picked up the framed photo of her beautiful mother in her wedding pearls. That's where Hayley got her enormous eyes.

Hayley's eyes were closed now as she slept on Bonnie's bed, snoring softly. She had only met her grandma once. Someday that necklace would belong to Hayley. Right now, it was still Bonnie's. What was she saving it for?

Bonnie pushed the quilt off the hope chest at the end of her bed and opened the wooden lid. She reached under her tissue-wrapped wedding dress for the small wooden jewelry box and pulled it out. It was stuck to a yellowed book of short stories. The cover ripped when she pulled them apart, but she could make out the name Tolstoy. A faded postcard of a giraffe was lodged in her mom's favorite story, "The Death of Ivan Ilyich." Her mom had sent it from Africa, where she'd gone on safari— it was her big splurge when she finally finished graduate school. She'd invited Bonnie, but Bonnie hadn't wanted to miss the Big Ten playoff games.

When her mother came back wearing that giraffe-print scarf, Buck and her dad had made jokes about menopause. Then she got sick. And Bonnie got married.

Nearly a hundred people showed up at the funeral, more than Bonnie imagined her mom knew. They shared postcards her mother had sent from the safari—and every one of them mentioned how much she loved Bonnie. They knew all about her. Bonnie looked at Hayley, sleeping peacefully on the bed, and hoped she would go on an adventure with her someday. Bonnie was ready for an adventure.

She fastened the necklace around her neck. The cool pearls

warmed quickly, smooth against her skin. She would still give them to Hayley, but why not wear them first? Bonnie looked in the mirror over her vanity table. She had tried so hard not to end up like her mother, and look at her now. Bonnie closed the lid of the hope chest quietly so it wouldn't wake her daughter.

Then she called Dr. Fisher for another appointment.

Chapter 16

DIANE

. . . you call your mother back.

At 7:20, Diane squirted lemon juice on the guacamole and stirred it to hide the brown spots. Bonnie carried another platter of chocolate buckeyes out from her kitchen to fill in for the ones she'd eaten. Lana rearranged the products on the linen tablecloths so that the anatomically correct ones were in the front row of the display table, while the faux lipsticks and scented candles were nearly hidden. No matter. They could replay Aretha Franklin on Lana's I-Pod speakers to as many times as they wanted, but there would be no "R-E-S-P-E-C-T" tonight. The Instant Pleasure party was a bust.

Diane turned down the volume and heard the electronic trill of "Satisfaction." She loved the Stones so much, she got Cody to download it for her ringtone. Unfortunately, the lyrics were starting to bother her. Diane wasn't sure what she wanted: Money? Love? Cody to change her ringtone?

By the time she found her purse under the first row of folding chairs, it was too late to answer. She punched in the call list, wincing from a paper cut she got folding flyers. She was expecting a call from Ben Hunter, her old business school friend, to make plans to discuss marketing. But, no, it was "X." Diane still got satisfaction from that bit of programming. He could wait. If Quinn or Cody were bleeding, he knew enough to call 911. If not, Quinn would remind him—she had Bonnie's kids with her. Diane put the phone on vibrate and straightened the dozen pink gift bags filled with discount coupons and scented candles. She went to the refreshment table and poured a glass of wine. It was nice of Annette to send a case over; it would be a shame to see it go to waste. "Want a glass, Bonnie?"

"No thanks." Bonnie came back in with the half-full tray and wedged it into her full refrigerator. She paused to seal the plastic wrap over her homemade birthday cake. "Do you think Annette will make it in time for us to sing "Happy Birthday" before the kids get home and destroy this?"

"Sure," Diane nodded. "She admitted it was a first date—how late can it go? Unless you think we should start packing up now . . ."

Bonnie closed the fridge. "I don't know. I gave the flyer out at preschool, but people can be squeamish."

"But I thought you said—"

"I know, even my Baptist cousins down South are into it. Mostly they like how they learn how to do stuff at the parties, since no one talks about it at home. Unless they have HBO. Maybe with the porno industry so close, it seems related."

Diane nodded. "I saw a TV show where an actress whipped out a vibrator last year. Her character was supposed to be edgy and evil, so it just added to that whole nasty perception. I was embarrassed watching."

"Men are the ones who like to watch," Lana called.

Diane laughed. The doorbell rang, then she heard Lana welcome some women in. Diane hugged Bonnie in excitement and hurried out toward the foyer.

Standing in the door was a short, white-haired woman in a turquoise suit. Diane blinked. "Mom?"

"Hi, honey. What's wrong with your phone?"

Diane looked back at Lana, who was peeking around the corner of the great room. She made motions with her arms to hide the plastic penises. Then she leaned over to hug her mother hello. "Must have had the ringer off, sorry. What are you doing here—did Cody tell you where I was?"

"No, honey, his father was just picking him up when we stopped by. I got your e-mail." Diane smiled at her mother's friends. Boy, had she messed up when sorting out the old addresses from the new ones.

"Natalie's car has one of those navigation systems, and there's no traffic from Palm Springs on a weeknight—so here we are!"

"Would you like some bottled water or tea?" Bonnie offered.

"Thanks, honey, but do you have any liquor?"

"We have wine, Mother, but . . . do you know what kind of party this is?"

"Oh, honey, we didn't drive three hours to buy Girl Scout cookies. Who needs the extra calories when you can have more fun burning them off? Personally, the whole idea is a bit scary to me, but you know I'll help you out however I can. Just don't let's talk about insurance policies." She pointed at the statuesque southern blonde to her left. "The Peach, here, is still looking for a new provider." She and her friends laughed hysterically at the pun.

"Welcome," Diane said. For the first time, she realized that most of her mother's friends were divorced or on their second husbands. She hugged the Peach and pointed inside to where the chairs were set up. Diane was ready for some liquor herself, but she needed to concentrate for her sales presentation. She had memorized an entire medical study proving that these products improved circulation and reduced depression by increasing serotonin levels in the brain. All her mother would care about was whether Diane was wearing lipstick in front of her friends. She went to find it in her purse.

The scent of jasmine wafted in as another group pushed their way inside. Whitney, the gal from Coffee Bean, had brought a bevy of beauties. She dragged one of them to the portrait of Bonnie's daughter with the big eyes. "Hannah, didn't I tell you? I only saw the headshot, but you could have her photograph Josh and Sophie for your holiday cards."

Diane went to tell Bonnie, who ran to the kitchen drawer for the stack of cards she had printed at Kinko's and set them under the portrait. Diane could see the training wheels turn in Bonnie's head. She needed proper lights. And a proper chaise longue. And so many other things to make this work.

Bonnie folded her hands calmly and approached Whitney's group. "Hi, I'm Bonnie, the portrait photographer. In case you haven't heard, in honor of the Instant Pleasure launch, we're offering an Instant Discount. Ten percent off if you put a deposit down today."

Diane nodded. Bonnie was a quick learner. She peered out the door to make sure there weren't any stragglers. Cathy, Bonnie's neighbor, was standing on the sidewalk, smoking a cigarette.

Diane knew Bonnie felt rejected by her neighbors. Buck had "kept them" by unspoken agreement. Couples usually had a say in divvying up the furniture, but that wasn't always true of their friends. Why was it more acceptable for men to be single? They had a much worse time living alone than women did. Maybe people felt sorry for them, the bastards. They won either way.

Diane started to shut the door, then thought of her old neighbor, Olivia. It took two to be friends, so it was partly Diane's fault they were estranged. She should have kept in touch. Diane hoped she was brave enough to invite Olivia next time. If there was a next time. "Hi, there!" she called to Cathy. "Would you like a glass of wine? We're having a party." She wasn't sure if she should mention the purpose. Even though men cruised porno sites so much that there was an entire mutual fund opening for investors, this kind of party wouldn't change anything. Except make women happy, one by one.

Cathy glanced at Diane, then wrapped her cigarette in a tissue, and disappeared inside her own house.

Oh, well. Diane checked her Cinderella watch: time to start the show.

"Good evening" Diane said, once the women were settled in the great room. "I'd like to welcome you to the launch of my new line of products, designed to enhance both relaxation and intimacy so that we can all have what we deserve: Instant Pleasure."

The women giggled and toasted her. Bonnie passed small clipboards around with order sheets and pens attached. "The unique aspect of our line is that we focus on helping women get through the stress of divorce and all its related physical ailments, from insomnia to lack of a partner. We stress personal pleasure."

The natives were getting restless. She nodded at Bonnie, who circulated and poured more drinks. Diane checked her notes and hurried on.

"Let's start with one of my favorite products, an aromatherapy candle with a waterproof base, so you can rest it by the bathtub without fear of having it go out. It comes in three scents, the same as the matching bath oil in this waterproof container, so . . ."

Her mother yawned politely.

Whitney spoke up. "Excuse me, what about something to use *in* the bath?"

"In the bath?" Diane asked. She saw an older woman look at her watch. Diane picked up a lavender-colored wand but was distracted by Whitney, who was whispering to the woman next to her. Diane was losing them to one of her mother's friends, who had picked up a remote-control unit wired to a silver bullet and turned it on. When it started vibrating, the women around her laughed. Diane looked to Lana for help.

Lana spoke up. "Good call, ladies; that's the vibrator featured on *The View*. It's called Seventh Heaven, 'cause it has seven ways to get there, bless its little double-A batteries." The women laughed and sat up. Lana smiled and took the lavender wand from Diane. "But this is my favorite." She paused until all the women were watching.

What was Diane thinking, to do a business speech when she had an actress right here?

Lana smiled and raised the wand so all could see. "Once you light the candle and oil your skin—and of course after those of us on birth control pills, hormones, or libido-blocking antidepressants have rubbed natural stimulant cream on our nether regions . . ." She did her Vanna White gesture, pointing elegantly at the lotion products Diane had just presented. Then she rubbed the wand ever so slowly down her impossibly long leg. "Then, my friends, you are ready for some fun."

Lana perched herself on the edge of the table and ran the wand up the front of her short skirt and her silky blouse until it was pressed to her neck. She closed her eyes and started moaning. She panted and kicked one leg up, then pointed her toes.

Diane covered her mouth and tried not to laugh. But she was drawn in like the rest of them when Lana undid the pearl buttons of her blouse.

Lana broke into a sweat and put the back of her hand to her forehead. She panted. Then she imitated an orgasm so loud, they could hear all the cats in the neighborhood yowling back.

Immediately, the women burst into conversation. "How much is that one?"

"I want the one with seven speeds!"

"What about the 'rabbit'?"

Lana handed the vibrator to Diane and winked. Diane mouthed "thank you" and started calling on the women who raised their hands with questions. She pointed at an elegant silver-haired woman with a jeweled brooch on her silk blouse.

The woman stood up and introduced herself as Doris, the highest-selling real estate agent in Palm Desert. She had an oversized Texas drawl and a crocodile purse to match. "Let's get real, sweetheart. I've had six children and two husbands." She unzipped the enormous bag and pulled out a two-foot plastic back massager, the cylindrical kind from Sharper Image. "This is the most reliable lover I've ever had. I'd like something that fits under my pillow, but are you trying to tell me that pretty little thing is going to do the job?" After some gasping, the room filled with laughter.

Lana held it out and twisted the fur ring. "Try it yourself, Doris. Here's a perfect example of how size doesn't matter."

The women laughed and reached for the toys Diane passed around. Whitney's sister asked for a product list to check off her purchases. "My husband had prostate cancer," she said. "This stuff saved my marriage. You should advertise in the medical journals. I could put a flyer in our oncologist's office!"

Diane nodded. She felt like an explorer opening a new trade route. The orders were pouring in, and they had run out of gift bags. The doorbell rang over the chatter. Diane put another bottle of wine on the table and went to welcome the new guests.

Her mother beat her to it. "Oh, hello, Steve," she heard her mother say. "They let you out of jail already?"

Diane ran to the front door, praying the kids didn't hear that. Asshole looked up from her mother and rolled his eyes at Diane. It was the first time they'd seen each other since the move. He was so proficient at lying, she was surprised he didn't come up with a quick retort. Diane stepped into the doorway. "Mother, I think Lana needs help in the other room."

"Whoop-de-doo," she said, and she jabbed her finger at his chest. "You were supposed to take care of my daughter and—"

"Mother, it's okay. I can handle this." She put her hands on her mother's shoulders, turned her around, and gave her a little push. "Thank you, Mother." She stopped short, horrified. She sounded just like Quinn.

"Our son needs a new inhaler," Asshole said.

"Tell me something I don't know," Like why, in the darkness, behind him, the kids were getting out of the car. "Lana!"

Lana tap-danced to the front hall. Diane pointed. Lana squealed and ran back in the great room to corral the women and hide the X-rated objects.

"You're having a party? Your son was choking to death and you weren't answering your phone. Why do you even have it?" He shook the empty inhaler at her. What would you do in a real emergency?"

"I would call 911. What did you do?"

"Quinn ran a shower and put him in the steam."

Diane nodded. "Gee, what would we do without you?"

"Nana!" Cody cried as he raced past her. He seemed fine now, thank God.

Whitney wandered out to see what all the commotion was about. "This isn't illegal, is it?"

"No, honey," Diane's mom said, sweeping Cody into her arms for a hug. "But it's time to go."

Diane nodded. "Thank you so much for coming, Whitney, and for bringing your friends. You'll have your goodies in a few days."

Another young woman followed Whitney out. She gave Steve a flirty look, which he had the audacity to return. Diane used to think he was handsome in his denim shirts and cowboy boots. He was going out with a buxom blonde when they met at a management conference; she couldn't believe he would be interested in a petite brunette like her.

It was like at the bar last week, when the twentysomething guy in the Armani jacket over jeans sent her a drink—her, instead of the young gals. Why was she so insecure? Then Diane remembered that Steve's ex-girlfriend warned that Diane would never marry him. Diane took it as a dare. She hadn't been interested in marriage, but he was awfully cute right when her hormones kicked in. She doubled down and proposed. Diane had been the real gambler.

Quinn carried Lucas up the walk. "Why is Quinn wearing my wedding dress?"

"I thought it looked familiar," Steve replied. "She said it was her Halloween costume."

"Quinn, honey, you look beautiful," Diane said. "Frightening, and beautiful. But it's only August." She kissed her daughter's cheek as she passed.

"We were playing dress-up." Quinn said. She shifted Lucas into a different position. Hayley rocketed past to her mom. Bonnie hugged her, then did a double take at the vision of a young bride with her baby. She looked at Diane, stricken, as many of the women filed out around Steve.

Someone dropped a flyer. Diane tried to pick it up, but Steve put the pointed toe of his boot on it. He picked up the flyer and read it. "This is what you left me for? Porno toys?"

Diane wanted to say, "So I could buy Cody a new inhaler,"

but she had more immediate concerns than arguing with him. "Quinn, take the kids inside. We have birthday cake going to waste in there." Diane waited until the kids were out of earshot. When she turned back and saw him, arms crossed and ready for a fight, she changed her mind. She would not sink to his level. It had only been two months since her rent check bounced. Saying he was sorry would not wipe the slate clean. She didn't owe him an explanation. Besides, Steve would use any excuse to engage. She had to learn not to react.

"Ready to talk?" he asked.

Diane thought of that scene in her favorite Sandra Bullock movie, *While You Were Sleeping*. "Talk to the hand," her character said when the creep was annoying her. Diane would do it one better. "Talk to the door," she said. Then she closed it.

She smiled, then went to the kitchen where she had left her purse to check her phone. Sure enough, she had missed four calls from Quinn. For a moment, she was crushed with guilt. What if Steve's concerns were credible? What if she was a bad mom? Now she knew just how Annette felt after the fire.

Then Lana came in and handed her a stack of checks. Diane put them in an envelope. The kids were definitely getting cable now. Diane was proud to know that she was capable of supporting them. If only she felt a little more comfortable with their knowing how she was doing it.

"Those older women looked so happy, didn't they? One lady told me how she and her girlfriend just got back from Europe and now she's off to New York to shop for fall clothes."

Diane started cutting the cake. It was late; Annette was obviously not going to make it. "Be nice to do that married, too."

Bonnie came in to help. "Sure, but if we can do everything ourselves, what do we need men for?"

Diane and Lana looked at each other. "Go ahead," Diane offered.

"No, you," said Lana.

But now, neither of them had anything to say. Diane took a bite, then wiped her mouth with a napkin. "Good cake."

Bonnie laughed and took paper plates piled with cake down the hall to the kids.

Diane wiped her mouth and wondered what satisfaction would really be for her—beyond getting a job with health insurance. Once upon a time, all she would be worrying about was the grams of fat in this slice of cake. On second thought, that was how she ended up here. Ignorance was not bliss. Then she realized the question was prompted by the ringtone emanating from her purse. She couldn't wait to answer the phone when her legal name was Diane Taylor. She found her phone anyway. "Hello?"

It was Whitney. She was driving down P.C.H. on her way home, but her friends were so excited, she wanted to thank Diane personally for the invitation. "We want to be fabulous—just like you guys—one day. Like goddesses."

"That's us, all right." Diane said, hoping her sarcasm wasn't obvious. "The goddess group." She thanked Whitney and hung up. If she had learned one thing from Asshole, it was how to bluff.

Chapter 17

ANNETTE

. . . you believe everything your first date tells you.

Annette spent an hour battling the traffic between her Century City office and Paul's downtown penthouse a few miles away, but the moment she stepped out of the elevator on the forty-second floor, she relaxed. When she heard the seductive horns of Carlos Santana, she pressed her red lips together to suppress a chuckle. Had Paul asked what kind of music she would most like to make love to, she would have chosen this. He either knew her better than she had imagined or had excellent taste. Excellent, meaning: identical.

Annette shifted the gold box of Godivas to her left hand and smoothed her pencil skirt down over her new black satin garter belt. After years of pantyhose, the breeze on her thighs felt liberating. She had skipped the usual birthday lunch with the partners to peruse the lingerie stores in the Century City mall. What a relief to skip the endless teasing about being twenty-nine again. At thirty-five, she was still learning valuable lessons. Today, a saleswoman taught Annette how to properly attach garters to the top of silk stockings. Annette hoped the stockings would hide the scar on her knee, but with garters, they accomplished quite a bit more. Clipped correctly, they framed one's derriere in the shape of a heart.

Annette took a deep breath and knocked on the door. There was no answer. Of course there was no answer; the music was too loud. Thank goodness Paul couldn't hear the pounding of her heart. Annette flexed her ankle, still weak without the ankle support she'd worn since the fire, pushed the door open, and stepped inside.

Paul stood in shadow, backlit by the most amazing view Annette had ever seen of Los Angeles. She could see the entire city, past the last line of lollipop palms in Palisades Park and the brightly lit Ferris wheel on the Santa Monica Pier. The ocean glowed all the way out until the horizon dipped down to the Pacific Rim. From this spot on the bamboo floor, the world was undoubtedly round, and Annette was standing on the very top. King of the world, indeed.

Even on the few occasions when Annette got home before dark, the sun usually disappeared behind the mountains to the north, rather than over the ocean. The Malibu coast didn't face true west. And since Annette was not a surfer like Jackson, proximity to the water mostly meant chilly fog, storm damage, and the annual cost of replacing electronics due to salt erosion. Why would anyone want to live on the beach with all that messy sand? Here was the ideal way to enjoy western civilization: from above.

Paul was the kind of man she should have been with all along. Annette could easily see herself living in this Beaux Arts building. It had all the amenities of a five-star hotel or a full-time housekeeper. Groceries and dry cleaning and mail were all taken care of, while residents swam in the lap pool beyond the terraced garden café. Paul did not waste energy on unessential acts; it was apparent in his décor: the simplicity of Japanese lines in luxurious materials like handmade silk rugs and long leather couches and a polished stone table. Everything was designed to enhance the view. The sun was beginning to set, and the show was going to be spectacular.

"You look gorgeous," Paul said. He kissed her softly on the lips, then disappeared into the kitchen. She stood there, not sure if she should follow. A moment later, he emerged with a silver cocktail shaker. Annette smiled; he looked gorgeous, too.

Paul's hair had turned white since she saw him last, several years ago, when they met to discuss his prenup. The divorce was handled by phone. And e-mail, of course. He was as understated as his décor: unremarkable until you looked right at it. Then you could appreciate the classic line, the subtle textures, and the quality of construction. When he looked directly at you, the intensity of his blue eyes kept you from looking anywhere else. His white linen shirt was rolled up to the elbows, revealing muscular forearms. She was surprised to see him in baggy jeans, but she knew enough about the closet full of Armani jackets at his Beverly Hills office to be flattered that he could relax with her. She admired the Zen approach of his leather sandals, worn for ease and comfort, allowing things to come to him. And yet he was always in control. So different from a childlike man who interrupted meetings to whine about what time she was coming home.

The heady scent of garlic and basil reached Annette's sensitive nose, and she realized he could cook, too. Annette loved the elegance of martini glasses, but she was not one for hard liquor. She was relieved to see he had only one glass out. She set the chocolates down on the sofa table and met him at the wet bar. "Dessert."

"Thanks, but I had something sweeter in mind." He winked, then poured his concoction over a strainer into the glass. He picked up a lemon wedge and pointed at the black marble bar in the living room behind them. "Would you like a glass of wine? I took the liberty of allowing them both to breathe."

Two bottles of wine were open on the bar. Annette read the wine labels. One was a chilled Vouvray, and the other a Bordeaux of such a caliber that Annette closed her eyes to drink in the scent. "Seems like a waste."

"Not if one pleases you," Paul said. He handed her a goblet

as big as one of the pomegranates in the wooden bowl on the bar. He stood so close that she could smell his eucalyptus after-shave.

She flinched.

"Are you going to be nervous all night?"

"I hope not." Annette savored the first delicious sip. Her Fire lipstick made a perfect impression on the rim of the crystal. They toasted to finally meeting face to face, then she drank some more. She couldn't remember the last time she had felt so nervous. She needed to relax. All the e-mails, communication so constant and insightful that he seemed to be inside her head, should have made her feel comfortable, but they only made it worse. Annette was overwhelmed by her senses. She took another sip. Ah, there was the gentle buzz she was looking for, like a soft cushion around her head.

When Paul took her hand, she thought she saw sparks. She certainly felt them. There was so much heat in the touch of their fingertips, she feared they would ignite. He led her back to the living room, where tapered candles were already aflame.

Annette finished her wine while they watched the sun glimmer and fade to light the other side of the earth. Paul sat down at the baby grand piano. She sat a few feet away by the wet bar, on a padded stool. He moved slowly, deliberately, tortuously. His light touch provided great contrast to the rich notes that filled the room with blues. His long fingers touched the keys with controlled power. She didn't know he played, how could she not know?

And yet, she was not surprised at how expert he was; he was expert at everything. Annette couldn't wait a moment longer. She had to have him. She slipped off the bar stool and pulled her black panties down around her stockings, then over each patent leather stiletto. She stepped out of them and held the offering out to Paul.

He rose from the piano bench and accepted it, then drew close for a kiss. Maybe it was the wine, or the music, or the lights flickering across the vast city below, but it felt as if they had been kissing forever. He placed his warm hands on her hips and slid them down over her skirt. Annette held her breath until he reached the hem. She exhaled as he pressed his finger-tips underneath and slid his hands slowly back up along the sides of her silk stockings. The room, the light, the rest of the known world disappeared—until he touched the bare skin of her thighs between the lace border and the garter belt. Annette had goose bumps.

Paul's BlackBerry rang. He turned it off and slipped it in a drawer. Good manners. And breathing room. Annette stepped back against the barstool. "How do you like my lingerie?" She asked.

"It's what's underneath that matters," he said.

Annette opened her eyes, disappointed. After all, she had skipped her birthday lunch of lobster salad. But Paul had a point, and it was flattering. She was the one he wanted. Her parts were more important than the scraps of fabric that adorned them. But while she wanted her present, she had to be smart. The fax machine had been busy and she never received his evidence of his physical. She trusted him, but still. "Do you have a condom?" she asked.

"Yes," he said, smoothing her hair back. "I like your hair down. You usually wear it in a bun, yes?"

"Yes." Annette nodded. *Oui.*

She pretended to admire the view while he left and came back. She waited to turn around until she heard the foil tear. She thought of the pamphlet in Diane's product line that illus-trated how to put a condom on a man with your mouth. An-nette wasn't ready for that yet.

Then she felt the heat of his body behind her. She looked back at his face and those eyes and turned toward him again. He kissed her as if he were starving, then he pulled her close. She hugged his broad back, so warm and strong and hard. She dragged her nails up his chest, then unbuttoned his shirt and pushed it down over his shoulders. She felt her skirt unclasp from her waist and drop to the floor while a button burst on the front of her silk blouse, then she pushed down his jeans and rubbed her palms over his hip bones, so smooth . . .

She reminded herself to breathe as he lifted her up to sit on the padded bar stool. She felt the rush of air to the flesh over-flowing her lace brassiere as he unbuttoned the remaining but-tons of her blouse—so polite when he could have just ripped them. She wrapped her legs around him. The wrought iron pressed against her midback, so she stretched her feet to the marble bar behind him, trapping him like a Bermuda triangle. A murmur escaped his lips between kisses, then his hands traced parallel lines from the point of her stiletto shoes along her stocking-clad legs, over her knees, and up to her thighs. He caressed the skin around her garter, then clutched her bare hips and kissed her again, and she was wanton, pulling him close between her legs until he grabbed the stool, and the legs scraped the floor, and then he was inside and the heat burst through her flesh and she was gone.

A mist circled and then she felt her body lifted. Something crashed and her eyes fluttered open to see the bar stool on the floor and a blur of city lights. She felt dizzy. Annette closed her eyes and relaxed, floating across the room in his arms, landing gently on something very soft. She sat up to kiss him and was pressed back until she fell against the feather bed. She sat up enough to reach down between his legs but he intercepted, took her hand until she relaxed, then climbed higher, until their eyes were even. He looked deep into her eyes and stroked her hair until she relaxed and closed her eyes, then he plunged inside her again. She felt sexy and soft and beautiful and hard and hungry all at once as she pressed her breasts against his chest, and then she was screaming. He flipped her over and she pressed her cheek against the soft bed and closed her eyes against the starry sky and held on. He pulled out and lay on top of her, a river streaming between her buttocks. She had never told him of her inability to bear children and he had never questioned her about birth control. He was kind to take control and protect her from pregnancy. As she panted, her mind flicked over to the question of condoms, if there had been a second one, or if something broke, she was only sure of shaking and catching her breath and feeling so beautiful. And that she was right about him being expert at everything.

She rolled over and caught her breath. She sipped from the bottle of Fiji water by the bed. She felt like a dormant volcano that had finally erupted and covered the land with lava. The geography would forever be transformed. She felt her skin cool. "I'm not nervous anymore."

He laughed and got up. He stepped over the heap of lingerie and went to rinse off in the glass shower next to the bedroom. She pulled the covers up above her collarbone.

"Oh, now you're being shy?" he said when he returned.

"No," she said, yawning. "Just chilly."

He went to the closet and tossed her a thick white robe as he stood naked, completely naked, before her. She was pleased at how comfortable he was, but she wasn't sure how to respond to a naked man, how to keep her eyes on his. "Hungry?" he asked.

She nodded.

"Dinner or another moment of bliss?"

She laughed and waved him toward the kitchen. The phone rang and she heard him answer, so she tiptoed to his bathroom. She had a feeling he'd burst in to say hello if she wasn't quick. She washed her hands and admired the fresh orchids sprouting from a basket by the pebble sink. She debated over whether to join him in the kitchen, but she didn't want to set a precedent. Let the man cook.

Besides, she could barely walk. She crept back to his bed and lay back, her hands behind her head on the fluffy down pillows. A fresh glass of wine rested on the nightstand. She savored the drink and enjoyed the concerto of cooking floating in from the kitchen. There was a splash of liquid in a pan, then a sizzle, then the sound of her lover humming. She looked out at the city lights. How lovely to live like this.

He returned with a platter of pasta and seared scallops. He

put it on the bed and sat across from her, still naked. "Aren't you afraid of getting burned?"

"I wore an apron," he said. He handed her a fork and a cloth napkin that, surprisingly, didn't match his.

She stabbed a scallop, then dropped it on the silky white sheets. So much for being a perfectionist. "Sorry. This is why you're not supposed to eat in bed." She looked up at him. "A plate might be helpful."

Paul laughed. "Forget it. That's what bleach is for."

"And maids," Annette said, and he laughed again. She wondered if she should have said housekeeper, if it would have sounded less snobby. She certainly didn't grow up with a maid, but he did. Before his dad lost his business. They had covered their parents and siblings, all those personal details, in the first few e-mails.

Annette took another sip of wine, then another bite of scallops. She sat back against the pillows and rolled her eyes in delirium. Too many senses tickled all at once.

"I guess I should have mentioned the seafood before offering you the red wine."

"Oh, who cares," Annette said. "Everything is delicious." She was tempted to say "including you," but didn't. She chuckled.

"What's so funny?"

"I was just thinking I should play hard to get. Which makes no sense, since you just fucked my brains out."

He laughed. "I think you have some brains left." He watched her so hard she smiled again between bites. He still sat cross-legged across from her. His parts looked absolutely enormous. She tried not to look. "So what happened with that last marriage? You didn't learn from the first two?"

He shrugged. "When it comes to love, we're all in high school."

"You stole that," Annette said.

He nodded. "But I only steal from the best."

Annette had to cover her mouth as she laughed to keep her last bite in. She put her napkin down and leaned over to give him a quick kiss. Then she stretched out like a lioness, fully sated.

"Where have you been all my life?" he asked. He shoved the platter away. "You're perfect. You should have married me ten years ago! We could have had children."

"Down, boy," Annette said. She was thrilled to be the cause of his anger, to know how much he wanted her, but she had no interest in his frustration now. Besides, they could still have children. "I didn't know you then."

"You should have introduced yourself."

"If I had only known. But I do have children—a daughter, remember?"

"Morgan, the love of your life," he said. "But is she as beautiful as her mother?"

"More," Annette teased. "But by now we'd be divorced and I'd be the one living in that palace in Beverly Hills instead of what's her name." She liked the sound of his laugh, bold and rich—like him. But he was right. They were good together. This was the best sex she had ever had.

Paul relaxed and set the platter on the bedside table. He lay down beside her. "Do you like to ski?"

"I like hot chocolate."

He pointed to a picture of a snow-covered lodge in Aspen. "That's my real home."

Annette shivered. "What's this, your closet?"

Paul laughed. "I just do this to do that."

Annette looked at the photo. "It is beautiful." Annette turned to kiss his smooth cheek. He must have shaved especially for her. She turned back to nestle in the crook of his arm. She envisioned herself all bundled up around his stone fireplace, reading and watching the snow fall outside the picture window. Morgan had only seen snow once, on a trip to Yosemite. She could build snowmen and learn to snowboard.

"When can I see you again?"

"Call my assistant," Annette said.

He laughed.

She reached to set her wineglass down and saw her reflection in the curve of the crystal. Her hair was loose and wild. For the first time in a long time, she felt her power as a woman. Here was a man who cared about more than money. She listened to his steady heartbeat as he stroked her hair and hummed to Etta James on his hidden speakers. She could feel him getting hard as he stroked her hair.

"Ready for dessert?"

She picked her head up and looked at him. He was really in good shape. Must be all that skiing. "How old are you, anyway?"

He laughed. "I meant sorbet. How old do you want me to be?"

"Doesn't matter. You are a very good birthday present."

He smiled and pulled her close. When he fell asleep, she tucked him in and tiptoed out.

A lollipop bouquet of roses was waiting on her welcome mat when she got home. Annette opened the florist card. The message was typed on a tiny, preprinted Happy Birthday card.

Sorry I fell asleep. PC

Annette smiled and looked around. She didn't mind that he fell asleep; she considered it a compliment. She felt that she was glowing so much the neighbors would wake up. She carried the roses inside and shut the heavy door.

If this was what it was like to be old, then so be it.

Chapter 18

LANA

. . . you stop joking about denial being a river in Africa.

Lana was late for work. She parked her motorcycle between two white trucks and fluffed out her helmet hair. She had fucked up the color yesterday, left it on too long while watching Lucas on *Entertainment Tonight,* so she bribed her stylist to open early this morning. So much for saving money. And now she was back to being a redhead. Not exactly her original color, but Winston would never know the difference. He would, however, notice if she had forgotten about a furniture shipment.

Winston's vintage blue Mercedes was parked close to the building, so whatever the damage, he already knew about it. She prayed he hadn't tried to reach her while she was under the hair dryer. She took the Mermaid Café envelope out of her saddle-bag. The check inside provided a bit of consolation. Giovanni, the restaurant owner, recognized the bargain on Jackson's painting and bought it himself. Winston would have to be pleased about the quick commission. It was the first sale of Jackson's work, and there would be many more—at double the price—if Lana had anything to do with it. And she would if he'd give her a commission. That would help with the emergency hair care.

Not everyone was a born beauty like Bonnie Fornari. Men

had no idea of the time and money required for the regular styling, skin and hair care products, hair removal, facials, peels, eyebrow shaping, eyelash dying, bikini waxing, acrylic nails and pedicures, permanent makeup, Pilates classes, quality cosmetics, organic vegetables, and Vitamin Water—not to mention the occasional cosmetic surgery—necessary to maintain that natural look. But they always appreciated the results.

The scrape of furniture on the floor made Lana cringe. It was bad enough that Lana didn't recognize the shipment when she strutted inside, but she did recognize Guy, the art director, pacing as he spoke on a walkie-talkie. And it got worse. She had to weave through a maze of scrims and lights and director's chairs with the Paramount Pictures logo on the back just to get to the sales counter. Oh, hell. Winston had rented out the store for a shoot.

It was barely nine o'clock, and paper coffee cups were already spilling out of an industrial trash can edging off the craft paper taped to the floor with gaffer's tape. Not painter's tape, but extra-sticky silver duct tape that electricians favored for permanence. There would be such a mess here tomorrow, Mecca would lose business until he had it cleaned up. Crews rarely cleaned up completely; they were off to the next location. He'd better not be counting on her to do it. Trash is where Lana drew the line. She shook her head at a scratch on the floor. The hand-distressed planks would be truly distressed after this. And for what?

The set went quiet except for the clip-clop of Lana's high heels. A few heads turned. "Cut. Footsteps." Lana stayed still and held her breath. She was always heavy on her heels—her ballet teacher used to tell her the same thing. That was one reason she loved salsa and the rumba—she could prance around to her heart's content. The fat guy with headphones on the stool took his hands off the black keys of the sound board and raised a finger. She looked away from his butt crack.

The assistant director listened to his headphones, then nodded. "Quiet on the set. Take three, roll sound . . . speed . . . action."

There was talking behind the small crowd of messy people, but only loud enough for the fuzzy boom mike the audio assistant was strained to hold up over the heads of the actors on the white couch.

Lana chuckled when she recognized the Slurpee stain. A few heads turned and scowled at her. She spotted Winston behind the Ritter fan, took off her high heels, and tiptoed over to him. As she passed the sound board, she recognized the pink hair of Cherry Baby, the stylist who lined Lana's eyes with kohl back in Rome just before the Lucas disaster. Lana accidentally caught her eye. She closed her eyes and pivoted the other way. Then she froze.

When Lana was little, she thought that if you closed your eyes, you were invisible. That's how she learned to always be moving to draw attention to you in a camera shot. Lana was an expert at upstaging other actors, but right now, she prayed somebody else was upstaging her—picking their nose or scraping lint off their sleeve.

No such luck. She should never have dyed her hair back to red.

"Cut!" The AD called. The set roared back to life

Lana ran out of the store to the fountain in the center of the mall and attempted to compose herself. She wondered if it would help to go into Kitty's boutique and change clothes. She would pretend to be a regular shopper. She leaned over at the candy machines and slipped a couple of quarters in the Boston Baked Beans. Lana never ate the real beans, but it felt loyal to her hometown, and Lana could use the protein from the peanuts.

When she stood up, Cherry attacked her in a way that could easily be mistaken for assault. Lana looked around for a security guard, but no such luck.

"Let go, I can't fucking breathe!"

Cherry let go and giggled. "Since when did you start swearing like a Teamster?"

"Not very nice to say about Teamsters."

"No worries, I just married one." Cherry held out her left hand, which bore an enormous diamond ring.

Blinded by surprise as much as the sparkle, Lana nodded. "Good luck," she said. "I mean congratulations."

"Where have you been? No, don't answer that—your boss told me. Lana, is it?" Cherry lifted up her hair, checked out the roots, and rubbed the slight dye line still staining Lana's temple.

"I was in a hurry. So, how are you?"

"Great! We're trying to get pregnant."

Lana felt that familiar pang over her miscarriage so many years ago. When would she stop remembering that awful week so clearly? Then Lana remembered where, and who, she was. "Great. Good luck with that, too."

"So, Ms. Store Manager, your boss says you're the person to talk to about getting a deal on that mahogany crib." Her eyes twinkled almost as much as the damn ring.

Lana frowned. The windows were blacked out with craft paper, but when she peered around the sign that read QUIET: FILMING IN PROGRESS posted at the entrance, she could just see Winston. "What did you tell him?"

"Nothing. Just said I knew you from somewhere."

"Want some Boston Baked Beans?"

"No thanks, they give me gas."

Lana looked at the red candies staining her palm. "Funny." Lana looked at Cherry. "You still working with Marlene?"

"As long as Charles keeps hiring us, sure."

Lana definitely couldn't go back into Mecca. Guy was bad enough, but Charles was a line producer. He never forgot a name, a price—or a face. And while Dr. Levine had kept her skin nice and plump and youthful, it didn't make her look different so much as better. If only she had dared to age gracefully. Even five years' worth of laugh lines would have let her fade to obscurity like so many other B-list actresses in Hollywood. For once, Lana was grateful to not have won an Oscar. Or even a Golden Globe. "Cherry, can you make me disappear?"

"Maybe . . . but like I was saying, you know that crib?"

"I'll get you the damn crib, alright? And the matching glider, if you keep quiet."

"Lana! Hey!" Bonnie's voice interrupted.

Lana cringed. Bonnie was so enthusiastic; so fucking loud. Everyone in the mall could hear her, and in a moment all eyes would fasten on those munchkins of hers. Lana looked around to see where she could step discreetly out of sight. Too late. The director yelled "Cut" and Charles stomped out from the entrance of the store, dragging the PA on crowd control with him. He glanced through his Coke-bottle lenses to be sure the QUIET sign was still there—just as Hayley squealed and tackled Lana at the knees.

"Lacy?" Charles saw her.

"Look who I found, Charles!" Cherry put her arm around Lana. Lana wanted to pull every strand of pink hair right out of her head. Whatever happened to loyalty? Did it only go as far as a paycheck? Cherry could forget the glider.

"Oh my God, how are you, honey?" Charles came over, arms out for a hug. Charles was a big man who maintained his girth for intimidation purposes. That was the theory, anyway. Most of the rest of the crew was starved skinny by the long hours and intravenous Red Bull drip. "We were all relieved when that fire proved to be an accident, but then you disappeared, so . . ."

Lana wobbled. "Nice to see you too, Charles."

Bonnie looked between them warily and pulled Hayley away.

Charles's eyes lit up as if he'd seen God. Or a bump in his paycheck. "Ready for your close-up?"

"Very funny," Lana said. She crossed her arms, insulted by his *Sunset Boulevard* reference to Gloria Swanson's portrayal of a crazed leading lady.

Cherry stepped in to explain to Charles. "Lacy just happened to be—"

Bonnie screamed and clapped her hand over her mouth, but not before Lucas started screaming, too. She pulled him out of the carriage to calm him down. "I can't believe I've been so stupid. I *knew* you looked familiar!"

Now it was Cherry's turn to look confused. Bonnie, starstruck over her friend, started jumping up and down again. Lana stood in the middle of this craziness. She was the only sane person in the bunch. Go figure. She gave Hayley her Boston Baked Beans, hoped she wasn't allergic, and pulled the squirming baby from Bonnie's arms.

Winston stepped outside the store, wearing the blue pinstriped shirt. Always a bad sign. And worse, he was smiling. Lana knew him well enough to recognize that smile. He knew all along.

Lana wanted to run away, but she knew this little scene would make the trades no matter what happened next. She tried to think up a good story, a way to spin the *Daily Variety* gossip column without promising her firstborn to a publicist in the next ten seconds. She set the baby down. He immediately pulled himself up to a stand against the fountain. She pointed Bonnie toward the baby and turned back toward the store, but Winston had gone back in. She couldn't help but be pissed at him. What, a movie star wasn't good enough for him? Her fall from grace made her pathetic in his eyes? If he was trying to give her privacy, why didn't he mention it? She thought they were friends.

Eli appeared at the entrance to the store and came out to get her. "Boss wants to know how much commission Mecca got for the painting."

Okay, so maybe they weren't friends. She was just another employee. Lana took the check for Jackson's painting out of her purse and offered it to him. Eli shook his head. "He wants to talk to you. The production company wants to use one in their shot and he's not sure what to charge."

Lana followed him back in the store with Charles and Bonnie tagging along close behind. Lana stopped at the counter to grab a pen and wrote Jackson's phone number on the envelope. Winston could handle this himself; she was done. She still had the envelope in her hand when Charles looped his arm through hers and escorted her toward the set. She had to be careful to avoid bad press at this point, so she accepted his VIP treatment. She smiled—a vague #14—as he introduced her to the director, the unshaven prodigal son of a studio suit, who was perched on one of the uncomfortable extra-tall director's chairs. He stepped down from his perch, turned his USC baseball cap around, and asked if she'd do a cameo in the commercial they were shooting. As if.

Lana had to at least pretend to be interested. She looked at the script. She saw Winston approaching and turned away. She was dying to grab her helmet and get the hell out.

Bonnie was trying to keep her kids from knocking over the cameras and yet stay close enough to hear every word. Lana looked over and saw the camera assistant snatch Hayley and raise her up in the air. Bonnie was apologetic as she held out her arms to retrieve her daughter. "Omigod, I'm so sorry. I just don't want to miss anything—there she is—" She waved at Lana.

Lana waved back, then skimmed a page of the script, but she could still hear Bonnie's nervous tirade.

"Do you have any idea how generous that woman is? When I first came in here I was a basket case, let me tell you, and she actually broke a table to give me a deal."

"She what?" Winston, en route to the counter, overheard and stopped just behind her.

"Oops." Bonnie looked at him. "Wait, I know you. Your boys go to Farm School with my Hayley, don't they? The brothers in pre-K?"

"Twins," Winston said. "But tell me more about the table."

"Oh, I forget," Bonnie said, blushing. She put Lucas down and held his little hand as he took a few steps. "Good boy, Lucas!" The entire crew heard the name "Lucas" and turned to look.

For the second time that day, Lana wished she could disappear.

Winston gave up on Bonnie and came over, stopping close enough for Lana to smell the Irish Spring. "You broke a table?"

Lana slapped the envelope with the check for Jackson's painting into his hand. "It won't happen again. I quit!" She looked around for Marlene and spotted her signature head-wrap bobbing on the set by the actors. At least someone was working.

Marlene straightened the pretty boy's collar and pinned loose fabric back from the long-legged actress's waist with clothespins. The actress kept pulling away, turning to face the other way. Marlene yanked her face-front. Lana opened her mouth to call to Marlene, then caught the eye of the actress, who immediately looked away. As well she should. She was that slutty slave girl. The bimbo on the set with Lucas.

Lana inflated to her full height, dropped her shoulders, and swung her hips in a showstopping figure eight as she crossed the room to them. When she reached the set, she gave her most blinding smile—the price of teeth bleaching was so worth it—and held out her hand. "Hi, there. We haven't met, but I think you know my husband. I mean, my ex-husband."

The slut stood up, barely reaching her armpit. "I'm really sorry, Miss Lerner. I didn't mean to hurt anybody. I just wanted to be a star."

"Don't we all. And look at you now, starring in some lousy TV commercial. Nobody watches commercials anymore."

The director laughed and popped his bubble gum. Charles spoke up. "Not true, babe. This one will play on every wide screen in the world. On Superbowl Sunday."

Fucking football. Last Lana heard, the airtime alone cost millions of dollars per second for those spots. The productions were more pricey than all the Oscar-winning independent films put together. "Is that so?"

Lana was unaware of the camera until she was blinded by a klieg light. There was no red light indicating the camera was on, but they were sure checking her out. She wondered if she was still as photogenic as she used to be.

Charles exchanged a nod with the director of photography scrutinizing her image at a bank of monitors. He caught her elbow and pulled her aside. "How you doing for cash, Lacy? Must be raking it in here."

Lana didn't reply. If they expected her to apologize for doing honest work, they had the wrong woman.

"I'll give you scale plus ten to read one line."

"Charles, you're sweet, but I don't get out of bed for—"

Winston coughed. He knew all about the beds she got in and out of. Dining tables, too.

Lana shut up.

"Wait here," Charles said, and steered a half dozen kids with pouches hanging from their belts to the production manager, a pregnant woman sprawled on the modern leather chair from the new Truby collection. She gnawed on a Twizzler as they handed over their stacks of petty cash. Then she counted hundred-dollar bills out loud to her young production coordinator. He tapped a calculator, ripped off the tape, and handed it back to her. She handed the tape on up the food chain to Charles.

He read the total and looked up at Lana. "I'll give you thirty-seven thousand, two eight-seven in cash, to say whatever you want."

Lana didn't want to say anything. She felt like Greta Garbo, the legendary film recluse famous for saying, "I vant to be alone." Lana thought about the offer, so much more than her Mecca paycheck. Now that she had quit, it could go a long way. She wasn't surprised that there was so much cash on the set, they had to pay the caterers and be prepared for any emergency. Throwing cash at problems always made them go away. Lana played with a lock of hair for a moment, wishing that happened in real life.

Then she realized that it could.

Lana wanted to move back to the beach. She loved the house that had burned down. She hadn't meant to drop her cigarette. She just wanted to know what Lucas was up to. He wasn't talking, and his lawyers were assholes. It was as if he'd forgotten she was even pregnant with his child before he left for Rome, let alone had a miscarriage three weeks before she caught him on the set with the slave girl. How had Lana become the enemy, as if all she wanted was money?

They were waiting for her answer. Lana had waited long enough for the question, so now she took her time. Did she really want to do this?

Guy's voice echoed across the store; he was bitching at the set decorators who were hanging a yellow painting, behind the set. Those poor guys never had enough time. Guy had obviously forgotten how stressful it was back in the day, when he was hustling props. She sure gave him trouble in Rome when she didn't return that spear to him. He saw her throw the spear at Lucas on that legendary day. But the legend was never the true story. And the fire that burned down Lucas's beach house was still a public mystery, one only she could solve.

The truth was, when she had finally had the nerve—and enough liquid courage—to go back and pick up her stuff from the garage of the beach house, she had overheard Lucas on the phone with his lawyers. She just happened to be able to hear him on the phone, if she stood in the corner just so. If he hadn't hung up so fast, the ocean air would have carried her cigarette smoke away in seconds. But she wasn't a litterbug, or a pyro, just a jilted wife. She didn't realize the stupid Jet Ski leaked. It really was an accident. That was her story and she was sticking to it.

Lana chuckled.

The prop guys climbed down the ladders. The set was gorgeous. By now, a few reporters had joined the crew in the store. If Lana was going to be publicly humiliated, she might as well make a profit off it.

Bonnie was still standing there. "No matter what you decide, Lana, I'll like you for you, but you have to sign an autograph for my sorority sisters. Please? I'll do your headshots for free."

Lana laughed out loud—at Bonnie's enthusiasm, at this bizarre situation, at everything. She put her hand out for the cash and a written guarantee for a million dollars more. Out of the corner of her eye, she could see Winston hovering by the counter. He was sweet, but he was history now. She felt a twinge of regret and pushed it out of her mind. She had to pay attention, act the part.

An hour later, the Pretty People had worked their magic and Lana was camera ready. And not just for the main camera. Now, outside the store gate that Eli had closed, there were paparazzi jostling each other, hungry for a hit. She was a comeback and comeuppance all wrapped up in one pretty little picture. But she controlled the sound bite. Thank God she'd had her hair done.

Lana let Marlene zip her into a white leather minidress and strolled onto the set.

She perched on the leather Truby chair, crossed her long legs, and arched her back just so. She opened her glossy lips and gave the camera the smile that had made her famous: Superstar #1. Within minutes, she would be famous again, all over the world. And yet, Lana didn't care about the office workers surfing the Internet in India, or the mothers nursing while they watched the E! channel, or even the freeway commuters listening to satellite radio. Lana only cared about reaching one person.

She leaned toward the red light over the camera lens, lifted a slim cigarette to her mouth, and spoke three words directly to him: "Got a light?"

Chapter 19

BONNIE

. . . you're not bitter, you're effervescent.

Gillian's Gourmet Grocery was busier than Bonnie expected on a Saturday morning. All Bonnie wanted to do was pick up some Perrier for Lana's photo shoot, but the dad in the sports team jersey was filling a cart with Gatorade in one lane, and the checker in the other was clearly new. Bonnie usually shopped at the larger discount market, but since Buck had that tantrum about Gillian's not carrying his potato chips, she felt safe that she wouldn't run into him here. She even got a club card for her keychain.

Bonnie pushed her nearly empty cart to the line behind a woman with a large pink bakery box. Bonnie shifted Lucas, who sat slumped in the front sleeping, and tried not to look. She had already resisted temptation when she filled the cup with cookie samples for the kids. Cathy bought éclairs for all her parties here, back when Bonnie was still invited, and she always had at least one. Bonnie licked her lips at the thought of the shiny ribbons of chocolate frosting on the long crisp shells. She liked to stick her tongue in the hole where they injected the filling—this was the only place in town that still used real custard. Bonnie could use the sugar rush after staying up half the night bragging about her celebrity friend to her sorority sisters back in Ohio. It was practically a medical emergency. She made sure Hayley was still holding on to the cart and grabbed the handle to turn back toward the bakery.

The lady in line in front of her turned and smiled at the sight of Lucas. "You want to go ahead?"

Bonnie shook her head but stayed in line. She pointed at the sheet cake just visible from the opening of the large pink box. "Birthday?"

"Wedding."

"Is that a new trend? To not have the traditional tiered cake?"

"It wasn't a traditional wedding. They eloped." She opened the cover so Bonnie could see the words *Enjoy the Honeymoon.*

"While it lasts," Bonnie muttered.

The woman laughed.

"Sorry," Bonnie said.

"No worries. My sister's sorry, too. It's her eighteen-year-old daughter. I told her it was a blessing not to spend a fortune, but she just watches too many of those wedding shows. Thinks a bigger wedding guarantees a happy marriage."

"More like a distraction so you don't have to think about the marriage," Bonnie said. She nibbled a cookie and pointed at the cake. "Why don't they just fool around and be done with it?"

"Then she wouldn't get a diamond." The lady opened the cover higher to reveal the plastic wedding bell. Plastic rings adorned with crystals were glued to a spray of white netting atop the bells. "The groom has a trust fund."

Bonnie shrugged. "There is something to be said for diamonds." Bonnie still daydreamed about her ring ceremony just after she'd gotten engaged. The sorority president turned the lights out for the ceremony after their regular Sunday night dinner, slipped Bonnie's ring over a white taper candle, and passed it silently around, until every girl had a chance to admire the diamond in the candlelight. The gem glittered with the promise of a sparkling future. They took turns guessing which sorority sister was the lucky owner, the chosen one. When the candle finally reached Bonnie, she blew out the flame. Everyone started screaming and hugging her.

Bonnie spent the rest of that year gazing at her hand to see that solid proof that she was real, that she had value, that she was loved. Bonnie automatically looked at her hand now and nearly choked on the cookie. Her rings were missing.

Bonnie pulled the juice bottle from beneath her son's arm and took a sip. She coughed until her eyes stopped watering. Lucas woke and started fussing. He hated being buckled in to that cart, but he was too fast a crawler for her to let down. Bonnie gave him his bottle and asked Hayley to distract him. Hayley was such a good girl.

Bonnie stared at her fingers, trying to recall when she saw her rings last. The pale polish on her thumb was already chipped from opening a container of applesauce. That manicure was such a waste of money to begin with. She wasn't biting her nails anymore, but they still wouldn't grow. That was it! She took her rings off at the nail salon before the Instant Pleasure party. She was so consumed with trying to decide if she should just give up trying to grow her nails and splurge on acrylic ones that she had forgotten to put her rings back on. They were probably still in her pants pocket . . . at home, being whipped around inside the hot clothes dryer. At least Bonnie hoped so.

She patted Lucas and smiled at Hayley. Cookie crumbs covered the little pink halter that matched Bonnie's top. She had turned back to the candy display. "Eight, nine, eleven . . ."

Bonnie knew better than to correct her. "Whatcha countin', cutie?"

"Numbers," Hayley said.

Bonnie nodded, at least someone made sense. Had she forgotten to put the rings back on purpose, or was she just distracted? She found a wedding photo under her pillow this morning. Buck had to have snuck in and put it there. She saw his truck at Cathy's last night. She wasn't sure if he was allowed to come in the house with the temporary restraining order. She had almost called Annette. She couldn't pay her, though, so she didn't really want to bother her. Besides, the picture wasn't threatening, it just creeped her out. A lot.

The light flashed over the express checkout a few aisles over. Bonnie checked her watch and pointed Hayley over. "Enjoy the reception," she said to the lady. She pushed the cart away without waiting for an answer. She wanted to get home in time to find her rings before Lana came over to take new head shots.

Those two words thrilled Bonnie. Until recently, she thought that expression meant dirty pictures, not the glossy photos that casting agents used to hire actors. Who would have thought Bonnie Fornari would be taking head shots of Lucas Hatteras's ex-wife? Tonight she would call her friends and report back. Two calls in two days was a record. She was too embarrassed to be in touch when Buck left, and it was worse when she didn't let him come back. Now she had something fun to talk about. Now, she had a life. She tried not to think about the phone bill.

Bonnie grabbed Hayley's hand and pushed the cart into the express line. Two shoppers had already beaten her to it. Neither had children to slow them down. In fact, both were single—it was obvious by their purchases. The woman was buying a tomato, a rotisserie chicken, and six cans of cat food. Bonnie shuddered. She did not want that to happen to her. Bonnie opened a new box of Kleenex and told Hayley to wipe her mouth. She would never have done that—opened something she hadn't paid for—when she and Buck were together.

"Hayley, would you please count our items?" She knew she had less than twelve, but the task gave Hayley something to do. Bonnie gave Lucas a roll to munch on. By the time the man in front of her stopped fussing with the checkout woman over an expired coupon, she would have even fewer things to count. The man was right not to want to pay so much for frozen macaroni and cheese. Why couldn't he boil his own water? Bonnie was tempted to tell him that Kraft made it in single serving microwaveable pouches, but she decided to let him figure it out for himself. If he wanted to save money, he should have gone to a different grocery store. Most of the stuff here was worth it; the éclairs were a perfect example, but mac and cheese? But you couldn't tell men anything; they had to learn for themselves. Dr. Fisher was helping Bonnie realize that she did try to tell Buck what she wanted. He simply chose not to listen.

As she inched forward in line, she spotted a celebrity magazine and did a double take. It was Lana! That didn't take long.

"Ten," Hayley said.

"Good girl," Bonnie said. Then she corrected herself. She didn't want her daughter to think being a good girl was so important, or she'd end up being a people pleaser, like Bonnie. "You are great at counting, Hayley. You could be an astronaut someday. Okay, let's put the groceries on the counter." Bonnie tossed the magazine on the conveyor belt.

The checkout gal paused to read the cover before scanning the price. "That's Mommy's friend," Hayley said, pointing at Lana's picture.

Bonnie nodded. "No matter what it says in there, she's really nice."

The checker, a large Latina woman with gold stars covering the name on her badge, nodded. "I heard she lost a baby, poor thing." She tsked.

Bonnie nodded. She forgot that. Or maybe she never knew.

The checker gave the magazine to the bagger. He smiled aimlessly and put it in the plastic bag. "Sure'd be romantic if they got back together, though."

"Hmm?"

"Lacy and Lucas. I hear they're hosting some awards show together. Do you have a club card?"

Bonnie nodded and dug further in her purse for her keys. "Just a sec." Bonnie looked between Lucas's bottom and the shopping cart seat. Sometimes she let him play with it. She wiped soggy crumbs from his face and picked up fallen chocolate chips from around him. He was straining to get out now. "Baba!"

"Hang on, honey, we're almost done, okay? High five." She reached between him and the safety belt. Nothing but crumbs. Bonnie looked around on the floor. She turned to Hayley and tried to speak calmly so her daughter wouldn't think she was a complete space cadet. That's what Bonnie's dad used to call her. Cracked Buck up. "Did you see my car keys, cutie?"

Hayley shook her head and snatched a package of gum from the rows of brightly colored candy.

"Not until you're five, you know that." She looked back at the aisles of food. She remembered having them at the bakery.

The clerk looked up from the register. "Need some help?"

"Mind if I leave the cart here for a minute?" Bonnie paid for her groceries and said a prayer of thanks that she hadn't lost her wallet. It was bad enough she had lost her mind.

"You can't leave the kids here."

"Of course not." Bonnie said, as if the thought had never crossed her mind. Bummer. She started unbuckling Lucas. He practically jumped to a stand. She held on to his ankles so he wouldn't fall and crack his head open, then she tickled him behind one knee until he crumpled down. He was "cruising" already, holding onto the coffee table and stepping to the side. He'd be walking in no time, but now was not the time. Bonnie rammed his feet through the space beneath the handlebar.

"You know what, I'll just take the cart." She took the receipt and hurried off. "Okay, Hayley, whoever finds my keys first gets a reward."

"What's the reward?" Hayley said.

Bonnie squatted down to her daughter's eye level. Negotiating with a child was so much fun. "It's a surprise."

"What kind of surprise?"

"The kind you get for being a good helper."

Hayley took off. Bonnie called after her. "If you can't see me, I can't see you!" Hayley turned to see her and bumped into a woman using a walker.

"Sorry!" Bonnie searched up and down the aisles, but all she saw was more groceries she needed, so she tossed them in as she went. Lucas was pulling Kleenex out of the box one by one. At least he was quiet. Bonnie stepped it up and raced her cart past a man scratching his head over all the choices in the shampoo aisle. She pushed the cart like a kamikaze past a young couple mooning over baby food, then slowed to go around what looked like the same couple a few years older herding their brats by the frozen pizzas.

She turned the corner toward the bakery and heard a familiar voice. Cathy was offering another cookie sample to Hayley. Bonnie hid her ringless hand in her pocket and steered the cart toward them with the other. She smiled as if she saw Cathy every day. She wanted to take the cookie away from Hayley, who had already eaten enough sugar, but she let it go.

"Hi, Cathy. Hayley, did you say thank you?" She turned to the bakery lady. "Excuse me, have you seen a set of car keys?" The bakery lady was boxing up Cathy's pastries. Another party, no doubt.

The bakery woman shook her head.

Bonnie looked through the baguettes and on the floor in front of the cake display. She found a silver bracelet and put it up on the counter. Finally she gave up and took Hayley's hand to go. She smiled uneasily at her former friend.

"How are you, Bonnie?"

As if she really cared. "Hanging in there."

"Your husband is devastated. Tom said you threw him out because you got tired of cooking." the bakery lady put Cathy's pink box on the counter. Cathy told her she'd be back in an hour for the rest, then she frowned and turned back to Bonnie. "Food is love to them, you know."

"It's not that simple." Bonnie said. She looked at the bakery lady. "Excuse me, could you please ask in back if any keys have been turned in?" The bakery lady nodded and disappeared into the back room. Bonnie pretended to peruse the bakery case to avoid Cathy's gaze. She definitely deserved an éclair now, but the bitch was buying them all.

Cathy put the box in her cart. "Don't your vows mean anything?" She didn't wait for an answer before pushing her cart out of the bakery area.

"Mommy, I have a tummyache."

"Me too, honey." Bonnie held Hayley close and watched Cathy leave.

She wished she had made some snappy retort, but she still couldn't think of any. The bakery lady came back, shaking her head. When she smiled, Bonnie thanked her, not just for her time, but for acknowledging her right to breathe.

Outside, the heat consumed them like a microwave. The sun was glaring and the kids' hats were in the car along with her sunglasses and the case of bottled water, boiling by now, in the trunk. Maybe the Jetta keys were in there, too. She had AAA; they would come and unlock it.

When she got to her space, a BMW was parked there. Next to it was a Lexus, then a Porsche Boxster. Maybe she hadn't parked right in front. Maybe she was losing her mind. Her armpits gushed like a waterfall. Bonnie pulled her hair off her sticky forehead. She could have sworn she parked right in front. But she could have sworn she had the keys in the bakery, too. She could have sworn she put her wedding ring back on.

Now she wouldn't swear to her name.

Bonnie prayed for a big arrow to point down from the sky to show her that she had actually parked a few rows over, but that didn't happen. Cars didn't just vanish. It was time to face facts. She had lost her car keys and now her car was gone.

Bonnie took Hayley's hand and walked around the parking lot. Obviously, there were far better cars to steal. Why hers? Thank goodness the heat had put Lucas back to sleep. He was slumped over, pinned by the little safety strap. Bonnie walked faster and faster down the row, dragging Hayley by the hand until they slammed to a stop by a car backing out.

Hayley threw up. Her vomit sizzled on the pavement, chunks of cookie and scrambled eggs.

Bonnie emptied the box of Kleenex and cleaned her off. She didn't dare show the kids how upset she was, so she pushed those feelings away, She hugged Hayley with one hand, never letting go of the cart with the other. She was Mom, she could handle this.

What would Diane do? Bonnie considered her options, then marched back into the grocery store. She gathered the strength to approach the customer service desk by the entrance and asked for the manager.

A geeky guy in a store apron came out of a tiny office. "May I help you?"

Bonnie blinked back tears and coughed to clear her throat. She smiled at Hayley and rubbed a speck of chocolate frosting off her top. This probably happened all the time. Why should he care? And where was the real manager, at lunch? Oh well, she couldn't wait; the geek would have to do. "My car was stolen," she told him.

"Oh my God," he said. "That's horrible!"

At first she thought he meant it was horrible for the store that she might sue them. But then he gave her a little hug, which surprised her. The checkout lady looked over. So did the autistic bag boy and the assistant manager counting lottery tickets, and the few customers within earshot. They all looked at her as if she were on fire. "I must have put my keys down when I gave the kids a cookie sample. I don't know . . ."

The young manager rifled through a drawer full of sunglasses and baby rattles, but her keys weren't there. His name tag read: Henry. "Don't beat yourself up." he said. "Any normal person who found your keys would have turned them in."

Henry had a point. She didn't tell someone to steal her car. The truth dawned on her slowly, just as it had the night Buck left. It wasn't her fault!

Bonnie took a deep breath and looked down at Hayley, who was clutching her bare leg. So what if her car was stolen? Far more horrible things could happen—and had. Her mom was dead, for one thing. She was getting a divorce. If Lucas sat in his diaper any longer, he'd have a raging case of diaper rash. And not one of those things was entirely her fault. Bonnie smiled at Henry. He was kind of cute. "It is inconvenient," she said. "But it's only a car."

"Do you want me to call the police? You usually have twenty-four hours to report it to your insurance company."

Bonnie nodded and looked out the window at the parking lot. Maybe she'd end up with a new car. A convertible would be nice. Bonnie had always wanted to be a California girl, driving a convertible along the Pacific Coast Highway, her long blonde hair trailing behind her in the breeze. She remembered Lana's photo shoot. "How long do you think it will take? I have company coming."

The manager shrugged. "Hard to say. It wasn't a violent crime, so . . ." He was sort of adorable, and Bonnie couldn't help but smile. He seemed more upset about her car than she was. He was older than Bonnie, maybe thirty, with dark hair, and brown eyes magnified by wire-rim glasses. And that Adam's apple bobbed with every word out of his mouth. She would bet a carton of diapers that he never played a first down in his life. She was tempted to toss him an orange just to see him drop it. "We could put your perishables in the freezer while you wait. Do you want a sandwich or a Red Bull or something?"

"No, thanks," Bonnie said. If there were any éclairs left, she might have asked for one of those. "But I will need some diapers. And a key to the bathroom, if that's okay." She remembered she had a new business card now, and handed it to him. He studied her picture, then turned it over as if hoping for more. When he picked up his clipboard and attached it to the top, Bonnie could see the airplane stickers covering the back. They reminded her of Lucas's puzzles. She lifted him from the shopping cart. "Guess I might as well finish my errands."

He nodded. "When you're done, I could give you a ride home."

Bonnie thought the police would do that. She saw his eyes go to her left hand. She glanced at it. No rings, that was true.

He got a card from the drawer and wrote his cell phone number on the back in precise block printing. "I've got to go check on a few things in the back. When you're ready to go, call me. Henry." He pointed to his name tag. Then he reached in his pocket and pulled out a pack of sugarless gum with one stick left. There was a whole display of candy and gum about three feet away, but he was offering his own.

Bonnie thanked him and gave it to Hayley. It was her reward. Plus her breath was still vomity. Bonnie turned to go.

"You might want to call a locksmith right away."

"Why?"

"Your house key is on your key ring, right? Registration with your address in the glove?"

Bonnie nodded, already fretting about the cost of new locks and keys.

"You don't want anyone getting in your house." He got out the phone book.

"That's true," Bonnie thought. Especially Buck, he'd need a new key, too. But she didn't have to give him one, did she? No more pictures under her pillow! She gave Lucas a high five.

Henry shook his head. "Most women would be freaking out now."

She wanted to tell him he underestimated women, especially almost-divorced women, but why bring up the competition? Henry was cute. And he had access to really good éclairs.

Chapter 20

DIANE

. . . you have far too much in common with your teenage daughter.

Diane got up from the chair in the hospital clinic waiting room. Her butt was sore even before Quinn was called inside for her checkup, but since it was Diane's idea, she couldn't complain. There was coffee at the Hospitality Desk, so Diane put the folder with Ben Hunter's marketing plan under her arm and headed over.

Calling Ben had been a stroke of genius, in more ways than one. He was just as smart as she remembered, and he was an expert at global marketing. According to Ben, Instant Pleasure could have the illusion of being huge in cyberspace without much investment beyond the design of a multifunctioning Web site storefront. Ben was also just as cute as she remembered—and blessedly single. They had three more meetings over the next ten days, but by the second one it was clear that when they got together, it was far more than business. Tonight would be for their first concert.

Diane smiled to herself, took a cup from the stack, and filled it all the way to the top. Who knew how long Quinn would be in the examination room? The unmistakable sound of the Rolling

Stones emanated from her purse. She picked it up to follow hospital rules and turn it off, but she was so surprised to see Annette's number on the screen that she couldnt resist answering. A week ago, queen of the world would never have gotten on the phone to speak with a mere civilian. Now, ever since Annette explained why she missed her birthday cake, the woman wouldn't shut up. Oh, what an orgasm will do.

Diane took one sip of the burned coffee, then tossed it in the overflowing trash as she listened. Her napkin fluttered down. When she picked it up next to her simple sandals, she pictured Annette's ankles in their fancy pumps crossed on her fancy desk in her fancy high-rise office. It was more fun to picture her wincing when she tried to sit up straight. Such are the challenges of rampant sex. "I'm glad it was so great, Annette. Maybe you can sweet-talk your Mr. Chambers into loaning me more money. When do you see him again?"

"Tonight," Annette said on the phone. "If I can walk by then. The man is huge."

"Can't be that huge." A man with diamonds in his teeth swaggered past. "He probably shaves his balls to make them look bigger."

"Did I mention he cooks?"

"Twice," Diane said. "That's more impressive than the acrobatics. Seriously, Annette, he didn't get to be an expert without a lot of practice. Be careful."

"Oh, you're just jealous. Should I ask if he has a friend?"

Diane considered the question, until she heard familiar typing in the background. "If that's him you're writing to, tell him to buy some condoms."

Annette chuckled. "Oh, he had one, but one wasn't enough."

"Then give him a case as a gift. Did you know the drugstore sells one that glows in the dark—and another with vibrating rings? Toys for men don't even need plain brown wrapping."

"And the double standard continues. *Quelle surprise.* But Paul doesn't like condoms."

"Another good reason to date younger men. They were raised

to use them, like seat belts." She thought of Quinn. "At least, I hope so." Diane was met with silence and more clicks of a keyboard. "Annette?"

"I'm here. Paul just pushed back our date. 'Bliss will have to wait,' he said."

"Your bliss or his?"

Annette chuckled. "That's what he calls his unit—isn't that a riot?"

"Men are so strange," Diane said.

"What did Steve call his?"

"His penis?" Diane asked. An older woman looked over. She lowered her voice. "He was a gambler, remember? He called it Ace."

"And the new guy, Ben?" Annette asked.

"Not sure."

"I thought you fooled around already. Didn't you say something about that three-date rule? You're way past that."

"I know. I just wasn't ready. And last time he ended up being so interested in, um, pleasing me, we never got around to, you know. He thought I was so beautiful down there, I had to go home and get out a mirror. Still not sure what he meant."

"Lucky bitch."

"I know. It was weird. Good, but weird."

"Things have changed since you got married, Diane. The Kama Sutra and all that."

"Evidently." Diane looked around to see if the old lady was listening. She was. Diane whispered. "Anyway, I'll find out when he calls it tonight."

Annette chuckled. "If you want to fax the proposal over, I'll review it."

Diane checked her watch, an inexpensive Timex, but new. "I'll get it to you later today." She glanced at the door. Quinn was in there somewhere, spread-eagled on an examining table. Probably scared out of her mind.

"Sure."

Diane saw the rack of information pamphlets and took a

bunch out. "Want me to grab some birth control information while I'm here? There's some new stuff out."

"No, Diane. That possibility is moot."

Diane put the brochures back. "Sorry. I forgot." She glanced back at the door her daughter had disappeared behind. She should count her blessings more often.

"Call my assistant when you're ready." Annette hung up.

Diane found a seat next to the blaring TV and sorted through the magazines on the table in front of her. One cover featured a photo of Lana posing seductively, with a cigarette to her mouth. She picked up the magazine and leafed through to the article about her friend.

"Mrs. Kowalski?"

Diane winced at the name. She put the magazine down, cleaned her hands with her purse-sized hand sanitizer, and headed over. It was the same nurse who had comforted her six months ago when she kept getting sick. "Hi! How are you—how's your little boy?"

"Better, thanks. How are you?" the nurse said.

"Better, too. Time heals and all that." She and the nurse smiled at each other. "Okay, that's not really true, but I am feeling better."

The nurse nodded. "We're petitioning the board to create a diagnostic code for marriage-related immune system deficiencies. We see it all the time."

Diane nodded. "The mind-body connection is scary. So how's my girl?"

"She's getting dressed. The doctor had an emergency call, so the nurse-practitioner is with Quinn. She wants to see you. Go on into the examining room."

Diane's stomach seized—she regretted that coffee now. "Is she alright?"

The nurse smiled like Mona Lisa and led her into the room where Quinn was pulling her shirt on. She put her hands up as if Diane had never seen her chest before. "Hey."

"Hello, I'm Liz Amagi." She gestured for Diane to have a seat in the chair at the end of the exam table. "Quinn is a fine, healthy young woman. I just wanted to get your signature before prescribing birth control pills."

Diane's lost her grip on the file folder. A sheaf of papers and a Ticketmaster envelope wafted to the floor.

"For my skin, Mother." Quinn pointed to a few pimples on her chin.

"Not so fast." Diane looked at Liz. "They really help the skin?"

"Studies show that they can." She crouched to help pick up Diane's papers and looked directly at her. "Better safe than sorry, in any case."

Diane was dying to ask if her daughter had been sexually active, but she was equally afraid. She had been sexually active at sixteen, but she was in love, whatever that means. And that didn't mean she wanted Quinn to be. It wasn't just pregnancy that worried Diane. Things were different now. She had lectured Quinn for years on how you could go blind from syphilis and get a recurring rash from herpes. But now, you could die. Call it progress.

Liz picked up the Ticketmaster envelope. "I understand you're recently divorced."

"Yes. Almost." What did that have to do with anything? Were children of divorce more sexually active? Looking for love? Please say no. Diane was happy now; the kids should be too, right? Okay, that sounded stupid, even in Diane's head. She stole a look at Quinn, who was studying her pimples in the wall mirror. "But I think we're fine. I mean, she is a teenager, you know. And I'm busy starting a business. But I'm not filling the house with misery. I actually have a date tonight. To see the Stones, how lucky is that?"

"Take condoms with you," Liz said, handing Diane the ticket envelope.

Quinn turned away from the mirror.

"Excuse me?" Diane slipped the envelope back in the folder. A note she had missed slipped out of the small envelope.

The doctor made a note on her electronic chart, then looked

from one to the other. "You and your daughter share the honor of being in the highest-risk group for STDs."

"STDs?"

Quinn woke up. "Sexually transmitted diseases, Mother. Duh."

"Right. But—I'm not about to, you know."

"Neither am I, Mom." Quinn stared at her.

This was the part Diane hated about being a mother. There was never a right answer, but every decision could be the wrong one. "Fine! Give her a prescription." Diane walked out.

She went back to the waiting room and tried to catch her breath. She tried not to think about her daughter having sex, not with Kyle or anyone else. Hormones were to blame for so many things. Okay, she was overreacting. Hormones were what made women great. It was natural. It would be okay. Trusting anyone was hard these days, but she had to trust her daughter.

She looked at her watch, wondering how long it would take at the pharmacy. She had to pick up Cody's inhaler, anyway. She wondered how much it would cost, whether her COBRA policy covered birth control. It took thirty years for insurance companies to cover the Pill, thirty days for Viagra. Funny how that worked. Diane pushed the image of Mr. Excitement out of her mind and calculated how much time she would need to pick up Cody from camp and get him home where Quinn would have to babysit instead of having sex. How was she going to remember to take a pill every day? She didn't remember to make her bed every day. Should she be carrying condoms, too? No, Kyle probably had plenty of those. Somehow, that wasn't very comforting.

Diane wondered if Ben carried condoms. She grabbed some birth control pamphlets for herself. Then she remembered the note and opened it. *Dear Diane, Your business is promising. Unfortunately, I don't feel comfortable with it personally. Hope you find someone more deserving of your time. Enjoy the concert. Best, Ben*

Best? Best what? Best of luck finding a man with balls—unshaved ones? Diane read the note again. Then she stuffed it in the envelope and pulled out the tickets. At least she wouldn't have to pay half, like she had offered. If she wanted to pay for herself, she could be with her girlfriends.

Liz emerged from the examining room area. Diane hurried across the room to speak with her. "Excuse me, can I ask you a strange question?"

Liz put her clipboard down. "Shoot."

"What do you think of intimacy aids?"

"Excuse me?"

"Sex toys."

Liz started laughing.

"Sorry I asked." Diane said.

"No, I'm sorry, it just came out of left field, reminded me of this picture in one of my old textbooks in medical school. It showed a doctor curing what they called "feminine hysteria" by putting an electronic stimulator up her skirt. It was a real product, made by one of those companies that still make blenders. They advertised in the back of *McCall's* magazine."

"It worked?" Diane asked.

"Oh, yes." Liz pulled herself together and spoke with expertise. "It's a scientific fact that orgasm promotes good health. It raises seratonin levels, increases circulation, induces rest. Anything that promotes good health, I'm in favor of."

Diane nodded. "And talk about safe sex."

"Exactly."

Diane thanked Liz and said good-bye. She kept the birth control pamphlets for Bonnie, but she threw Ben's note away. By the time Quinn emerged, Diane had zipped the concert tickets in her purse and devised a plan.

She took Quinn to the pharmacy, then took her cell phone outside to call Cody. She asked his friend's mom if he could stay over tonight. When she heard the moment of hesitation, she went for broke. "Oh, and we're going to Universal Studios Saturday, do you think your son would like to join us?" Diane knew how to barter as well as Lana, but the currency for moms was time, not money. And the bonus of having your kid enjoy the splendors of a theme park without having to endure them yourself, well—that was an offer no parent could refuse. For

Diane, the deal would buy time with her daughter. And that, as the commercials put it, was priceless.

Details set, she went back inside the pharmacy, paid for the medication, then snatched the bag before Quinn could take it. She was dying to talk, but she bit her tongue until Quinn was trapped in her seat belt.

"Okay, sweetie, here's the deal. I'll let you go on the Pill on one condition—I mean, beyond promising to not have sex until you're twenty-five, after you've graduated from college, and if you are truly in love." They both laughed, but Diane wasn't really kidding. She'd like to have her daughter's body hermetically sealed, just like her old wedding dress.

"Well?" Quinn asked.

Diane opened her purse and waved the concert tickets.

Quinn groaned, just as Diane expected. "You're bribing me?"

"Think of it as a reward." Diane said. In a perfect world, Diane would birth a child who was excited about seeing a concert with her mother, especially one with a band as legendary as this. Diane had learned the hard way that it wasn't a perfect world. But she could try.

That night, high up in the nosebleed seats at the Hollywood Bowl, Diane handed her daughter the binoculars and looked down below at the tiny figures doing the same dance moves they had done for decades. Above them, the stars glowed like pinpricks through a dark blanket of calm.

As the first notes of "Satisfaction" reverberated from the monster speakers mounted on the towering video monitor to her right, Diane chuckled to herself. Then she sang along. A nice-looking man in his midthirties carrying a beer up the stairs nodded at her. Quinn looked up. He nodded at her, too. Then he looked between them and dropped the beer.

Quinn and Diane laughed.

As the sound rose, the music seemed to flow through Diane. The swell of voices around them was intoxicating. Down to the left, several skinny boys in tie-dyed T-shirts rocked side to side with their gray-haired parents. It would be nice if Quinn was like that, but you *can't always get what you want*, right? Broad middle-aged backs rose and blocked their view. When Quinn handed the binoculars back to Diane, her hand brushed against Diane's. Diane reached out and pulled her up to a stand. For one split second, Diane felt the warmth of her baby's blood radiate through her skin.

Then Quinn pulled her hand away.

Diane glanced at Quinn's profile, then peered down through the crowd to the glowing stage. She sang along: *If you try sometime, you just might find . . . you get what you need.* Quinn gave her a dirty look. Diane laughed and sang louder.

Chapter 21

ANNETTE

*. . . after your first date, you no longer believe
anything men say.*

"Is there a last name?" The antiseptic young woman in the smart black dress at the reception desk had two fingers covering the microphone of her headset. Her male twin in the black suit beside her quietly answered another phone line, "Pacific Investments, please hold."

"Paul knows who I am," Annette said. She smiled patiently and looked down over the marble counter. While text messages were private, Annette had returned enough "urgent" phone calls that it was hard to believe this young woman was so ignorant about the boss's private life. How could she not know that Annette wasn't just any business associate? Seriously, how many Annettes could there be?

"Would you like to have a seat?" the other receptionist asked, as the young woman whispered into her headset. He pointed over Annette's pinstriped shoulder at the black leather banquette modeled from a row of theater seats. Annette shook her head. She preferred to enjoy the view of Beverly Hills behind them. It was so much nicer than her chrome-framed sliver of Century City. Besides, she couldn't imagine that Paul would keep her waiting.

When she texted a few minutes ago that she was en route to a meeting nearby, he begged her to stop in for a quick visit before his one o'clock lunch. She was so pleased that when Bonnie called about her restraining order hearing, Annette volunteered to help. Annette popped a pastille and strolled around the waiting area. She paused to admire the vintage black-and-white photographs of grapefruit groves and the dusty fields of the San Fernando Valley.

Another sharply dressed young man emerged from a hidden door to escort her to Paul's office. He offered her bottled water or green tea. This was more like it, Annette thought. He led her down the long corridor lined with assistants half hidden by tall counters. Discretion was a good thing, she decided, and logical for a company that handled so much money. Annette undid the top buttons of her silk blouse.

Paul was all business until his assistant shut the door. Then he leaned against his corner desk and reached for her.

Annette took her time crossing the white Berber, pretending to admire the autographed artworks hanging on the paneled walls. She allowed him a quick hug, then walked over to the conference pit at the intersection of the picture windows and sat down on the longer side of the suede sectional. A leather-framed photograph of his snow-covered chalet lay open on the steel table, but she couldn't sit back comfortably on the couch and still see it. She crossed her legs at the ankles and tried to act blasé.

He lifted his eyes from her legs and met hers. "You look amazing."

Annette smiled, of course she did. Why would she show up looking any less? Before her visit, she had stopped in the ladies' room downstairs, took her hair down out of the bun, and glazed her lips with a final coat of Fire. "I have a lunch," she said, and checked her watch.

He pouted. "I rescheduled my flight to San Francisco."

Annette was flattered, but she wasn't about to take her panties off here. "So, how are you?"

"Fantastic, now that you're here. What a treat."

Annette smoothed her skirt over her knee. He was staring so hard she felt like he was studying her. What was he looking for? Annette reached for the photo and stole a glance at her reflection to make sure there wasn't lipstick on her teeth. Nope, all good. "Is that your place?"

He nodded. "It's gorgeous when the leaves turn. Do you like to travel?"

"Doesn't everyone?" Annette asked, daring to dream of a trip to Aspen in the fall. She could switch Morgan's weekends ahead just in case. Jackson was in a far better mood now that his paintings were selling. If she hadn't just confirmed Bonnie's court date, she could fly to San Francisco today.

She took a sip of water and tried to think what else to talk about. His cowboy boots? His view of the Hollywood sign? His silence wasn't helping. She felt awkward; so different here in the bright light of his office. "I should go."

Paul looked stricken. "Can we just grope for a minute?"

"If we must," Annette said. She followed him toward the desk, out of view from the windows.

He kissed her softly, then pulled her close until her breasts were squashed against him. The urgency rose like heat—had she ever felt so much chemistry with a man? He plunged his hand down her skirt, but she pulled it back out. Her red nails were clicking against the buttons of his white linen shirt when the door opened. She pulled away to examine a cuticle. He turned and leaned over his desk to button up as if checking a spreadsheet.

"Victor on line one," his assistant said. He pointed at the blinking light on the phone.

"I'll call him back," Paul said.

Annette smiled at the assistant, who nodded as if he had expected as much.

Paul shook his head and took a deep breath. "Walk you out?"

He touched her lower back lightly as they left his office. A few steps down the hall, Annette turned to smile at Paul. He had a smidge of lipstick on the corner of his lip. Annette reached to brush it off with her thumb, but Paul jerked away from her touch.

They walked quickly down the long hall past the assistants. Not one looked up. Annette understood that this was his place of business, but she felt disappointed at Paul's sudden dismissal of her. She played it cool as she passed the receptionists, who simply nodded. Bunch of snobs. Paul got her parking stub validated and escorted her out to the elevators. He pushed the button.

Before they could speak, a big-bellied businessman greeted Paul and joined them. Annette stared at the numbers and said nothing. When the elevator dinged and the doors opened, he waved the man in, then leaned in for a quick kiss. Annette let him press his lips to hers, then stepped inside. She punched the Close Door button and descended twenty floors in a dark cloud. She shook it off as she emerged in the parking structure. The valet brought her Mercedes around. She turned off her PDA and drove out into the glaring midday sun.

When she turned it on after her lunch meeting, he had sent four text messages. She laughed at herself for getting so worked up. He was contrite that his San Francisco trip had moved up— that was the call from Victor. Paul had to go put out a fire, bail some company out of a restructuring deal that was burning money. Annette didn't respond right away. Paul texted every few minutes, all the way to the airport. Finally, she texted back and admitted she had been uncomfortable in his office. Why would she lie?

By the time he responded, she was back in her own office, finishing another deposition. He apologized for the delay and described his four-star hotel. In blue. *You'd love it here. I have a view of the Golden Gate.*

She changed to pink. *How's the weather?*

Who cares? We'd never get out of bed.

When do you leave for London?

Thursday, he typed. *Back Sunday, then Boston. Hong Kong a week after.*

Busy man. Do you even have time for a relationship? She giggled and hit Send.

There was no response; he was probably in the elevator, then at his meeting.

Six hours later, she was cozied up in bed. She had just topped off her glass of Bordeaux—when the flag went up on her PDA screen.

Relationship?

Pardonnez-moi? Annette typed.

I can't do this.

Annette scoffed. She wasn't looking for marriage, but it would be nice to have a date for her boss's annual Labor Day yacht party. But there was nothing more.

The next day, still nothing. All day. She watched the digital clock on her computer screen and stayed in for lunch just in case. She finished the entire bag of chocolate Kisses as she watched executives and office workers stream out of the Century City towers toward restaurants across the street. Finally, she called his office to see if something had happened. Maybe he was in a car accident, or got hit by a bus.

His assistant was all business. Nothing had changed. Except that he was not communicating. Could he really not do a relationship? Or did he mean he couldn't do it with her? He had already done her, and done her well. Fine, they were grown-ups, and sex didn't equal a relationship, but what about all the e-mails? She clicked on her mailbox: over 800 messages in the last ten days. Wasn't that a relationship?

There must be some mistake.

Annette checked her PDA again. She put new batteries in it, then used it to talk to Morgan. It worked now, but the magic was gone. By the end of the day, he still hadn't written. Annette drove home in a daze.

Once home, she paced the living room and then the kitchen. She picked at a chicken that Carmen had left. She chose another bottle of Bordeaux from the wine cabinet, poured herself

a glass, and considered the evidence. He said she was perfect!
Where had she been all his life? Could she travel?

How could he have said those things if he didn't mean them?
She had seen him in depositions and negotiations. He was a
credible witness. She spent an hour hunched over the marble
kitchen island, composing a request for an explanation on her
PDA. She tried to be objective and businesslike. Usually, she
was good at it. Unfortunately, this wasn't business; it was personal. Three-quarters of a bottle of wine later, she deleted it.
This was the modern equivalent of drunk dialing. She wouldn't
stoop so low.

Annette sat down by the window and looked out over the
yard. She was horrified that after all the dreams she had about
providing this wonderful home for her daughter, she had imagined moving to his penthouse and jetting around the world. Finally, she sent him a message, in pink: **??**

Thirty seconds later, the flag on Annette's mailbox icon went
up. She was so relieved she nearly cried. She put the PDA down,
went to the bathroom, and washed her face. She didn't want to
seem anxious. She told herself it was just another e-mail, then
clicked on the flag.

I'm not ready for a relationship, he wrote.

But—all those e-mails?

I apologize if I hurt you.

If he hurt her? Every cell of her body ached. This was different from Jackson; he was a battle she couldn't win. But Paul was
worth fighting for. After all this time, she had a taste of victory.
How had she lost? Annette should never have said the "R"
word. She could have been happy in a little compartment of his
life.

Annette took her jacket off, and her high heels, everything
down to her slip. Fuck Paul. That's all she wanted to do, really.
They could be having sex right now.

She slipped into bed. She put the PDA on the pillow next to
her, the pillow she had imagined his head resting on. She had
male clients who were staunch believers in having Friends with

Benefits. Why couldn't it work for a woman the way it did a man? She shouldn't have let her guard down.

Annette threw the PDA across the room. It dented the wall and landed next to the fireplace. She reached for the wineglass, then reached past it for the bottle, took a swig, wiped her mouth on her sheet, and took another gulp. She wanted to feel numb, but it wasn't working. She saw the lights of a migraine coming on and pulled the pillow over her head. Then she passed out.

In the morning, the sunlight was blinding. Annette threw an arm over her face and blinked to see Carmen's rotund backside as she tied up the damask curtains at the window. Annette threw a high heel at her. Carmen dropped the curtains and scurried out, swearing in Spanish.

The phone rang. Annette knocked it off the nightstand. When that annoying recording began, Annette rolled off the bed far enough to yank the base cord out of the wall. Annette wasn't even going to call the office. Nigel would be the first to respect the pain of an Internet affair gone bad.

Annette glared across the room at her PDA. It was glowing. The thing was indestructible. A tiny bit of her was relieved. Especially when she heard the buzz. Maybe it was Paul. Apologizing. Annette got out of bed, crawled over her skirt, tossed a shoe out of her way, and reached under the chair to pick it up. The sex was like morphine, she had to have more. She hit Return Call before she thought better of it.

Diane picked up. "Hi, Annette, just checking in. Was Mr. Chambers pleased about Instant Pleasure?"

"Yes," Annette said. "You could say that."

"Great. See you at the courthouse."

Annette hung up and fumbled in the drawer for her sleeping pills. She was tired of the courthouse. She was tired of working so hard. She was tired of so many things . . .

Chapter 22

BONNIE

. . . when you stop being a pushover.

Bonnie parked her rental car in the lot across from the county court building downtown. She watched the mass of humanity heading toward the long gray building while she waited for the ragtop of the Mustang to rise. She locked down the clamps, then brushed the knots from her hair. She had been thrilled to rent the Mustang, but it wasn't any fun driving a convertible on the freeway, especially during the rush hour. Even her face felt grimy. If Lana hadn't worked so hard on her makeup, she'd get a baby wipe from the trunk and scrub it all off.

Bonnie clutched her file of physician letters and her schedule of phone calls. She had checked that her miniature tape recorder was cued up to the last recording of the "C" word. All in all, she was feeling pretty confident. Yesterday, Henry from the grocery store took her flying in a cute little airplane. Buck practically forbade her to cross the street. He made her take Dramamine that time they went whale watching, but she didn't even get airsick yesterday. She felt like Supergirl. Or Superwoman. Whatever. She was ready.

Twenty minutes later, as Bonnie waited to go through the

metal detector at the entrance, her cell phone rang. It was Henry's number. She was dying to hear his reassuring voice, but he had no idea where she was. It had been hard to keep this a secret, but she was afraid of scaring him away. She let the call go to voice mail. This was too much baggage for such a nice guy. Her confidence was wilting as quickly as her ponytail.

She checked to see if Annette had called, but there were no other messages. The odor of boiled hot dogs from the street vendor on the corner was making Bonnie nauseous. She tried not to look around too much. What if one of these angry-looking people really did have a gun?

Finally, after being prodded and X-rayed and everything short of a strip-search, she was in. A man at Information directed her to the sixth floor. She squeezed into the crowd in front of the elevators. After a few minutes of fighting for elbow space between the bored lawyers, the nervous women with crying babies, and the unshaven men in windbreakers, Bonnie decided to take the stairs.

She ran up the smelly stairwell as quickly as she could and exited at the sixth floor. She found the C hallway and took a deep breath. There he was, bigger than life. She had dreaded this moment. He was wearing his Buckeye jacket and was all spruced up with a new haircut. He had lost weight, too. He looked eerily similar to the Rose Bowl injured football jock that she remembered. Had it really only been three years ago? Bonnie tasted bile.

He glared at her, and Bonnie wished Diane was here. When she dropped Quinn off to babysit, she promised to meet her here after dropping Cody off at camp. Bonnie focused on the tile floor. When she noticed that Buck was wearing white tube socks with his loafers like a total dork, she relaxed. She slipped past him and went into the courtroom.

Buck came in and sat right behind her. She could hear him breathing through his deviated septum but pretended not to notice. She straightened her flowered skirt and touched the pearls at her throat. Lana told her what to wear to look sympathetic, but she added her mother's pearls herself. She didn't believe in luck much anymore, but she liked feeling like her mom was with her. She would understand.

Bonnie had read in a chat room that this could take awhile, so she got out her small-business loan forms. Diane had helped her figure out how to use the equity in her house as a collateral for her photography business. She had even found a bank officer who helped her with the interest rate. The club discount, of course.

A white-haired man with a red-veined nose sat down right next to Bonnie. She uncrossed her legs to avoid touching his rumpled seersucker suit. He stared straight ahead as another case was called, then turned to face her.

"Bonnie Fornari?"

"Yes," she said.

"This is for you." He slapped an envelope in her hand and got up.

Bonnie recognized this from TV. She had just been served! She heard Buck get up and change seats, then heard him whisper in the back row to that clown. She put her business forms away and opened the package. Inside was a sheaf of legal papers. Buck had hired a lawyer and was contesting the restraining order. It was almost flattering, that the cheapskate had spent money on her. She hadn't spent any on him, that was for sure. But Annette had said she'd come. Bonnie looked around. Where was she?

Bonnie took her cell phone out of her purse to check the time and then saw the sign: NO CELL PHONES. She turned it off.

The typed document in the legal envelope was a sworn statement. According to this, Buck "did not recall making any phone calls using improper language." Bonnie chuckled. Of course he didn't remember—he was drunk. She read further. Buck "did not have a drinking problem." This was no longer funny. How could he lie like that? The judge said something, but Bonnie missed it. She didn't have time to read everything, but the next page was an affidavit signed by a doctor. She wondered who paid him. There must be some legal fund for wayward athletes. It must be huge.

The judge called their names and ordered them to go to Social Services on another floor. Bonnie trudged a few steps ahead of Buck. Once inside the small room, she sat as many rows away from him as possible. The families between them made quite a racket, arguing in a zillion foreign languages. Despite the No Children sign, there were plenty of crying babies and a few sulky teenagers. From the McDonald's wrappers spilling out of the trash can, it looked like many had been there all morning waiting to meet with the social worker.

Bonnie pulled the documents from the legal envelope to read, but she couldn't concentrate. She hadn't eaten breakfast or read her horoscope yet. Why hadn't anyone told her to bring quarters for the candy machine? Bonnie watched the door for Annette, who had probably never been there. Her clients paid her to keep them away from places like this.

The wooden door with the safety-glass window banged opened. A woman with a coffee stain on her sweater stopped speaking Spanish with a coworker, leaned out and called Bonnie's name. Bonnie followed her through a maze of hallways to a tiny cubicle. A young black woman waved a fly off the cake donut on her desk and asked if Bonnie would compromise on an interim custody agreement so that Buck was not prohibited from seeing the children.

"Of course," Bonnie said.

The woman sent Bonnie out and called Buck's name. He didn't even look at Bonnie as he left his lawyer's side and marched past. Bonnie went out to the hallway to call Annette's office. Nigel, in his adorable accent, barely had time to tell her Annette wasn't in before the Social Services door creaked open and she was summoned back inside. She passed Buck, who was already sitting down with his lawyer. That was good, right? The black woman was waiting at the door. She led her back through the maze to the cubicle.

"Your husband did not agree," the social worker said. "He wants full access."

Bonnie looked at the donut. Her stomach turned over. "Will he stop calling?"

"That's not under our jurisdiction."

Bonnie fanned her file of papers and set them on top of legal documents Buck had filed. Had she gone to all this trouble for nothing? All that worry? All those fingernails? "He can't just call anytime and say whatever he wants in front of the children!" she said. *It's not reasonable,* she thought.

"Okay." The woman stood up.

"Okay?" Bonnie wanted to hug the woman.

"Okay, back to court. Since both parties were unable to come to an agreement, you have to appear before the judge."

Bonnie tried not to bite her nails as she went back to the courtroom. She called Diane before going back in. Diane was on her way, but she hadn't heard from Annette at all. Bonnie patted the tape recorder. She had evidence; it would all be okay.

Bonnie squeezed through the people milling about in the hallways and found the one she had been in earlier, 612c. Hard to believe that behind every door in this hallway, and the doors above and below, were courtrooms. So many unhappy people. The bailiff signed her in. He was nice, but he couldn't predict when her case would be heard. This could take all day.

Bonnie started reading the papers she was served. It felt weird reading them right in front of Buck. The lies made her furious. She stole a glance at the smug lawyer. Did he know his client lied? Did he care? How could Annette do this job?

The next case was an uncontested divorce that was approved immediately. The husband didn't show up. Wouldn't that be nice?

Ninety minutes later, the bailiff called, "Bonnie Fornari versus Robert Fornari." Bonnie had never, in her wildest nightmare, imagined hearing that word, "versus." How did they get here? Now she understood the futility of her favorite beauty contest plea, for world peace. How could two foreign countries get along when two people who once loved each other enough to bring babies into the world couldn't share a friendly word between them?

The bailiff pointed to the long wooden table on the right

side of the gallery in front of the tall judge's bench. The bailiff acted like he didn't mean to boss her around, he was only working there so he could wear the shiny badge over his clip-on tie. The judge scanned the papers before her as quickly as possible. That was a hard job, Bonnie thought.

Bonnie stood alone at the plaintiff's table until the bailiff ordered her to be seated. Buck stood at the table on the left surrounded by that creepy lawyer and three other men. They were all old and white—an island of rednecks in a courtroom packed with so many other races and ages. She wished Annette were here, she was so much more hip. Bonnie went to the witness box and sat down. She folded her hands in her lap just like Lana did in the movie when she got away with murder.

"Are you afraid of your husband, Mrs. Fornari?" the judge asked.

"Yes," Bonnie said.

"You believe he is a threat to you physically?" Bonnie hesitated. She had to be completely honest, even if Buck wasn't. He could get really mad, that's what scared her, but she didn't think he'd hit her. Not on purpose. He might try to beat up Henry, though. Anyone she dated was at risk. But that wasn't the question. The judge was waiting. What would happen if she said yes? She couldn't send the father of her children to jail. "No, Your Honor."

"Have you received Buck's supporting documentation?"

"Um, yes," Bonnie said.

The judge pushed her cat's-eye glasses up on her bumpy nose. Maybe she was a grandma. "And you, sir, swear to the authenticity of your statement?"

Buck stood with his hands behind his back. "To the best of my knowledge, Your Honor."

Liar! Bonnie crossed her arms. Enough already. He had lied on the very first page.

The judge saw her. "Do you have any questions?"

Bonnie thought about it. He had just perjured himself on paper and right here in front of the judge. Then again, he did say it was to the best of his knowledge. Clearly, his knowledge was limited. How could she argue with that? "No, Your Honor, but I do have evidence to the contrary." She held up her tape recorder.

The judged raised her eyebrows.

Buck wiped his forehead with a handkerchief. He didn't own a handkerchief that Bonnie knew of, but she didn't care who paid for it. She was pleased that the mere sight of her tape recorder was making him sweat.

The judge pointed her pen at the opposing council. "Have you reviewed the plaintiff's evidence?"

"No, Your Honor," the creepy lawyer answered. "It's the first I've heard of it."

The judge looked at Bonnie. "Then it's inadmissible at this time."

Bonnie's mouth dropped open, like Hayley's turtle. How could she give Buck's lawyer a copy of anything when she didn't know he had a lawyer until today? She hadn't even had time to read his stuff. Bonnie had followed all the directions on the government Web site about how to do this whole restraining order thing. She had studied two sites posted by divorce lawyers. And she had done everything Annette suggested. What she hadn't done was hire a lawyer. Penny-wise and pound-foolish, her mother would have said. Her mother would have given her the money.

"Case dismissed," the judge said.

"What does that mean?" Bonnie asked.

Buck sneered. "It means you lost, babe."

The judged rapped her gavel. "The record will show that in the case of Fornari versus Fornari, the case was dismissed—with prejudice."

"Judge," the creepy lawyer argued. "My client has—"

The judge held up her hand. He shut up. "It is the opinion of the court that this kind of case does not belong on the legal docket. It's a private matter that wastes taxpayer money. Mr. Fornari, please consider what is in the best interest of your children before opening your mouth in their presence and on the telephone." She turned to face Bonnie. "Mrs. Fornari, 'with prejudice' means that if another situation should arise, you may use the evidence collected in this case so long as it is shared with the defendant and his council. Understood?"

Bonnie nodded. She supposed that was good. She glanced at Buck. She only wanted to give him a wake-up call. He was awake now, that was clear. She glanced over. Buck put his hand up and spread his thumb and forefinger into the shape of an L. Loser.

Bonnie blinked back tears and snatched a Kleenex from her purse pack to blow her nose. She felt so stupid! She walked out as fast as she could without running. Diane was in the hallway, thank heaven, with Hayley and Lucas. Bonnie had never been so happy to see her babies. She hugged Hayley, then heaved Lucas out of Diane's arms. She staggered under his weight.

"How'd it go?"

Bonnie burst into tears. "I lost."

"Oh, honey, I'm so sorry."

Bonnie nodded. "I didn't know what questions to ask."

Diane looked around. "Where's Annette?"

"I don't know. But I don't think she could have helped."

"What are you talking about? It was her job to help. That's what she does."

"Not really, Diane. Not if you don't pay her." She wiped her eyes.

There was a commotion in the hall as Buck gave a quick interview to a sports reporter. He high-fived his creepy lawyer. Diane looked at Bonnie. "He hired a lawyer?"

Bonnie nodded. Lucas was squirming. Bonnie sat on the bench and let him stand between her knees. He took a step away from her. His first steps.

Bonnie screamed with excitement.

Hayley screamed, too, of course, so everyone in the bustling hallway stopped and turned to look. An armed guard burst through the crowd. He stopped right in front of them with his hand on his gun.

Lucas took another wobbly step.

"That's my boy!" Buck said, just as Lucas fell down. Buck rushed over and picked him up. Lucas looked tiny in his arms.

"Hey, buddy, look at you!" Buck looked at Bonnie, and when he spoke to her, his voice was cold and accusing. "What else are you keeping from me?"

"Nothing, Buck, I swear. Those were his first steps!" Bonnie was still sniffling, but now she couldn't help smiling. Her baby was walking.

Buck was grinning, too. She caught his eyes.

Then Bonnie remembered where she was and turned back to Diane. This was all too confusing. She sat on a bench along the wall to collect herself. Diane handed her another Kleenex and hugged her.

A moment later, she felt Buck towering beside them. She turned and looked up over her squirming son to face him. *Liar,* she wanted to shout. But she waited.

"I had to say those things," Buck said. "I didn't want to lose the kids."

Bonnie tied Lucas's shoelace as it dangled in front of her. "That wasn't the point, Buck."

He reached for her. "What was the point?"

"I want a divorce!" She clapped a hand to her mouth. That wasn't what she meant to say, but it *was* the point.

He handed Lucas back to her. "Fine. I'll do the mediator thing."

Bonnie pulled off her wedding rings and held them out. He shook his head. "Keep 'em. But I get the kids Saturday. Every Saturday."

"Fine." Perfect, actually. She could go flying with Henry every week. She put the rings inside the diaper bag. She knew just where they would go in the hope chest. Or was it a No Hope chest? A Hope for Something Better chest? She felt out of sorts. Sad, yet strangely light.

Diane and Bonnie waited for an elevator. No way were they carrying the kids down six flights of stairs. When each packed elevator opened, Bonnie studied the faces to find Annette. "Maybe she had a car accident."

"She better have," said Diane.

Outside, the sun had broken through the haze. People in lightweight suits and slacks were sprawled on the steps eating sandwiches and hot dogs. Families speaking foreign languages picnicked in the small patch of grass between the courthouse buildings. They both turned when a sharply dressed woman marched past, but it wasn't Annette. They walked down the steps and onto the sidewalk toward the four-lane traffic of Spring Street.

A just-married couple left the courthouse and skipped past holding hands. The bride's green-streaked hair flopped down the back of her lace sundress. Her groom, who had a bow tie clipped to his T-shirt, waved a white certificate as if he'd won the lottery. Diane shook her head.

Bonnie saw her reaction. "You don't want to ever get married again?"

"I don't want to ever get divorced again," Diane said, as they approached the intersection of one-way streets.

"Who does?" Bonnie laughed at the memory of Diane saying those same two words to her the day they met at Mecca. She let Hayley pound the red button for the Walk signal. "But don't you think the folks who marry a bunch of times are the real romantics?"

Diane laughed. "Hopeless optimists. Lunatics." A car honked and Diane pulled further back on the curb as the traffic rushed past. "Wonder if it's different every time."

Bonnie nodded. "Like that Russian dude said, 'Every happy marriage is happy in the same way, every unhappy marriage is different.'"

"I take it you flunked Tolstoy."

"C minus. But I got the drift. And I don't care what anyone says: it's way harder to get divorced than to get married. But now I feel like . . . like when Henry takes me flying. It's so freaking great—but I'm also scared to death of crashing." Diane's cell phone rang. Bonnie looked over. "Annette?"

Diane shook her head but looked puzzled at the number. She let it go.

The smell of grilled onions wafted over from the hot dog stand. "Mommy, I'm hungry." Bonnie looked down at Hayley. Lucas was smacking his lips, too. "Baba."

Diane got up. "I'm going to get some hot dogs. Want to sit down and nurse him?"

"I'll sit down, but Lucas is drinking apple juice now, right, big boy?" She pulled him onto her lap and waved bye-bye to Hayley as Diane took her hand and led her to the hot dog cart. Bonnie opened a juice box for Lucas and turned on her phone. There was a text message from Lana.

She waited for Diane to get back, then showed her the message. "Lana's looking for Annette, too. She hasn't heard from her in two days. Could she have gotten the date wrong?" Diane gave her a hot dog. Bonnie was so ravenous, she didn't take the time to open a packet of mustard before taking a bite.

"I dunno. I mentioned it when I called her about my loan. She's having quite a fling with my investor, did I tell you?" She dialed Annette's office.

Bonnie swallowed and grabbed her phone back. "I already talked to her assistant. Nigel."

"Have you met him? Adorable. He'd be good for you if Grocery Boy doesn't work out. He moved clear across the ocean for some babe he met online, then—" They looked at each other at the same time.

Bonnie took another bite of her hot dog, then threw out the rest. "Take the kids for me, will you?"

"I'll go."

"No. This one is mine." Bonnie kissed her kids. "Go take care of Cody. You have a camera on your phone?" Diane nodded. "If he walks again, take a picture, okay?" Bonnie hurried to the parking lot.

Half an hour later, Carmen opened the door of the Brentwood estate and pointed Bonnie upstairs. Bonnie took a brownie from the plate on the table below Jackson's painting and looked around. What a waste of space for one person. Even for two. It was practically a compound. Bonnie nibbled the brownie and trudged up the circular stairs. She was surprised to hear Dr. Phil lecturing on the TV.

Bonnie knocked on the bedroom door. There was no answer, so she went in and turned off the TV. Once her eyes adjusted to the darkness, she sank her feet into the plush carpet and waded over to the heavy curtains at the front windows. Her nose twitched from the lingering scent of smoke. When she pulled the heavy curtains open and turned from the glare of sunlight, there was no mistaking the lump on the enormous bed.

Annette wasn't asleep; she was passed out, drooling on her satin pillowcase. Kleenex was bunched on the floor. Hershey's Kiss wrappers littered the bed like silver snowflakes.

Bonnie's stomach fluttered when she saw the bottle of sleeping pills on the table. When she picked it up, the remaining pills shook like Hayley's plastic maracas. Bonnie was relieved that the bottle wasn't empty, but selfishly so. If Annette had died of an overdose, Bonnie couldn't strangle the woman herself.

On the night table, a wine-stained florist card stuck out from beneath the empty wine bottle. Bonnie could make out two initials: P.C. Prince Charming?

Bonnie rolled her eyes. Buck would have moved his hand up and down as if he were masturbating. That was gross, she knew. When would she stop thinking of how Buck would react?

Then Bonnie saw the enormous bouquet of wilting roses on the vanity across the room. It was gorgeous; two dozen roses all pressed together like a big lollipop, not the usual corner florist variety. This bouquet must have cost a fortune. Bonnie pulled the roses out of the vase, one by one. There weren't even any thorns on the long stems. Once she had laid the flowers carefully across the table, she picked up the vase, walked to the bed, and dumped the water on Annette.

Annette sputtered to consciousness.

Bonnie went to the door and called down to Carmen. *"Señora, mucho agua, por favor!"* Thank goodness for college Spanish.

"What the hell?" Annette sputtered.

Bonnie went to the enormous bathroom and got a towel that was so soft it should have been illegal. She handed it to Annette, then sat down against the corner column.

"What are you doing here?" Annette wiped her face.

"I should be asking you that."

The fog cleared and Annette sat up, stricken. "Is today your hearing?"

Bonnie nodded. "Was. Past tense."

Annette fell back and covered her face with a silken pillow. Her words came out muffled. "I'm so sorry." Then she sat up and took a sip of water. She pressed her hand against her head. "I had a migraine."

"Self-induced?"

Annette frowned. "Isn't Diane more the Mother Superior type?"

"My turn. I came to give you hell, but apparently, you're already there." Bonnie waved the wine-stained card and sighed. She could have said a million things, but they all sounded so clichéd. It was only in real life that when your heart was broken, it truly hurt.

Annette sat up. Her slip was stained and clinging to her. She put her hand across her chest.

Bonnie searched in Annette's enormous walk-in closet. She had never seen so many suits, even in a store. She found Annette's robe and went back out to her. Carmen was there, pouring water into a glass. "*Gracias, Señora.*"

"*De nada,*" Carmen smiled and left the pitcher. Bonnie waited for Annette to take a sip, then handed her the robe.

"Shouldn't this be coffee?"

"Nope," Bonnie shook her head. "You got it all wrong. I can't believe I looked up to you so much. Miss Perfect. You remind me of Hayley's turtle."

"Slimy?"

"You do look a bit green, but no. I mean the hard shell on the outside, safe from attack. But turn the turtle upside down and there's nothing but soft tissue. Can't get back on its slimy little feet."

Annette wrapped the robe around her and snatched the florist card back. "He said I was perfect. He was mad we didn't marry."

Bonnie stared. Annette reminded her of her younger sorority sisters. "He probably meant it when he said it. Men say a lot of things."

Annette ripped up the card and threw it like confetti. "You've never been alone, have you?"

Bonnie opened her mouth to argue, then closed it. She put her hand on Annette's arm. "You're not alone, Annette."

After a moment, Annette looked up. "I'm sorry about your trial. How was it?"

"Wasn't fun." Bonnie got up to go.

Annette picked up her water and leaned against the headboard. "You seem okay, though."

Bonnie paused at the bedroom door. "There's nothing I want from Buck anymore. Be nice to be friends with him someday, but I'm not holding my breath." She smiled. "Lucas took his first step today."

"Ah. So he isn't 'slow' after all."

"Nope." She watched Annette brush a bit of confetti off her lap. "We all take that first step, eventually." Bonnie shut the door and went home.

Part Three

CLUB BENEFITS

You know you're in the club when . . .

Chapter 23

LANA

. . . you stop cranking up the stereo to drown out the noise in your head.

"Pleasure doing business with you, Jackson." Lana stood in the living room of the beach house, admiring the seascape reflected in the mirror on the wall. It was hard to understand how the light could play below the blue surface to give it such depth. And the shimmer of silver. It was better than a painting. Lana pulled herself together and leaned closer to the large mirror to see her hair, which was back to its natural shade of amber. The real thing was always best. She turned to face the wide expanse of ocean. Her chuckle was drowned out by the sound of the surf crashing against the wooden pylons. "Can I see you out?"

"I know the way," Jackson said. He carried the last of his boxes out the back door of the empty beach house just as Lana's herd of moving men came in.

A familiar voice from Mecca rang out above the heavy footsteps. "Five seventeen Malibu Cove?"

"Eli!" Lana said. "Come on in!" Her old associate was just as shiny and sweet-smelling as ever. She hugged him.

"You never did come over for that vegetarian barbecue. And Owen promised to cook it up special."

"I'm sorry, things have been crazy. How'd you tear yourself away from the store?"

"Special delivery. I don't lift much, but I point really well."

A toilet flushed, then Diane's voice called toward Lana. "Think you'll get enough selling the loft to get any equity in this place?"

"Hope so." Lana answered. "I'd like to buy one of Jackson's paintings for the back bedroom."

Diane was looking at the wisps of cumulus clouds drifting over the horizon as she entered the room. "Where's he moving to, anyway?"

"Didn't ask. I thought you'd know."

"Nope. Not my problem."

"I thought everything was your problem, Diane."

"Not anymore." Diane looked up and saw Eli. "Hey, you're the wedding registry guy, right?"

Eli snorted. "I like to think I'm more than that."

Lana laughed. "I wish I had something to offer you guys to drink, but . . ." She gestured around the empty room. They heard a bang, then two guys carried a couch in through the back hallway. "For crying out loud, who do you have to fuck to get delivery at low tide?" Eli opened his mouth, but Lana put her hand over it. "Don't answer that. Where's my leather chair?"

"The Truby's out of stock, sweet cheeks. After your commercial aired, the warehouse sold out. The floor model is damaged. Not to worry, the rest of the grooviness you ordered is here today."

"Cool." Lana pointed to the two wardrobe bags lying on the bare floor by her purse. "So, Eli, I was thinking of wearing that white leather minidress to the awards show tonight, but designers sent all these gowns over. What do you think?"

"Just because I'm gay doesn't mean I know about women's clothes," Eli said. There was another bang. A burst of swear words erupted from the back door. Eli ran off to investigate.

Diane looked at Lana, all wide-eyed and innocent. "Will Lucas be there tonight?"

"Shut up," Lana said. "The whole world knows Lucas will be

there." Her hip throbbed at the thought of it. Lucas had been quoted about their reunion in the press, but it was just fluff. There was little indication of whether he'd be angry about the fire, was sorry he hurt her, or if he wanted to get back together. Probably none of the above. Just publicity.

Eli was back, pointing the men carrying furniture crates toward the right rooms. The furniture was all new, the best that Mecca offered. Lana was back at the beach and had every intention of staying there. Except not right now. She picked up the Stella McCartney duffel. "Ready to roll?"

Diane nodded and grabbed the Dolce & Gabbana garment bag. "You okay to leave them?"

"'Course. Plus, I promised Eli my Harley if they don't scratch the floor."

Diane grabbed her car keys. "Why?"

"Studio can't get insurance for the film if I'm riding a motorcycle. With what they're paying me, I can lease a Porsche."

"Why not just buy one?" Diane asked.

Lana followed her outside to her car, ready to explain how the million for the commercial went to Uncle Sam, her lawyer, her agent, and the down payment to Annette. But Diane was no dummy. Lana would be getting a hefty salary for the film as soon as they started principal photography. "Guess I'm getting cautious in my old age," Lana admitted.

"Bonnie, too. She gave up the convertible." Diane said. "They found the Jetta; some kids took it on a joy ride. Personally, I'm on the waiting list for a Prius. Even Quinn's happy about that— she'll get this piece of crap." Diane unlocked the old Volvo. They had just set the clothes bags over the plain brown boxes containing the Instant Pleasure inventory, when a vintage Mercedes rattled up behind them.

Diane whipped around to the car that was now blocking them. "Excuse me!"

Lana turned and saw Winston's shiny head rise from the driver's seat. She hoped he used sunblock. She smiled, #18, mostly real with a twinge of false cheer. "Talk about customer service."

Winston blushed. Lana wasn't sure she'd ever seen him blush before, except once when he had mentioned a girlfriend. He was usually all business, unless he was talking about his twins. Bonnie had kept her up-to-date when she saw him in the pre-school parking lot.

"Hi. We were on the way to the soccer field, so I thought I'd see how the delivery was going."

Diane looked at Lana. Winston didn't notice. He was leaning down to scold a beautiful Irish setter. Lana didn't know he had a dog. His twins were buckled in the backseat wearing bright green soccer jerseys. Lana wished he'd stop dressing them in identical clothes. She leaned down. "Hi, boys!"

They waved. "Daddy says you're on TV tonight."

The dog jumped into the back seat. Lana petted him. "After your bedtime."

"We have DVD," the other one said.

"Oh, you do," Lana laughed. She didn't bother to correct him. Now Winston was like all the others; he just wanted to know a celebrity.

He held out a square wrapped in the familiar brown-and-gold Mecca gift wrap. "Brought you a housewarming gift."

"The discount was more than generous, Winston." But she tore off the wrapper and read the CD cover: Mecca Music: Take Two. "More salsa?" Lana's hips swayed beneath her drawstring pants.

Winston nodded and held out his hand for hers. She took it, an automatic response. Winston fell into the beat and led her in a few steps. When he released her, she felt that odd pang of disappointment. He was a natural. She tried to shake off her surprise. "Thanks, Winston."

They hugged awkwardly, then she waved good-bye. "Have a good game, boys."

Winston saluted and got back in his old Mercedes. Lana watched him back the car out. The road not taken, and all that crap. It was just as well that nothing had happened between them. She'd be stuck in his condo in Westlake Village making peanut butter and jelly sandwiches and walking the damn dog.

"Lana!" Diane was tapping her watch.

Lana slipped the CD in her purse and went around to the passenger side. "I should have let him look around. I'm a bad hostess." She sat down and slammed the door shut.

A loud buzzing noise filled the car.

Lana panicked. "Maybe I should have agreed to take the studio limo. It's one thing to be lonely in a limo full of champagne, but it's entirely different to miss your debut at the Emmy Awards because your friend's car broke down."

Diane laughed. "That noise isn't from the car."

Lana looked behind her. The back seat was full of the same kind of plain brown boxes as the trunk. The pink labels were printed with the initials I.P. Diane shifted some boxes from the backseat onto the floor. "Customers love having the batteries included, but it does make for some embarrassing moments at the post office. Buckle up."

Lana laughed and slipped the CD into the deck. They cruised down the Pacific Coast Highway, past the palm tree arches leading to hidden estates. Lana sat up when they slowed for traffic by the pier where the locals were riding the waves at Surfrider Beach. She yawned past the miles of garage doors of smaller beach houses. Then she took off her sandals to check out her French pedicure. She picked up the stack of mail Diane had moved to the floor. *People* magazine was on the bottom. "You get a lot of mail."

"Mostly bills." Diane nodded at the magazine. Lucas was on the cover. "Quinn pays for that from her babysitting money."

"Diane, if you need a loan, let me know."

"I'm fine. Thank God for rent control."

"Okay, but my loft is bound to sell any day and I can always renegotiate my mortgage. Much as I hate landlords, there is an advantage to having one as a friend."

Diane shook her head. "I'd use a different F-word for Annette. It's not that I blame her for buying my house anymore, but I still can't get over how she missed Bonnie's hearing."

"Bonnie's not pissed at her, so get over it." Lana said. She spotted the WELCOME TO SANTA MONICA sign. Time to get ready.

She slipped her bra off from beneath her cashmere tank and started primping.

Diane glanced over. "If you didn't get paid yet, how'd you get all those gorgeous clothes? And don't tell me you bartered."

"People who don't need shit get it free. Law of the jungle."

"The Hollywood jungle. So, what's it like? Is that weird, being on a magazine like that?"

Lana looked at Lucas on the cover of the *People* magazine. Her face was an inset at the corner. It was a close-up from their wedding. She recognized part of a swan just behind her head. "Depends on the picture." Lana put the magazine down. "On the other hand, it makes me think I should be traveling by limousine."

"You don't like being serenaded by the hum of plastic penises?"

They laughed so hard, Diane automatically slowed down. The car behind them honked. "Can I ask you a weird question? Sort of an informal poll—I promise not to tell the tabloids: did Lucas have a name for his penis?"

"Boss," Lana nodded. "But that's only because King of the World was taken." They laughed again. "Go ahead and leak it. Or let Bonnie leak it and split the profit with her."

Diane's cell phone rang. "You mind if I answer that?"

Lana shook her head. She needed to chill, anyway. She didn't know what would happen tonight, but it was bound to be big. She could see flashes of the ocean between the buildings as they drove past. The low clouds reflected like silver on the waves. Lana leaned her head back against the seat and took it all in. It was a wonder anyone could drive here, along the edge of the continent, without falling off.

A gal wearing nothing but a string bikini and a helmet was rollerblading along the bike path. Just a few weeks ago, that had been Lana, torn between watching the waves crash on the beach side and looking for rooms to rent in the apartment buildings along the road. Now, she wasn't even considering Santa Monica; she was back in Malibu. What a difference a day makes, or a few months, or a year.

She looked at Diane, who was talking to Cody on the phone. At the beginning of the summer, she was a tortured soul with frizzy hair and boring panties trying to hide a Slurpee spill on a couch at Mecca. Now, she was a classy businesswoman being ogled by the gentleman in the Jag to her left. Lana was never ogled without makeup; she was a blank canvas, all the better to become the character she portrayed. But those nay-saying folks down in Venice carrying placards past bare-chested chainsaw jugglers were wrong about the world coming to an end. Things could change dramatically, but only if you believed it enough to make it happen.

At the first glimpse of the Ferris wheel on the Santa Monica Pier, Lana tapped Diane's suntanned shoulder. She hung up the phone and took a left up the California incline. She stopped at the light by the Palisades Park overlooking the ocean. Lucas had proposed in the rose garden by the green gazebo. Lana had been so busy smelling the different blooms that she didn't know what was happening until Lucas was down on one knee pointing to the letters spelled out in the sky. He was always one for grand gestures. Bonnie probably knew Lana's tearful acceptance verbatim. What a strange world it was.

Diane turned right past the Mermaid Café where they had first plotted their escape, then turned left toward the Santa Monica Civic Auditorium. They approached the enormous outdoor parking lot shared by the courthouse, which was crowded with production vehicles and news crews setting up at the round white theater. When mold was suspected at the Shrine Auditorium, the Emmys had downsized to these cozier quarters.

"Want to do Thanksgiving here?"

Lana looked at her. "Don't they hold the homeless dinner here?"

Diane nodded. "You should see Cody in a hairnet. He was too young to stir mashed potato mix in the kitchen last year, so he gave out the rolls on the buffet line."

"Pretty altruistic."

"Not really: Quinn needed the volunteer hours for school.

Plus, we went to San Francisco for the rest of the weekend. The dinner thing made me feel less guilty about blowing the last of the mortgage money to show the kids the Golden Gate."

Lana thought about this. "You lost the furniture because you went to San Francisco?"

"No. Okay, maybe a little. But I begged Asshole to take me to San Francisco for years, and we never got any farther than the Indian casinos in Barstow. It's true that I wasted too much money fighting Asshole for money he didn't have. He was so good at forging my name . . . never mind. But I did have a grand stashed for emergency. And it was an emergency, to feel like a family again, the three of us, out of the war zone. It was our first fun in a long time."

"So you want to do it again this year?"

"Definitely. Except for the San Francisco part. That was freezing."

Lana laughed as they pulled up through the open gate. "Count me in," she said. "But only if I get to wear the hairnet."

"Deal." Diane got out and opened the back. She shouted over the noise of the generators lined up in the parking lot, "See you tonight."

"You coming?" Lana lugged her wardrobe bags out of the back, surprised. The promoters had canceled all the guest passes when they switched venues. This place was so small, tickets were selling on eBay for a thousand bucks a pop.

"No, on TV. We're feasting on Tahitian Tuna Toss this evening. It's essentially casserole with shell-shaped pasta, very exciting. Welcome to my world." Diane got out to help shut the trunk and pointed to the wardrobe bag. "You decide what to wear yet?"

Lana shook her head. She knew exactly what would turn Lucas on—or piss him off, but she wasn't sure which way to go. It pissed her off just to be thinking of it. A production assistant with an ID badge hanging around her neck ran over to take the garment bags.

Lana rubbed the scar on her hip, healed now, but it tingled in the salt air. The tattoo commemorating the date of her wedding anniversary was gone, but it would forever be burned into memory. It was today: August 25.

She could feel the sting of tears in her eyes. If only that was from the salt air, too.

"You okay?" Diane asked. "This is supposed to be fun, remember? Your comeback. You worried about your ex?"

Lana leaned down to the open window. "Location romances are sort of expected. It's lonely on the road. Too much power for a guy like that to turn down. Maybe I was too clingy or too wild or too neglectful, who knows? I'm not saying what he did was right. But if I hadn't just lost the baby, maybe I wouldn't have reacted so strongly."

Diane pulled down her sunglasses and looked Lana in the eye. "You still love him?"

Lana sighed and stood up. "Doesn't everybody?"

She waved as her friend drove off. Then she turned and followed the PA, a film school kid in trendy eyeglasses who could barely keep from tripping over the power cables snaking across the lot. Lana followed her past the production crew in black T-shirts eating an early dinner at a long table, then over to the far left of six doors in the back of the building.

A sweet-faced security guard with arms the size of the entrance columns at Mecca adjusted his high-tech headset. He flipped through his 8x10 glossies and compared the image Bonnie had shot weeks earlier to her face. Lana dipped her shoulder and gave him smile #2, Kiss-me-I'm-gorgeous. He winked and opened the door.

Inside, the swirling mass of humanity was like a tornado. Lana took deep yoga breaths to remain calm in the eye of the storm. A few handlers led her past chatty models at makeup tables. TV stars gave interviews to E! Entertainment reporters in make-shift lounges. Marlene, the stylist from the commercial was waiting in a small tented area with an empty wardrobe rack. She squealed and took Lana's wardrobe bags while introducing the rest of her team of pretty people. It was a bit more cramped than the Oscars, but with the advent of Internet entertainment,

TV, and film had a more level playing field—everyone was treated the same. Lana wondered where, among the flashbulbs and makeup and cases of champagne, was Lucas?

She would know just how to feel if her ex was a gambling asshole or an abusive redneck or homosexual artist. But how was a woman supposed to feel when her ex was known as The World's Sexiest Man?

Chapter 24

DIANE

. . . you feel less alone now than when you were married.

The sight of another note from the landlord taped to the door of Diane's apartment made her fists clench, ready to pound the cheap plaster walls. After an hour in line at the post office shipping Instant Pleasure boxes, all she wanted to do was make some microwave popcorn and watch Lana on TV. What was the point of scoring a rent-controlled apartment if she had to give kickbacks to the borscht-swilling landlord? Diane had run into his wife Natalia, crying in the laundry room last night, and she hadn't noticed her diamond ring on any fingers.

Diane ripped off the notice and read it. The building was going condo. So much for rent control. Was this even legal?

No one was home begging for dinner yet, so she got right on-line to do some research of her own. There was an e-mail from Asshole, that he was taking the kids for dinner at his brother's. So that's where he was crashing these days. Diane had been looking forward to hanging out with her kids. They needed more family time, but oh, well. She wished Asshole would just call her—what if she hadn't gone online? He was afraid she'd say no, and he was right. She wished they had a regular schedule, but any time with their father was good for the kids. Or maybe it wasn't—how the hell was Diane supposed to know? She vented in an e-mail to Bonnie.

Now that the kids were gone for the night, Diane decided to skip the tuna and go out for dinner. She hit Send on Bonnie's message and picked up her purse. When she reached to turn off the computer, she noticed that her e-mail still hadn't posted as sent. Diane put her glasses on and looked closer. *Shit.* She had vented to her entire sales list, consisting of Steve's old insurance clients and the majority of the middle school PTA.

"No, no, *no!*" she muttered, pounding the keyboard to Unsend. But it was too late. Everyone she had ever known or done business with would know her private angst. Screw dinner, what she needed was a glass of wine. Out. She grabbed the mail, put on lipstick, and was halfway out the door when she heard Lana's voice in her head—*Every time you wear a jacket, it raises you a notch above the crowd*—and went back inside to get one.

Diane waited in the cool entrance of Mi Piace, the trattoria close to their old neighborhood. She had been dreaming of their angel hair pomodoro all summer. It was a simple dish, but sometimes the things that appeared simple took the most finesse. How anyone could think that getting divorced was a simple solution was as wrong as a soggy plate of noodles. Unless you didn't have kids, of course, like the cute young couple putting their names on the waiting list. These two had all the time in the world to have drinks before dinner without worrying about the babysitter. And engagements were more fun than simply going steady—there were great parties involved, after all. But for everyone else . . . Diane's growling stomach brought her back.

Diane looked around at the couples and the families and the groups of women, and for a moment wished she wasn't alone. That's why she had robbed herself of the enjoyment of her favorite dish—not because it was too far, or too expensive, but because she was afraid. She didn't want to feel embarrassed or unwanted or pathetic or sad. But right now, she mostly felt hungry. Diane often ate breakfast out alone, and lunch out alone . . . she deserved a good dinner in a nice restaurant. It was about time, wasn't it?

"Are you waiting for someone?" the hostess asked.

Diane counted to three and tried to sound patient. "Nope, just me."

"Do you have a reservation?"

"You don't take reservations for parties of less than four."

"Oh, right." The hostess squinted through the low light of the large Tuscan-style room, then waited for the other young hostess to finish the phone call and jot down the time of her next audition. Diane could hear their loud whispers as they discussed the seating. "The four-top in the corner is clearing, but the server just got stiffed and there's a VIP party due. We need a loser table."

"I beg your pardon," Diane said.

The waitress turned around. "Oh, I'm sorry. That's just an expression. It means 'table for one.'"

Diane knew exactly what it meant. Her fingers clenched around the pile of mail she had brought inside to keep busy, but the other hostess ushered her into the main dining room before she could use it as a weapon. Diane seethed as she followed the cute young wannabe—the very reason Lana made Bonnie take her photos four times—across the hard tile floor. Once Diane inhaled the scent of fresh garlic and warm bread, she relaxed. This ignorant girl was too young to be worth her anger. She might find out how it felt herself, some day. But Diane didn't wish that on anyone. She smiled benevolently, and followed.

They passed tables with a smiling man dipping his calamari into marinara, a young couple pulling apart an eggplant pizza, and a family diving into bountiful bowls of risotto. Diane's mouth watered. She hadn't been here since she moved. She was dying for a decent meal. But the hostess put her at a distant table by the kitchen, where she could hear the waiters yell at the cook. She tried to be positive, but when she sat down, the table wobbled. Diane got up and marched back up to the front.

She didn't come here to be shoved into some depressing back corner. "Excuse me," she said to the hostess, "but if I wanted a view of the kitchen, I would have stayed home."

The hostess looked over Diane's head as a large shadow loomed behind her. She turned to look up at a beautiful black man in a pin-striped suit.

"Is there a problem here?" his booming voice was softened by a French accent.

Diane nearly said no, but for crying out loud, this was her life. Every moment counted, and all she wanted was a damn plate of pasta. "Yes," Diane admitted. "Are you prejudiced against divorced people?"

The man chuckled. "If we were, we wouldn't have much business, now would we?"

"I mean women. You know, single women?"

The man shook her hand in both of his. "No, ma'am. We love women, they just don't seem to dine often by themselves. It's a loss for all of us. I'm Philippe, the manager. Let me see what I can do."

Diane waited contentedly while he conferred with the pretty idiots.

"Unfortunately, there are no tables right now," Philippe said. "I could seat you at the bar."

Diane looked across the room at the empty seats at the granite-topped bar. A baseball game played on the TV screen hanging discreetly in the corner. The sound was turned down, so Diane could probably bear it. Or she could pretend to care about the game, since the cute rough-hewn type watching it might be single. On the other hand, she'd have to be friendly and upbeat when she'd rather relax and read her mail. Maybe she could sit next to the couple a few seats down who had empty shot glasses lined up in front of them. Or she could wait. Thanks to Annette's tale of her wild night of passion, she would never look at a bar stool the same way again.

Philippe, sensing her hesitation, offered, "We're turning the game off in a few minutes for the award show."

Diane perked up. "That would be great. I'm taping it, but

live is more fun." Diane followed Philippe to the bar, checking tables with food along the way. She should look for attractive men, she realized, but she was too hungry. She spied someone eating the pomodoro—bright chunks of tomato flecked with garlic and basil, just the way she remembered it. Philippe seated her by the single man and winked. "Can I get you a glass of wine?"

"Please." She reached for the wine menu, but Philippe stopped her.

"Our new pinot noir is excellent," he said, then directed the bartender to pour her a taste. Diane sipped it. The man knew his wine. She nodded. He signaled the bartender, an older man in a vest, who poured her a glass immediately.

"On the house," Philippe said. "We're thinking of doing a wine tasting event once a month. Would that be something you'd invite your friends to?"

"How do you know I have friends?"

He laughed again. "You don't look lonely."

Diane smiled. He was right. Except . . . "We're not into the singles scene."

"Neither are we. We just like to class the place up with quality people."

He tipped his head and left the bar. Diane ordered her pasta and got out her pile of mail. She shuffled the condo notice behind the unopened envelopes and noticed scribbling on the back. *Miss Taylor, please call.* The cramped cursive ended with a phone number with slashes through the sevens, but no name.

Diane recognized her landlord's phone number. Natalia probably posted the condo notices herself; it had to be from her. She reached to the bottom of her purse, where her phone was buried. Evidently it was buried so deeply, she hadn't heard it over the restaurant music. The screen blinked: *7 messages.*

Diane scrolled down, afraid something had happened to Quinn or Cody, but these numbers did not belong to them. She listened to one of the messages. It was from her former VP of the PTA. She had taken over as president when Diane quit in disgrace during the divorce. Lovely. It wasn't bad enough that

Diane had lost her husband and her house, now the Super-
moms were going to give her hell for it.

Diane braced herself, in case there was just cause for some
real drinking, but the message wasn't angry. The woman was
apologetic, nervous, and ended by suggesting a coffee date.
Diane listened to the next one, a woman she vaguely remembered from Steve's insurance business, who read her rant to
Bonnie and was now doing some ranting of her own. Diane
stared at her phone as the number of messages blinked higher.
First 10, then 11, then it jumped to 14. People had always come
to Diane with their problems, even in the grocery store. She may
have looked like she was in control, but she was really just a control freak. Maybe that's what happened to wives when they had no
life of their own. Diane had a life now, as the poster child for divorce. How ironic. A few months ago, this would have bothered
her. Now she looked at these people as potential customers.

Still, there was something unsettling about it. She flipped
through the mail, hoping for one of the catalogs that had
stuffed the mailbox before she declared bankruptcy. Soon, she
would be able to order from them again. She shuffled through
several bills, then came to a white envelope behind it. The return address read: L.A. County Superior Court. It was better
than any catalog. Diane opened it. Sure enough, it was her official dissolution document. She read the date stamp: August 21.

Diane looked up to see if the world had stopped spinning,
but everything went on as if nothing had changed. Yet something *had* changed. Diane had been divorced for four days, and
she didn't even know it. Her life had split into Before and After
without a pause. The future was officially now. Diane felt her
heart clutch even after all this time.

Then she saw the typed words near the bottom of the front
page: *The petitioner's formal name is restored to: Diane Joyce Taylor.* A
smile spread slowly across Diane's face. Time to celebrate! She
took a sip of wine then gestured for the bartender.

"Something wrong with the pinot?" he asked.

"No, it's fine." She waved her stamped dissolution document.
"But I just got my divorce papers."

His face clouded. "Is that good or bad?"

"Good. Got my name back!"

"Congratulations."

"Thank you! But now I'm in the mood for champagne."

"Champagne it is," the bartender said.

"No, forget it, I already have this."

Philippe was back to check the baseball score. He nodded at the bartender, who popped a cork and poured. Philippe slid the champagne flute in front of the wine and leaned down to look at her squarely in the face. "You should have exactly what you want."

Diane laughed and toasted him. Her nose tickled as she took a sip. The man next to her eating the steaming bowl of penne eyed her. Diane guessed what he was thinking: another difficult woman. Diane sighed and took another sip. She smiled as the bubbles tickled her throat.

The long-haired guy with his arm around his tattooed girlfriend was eyeing her also. That's right, I am the enemy, she thought. Either that or easy prey. Two men with gold necklaces and slick-backed hair glanced at her as they cruised over to the far end. They looked up at the TV. The bartender waited for the final score, then muted the sound and changed the channel to the Emmys.

"So, you're divorced?" The guy next to her pushed his bowl away.

He was not going to ask for her number, she could tell. Which was fine. So what if he was cute? Why would she want to date someone who ate dinner in a bar? Although here she was, doing exactly that.

He shook his head. Uh-oh. She thought about playing the sympathy card and reminding him of the odds: One out of every four women of childbearing age was bleeding from their time of the month. But Diane was already having hot flashes. So she sipped her champagne and waited politely for a venomous lecture on the impossible standards of modern women.

"My sister is getting divorced," he said.

"Oh," Diane said. "Sorry to hear that."

The man nodded. "I want to give her some money, but I'm not sure how my wife will feel about it. I've already been helping her out."

"She's lucky to have you," Diane said. "Your sister, I mean."

"Not my wife?" He cracked up. "She took the boys skiing. I had to work. Rob Johnson." He held his hand out and she shook it. Then he took his wallet out and opened it to photos of Josh and Jason, his sons.

Diane nodded. Turned out she knew his wife, Janet, from Boy Scouts. Bad enough they played the name game with that alliteration, but Janet had one of those personalized decals with stick figures of the family members on the rear window of her Navigator. Now Diane was stuck; she had already ordered dinner. Phillipe had turned on the awards show, and she desperately wanted to watch it, but Rob was still talking. On the screen over his head, she saw a snippet of a nighttime soap opera.

"She hasn't worked since she had the kids."

"Your wife?"

"My sister. The jerk was having an affair for two years and now he's moved in with his hairdresser. Like to kill him."

"Ouch," Diane said. She sipped her champagne. Real life was so much more interesting than soap operas. So randomly visceral. "What did she do—for work, I mean?"

"Lawyer."

"Oh, good," Diane said. "She'll be fine."

He shook his head. "She never practiced. And she can't afford a baby-sitter. I bought her a computer program to learn to do wills and estate planning. I thought she could do that at home."

"What a great idea," Diane said. "I should get a new will. I bet a lot of women need one. She could specialize in divorced people." The guy looked at her and nodded. "There must be some moms she could trade babysitting with. That's what I do."

"That's what you do?"

"No, well, not for money. I do trade baby-sitting, though." Diane dug in her purse for her business card, then thought better of it. As much as she believed in Instant Pleasure, she had

the feeling his sister might be too intimidated to call her. Diane
would have been. She was such a mouse not so long ago. But
here she was, four days free. She grabbed a cocktail napkin and
wrote down her number. "Tell her to call me anytime."

"Are you some kind of divorce expert?"

Diane laughed. "I guess."

Rob looked at the napkin. "I thought you might be. You
seem together."

"It's the jacket," Diane laughed. "But thanks."

He shook his head and pointed at her champagne. "My wife
would never admit to wanting something else; she'd just drink
it."

"Easy to please is an underrated quality."

Rob shrugged. "Makes it hard to know exactly what she wants."

Diane took another sip of champagne. Maybe his wife didn't
know what she wanted. Or maybe the bubbles were going to
Diane's head. The sex toy business was paying the bills these
days, but there was a bigger picture, and Diane was tempted to
paint it. "Tell your sister not to worry. It gets better."

He shrugged as if he wasn't sure how. That was the mystery,
all right. The divorce process had such a steep learning curve,
and once you climbed it that information was useless—except
to someone else.

Diane toyed with her glass. Maybe the sex toy business was
just a small part of what she could do. Plus, there were so many
smart women like Rob's sister in need of part-time work or new
careers entirely, that maybe Diane could string together a net-
work of consultants and businesses to help other women going
through divorce. Diane thought of all the help she and her
friends had shared, with their unofficial club. Not just therapists and lawyers and sex toys to get through the dark days, but
furniture and fashion makeovers and career counseling and . . .
it was definitely time for a party. The idea was making her dizzy.
Or maybe that was the champagne.

Philippe came back and asked how she was doing. "Excellent, thanks. Do you guys cater? I'm having my divorce party
soon. Next week. I just decided."

Philippe eyed the bartender. "We had one of those last week." The bartender pulled a dartboard out from under some table- cloths. When he held it up, the holes in the photograph of the man pinned to the middle of the board made it impossible to identify him. "They left this behind."

Diane shook her head. "Much as I'd like to throw darts at my ex's face, if my kids found out they'd be scarred for life." Rob nodded, visibly relieved. "I want my party to be more of a shower, you know—a coming-out party. For me. A real wing-ding." She lifted her glass to admire the bubbles and spotted Lana on TV. "Oh! Could you turn it up, please?"

People started gathering around and talking about the show. "Oh my God, is that Lacy Turner with Lucas Hatteras?"

"They used to be married, you know."

"She didn't really burn his house down."

Yes, she did, Diane was dying to say. She listened to the chat- ter and admired Lana's guts. She was stunning in an Egyptian slave dress, probably the same one she wore in that clip a few years back when she caught Lucas making out with some extra. Lucas was all smoldering eyes and glistening chest in his Caesar toga as he stepped up to the podium. He turned and offered his arm to help her up. Lana took it, looking dead calm, but Diane could tell she was nervous. She scratched her hip.

Philippe turned the volume up.

"Hi there!" The TV audience went wild. When they quieted, Lana continued. "We're giving out the award for best comeback."

"That would be you, darlin,'" Lucas said.

The crowd behind Diane hushed. There was definitely a siz- zle between the two actors, but that was the tricky thing about chemistry, as Quinn would be the first to tell you. Or Annette. A little too much of this, or not enough of that, and things could blow up without warning.

On-screen, Lana pointed at the TelePrompTer below the camera. "Follow the script, Luke." They read off the names of the nominees.

Then Luke interrupted. "You really want to know who the winner is?"

Lana looked at him, and Diane could see her soften. He really was gorgeous. And he had been doing a bunch of charity work, according to the *People* magazine article. It was a puff piece, sure, but maybe he had changed. Maybe they'd start dating again. The crowd in the bar certainly wanted to know.

Lana nodded. "I do."

The crowd tittered. Diane looked at Rob: even he was riveted. She took a sip of champagne.

"I don't," Lucas said.

Lana blushed. The crowd booed.

Then Lucas dropped to his knee. The camera dollied around behind the podium. Two stagehands in black turtlenecks crept in and pulled the podium aside.

Now it was Lana's turn to look around. "What's going on, Luke?" She was annoyed. Diane recognized the phony smile, but she wasn't so sure that Lucas did.

"There's another comeback that's more important." He put his hand on his bare chest over his heart. "I loved you once and I love you now."

A woman behind Diane scoffed.

The bartender piped up between pours. "Is that guy for real?"

Another woman murmured, "Sounds sincere."

"That's because he's an actor."

"I'd do him."

Diane bit her lips to keep from laughing.

"I'd have his baby."

Diane stopped laughing.

On-screen, Lucas stared with puppy-dog eyes at Lana. "I'm sorry about what happened."

"So am I," Lana admitted. Diane saw the honesty in her eyes and leaned in closer. "You know," Lana continued, "my friend Bonnie named her baby after you." The crowd laughed. Diane smiled. Bonnie was at home, watching this with Henry. After hearing her name on TV, she was probably jumping up and down on her new couch.

Lucas reached between his legs as if he was going to play with himself, but there was a leather pouch hanging from his toga

belt. He untied the drawstring and pulled out a diamond engagement ring identical to the one the celebrity magazines
showed when they first got married. Or maybe it was the exact
same one that Lana, aka Lacy, had thrown at him on the set. He
gazed back up to her eyes. "Will you marry me?"

Lana looked at the stage manager behind her to see if this
was a gag. But clearly, she recognized the ring. Who would forget a five-carat pillow-cut diamond set between a double strand
of pavé diamonds? No one in this bar, that's for sure. They were
all whispering about it.

"Coming through," the waiter shouted. The people moved,
but not much. Diane leaned back to allow the steaming bowl of
angel hair pomodoro be placed in front of her. She thanked
the server and inhaled the perfect blend of garlic and tomatoes
and basil.

On the screen, Lucas was still kneeling and Lana was still
standing there. The bar patrons were making such a hubbub
that Diane missed part of the conversation, but she could replay it at home later. She was savoring her first bite of pasta
when the phone rang with the opening notes of "Satisfaction."
She had to change that ring tone; it was getting old. Shit. Diane
considered letting voice mail pick up. But what if both kids
were bleeding and Asshole forgot the number for 911? Diane
dug in her purse to deal with it as fast as possible so she wouldn't
get escorted out. "Hello?"

"Diane?" The voice was familiar, but there was an echo.

"Lana?" The crowd around Diane shifted away to look at her.
They looked from her to the screen. Diane looked up, too.
Lana stood there with her red cell phone pressed to her ear. "I
mean, Lacy? Are you calling me on live TV?"

Lana pulled off her black-jeweled earring, pressed the
phone back to her ear and nodded. "I need your advice."

Diane's gaze swept around the faces staring at her. The bartender raised his hands. "I'm trying to eat dinner."

On-screen, Lana laughed. "You're not watching?"

"I am." Philippe saw what was happening and pointed at the
bartender. He refilled her champagne and put the bottle on

the bar in front of her. Diane had a feeling Philippe would come in handy in the future, and not just for champagne. "At my favorite restaurant, Mi Piace."

"Mi Piace," Lana said, playing along. "I love that place."

The bar crowd cheered.

Diane laughed. "Anyway, I said I would watch, and I always keep my word."

"Unlike some people," Lana said, throwing a backwards glance at Lucas. Even on the screen you could tell he was starting to sweat. "But he is kind of cute. And he would make nice babies. You think I should marry him?"

It was Diane's turn to sweat. She dabbed at her forehead with a cocktail napkin and got up from the bar stool. She squeezed through the crowd that was watching her and found a quiet corner by the restrooms. Then, she put her hand over the phone and whispered.

On the screen, Lana nodded. She closed the phone, gave it back to the stage manager, and pulled Lucas back to a stand. "May I have the ring, please?" He aimed it for her ring finger, but she turned her hand up. He dropped it into her palm. She picked it up and studied it closely. "This sure brings back memories." The camera zoomed in on the five-carat sparkler, then cut to a reaction shot of Lana. She smiled.

Lucas smiled, too. The camera panned across the smiling TV audience. The bar patrons cleared a path for Diane to get back to her seat. She smiled and put her phone back in her purse. They all leaned forward to hear the television.

Lucas cleared his throat. "So, Lacy—"

"You know what? It's 'Lana.' I don't know where Lacy came from, some agent probably." She made a face at the camera. The TV audience cracked up. They loved her.

On-screen, Lucas nodded. "Okay. So, Lana, love of my life, tell me you'll do me the honor of marrying me again."

Lana smiled sweetly and put the ring on her pointer finger. "May I have a glass of something bubbly, please?"

Diane could tell she was stalling.

A stagehand ran up with a flute splashing like the waves at

Lana's beach house. "Oops, I meant Perrier. I quit drinking a few years back. Went through a rough patch." Lana looked at Lucas and laughed. The stagehand returned with a small bottle of Perrier and a straw. Lana tossed the straw over her bare shoulder and toasted the camera with the bottle.

Diane held up her glass, too.

Lana looked directly at the camera, at the millions of viewers at home, and especially at Diane. "To life, liberty, and the pursuit of happiness!"

"That's a yes?" Lucas said, his arms wide for an embrace.

Lana pursed her puffy lips. "Oh, baby, I don't fucking think so." There was a delayed beep. Lana handed Lucas the bottle and walked off. The crowd could be heard roaring on-screen. The camera switched over to a crowd shot and went to commercial.

The bar patrons broke into chatter and shook their heads at her. Rob signaled for his check. "That was harsh. You told her to dump him? On national TV?"

Diane shook her head and smiled as Philippe turned off the TV. "Nope."

"Then what did you say?"

She took her last sip and set the glass down. "I told her . . . she should have exactly what she wants."

Chapter 25

ANNETTE

*. . . you start giving people the benefit of the doubt.
Women, anyway.*

Annette crossed and recrossed her legs under the conference table as the plantiff gave a halting list of arbitration
demands in heavily accented English. She used to look out this
window and admire the view of the office building across from
theirs while she waited for her turn. The anticipation of reject-
ing every demand was delicious. Not anymore. This woman was
in tears already. Annette wanted to get this bullshit over with.

Still, Annette took notes as if she had never been pierced by
the slings and arrows of a failed relationship. The woman's
lawyer, a night school graduate who provided a package deal
no better than a do-it-yourself divorce kit, patted his client's
hand on the mahogany table. He knew his client was a lost
cause; showing emotion always proved fatal. He got paid either
way.

Annette's client, Mr. Orloff, whose English was far more ad-
vanced than that of his estranged wife, sat smirking with the
confidence that he would keep his real estate holdings in Santa
Monica and send this sexpot back to the old country. Annette
was used to Beverly Hills couples fighting over yachts and vaca-

tion homes, but this guy was a referral from Diane. Annette took him on to appease Diane's anger over Bonnie's case. Annette wasn't sure how this creep knew Diane, but he paid his retainer in cash. Besides, Annette believed people had the right to live as they chose. She was like the ACLU, protecting their rights. But even the ACLU went overboard sometimes.

The woman was crying now. *Quelle surprise.* Annette offered her a tissue, right on cue, but the woman had a lace handkerchief. She looked Annette right in the eye. "He said he loved me."

"I did love you, Natalia."

"Then how can you take back? I leave son with babushka for you! You promise to send for him and now two babies more. It is six years—my good years!" Natalia looked at Annette, the only other woman in the room, as if she'd understand.

And for the first time, Annette did.

Mr. Orloff snorted. "That's bullshit—unless you mean the years before your ass spread."

Annette turned to her client and spoke in her usual quiet manner. But nothing about what she said was usual, not for her. "That's exactly what she means, Mr. Orloff. The wear and tear during childbirth alone could cost millions in reconstructive surgery; the monetary value of full-time motherhood is over a hundred thousand dollars per year. Any work she's done for your business, in addition to the loss of those years at the peak of her greatest earning period, are irreplaceable. And just to clarify, Mr. Orloff: the definition of cliché in the English language means something that happens often enough to be expected."

Annette turned to Natalia. "As for you, ma'am, have you ever heard the American expression, 'He's just not that into you'? How about, 'Get over it'?" Annette saw no flash of recognition, so she tried again. "It's over, hon."

"Hon?" Natalia turned to her lawyer. "What is this 'hon'?"

"Ms. Gold," Natalia's lawyer shook his head.

Natalia figured out what Annette meant and looked directly at her. "What kind of woman are you?"

Annette sat up. Now, *there* was an interesting question. American women never questioned her authority. Annette caught a glimpse of herself in the sliding glass doors. Her hair was collected in a bun today, but not a tidy one, and her Fire lipstick was chewed down to pink embers. She couldn't bear to look at her pencil skirts, so her personal shopper sent over some trousers. They weren't as uncomfortable as she had thought. Annette was not the woman she thought she was. Or used to be. Or wanted to be, for that matter. She used to choose only those battles she could win. Now, she was more interested in choosing battles that she wanted to win. In fact, at this very moment, as her client rolled his eyes at the mother of his children, Annette felt a strong desire to punch him.

She took a sip of coffee instead. She needed to get out of here. They were all looking at her, waiting for her to make the next move. Opposing counsel knew she wouldn't open her mouth. This was a chess game that she was expected to win. The only question was: how fast she could rob this poor woman of her future, not to mention any coin rolls she may have stashed in her pillowcase. This was a lose-lose. Annette put her coffee cup down and looked at her copy of the list. "Plaintiff gets the apartment building on Fourth Street."

Mr. Orloff was startled. Annette had told him there was no need for disclosure if they settled out of court. But she felt a need for disclosure, so she continued. "You can keep the building on Main."

"What building on Main?" Natalia asked.

"The one in Santa Monica. The property in Venice will be liquidated to set up a trust for your children."

The woman was stunned. "Property?" She looked at her lawyer, who shrugged. He had obviously not consulted with her, since he expected to lose. "I miss my son to make better life." She turned to her estranged husband. "I do not get wedding ring and you have buildings?"

"She's making it up, Natalia. You don't understand."

"I understand all but lies."

"This is business, not to worry your pretty head."

Natalia looked at Annette. "I am doctor in Russia. Not pretty head."

Annette put her hand up and turned toward Mr. Orloff. "Is it true that you promised to take care of her 'until death do you part'?"

"Sure. Everybody says that."

Natalia crossed her arms. "You say even after you sleeping with three ten." She turned to Annette. "He say it is just sex, like that is good thing."

The sleazeball put his feet up on the table. "You want me back."

"*Nyet.*"

Annette pushed his feet off the table and turned to Natalia. "What do you want?"

"Excuse me," opposing counsel said. "Hate to interrupt the girl talk . . ."

Annette and Natalia locked eyes at the condescending remark. Annette sat up straight and turned to Natalia's lousy lawyer. "No worries, Bob. From where I sit, it looks like those terms were binding." She turned to her client and stared at his cheap shoes resting on her firm's conference table. "Mr. Orloff, your wife could sue you for breach of contract. Possibly international fraud. And when you are divorced she can testify against you should any zoning laws be compromised in your real estate holdings."

Mr. Orloff put his feet down. "You gotta be kidding me."

Annette looked across the table at her opposing counsel. "Do I kid, Bob?"

"Not that I know of," Bob replied.

Natalia looked between them, confused.

"Far as I know, she's never lost a case." Bob patted Natalia's knee.

She slapped him.

Annette smiled. "I think we're done here."

Mr. Orloff jumped to a stand. "Whose lawyer are you?"

"That's an excellent question, Mr. Orloff. I find it difficult to believe that Diane Taylor would give you my number, especially since I saw her address among your assets—and I know just how happy she is with the accommodations. Therefore, you are here under false pretenses. Which makes me your wife's lawyer by default."

"Is true," Natalia said. "Ms. Taylor gave me number. You cost much money." She glared at her soon-to-be ex. "But I don't want building."

"You're going back?"

"No. I get my son here. I don't want winter."

Annette didn't want winter, either. She hated cold weather. Bothered her knee. She never would have been happy in Aspen. Her mind ratcheted back to the conversation with Paul Chambers. How could she have been willing to put up with early arthritis for a man? A man who didn't have time for her? Or her daughter?

With a flash, she understood why the end of her affair with Paul Chambers had been so devastating. She had been unhappy in her marriage, so the end of that was a manageable loss. With Paul, however, she had a view of the life she always wanted. Annette didn't want to be *in* Paul's life. She wanted to *have* his life. She didn't need a man to make her life complete; she could be her own prince, make her own dreams come true. She wanted to work for herself, not for the partners, nor for her ex-husband. She wanted to travel for fun, to do work that mattered, and most of all, to have her own view.

The other lawyer cleared his throat, snapping Annette back to the present. Natalia looked pleased. "Then it's agreed," Annette said. "And now, if you'll excuse me . . ." She shook Mr. Orloff's limp hand, wished him luck, and went to clean out her desk.

It took less than five minutes for Grant, the senior partner, to appear in her doorway. "What's up, Gold, you hormonal?"

"Of course I'm hormonal, Grant; I'm a woman." She popped

a Kiss in her mouth and offered him one before tossing the bag in her box.

He shook his head. "You know what I mean. Can't you just buy a little red sports car like everyone else?"

"Grant, it's too cold in this office."

"You can't quit."

Annette put her hands on her hips and savored the last lump of chocolate melting on her tongue. "Then fire me, Grant. I don't care what rich people do with their money. As long as they don't have children."

"What's in it for me?"

Annette opened her filing cabinet and waved the file pertaining to her partner's niece. "Sex. Your niece will get what she deserves from her divorce and your wife will be incredibly grateful."

Grant shook his head. "How so?"

"I'm going into collaborative law. Once your niece and her ex are sitting in the same room with an accountant, a financial planner, and a family therapist all working together, she's bound to get a more realistic support plan. Annette raised the blinds to get a good look at the rest of the files in the drawer. Nothing she wanted. She shut the drawer.

There was a commotion down the hall. A familiar redhead appeared in the doorway, and Grant hugged her as if she were an old friend.

"Lana?"

Lana waved and pulled free of Grant's bear hug. Annette held the door open so she could scurry in. "Be right there," Lana called, as Annette shut the door behind her. Lana plopped down in the chair across from Annette's desk. "Thank you! Grant's handling my movie contract, so he thinks we're BFF. I am so sick of kissing strangers, blech."

Annette pressed the intercom. "Nigel, bring me a Perrier for Ms. Lerner."

Nigel's voice came on the intercom. "We have Fiji, Voss, and Blue Italy. No Perrier."

Lana shook her head but Annette ignored her. "Find some,

Nigel." Annette sat on the edge of her desk for the very last time. "How are you liking the beach house?"

"What's not to like?" Lana got out her checkbook. "I know I owe you money; I was stalling until I can figure out how to write it off. Think Diane's divorce party would count as publicity?" She pulled a Mecca pen out of her leather handbag.

"Depends who you invite." Annette leaned forward and put her hand out to block Lana from writing. "But forget the check, Lana. There's been a change of plans. If your loft is still available, I'd like to make an offer."

Lana put her checkbook away and tipped her head at the box. "New office?"

"New home. I keep reading about the new developments downtown—restaurants and theaters and parks—and I'd rather have a view overlooking the city than one of my Brentwood neighbors scooping up Fifi's poop. The place is too big for me, anyway. You don't have a cat, do you?"

"Only a stray. Sort of a rental, like everything else there. Think he sleeps in the playground across the street."

Annette nodded and put her picture of Morgan in the box. Nigel came in and gave Lana a small bottle of Perrier. He started to explain where he got it. A few months ago, Annette would have listened patiently but done what she wanted anyway. Passive-aggressive, she realized. Now the passive part was gone. And yet, so was the aggressive. So, Annette merely pointed him out. And shut the door.

Lana's diamond ring sparkled in the sunlight through the window as she unscrewed the top of the Perrier bottle. The reflection danced across the door as if from a disco ball. She took a slug of water. "Would you take the loft as payment on the beach house?"

"Down payment, maybe." Annette pulled her eyes from the glittering door. But I think we can work something out."

"Excellent! I'll have my people call your people." Lana laughed. "I love saying that. Seriously, I'll call my agent today so I can bring the deed to Diane's divorce party."

Annette shook her head. "I'm not going. We're not friends."

There was a knock on the door.

Lana shook her head and stood up. "You two have more in common than you think." She put the Perrier on Annette's desk and paused before leaving. "Besides, once you're in the club, membership is for life."

Chapter 26

BONNIE

. . . you are ready to fall in love again. Whatever that means.

The shutters closed as Bonnie walked Lucas slowly past Cathy's house. She was tempted to hoist up her son and hurry past, but he was a slow and steady walker and she refused to be intimidated. Bonnie had just picked the kids up from Diane's and she had promised them once around the block before dinner. Besides, Hayley was having way too much fun circling them on her tricycle to be rushed.

Norah Jones crooned from a car stereo speeding up behind them. "Slow down!" Bonnie shouted. She looked to see if it was Kyle, who had just started classes at UCLA. Bonnie wanted to know if he had found a new girlfriend yet, so Quinn could start high school in peace. This was a yellow Porsche, way beyond Kyle's means. A turquoise sun hat flew off the driver and rolled across the street toward her.

The Porsche backed up. The silver-haired women sitting inside were laughing. The passenger climbed out and yanked her bathing suit cover-up farther down her backside. She hurried to retrieve the hat as an old Jeep turned down the street headed toward her. "Sorry about that," the woman said. She might have been sorry for speeding, Bonnie thought, but she looked pretty happy. Bonnie gave her the hat and automatically checked her hand: no ring. "What pretty pearls," she added. She pulled her hat back on, ran back to the convertible, wedged the beach chairs down in the cramped space behind the leather seats, and climbed back in.

Bonnie rubbed her fingers along the pearl necklace that had become her trademark. Those women were perfect candidates for a boudoir portrait. Or a new line—what was it Whitney had called them? The Goddess Group. Bonnie needed to start carrying business cards. She set Lucas on her hip and called to Hayley.

Henry parked on the street and got out of his Jeep with a pink bakery box. He put his keys in the pocket of his plaid Bermuda shorts and stopped to look at the picket fence. Bonnie had painted it with blue flowers and green vines as if morning glories were growing on it. "Didn't that used to be white?" he asked.

"It needed work," Bonnie said. "C'mon, Hayley, looks like we're having éclairs." Hayley pedaled faster.

Henry was humming when they reached the door. Bonnie had never known anyone who hummed so much. It was a happy sound, like the gurgles when Lucas woke up, but she still couldn't recognize a tune. If that was his greatest fault, so be it.

The smell of chocolate wafted into the front hall as they entered. Bonnie went to the kitchen and covered her cooling trays of chocolate buckeyes. Henry picked Hayley up, flew her into the kitchen, and swung her around like an airplane until she giggled so hard that Bonnie was afraid she might choke. Henry put her down and leaned over Lucas's head to give Bonnie a kiss. Bonnie put her son down and let her lips linger until he pulled away.

"Wow," he said. "Happy Anniversary."

She giggled and crouched down to get out the Tupperware. Baking pans rattled and crashed as she pulled out the plastic containers. "One whole month, is it? Time flies."

"So can we. Want to go tomorrow?"

"That would be great, except I need all morning to get ready for Diane's party. Don't you?" He popped a buckeye in his mouth, then helped her make room on the counter for the containers.

"No, the catering department will take care of her order. I just hope I can get off work in time to pick up my favorite girl."

"Woman. Favorite woman."

"Yes, of course. You are very womanly, but you are still my girl." He gave her a squeeze. "Do I need to wear a tie tomorrow? Say no."

"No," Bonnie said. "It's a beach party. But you can't wear that dorky swimsuit with the airplanes on it, either."

Henry kissed her, then took Lucas from her arms. He carried him like an airplane into the TV room and set him in the playpen. Bonnie played Lucas's favorite dinosaur DVD on the large monitor she had bought to screen her digital proofs. Then she settled Hayley with a coloring book near the playpen. Finally she led Henry back to the living room, where they could see through the open doorway and keep an eye on the children.

The Great Room was now divided into two: this room was now a plush sitting room with deep couches and armchairs around the coffee table from Mecca. Bonnie had replaced all the wooden knobs with flower-shaped glass pulls that matched the antique lamp. There was even a small stereo to help her clients relax before they had their pictures taken. When Quinn came over to babysit and saw the new décor for the first time, she told Bonnie that no man would ever dare enter such a girlie place. Obviously, Quinn had a lot of growing up to do.

Bonnie turned a violin concerto on low so she could still hear the kids in the other room. Then she pulled Henry down next to her.

Henry lifted the pearl necklace to kiss Bonnie's neck. Then he kissed her lips. She sat still to enjoy the feeling and lost herself in the feathery touch. She closed her eyes and murmured, "Are you this good naked?"

He laughed. They were way beyond the three-date rule, but he hadn't so much as unbuckled his belt. He was so different from Buck, whose handprint she still felt on the back of her neck. Sometimes Bonnie wasn't sure if she loved Henry or if she loved the way he loved her, but it was fun finding out. He was pretty lovable, no doubt about that.

She felt herself dip beneath consciousness and slipped her tongue in his mouth. He sucked on it for the slightest of moments until she woke up and pulled her tongue back out. "I'm sorry. I don't mean to tease you."

He pushed her bangs back toward her ponytail. "You're not. I like to kiss you."

"Oh, no. Are you gay?"

Henry laughed.

"I'm serious. One of my friends was married to a gay man, even had a kid with him."

"No. I like women. Can't you tell?"

"Yes, but how can you, you know . . ." She put her hand on his thigh. ". . . be so patient?"

He shrugged. "I want you to be comfortable."

"That's not what I mean." Now, she was worried. "Is twenty-eight past the age of caring?"

Henry put his hand on hers and gave it a squeeze. "There is no age past caring," he assured her.

Whew. Bonnie swung her feet in glee. Her sandal flew off, so she got down to find it. When she looked under the couch, she found a box of Instant Pleasure samples that Diane forgot after the party. That gave Bonnie an idea. "Do you, you know, take care of business before you come over?"

Henry pretended not to have heard her. "Is that Itzhak Perlman on violin?"

Bonnie took that as a yes, screamed, then clapped her hand over her mouth.

Hayley heard her and came running in. "Mommy, are you okay?"

"Yes, baby, thank you. Let's see what's for dinner, okay?" She took Hayley's hand and walked her to the kitchen. So he was normal, that was good. But he was nice all the time; it was spooky. She kept waiting for him to yell at her. At least he got impatient last week when he reserved air time and they still had to wait for takeoff. She called back to him. "So what do you want for dinner? I have hot dogs, or hot dogs, or maybe some hot dogs. I forgot to ask you to bring something."

He came in the kitchen. "Let's go out."

"I don't have a babysitter. Quinn had the kids all day and she's working at the party tomorrow, too."

"I meant out with the kids. You do need to find someone else, Bon. It's Labor Day weekend; school starts next week and Quinn won't be around. It's dangerous to get dependent on one person."

Bonnie nodded. No one had to tell her that.

"Let's just pack up the kids and go. I'm starved."

"How about an éclair appetizer?" Bonnie got the bakery box. He put his hand on it. "You'll ruin your appetite."

"We can share." She moved his soft hand and opened the box. There was another box inside, but it wasn't pink. It was small, black, and velvet. Bonnie looked up at Henry.

He grinned, less happy than bemused. "I was going to wait, but . . ."

Bonnie shut the bakery box quickly. "Can you excuse me for a minute?" She ran down the hall toward the bedroom. She could feel his eyes on her back and hoped he wasn't angry. He had every right to expect a big reaction, but she had no idea how to react. She had to talk to Diane. She saw the cat curled up on the bed, but where was the phone? She moved the cat and threw off the covers, then found the phone on her hope chest. She pounded the keypad, imagining that tedious Rolling Stones song blaring wherever Diane was at this moment.

"Diane Taylor."

Bonnie ignored the pride in Diane's voice—she had more urgent business. "Help! I think Henry's going to propose."

"You're not even divorced yet."

"I hope he wants a long engagement. He needs to meet my dad. Do you think I should check out that marriage insurance?"

"Bonnie, you don't even know who you are, yet."

Bonnie lay on the bed and stared at the ceiling. "I do when I'm with him. I'm me—but happy. I don't have to try."

Diane was quiet for a moment. "You don't need your panties to make you feel special."

Bonnie nodded until she found her voice. "And he's good for the kids."

"But he's not for the kids, Bon. You haven't had sex yet, right? What if he doesn't know what he's doing?"

Bonnie rolled over to her belly. "I said he hasn't unzipped his pants. I never said anything about mine."

Diane laughed. "So, he knows what he's doing. Still . . ."

"Too soon, I know." Bonnie got up and leaned out her bedroom door but didn't see him. She whispered anyway. "But what if I lose him?" The cat jumped back up beside her and nestled next to her side. She petted him.

"Bonnie, if you lose him because you won't make a snap decision about your life and the future of your children, then maybe he's not 'the one.'"

"You still believe in 'the one'?" She heard Diane sigh.

"I don't mean the only one. I mean the right one. There's probably more than one that could be right. So, no need to rush."

Bonnie nodded. "Thanks, Diane. It's just, you know, when someone wants you, it's pretty hard to resist."

Diane laughed. "It's what you want that's important, Bonnie. You deserve the best."

"Okay, now I'm confused again. What if he's the best? Do I miss out 'cause of bad timing?"

Henry's voice called down the hall toward her. "Bonnie? Someone's at the door."

"Gotta go. Thanks for being there." She hung up and glanced in the mirror. She tried to smooth her expression as if she didn't feel tortured inside. How did Lana do it? Bonnie could never be an actress. She hurried back down the hall to where Henry was holding Lucas.

"You okay?" he asked.

She nodded. It wasn't a lie if you didn't say the words out loud, right? This time, she heard the knock. Bonnie kissed Lucas's soft cheek and hurried past. She put her hand on the doorknob and prayed Buck wasn't on the other side.

He wasn't. It was Cathy, her neighbor and former friend. "Can I talk to you?"

"Not now, Cathy." She started to close the door.

"Hi, Mrs. Amsterdam!" Henry called from behind her. Lucas was nibbling on the buckeye in Henry's hand. Bonnie motioned for Henry to go back in the other room.

"Henry, is that you?" Cathy looked confused.

"He's, um, making a home delivery. No biggie." Bonnie felt horrible at the lie. What was she hiding? "Actually, we're dating." *More than dating*, she thought, but she wasn't sure how else to describe it.

Cathy stood there a moment and nodded in understanding. Then she burst into tears.

Bonnie had no idea what was wrong. She was tempted to say the same thing she said to her kids: use your words. She called to Henry. "Could you put the buckeyes away so the kids can't get them, please? They can have frozen peas as a snack." Henry made a face. "They love them, don't worry—and it's good for teething." She blew him a kiss. He nodded and disappeared.

"I don't mean to intrude when you have company." Cathy wiped her eyes. They flashed, and Bonnie could see the accusation in them. "You have a lot of company these days."

Bonnie sighed. "It's business, Cathy. I'm the same person I was back before you stopped talking to me." As soon as she said it, Bonnie realized it wasn't true. Bonnie wasn't the same person. The old Bonnie would never have asked someone else to check on the kids—she would have done it herself. She usually did everything herself. She wasn't a control freak like Diane or Annette, but she never wanted to inconvenience anyone. Now, she didn't care. She appreciated the help. It was a small but important difference.

"I was afraid," Cathy said.

"Of me?"

"No," Cathy said. She smoothed her sleeveless blouse down over the elastic waist of her khaki skirt. "But you're driving a convertible and you have all these people coming and going."

"Yup, it's just one big party here." She opened the door a little wider. The cat was back, meowing at her feet. Bonnie picked her up to keep her from escaping outside. "In or out?"

Cathy looked behind her as if to see if anyone on the street was watching her go inside the harlot's house. Then she sniffed the chocolate and came inside. Bonnie led her through the living room where she and Henry had been sitting and opened the door in the new wall so Cathy could take a look. A burgundy satin chaise longue was centered in the middle of a few spotlights. "A photography studio?"

Bonnie nodded. "The men were mostly carpenters and craftsmen working after hours. I couldn't afford the larger companies, so they didn't have company trucks. But now, they have beautiful pictures of their wives and girlfriends." Some of them, anyway. The others were amazingly generous with discounts. Amazing what a friendly smile could accomplish—with lip gloss, of course. Like Diane said, the root word of feminist is feminine.

Bonnie led her neighbor to the sitting room and showed her the new album on the coffee table. Cathy sat down on the couch and flipped through the sleek silver book of boudoir portraits. "Is our neighborhood zoned for business?"

Bonnie slammed the album shut. Enough already. "Did you want something, Cathy? Because I have a dinner date."

Bonnie was anxious to get on with her own situation, but she couldn't kick Cathy out when the woman was clearly in pain. She took a deep breath and sat down next to her. "I'm sorry if I seem rude, Cathy, but . . . it really hurt when you dropped me. If you want to be friends, I'm willing. But I don't need anyone judging me. I do plenty of that myself." Bonnie looked sideways at her old friend. "You have no idea what goes on behind closed doors. Or a white picket fence."

Cathy nodded. "The fence looks nice, by the way." She looked at Bonnie. "I just thought you and Buck were good together, you know. You seemed happy at our parties."

"You have nice parties," Bonnie said. "I miss them."

Cathy shrugged. "Sometimes I think we have parties just so we don't have to talk to each other." She twisted her wedding band around her thick finger. "But if you could split up, so could anybody. Including me."

Bonnie patted Cathy's back. "Don't give up." Now what? Bonnie hesitated, then pulled the Instant Pleasure box that Diane had left behind. She fished out a bottle of massage oil and a scented candle. "I keep hearing what a difference a warm touch can make."

"Didn't work for you, though."

Bonnie shook her head. Buck didn't like to be touched. Unless, of course, she "meant" it. She pushed the thought out of her mind and smiled appreciatively at Henry.

Cathy shrugged. "I thought you'd say go for it. Give me the name of a lawyer."

Bonnie put her hand on Cathy's arm. "I'd give you other names first. Like the name of my therapist. If you really love your husband, get help. Figure out what you want to do for the rest of your life."

"Is that what you did?"

Bonnie shook her head. "I'm a work in progress." Henry was now standing in the hallway, pretending to straighten the portraits of Hayley and Lucas while he eavesdropped. Bonnie looked up at him.

Cathy followed her gaze. "What you are is very lucky. I've seen that young man work his way up from bag boy. Could be coasting on his family's airport business like his brothers, but no. He's a keeper, that one." She got up.

Bonnie led Cathy out. Hayley ran out and strangled Cathy's knees, nearly tripping her. "Can we go swimming?"

"Sure, honey, how's my girl?" Cathy turned to Bonnie. "I miss this little cutie-pie. Let me know if you need a sitter sometime."

"How about tonight?" Henry called.

Bonnie shushed him. "You might regret that offer," she told Cathy. She gave her a little hug, said goodnight, and closed the door. When she turned around, Henry was waiting on the couch with a big hug and that little velvet box.

Bonnie sat next to him. "You are such a troublemaker. And yet, one of your most devoted customers claims I'm lucky."

"I'm the lucky one."

Bonnie kissed his cheek. "Just how lucky are you?"

He put the box in her hand. "Guess that's up to you."

Bonnie looked from him down to the box in his hand. She was dying to call Diane back, but just knowing that help was available gave her the strength to do this herself. "Henry, we barely know each other."

He shrugged. "The more I know you, the more I love you. And I know myself. I know what I want. And unless I mess up somehow, I intend to get it." He lifted the velvet box closer to her face. "Don't you want to open it?"

Bonnie shook her head. She knew his family had money; whatever was in that box was no bitty little thing. "I'm scared."

"Fair enough. It is scary."

"Everything is scary."

"Doesn't have to be." He put his arm around her.

Bonnie felt so fidgety, she sat on her hands. She had no idea what to do. Henry followed and cleared his throat and wiggled the box. "Dunno about you, but I'm so hungry I could eat this box. You going to open it or not?"

"You're not going to get down on one knee?"

A smile flickered around Henry's mouth. "Why would I do that?"

"You grew up with airplanes, right? Ever heard of the rule of wing walking?"

"Sure: don't jump off one airplane until you have firm grip of another." He blew on his knuckles and rubbed them against his skinny chest, pleased with himself.

"Exactly." Bonnie kissed him. "But I need to take that leap. Free fall. See where I land all by myself."

Henry looked at her for a long moment. He ran his hand through his unruly hair and grinned. "Don't you want to open it, just to see? Please?"

Bonnie counted to three and opened the lid. She covered her mouth and caught her breath. Never had she seen anything so beautiful.

Chapter 27

DIANE

. . . you have no idea what will happen, but you can't wait to find out.

Diane got out of the car, looked up at the back of Lana's beach house, and screamed. Quinn yanked Cody past her around to the beach side to avoid having anyone—from Lana's Hollywood friends to the valet parking attendants—think they were related. Diane didn't care. She found her phone in her beach bag and took a picture of the banner strung across the double garage: WELCOME TO CLUB DIVORCE.

Silver and white balloons tied to the balcony railing danced in the ocean breeze. A five-piece salsa group played barefoot in the sand, but the only dancer so far was Lana, who was being trailed by a hired photographer.

Lana danced over and gave Diane a hug. Then she shifted the skirt on her custom-made swimsuit to cover the scar on her hip, put her arm around Diane, and posed. The camera light flashed. Diane laughed. Lana would single-handedly bring back skirted swimsuits à la the 1950s. By spring, even Quinn would be begging for one. The average woman would end up looking like the ballerina hippos in *Fantasia*.

"Come on in," Lana called. She shooed the photographer away and dragged Diane up the newly painted stairs and through the sliding glass doors. Inside, all the furniture had been cleared out to make room for the bar and dance floor. A few early guests were already sampling chocolate buckeyes at the snack table. Others were perusing the booths lining the perimeter, where brightly lettered signs announced products and services. Lana led Diane over to a long table by the back entrance. Several large gifts filled one end; a champagne bucket was filling up with raffle tickets on the other. The former bimbo slave girl, now in paid servitude as Lana's assistant, wore a mini–wedding dress and broken handcuffs as she greeted each guest. Lana snatched one of the hot-pink membership cards that Diane had ordered. Diane read the fancy script with the words *Club Divorce* above the smaller print: *You've paid your dues . . . and then some.*

"Good idea to laminate these," Diane said. "But I'm not sure about your assistant's handcuffs. We are not anti-marriage."

"Lighten up, Diane. Look." Lana pointed to a mural-sized signup sheet for the Club Divorce mailing list, which already listed 122 e-mail addresses. A couple with matching wedding bands laughed as they signed up.

Lana nodded. "Everyone likes discounts."

"And free samples. Want a drink?" She pointed to Philippe, dapper in a white suit, who was setting out wine courtesy of Mi Piace. He'd become Diane's first official club sponsor. The cash bar would underwrite her newly redesigned Web site, which offered resources for both women and men who needed information about divorce. Next to him at a buffet table, Bonnie was lining up rows of buckeyes on a silver tray. Diane looked for a telltale sparkle on her hand, but didn't see anything. She didn't see Henry, either. Bonnie didn't seem bothered, though, so she must have made the right decision.

Diane looked at the end of the table and gasped at the five-tier wedding cake. It was as elegant as the wedding cakes on *Top Chef,* with bride and groom figurines on the top. Except that on this cake, the groom's head was missing. Diane turned to Lana but she was distracted by the diamond ring she'd taken back

from Lucas at the awards show. It was so massive that it threw
sparkles across the walls and floor of the house.

"All you said was no dartboards or shot glasses," Lana said.
"But the club needs to be fun, Diane. Isn't that the point? That
it ain't the end of the world?"

"No, I like it. But I was just kidding when—"

Lana interrupted. "Check out Natalia." She pointed to the
Instant Pleasure booth in the far corner, where the Russian
beauty was barely contained in a red Merry Widow corset with
black garters and fishnet stockings.

Diane glanced down at her modest tank top and skirt. "Who
needs an MBA when you look like that?" Diane congratulated
herself on selling the business to her landlord's soon-to-be ex.
Then she scanned the feather dusters and lotions on display to
be sure there was nothing inappropriate for the half dozen
children running about.

"Don't worry, she's a doctor," Lana said, "I swear."

Diane shrugged and checked out Bonnie's booth next door.
The sign was a freakishly large portrait of Lana in her white
leather minidress and long pearls between her teeth. Diane
turned to Lana. "Are you raffling off that picture or a photo
session?"

"Whatever it takes, baby. The spa and the travel agency in the
mall near Mecca are interested, too. You're the one who said
Club Divorce should be like the AAA, helping when there's an
emergency and providing discounts wherever you go."

Diane wasn't so sure. "I know, but people shouldn't get re-
wards for being divorced. That's not the point."

"Of course not," Lana said. "But what's wrong with getting a
break to soften the blow? Same principle as insurance. You're
the expert there, right?"

"There's always a risk with love, Lana, you know that. It's a
leap of faith. We may have better luck with corporate sponsors,
but I need to talk to a lawyer about it. Speaking of which,
where's Annette?"

"Haven't seen her."

Diane swore under her breath. "No surprise."

"Diane, you're the one being a bitch."

Diane looked at Lana. "So she had her heart broken, big whoop. We all have."

"That's the beauty of it, don't you think?" Lana toyed with her diamond ring.

Diane grabbed Lana's hand for a closer look. "Why do you want a million-dollar memory, if it hurts so much?"

Lana brightened. "Security. Thanks in part to this ring, I'm going to own this place free and clear."

Diane let go of Lana's hand. "Annette's going to let you pay her with the ring? That doesn't mean she's not a bitch. It's just real estate."

"Sure, but real estate isn't just about money." Lana adjusted her cleavage. "Forget business for now. It's your party, Ms. Taylor. Let's have some fun."

As Lana descended to the beach to entertain the guests who had gathered to dance on the sand, she inflated to her celebrity persona. The paparazzi went crazy, jostling each other for a clear shot. Security guards kept them behind ropes on the side of the property. Even a few of the surfers lining the break had cameras raised.

Behind them, the Pacific Ocean sparkled in the late sun. White triangles of sailboats lined the horizon. Half a dozen private yachts were anchored toward the Paradise Cove pier. Diane sighed. It sure was gorgeous here, no doubt about that.

Philippe joined her at the railing and offered her a glass with a taste of chilled wine. "You look thirsty. Pinot grigio?"

Diane accepted it and took a sip. "Yum. So, about that monthly wine tasting event?"

He chuckled. "I'll give you half price for members if you give me reduced rates for my online ad."

Diane laughed. "Don't tell me you didn't book every night until Christmas after my plug on the awards show."

Philippe laughed. Diane watched a surfer catch a huge wave. He reminded her of Kyle. She looked over to see if Quinn caught it, but she and several of her friends were busy building sand castles with youngsters in a shallow area patrolled by a private lifeguard. Quinn loved bossing kids around and she was saving money to buy car insurance for when she inherited the Volvo. The babysitting business was perfect for her. She even had business cards.

Diane pointed her daughter out to Philippe just as Quinn ogled one of the wake boarders, one with his skull-printed surf trunks slung low across his muscular hips. So she wasn't entirely immune. Philippe raised his eyebrows at Diane. "I'm not paying for a wedding until she's forty."

"They say forty is the new thirty," Philippe said.

"Great, then maybe fifty will be the new forty." Diane toasted Philippe and laughed. She looked back out at the surfers. "Maybe I'll buy a surfboard."

He raised his glass. She toasted it with hers, downed her wine, and noticed her hand. The white line from her wedding ring was completely gone, and so was her tan.

Philippe reached for her empty glass. "Get some sun," he said. "You're working too hard."

Diane smiled, put on her floppy hat, and walked down the stairs to the beach. In the roped-off playground area, Cody was helping Hayley make a giant sand castle with seaweed turrets, something his dad taught him. They were good kids. She wished they didn't have to start at new schools on Tuesday, but they'd ridden this summer like a rogue wave; they'd land on solid ground whether she bought the condo or not.

Lana posed by the security guard. She was a wonderful hostess, flashing that bright pink Club Divorce membership card to everyone. She waved to someone at the Spanish adobe next door. On the sand, handsome model types were playing volleyball, watched closely by a group of PTA moms, who had set up camp under Lana's rented blue umbrellas. They couldn't all be divorced, but they all knew someone who was. This could be the end of that scarlet letter D.

Diane wished Steve were here to see all this. She nearly tripped over a pile of seaweed when she realized what she had thought. If he were here, this wouldn't be happening. But after all those years, he was family. She did want the best for him. Just not in any way related to her.

Diane stepped to the edge of the water, wishing she'd brought her swimsuit. Maybe her bra and panties would do. They were red: power panties. Her toenails were painted to match. She wiggled her toes in the sinking sand and gazed out at the ocean. A dog barked. Diane looked up, surprised to see Ben Hunter, her old B-school friend and almost lover, holding his collie by the leash. Even unshaven, wearing a plaid fishing hat and baggy shorts, he was still cute. "Hey! Fancy meeting you here. Or did you hear there was free food?"

"I was just walking my dog; I walk him here a lot." He scratched his dog behind the ears.

"You forget I was married to a gambler. I know a 'tell' when I see one."

"You mean because I can't look you in the eye?"

She lifted his dark aviators and smiled. Why did men have the longest eyelashes? "Yup."

He met her eyes. "Okay, I'd like to walk my dog here a lot. Maybe with you and your dog. Scoot, right?"

"Scout," Diane corrected. "You missed a good concert, by the way."

Ben sighed. "Look, I was an idiot about the sex toys."

"Intimacy aids," Diane corrected.

Ben nodded and smiled. "I'm sorry. I'm a branding guy; I know the shortcuts. In real life, I don't even like instant tea. So Instant Pleasure . . ."

"No worries," Diane said. "Someone insecure about his masculinity would naturally be threatened by a few AA batteries."

"No, that part I'd be interested in seeing," he laughed. "But I'd like to get to know you for more than an instant. Beyond the business."

"I sold that business. I'm all-divorce all-the-time now."

"Sounds depressing." Ben said. The dog was pulling on his leash, so Ben crouched down to pet him.

"Nope. Liberating."

"You playing hard to get?"

Diane laughed. "No. I *am* hard to get." She crouched down to pet his dog, too. She wasn't sure if he was speaking in generalities, or if he wanted a shot. She didn't have an answer in either case. Of course she wanted someone to *want* to marry her someday. She just didn't know if she would ever do it. She loved being single. But it was always fun to fall in love. Oh hell, she was getting a stomachache just from thinking about it.

"Shall we make a deal?" Ben asked. "Take it out in trade?"

"You're so full of it." Diane kicked water at him.

He backed away. "I meant dinner!" His dog pulled loose and ran off barking. "I'll call you," he shouted as he staggered between sunbathers, trying to capture the loose leash trailing between them on the sand.

Diane laughed. She would do dinner, as long as it was a slab of fish on the grill after a day of surfing. Maybe in Hawaii. She was itching to travel. Maybe she could open clubs all over the world. Starting with Paris.

"Hey, Mom!" Cody called.

Diane looked up. A curly-topped teenager tossed a circular wooden disc at the water's edge and helped Cody hop on for a ride. When he waved at Diane, she was momentarily confused. Then Quinn appeared at her side and Diane laughed out loud. Of course he'd be waving to a cute girl in a bikini instead of her middle-aged mom. And thank goodness. "Hey."

Quinn pointed at Ben, who was still chasing his collie. "Who's the dog, dude?"

"Nobody. Who's the wake boarder?"

"Nobody."

"Sure, teenagers always help out random little brothers." Diane reached toward her daughter's top to pull it up a smidge.

Quinn swatted her hand away and scanned the waves full of surfers. "So many men, so little time."

"That's where you're wrong, sweetie. We've got all the time in the world."

"Diane!" Bonnie called from the balcony. Diane waved up to her, then turned to Quinn. "See ya."

"Wouldn't want to be ya."

"So original." Diane yanked Quinn's bikini top up quickly, then ran for the stairs.

Halfway there, she heard Quinn's voice. "Nana called!"

Diane stopped and turned around. "When?"

"Yesterday. Sorry."

Diane nodded, almost grateful that some things never changed. She climbed the stairs, squeezed through the guests on the balcony, and took Bonnie's bare hand. "What's the verdict? Is Henry gone for good?"

"Not a chance," a low voice said behind her. Henry leaned in and kissed Bonnie's neck. "Sorry I'm late," he whispered to her.

Bonnie touched his cheek. She took the small velvet box out of her pocket and held it up for Diane. "I wanted you to see it first."

Diane took a deep breath and nodded. She couldn't help but pinch her own naked ring finger.

Bonnie opened the box slowly. Something sparkled in the streaming sunlight. It was a pin: gold wings with a tiny diamond in the center. Bonnie clasped Henry's hand in hers. "He's going to teach me to fly."

"You're flying already, Bon," Diane said. Smiling.

"No, I'm not!" Bonnie blushed and looked at her pointedly. "But he's certified. He has his own equipment."

Diane laughed. "I bet it's huge."

"It's a Cessna," Bonnie said. Henry laughed, took the pin from the box and pinned it on Bonnie's bathing suit coverup. "What?"

"Nothing. It's beautiful. Not to mention a huge relief."

"Tell me about it," Bonnie answered. She gave Henry a kiss, then waved at someone across the room. "That's my lawyer," she told him.

Diane turned to see Annette squeeze through the crowd. She wouldn't have recognized her with her hair down and wearing drawstring pants, if she hadn't been leading Morgan toward them. "You're late," Bonnie called.

"I was packing up," Annette said. "Morgan was helping—you know how helpful kids are." Even Diane laughed at that.

Bonnie looked between the two women. "Morgan, you want to go build a sand castle with Hayley?" Morgan looked at her mom, who nodded approval. Bonnie helped Henry settle Morgan on his shoulders, then turned back to Diane and Annette. "Play nice, you two," Bonnie said. She led Henry to the stairs and down to the beach.

Diane looked around, but there was nowhere to escape. She looked up at Annette. "I heard about your job. What will happen to the Instant Pleasure file?"

"I told Natalia Orloff to call the firm if she needs the records. Mr. Chambers has been paid in full."

"And then some," Diane teased. She regretted it even before she saw Annette flinch. They weren't on teasing terms, and why would they be? Diane had been using Annette as the scapegoat ever since she lost the house. That was Diane's fault. And it was time she took responsibility. "I'm sorry."

Annette hesitated, then let it go. "In any case, I'm setting up my own group. No more nights or weekends."

"Or bonuses," Diane mused. "You want to share an office? I'll be checking out rental space this week, as soon as the kids are settled in school."

"You don't need more space," Annette said.

"You've got to be kidding. Have you seen my place?"

"I have," Annette said. She reached in her pants pocket and pulled out a key. "It's lovely, but not quite right for me and Morgan."

Diane looked more closely at the happy face key. She burst into tears.

"I told you she'd cry," Bonnie said to Lana, as they reappeared on the porch stairs. Lana pulled a twenty from her cleavage and handed it over.

Diane whipped around and saw them. She laughed, then sobered up. "Annette, I can't accept this."

"It's not a gift, Diane. You can have it back for the same price I paid and deduct a percentage of the mortgage for the club office."

"But you just quit your job."

"Don't worry, I won't need the money." Annette put her palm out toward Lana. Lana smiled, pulled the diamond ring off her pointer finger, and slapped it into Annette's hand.

"But, Diane, I get dibs on the guesthouse for my studio." Bonnie put her hand in Henry's deep pocket and pulled out the ring box. She gave it to Annette for the ring, still looking at Diane. "And you need onsite day care."

"Deal. But where will Annette live?"

"My old loft," Lana said.

Annette snapped the ring box closed. "Has a fabulous view."

Diane hugged her. "That's wonderful! And by the way, whatever you hear about me calling you a bitch isn't true. Anymore."

Annette laughed. "Keep that in mind when you smell smoke in the master bedroom."

Diane ran to the balcony and shouted down to her kids, "Quinn! Cody! We're going home! To Brentwood!"

They jumped up and down screaming. Then they ran and hugged each other. It was a rare sight, and it only lasted a moment. When Cody turned back to the sand castle where Morgan and Hayley were waiting, it was obvious that they had moved on.

Diane had mixed feelings, like during the Thanksgiving trip she had mentioned to Lana. Cody lost his beloved teddy bear at that hotel in San Francisco—and Diane was the most heartbroken. She spent weeks crying on the phone to Housekeeping, begging for them to find it while Cody slept peacefully beside her. And now, while the kids were thrilled to get their own rooms back, the old house was like that castle rising from the sand. Soon it would be a memory. Lana was right about real estate. Money was security, but home was a place in your heart.

The party was winding down as the sun dropped over the ocean. The light glowed over the last few partygoers dancing on the balcony. Lana chatted with Annette, who was at the railing watching her daughter play in the sand below.

Inside, the place was a shambles. Diane started picking up

empty wine cups, then remembered Lana had hired a cleanup crew. She went to her beach bag behind her to be sure she had put the happy face key on her key chain. She planned to use it first thing in the morning. If she was lucky, she'd be having Olivia's crème de menthe brownies for breakfast.

Philippe emerged from the kitchen and helped his bartender pack up bottles in a cardboard wine case. He tapped Diane on the shoulder. "Who's your friend?" He nudged his chin in the direction of the balcony where only Annette remained.

"My friend?" Diane smiled. "That would be Annette."

"Does Annette appreciate fine wine?" Philippe asked.

"Indeed, she does."

The front door flew open with a bang, and Eli trudged in stooped over, with a black leather chair on his back. "Lana!" Diane called. Eli dropped the chair in the middle of the empty room as Lana entered. "Housewarming gift."

"I already got one." Lana said.

"Wasn't my idea, believe me." Eli rubbed his shoulder. He glanced backwards at his boss, who walked in the back door with his twins.

"Winston?" Lana's cheeks glowed like the sunset. "This is too much, really."

"Sorry we're late," Winston said.

Diane saw how Lana looked at Winston and couldn't help thinking, *better late than never.* She stepped back out of the way as Winston continued.

"Hayley's mom invited us, but the store was shorthanded for the Labor Day sale." He turned to Diane. "Congratulations, by the way. Looks like it was a helluva party."

Diane plopped down in the chair. "The Truby, right? Classy. Comfy, too." She rubbed the wide leather arm, noticed a mark on it. "But this one's damaged."

Bonnie came over to take a look. "That's the burn mark from the commercial. Couldn't you get it out?"

Winston couldn't take his eyes off Lana. "Nope. Some people make a lasting impression."

Bonnie and Diane exchanged looks.

A new salsa beat started outside, and Winston reached out a hand to Lana. She looked at it. "You really like to dance?"

"Who do you think makes the CDs?"

Lana didn't answer. She just took his hand and followed his lead. The others backed away to watch as their hips swayed in unison and their feet tapped the floor. They moved as if they had been dancing together for years. And maybe they had, Diane thought.

Henry put his arm around Bonnie. "Can you do that?"

"Not as good as Hayley," she said. "But I can try." They tried a few feeble steps and fell together, laughing.

The sun was sinking fast now. The band stopped playing and packed up. "Lana," a photographer called. "Losing the light!"

Winston brought her back to the group. "Go on."

She handed him a cocktail napkin to wipe his forehead. "You'll wait?"

"I waited this long," Winston said.

Lana squeezed his hand and went outside.

"Come on, I'll buy you a drink," Diane said. She took Winston over to the bar and poured him a cold glass of wine.

He looked at the engraved champagne bucket full of dollar bills. "Looks like your club is going to be a success."

"Thanks. What do you think about Mecca offering a furniture discount to members?"

"Apparently, we already do."

Diane laughed. They headed to the balcony, where they could see the sun sinking to the right of the beach behind the cliff of Point Dume. There would be no sunset over the water, no green flash. Most of the party crowd had broken up and strolled along the beach. Lana was still close, moving around so that the photographers could only shoot her with the soft light in her face.

Bonnie came up behind them. "We forgot to cut the cake."

"I know." Diane was bummed, too. "I was counting on a great sunset, so we could make a formal announcement. Sort of anti-climactic, don't you think?"

"You can't always get what you want, Diane," Annette teased.

"Oh, yes, you can." Diane pulled out her phone. She looked around to ask Cody for help, but he was still playing with the younger kids in the sand. Diane pressed enough buttons on the keypad to figure out how to change the ring tone herself. Then she did.

"What did you change it to?" Bonnie asked.

"The sound of a telephone." Diane laughed.

The porch light clicked on as they looked out past the children at the inky water. The frothy waves glowed fluorescent. Lana rejoined them on the balcony and shooed the men inside. She signaled the photographer for one last shot. The women gathered with their arms around each other and smiled, but not at the camera. At each other.

When they were done, Diane called out over the balcony. "Who wants cake?"

"I do, I do!" The kids clambered up the stairs. Winston and Henry took charge of the commotion. Philippe poured four glasses of champagne, handed them out and went inside.

The four friends were left alone on the balcony, watching the waves crash on the beach below them. Bonnie looked around. "Feels like the end of something."

"Just the beginning," Lana said.

Annette looked at Diane. "I think it's time for that toast."

Diane nodded. Here she was, happily divorced, when she had never imagined there was such a thing. A calm settled over her. Slowly, she raised her glass. "Here's to living happier ever after."